THE DELILAH CASE

CASE

Mickie Turk

Mickie Turk

Cover Design by Benjamin Hovorka

DEDICATION

This novel would not have been possible without a lifetime of support from loyal and stouthearted friends. I could not have improved as a writer had it not been for my editors, Joan Hause and Kim Hines. And the picture would not be complete if I did not give a shout out from the mountain top to the members of my writer's group, who, after many years of reading my submissions, and always making careful and instructive suggestions, gave me the courage to do more, to be more.

PROLOGUE

May 20, 1968

Little Niqui didn't stop to catch her breath or fasten her shoe buckles. She knew the cracks and fissures in the sidewalks by heart, avoided them and ran as fast as she could. Past the quickly disappearing smear of faces. Past the arranged tableau of her childhood. The usual folk estivating like reptiles in the heat. Sipping iced teas on their porches. Endlessly fanning themselves with old newspapers. She never saw them.

But they always noticed her.

Especially today. The seven-year-old bolted up her front stairs and tore open the screen door with so much force that it snapped back against the window shutters like a heavy magnet and stayed there, letting in a spume of dust and all of the buzzing flies. Old men, weary women with small children, pre-teens whose parents didn't own fans, all gaped in astonishment because only once before had the little girl attempted anything so brash and bold.

Where was the fire? And what about Darnell, the block wondered. Why in heaven's name was she keeping him waiting?

Little Niqui flew into the dining room right before dropping to her knees and crawling under the table. When she found what she was looking for, the girl repeated her steps backward and was out in the street before the cone of dust had a chance to settle back to earth. The object of her quest, the new present from Miss Marta, safely swaddled in the crook of her arm.

The six-inch, brand new voodoo doll wore a tuxedo and top hat. Gede's hands were splayed in gleaming white gloves, and dark sunglasses with one lens missing hung rakishly on his head. A short fat stubby cigar poked out of the twisted mouth, and a carved wooden cane dangled from his right forearm. He looked drunk and lascivious, but this deity, the voodoo lwa, was the one you called when there was a serious illness in the family, and he loved the little children whom he defended against the seen and unseen.

Little Niqui was already halfway to Treasure House to play with Darnell when she realized she'd forgotten her protector. She had to run extra hard and extra fast because she knew full well that this mistake would cost her three-and-a-half minutes of play: one-and-a-half minutes back home, a half-minute for the retrieval, and another one-and-a-half minutes back to the place where she first noticed the doll missing.

Little Niqui never wore a watch, never looked at clocks, was terrified of them because everything in her life was scheduled—her mama Nadine, always making sure of that. Instead, she used her internal guides to tell time just the way Miss Marta taught her. She had taught Little Niqui that once you understood them, the spirits would always be there for her.

Nadine didn't approve of that kind of thinking, but what could she do? Miss Marta was Nadine's voodoo priestess, too.

Once again the skinny girl with legs like a gazelle was running past the neighborhood, a little less frightened now, and a lot more aware of her surroundings. She smiled and waved to the people talking all at once at her.

"You forget something Little Niqui?"

"Gonna catch your death running in the heat."

"Slow down girl, you hear."

"Careful or you'll wear out your shoes."

"Ummmhmm! Brand new patent leather Sunday shoes."

"Don't let your mama catch you."

"I have thirty minutes," Little Niqui said.

"Not no more you don't."

"Show us whatch ya hidin' under that arm."

"Better hurry, Darnell be waiting on you."

Darnell. Her everything. Her one true friend. She was truly sorry to be late. Three-and-a-half-minutes late. Darnell would say he didn't mind. That was how a true friend acted. Not like that crazy Delilah who would have screamed at her for one silly mistake. You never knew about Delilah, because as much she said she could be counted on, the older girl sometimes wouldn't come around for days, even weeks. And then, you'd have to be afraid of what kind of mood she'd be showing. Once in a great while Delilah could be a peach. That's when she brought them fun games to play and didn't even get too cranky when she lost. That's why she was invited back. But lately Delilah only made Little Niqui feel real bad about herself, even worse than before she showed up.

Her mama never mentioned Delilah, but she made her feelings very clear about Darnell. He wasn't smart enough or good enough. In her estimation, just another neighborhood runt. Still, Nadine believed if left to his own devices, that boy had the power to unravel all the good plans she had carved out for her daughter's future. Hadn't he already discarded her proper title of *Dominique*, for that low class nickname, Little Niqui? As if her perfect angel needed street cred. No, everyone knew that the prodigious child's destiny was to grow up and make a great impact on this 'ole world. Nadine would have to stay cautious. Ummmhmm!

If you had bothered to ask Little Niqui's opinion, she would have told you that her mama was jealous. Maybe Mama knew she loved Darnell as much as her. Maybe Mama knew that Darnell could keep her safe in a way she could not. Maybe Mama knew if she died, Little Niqui would be very sad. But if Darnell died, Little Niqui would die, too.

She might die anyway. More than usual, things were rocketing right out of proportion. Clutching Gede to her chest, the girl tried to squeeze out the memories of the day. It ranked among the worst. And it was happening again. She'd begun detesting every single thing she was forced to do.

That morning she woke up like every day, an hour earlier than the other children on the block, and was chauffeured to a private Jesuit school in the upscale suburb of Metarie. The first half of the day was spent in European-style classes for fourth graders—thanks to her mama's wheedling she had skipped second and third grade altogether. In the morning she studied her primaries: mathematics, English, history, geography, religion. Then after lunch she was passed from nun to nun, for individual tutoring in eclectic areas such as Picasso's Blue Period, or the discoveries of the Italian Renaissance. At three-o'clock she took a French vocabulary test and passed it with flying colors.

Little Niqui had the reading comprehension of a tenth grader, and the I.Q. of the current reigning Mensa champion. She could sing opera, play three instruments, compose music, recite a dozen sonnets, and on occasion, fix her mama's sewing machine and the old electric toaster when they went on the fritz.

When she thought things couldn't get any worse, after her last class, Little Niqui was summoned to the principal's office. He explained that because of her greater than expected academic progress that year, she would be spending the summer taking accelerated classes with a group of equally talented, although slightly older, children on the French Riviera. The principal beamed, saying it would be for the *whole summer*. Astonished to see a look of sheer terror cross those big bright eyes, he quickly added that her mama would be going, too. And that's when she burst into tears and ran into the bathroom to throw up her lunch.

They had a deal!

You didn't break deals, or go back on your word. Even if you were Nadine Doucette. Last winter after they took Darnell away from her, with only Delilah to witness it, Little Niqui jumped off her second-story veranda onto the brick courtyard below. And although she hadn't broken a bone, an examining doctor at Charity Hospital who was no shrink, but could recognize a suicide attempt when he saw one, reported the incident to the resident psychiatrist. A group of specialists was brought in, and, soon after, a conclave convened between the hospital and Dominique's school. And between Nadine and the Black Panthers.

One of the first things the latter group did after they had taken over the neighborhood was become Little Niqui's personal benefactor. Indeed, they supplied the cash for the expensive matriculation, after-school lessons, and of course the car and driver. They bought Little Niqui's mother a new stove and refrigerator, and when she asked for it, paid for the repairs to her porch and steps, and replaced the shutters on the front windows.

The senior members of New Orleans's Black Power movement were also Little Niqui's neighborhood-appointed child advocates. They had a big say in what happened next.

So it was settled that she would continue all of her schoolwork and activities. She would keep curfew and go to church and Bible study on Sundays. The tiny, precocious child also promised no more shenanigans like jumping off porches, or cutting—the ER doctor had also found a half dozen tiny unhealed slits alongside older scars on the back of her neck, mostly covered by her long pony tail.

In return, much to Nadine's chagrin, her daughter would be allowed to play with Darnell for thirty minutes each day after supper. No more, no less, and as much as Little Niqui wanted on weekends, as long as there were no special events planned.

That was the deal.

Until today.

Instinctively, Dominique knew this new life plan was different, that it would do no good to complain to Barry Beales, the leader of the Panthers, because most likely he was financing the trip. She would just have to find a way to bring along her best friend. Otherwise, how would she ever survive the summer?

Darnell sat on the top step carefully unwrapping a piece of chewing gum. Little Niqui watched him for a moment before taking the piece and popping it into her mouth. She never tired of looking at his face, briefly wondering why some of her mama's friends thought Darnell didn't quite "fit in". Almost the darkest kid on the block, nine-year-old Darnell had been born with European features, a short skinny nose, thin lips and steel-blue eyes. His jet-black hair fell in waves slightly over his ears, and, unlike Little Niqui's, it was natural and not processed. To her, he was the cutest creature she'd ever laid eyes on, and she prayed he would always belong to her.

"Come on, let's play." Darnell clambered up the steps and tore into the house. Little Niqui ran after him chortling, trying to catch up. She followed the narrow hallway and ran past three rooms until she found him in the kitchen. Darnell heroically ducked and feinted her grabs by running under the square metal table. When she finally tagged him, he fell into an exaggerated heap on the cracked linoleum floor and pretended to be dead. The girl pulled and tore at his sleeve. She laughed so hard she fell down, too. Then, like a miniature twister, she shot up and screamed, "Catch me if you can!"

The two kids always continued this exchange, in and out of the rooms for fifteen minutes. The house was laid out much like the rest of the shotgun houses on the block: three rooms with an unbroken hallway connecting them. But this one had the camel back edition, where a second bedroom had been built upstairs. It belonged to Davina and Dave Treasure, who a month ago up and left to take care of their ailing daughter near Vicksburg, leaving the keys with their next-door neighbors, the Davis'.

Once, when Larry Davis went to check on the house, he found the back door slightly ajar and that's when he discovered Darnell and Little Niqui jouncing through the front rooms. From that time on, he unlocked the back door at five minutes to seven and came back promptly to lock up at seven-thirty-five. If it so happened that his wife made cherry Kool-Aid that day, he filled two glasses and left them on the kitchen table where the kids would be sure to find them.

Their final ritual, to run up the stairs and jump up and down on the old feather bed, had to be cut short today, but they still managed to get in a game of who-could-jump-farthest-off-the-bed. It was when Little Niqui cleared her friend by almost a foot and rolled to her side, that Gede fell from her pocket and landed on the floor. Darnell swiveled his body and grabbed the doll.

"This new? When did you get it?"

"Yesterday, from Miss Marta."

"But you already got one."

"This one's better." Little Niqui took back the saucy patron of young children, sat up and balanced him on her knees. The children studied the cockeyed face staring at them.

"Why do you need better?"

"You know." Little Niqui twisted her mouth. "I'm getting scared. All the time now."

Darnell turned away to look out the dormer window. The glass was melting. He could feel Delilah's heat all around. "It'll be okay," he said, knowing it wouldn't be. "I'm here. Don't you worry."

"Look at me Darnell." Little Niqui's eyes were wide trying to contain a flood of rushing tears. "Look at me."

"Don't cry. I don't like that crying."

"I'm sorry. Darnell. Darnell."

When he looked back at her his smile was warm. Darnell couldn't bear to see his friend sad. "You have five minutes, then we gotta go." Darnell did own a watch, his own present from Barry Beales.

"You won't ever leave me, will you Darnell?"

"You know I won't." And then looking very serious in the manner of a grown up, he asked, "Have you seen her yet?"

"She'll be by soon."

Their evenings always ended with Darnell patiently reciting every article of whatever Little Niqui made him promise. He put up with it, because it seemed to make her feel better. Secretly he wondered why she bothered at all with the ritual when she already knew the ending to the story.

It most certainly wouldn't be him leaving her.

ONE

August 13, 2005

Sheriff Leroy Futrell drove with the radio off.

Sporting the usual dark shades and Stetson, the sixty-year-old lawman guided the skinny steering wheel of his black and pink 1955 Crown Vic along the endless banks of lime-green sugar stalks. He liked to scan all the old relics: nineteenth century farm houses, tractors as big as dinosaurs, and humanity's surviving hoary remnants—old men smelling of cigarettes and coffee, playing dominoes in the shade of their dirt-packed yards.

Sheriff Leroy Futrell surveyed the countryside around Elysian Fields Parish like he owned it. Until a month ago, he did.

Because a month ago, Dr. Dominique Doucette hadn't yet arrived in his parish to mess things up. A month ago, he was respected and listened to.

If things had stayed that way, she'd still be alive, and he'd still have peace of mind. More importantly, in a few hours the community would not have to watch their quaint villages get trampled by the march of news reporters and cameramen from all around Louisiana and the planet.

The sleepy little parish of Elysian Fields used to be clean, orderly, and mostly law-abiding. On weekends, Futrell and his posse responded to a half-dozen drunken disorderly complaints, and occasionally surprised teenaged joy riders with their first speeding tickets. Now and again, the sheriff had to issue a DUI, and once or twice a year, raid a marijuana field. Violent crime was almost nonexistent here, its proximity to New Orleans notwithstanding. In the twenty-five years that Futrell guarded and corralled his citizenry, there had been three killings: two domestics and one unfortunate hunting accident involving a five-year-old boy. Now they would have to add two more to the roll.

The one, they were still calling a homicide.

He didn't blame Dominique. Or himself. He put the onus squarely on hubris and his lunatic childhood friend, Governor Jedediah (Spike) Jefferson.

The governor never thought twice about using someone else to elevate his esteem among constituents, or finding new ways to fatten his bank account. It seemed it was his fate, or his doom, to be the only state chief in the country to invite Dr. Dominique Doucette and her newest experimental project—a reform prison for killers—to Louisiana.

Specifically, the invite bore the return address of the sheriff's own back yard, Elysian Fields proper.

The possibility of untold tax revenues from the untested scheme was by itself a delicious temptation. But good old Spike also liked to live fancy and in the headlines. He had willingly signed on the dotted line because he envisioned new heights of grandeur while getting photographed next to Dominique, arguably the country's most famous psychiatrist, dubbed as a hybrid between Oprah and Dr. Phil—many were inclined to throw in a big dab of Mother Theresa into that mix. And oh, so beautiful.

No matter, moving six treacherous murderers from state prisons into minimum security, within the sheltering walls of an antebellum Creole plantation, had always been, and would always remain, simply, a preposterous idea.

Not to mention Dominique's ill-fated volunteer program for the murdering scoundrels inside a New Orleans homeless shelter. Anyone with a pea brain and a beating heart should have known the very idea was irrational and dangerous to the community. So why was he, Leroy Futrell, a no-account sheriff from a small country parish, the only one capable of fully grasping the concept?

If he'd been able to stop her from the beginning, they could've saved themselves one bloody massacre. But he had done what he could and now had nothing to feel contrite about. Not so much as anyone could ever tell.

Futrell braked. The sight of the voodooiene in a white robe and purple headscarf wandering out of the tall sugar cane field gave the sheriff a start. Wilhelmina Young usually didn't sneak up on people, nor had he ever before seen her hoisting squawking chickens by their feet onto her bony shoulders.

They had always gotten along well. On Monday mornings, the old woman was usually returning from babysitting the Favro kids, whose parents worked long shifts on the weekends at the oil plant. Whenever he came upon her, Futrell would offer Wilhelmina a ride home. The old woman always declined with a shake of the head and a big toothy smile, but never failed to deliver a little salty gossip from the neighborhood.

Today, she didn't even look at him as she scampered across the road and ducked into another field. It seemed like Wilhemina was in an awful big hurry to oust some bad juju.

Futrell mopped his forehead with the back of his hand and gently accelerated. Ahead, the road looked like melting black plastic. He felt the first wave of nausea rise inside his esophagus.

A mile later he pulled into Roadside Ruby's and scowled. Three small cars blocked his usual spot near the door. He pulled his car perpendicular to the others, effectively blocking their escape until he could fill up his thermos. For the first time that day, the sheriff felt like smiling. The Crown Vic was almost as long as the other three cars were wide.

Futrell walked into the darkened establishment and sat in the middle booth. A regular at the bar held forth a steady drone of chitchat, while the bartender cut limes with quick precise movements. The TV buzzed a stream of snow while the bar's handyman and oldest employee climbed a ladder to fix the cable box. These familiar sights and the smell of brewing coffee gave Futrell cold comfort, but just the briefest break from reality.

The waitress was filling up Futrell's thermos when the TV came to life.

"Prominent psychiatrist and director of Elysian Field's new reform prison, House of Mithras, was shot and killed in the early hours of Monday morning inside her office. Details have not been released," the male reporter from CNN announced.

All movement ceased and a half-dozen pair of eyes flew to Futrell. He kept his own focused on the thermos. The sheriff unceremoniously poured a cup and inhaled two good-sized swallows of burning java before getting up to face the day that he knew would never end.

Futrell drove out of the parking lot and turned on the radio. Static and then:

"Many unanswered questions revolve around the shooting death of Dominique Doucette. Sources close to the prison staff say another person was also fatally shot in the director's office. No word yet if the fatality was a prisoner or staff, male or female. While investigators…"

Futrell fiddled with the radio always getting more or less the same account of the news delivered either by a caffeine-injected female, or a male shock jock trying to sound serious for once. He turned the radio off and grabbed the manila file lying on the passenger seat. Then he pulled into a parking spot a couple of blocks away from his office and switched off the engine.

In a few minutes he would walk into his office, where no doubt the first witness with her own file in hand, was waiting patiently. For the next few hours, she and the others would testify informally, to the best of their knowledge. But they'd have to wait a little longer.

Futrell had stayed up all night perusing the journal inside the *Delilah* file, but something still puzzled him. He wanted to re-read a few of the entries before going in. The sheriff had to be prepared to ask and answer any and all questions. Everyone, including himself, would want to end this day with a respectable version of the truth.

TWO

Four weeks earlier

If Guyla Ray Gansen could have leapt up on stage and stuck a finger down her boss's throat, she might have pulled out whatever obstruction was jamming up those golden words.

As it was, the eminent and normally unflappable Dr. Dominique Doucette was staring dumbly at the audience, like she'd just been frozen in place by an invisible entity. But this wasn't a scene out of Harry Potter; it was the most important reality show of the celebrated psychiatrist's life. And if she didn't start speaking soon, from all around the banquet hall Armani suits would begin a twitching dance inside their thousand-dollar-a-person velvet seats. Ostensibly, these medical professionals, statesmen and royals, had come to Washington, D.C., to watch the famous psychiatrist receive yet another prestigious award, presented by another notable organization.

But that was just the price of admission. These good people were really there to learn if the rumors about House of Mithras were true. They were dying to find out if Dominique's controversial reform prison for killers would indeed be opening its doors the following week.

So why wasn't she telling them? Maybe she's had a stroke and was suffering from amnesia? Keeping most of her vision locked on the stage, Guyla Rae sneaked a peak at their colleague Kevin Wadell, who not surprisingly had pulled an ear-to-ear plasticine grin.

Guyla Rae said, "This isn't part of the script. I know because I wrote it. What the hell is she doing?"

Kevin said, "I can't tell, but give her a minute. We've come this far."

Guyla Rae tried to relax, but as she looked past the pretense of tranquility to study Kevin's handsome features, she saw that he was as worried as she was. Known in some professional circles as Ken Doll, not just because he had the ultimate wasp Super Hero face found in comic books—a lantern jaw, sparkling blue eyes and the tousled, shapely blonde hair found on magazine models—he also possessed that lean sculpted body that only years of disciplined running could shape. Guyla Ray knew something else about him. Next to Dominique, Kevin was the most dedicated professional on the planet who used his waking hours preparing, planning, and working towards eliminating the disparity of mental health care for poor people. He had graduated from the best schools, worked in the worst neighborhoods, and rarely took a dime for his efforts. That his pretty boy appearance occasionally favored a largesse of donations aimed at worthy causes—well, what were good looks for in the first place, if not to create some justice in this big ole' cruel world?

They were The Three Musketeers. One for all, and all for one. While Dominique arranged and organized programs, Kevin acted as her chief advisor and head clinician. Guyla Rae's work ran the gamut of public relations duties: speechwriting, managing the flow of information between House of Mithras and the media, and marketing. In reality all of their responsibilities were in flux. On more than one occasion, Guyla Rae had traveled to interview and compile convict's histories, while Dominique stayed in her office negotiating building contracts. First and foremost they looked out after each other. That's what Guyla Rae was doing now.

How long had it been since Dominique had reached the podium? Five seconds? Ten? Thirty? Just before, Guyla Rae recalled, Dominique had been sitting confidently at a table on the stage alongside the visiting queen of Sweden, the honorable mayor of Washington, D.C., and the flamboyant populist governor of Louisiana, Spike Jefferson. After opening remarks, the chairman had begun his introduction.

"The International Psychiatric Association has decided to bestow the Creative Humanitarian Prize in the Field of Applied Psychiatry to Dr. Dominique Doucette." As she sat, the sleek African-American woman discreetly arranged papers in front of her and straightened a pen. She looked up at the chairman and threw him a warm, earnest smile.

"By combining her revolutionary Desire Therapy with community partnerships, Dr. Doucette has shepherded peaceful solutions to ending civil strife in Haiti. After months of negotiations, Dr. Doucette facilitated the signing of a temporary peace agreement between security forces and a tribal separatist group in northeastern India."

While the chairman spoke, a young intern brought a tray of coffee and water to the table on the stage and began filling the guests' cups and glasses. When Dominique turned her body slightly to better hear the chairman, she spilled coffee on her sleeve.

"Dr. Doucette mediated talks between police and community leaders in South Central, Los Angeles, during riots. And most recently, by treating the prison environment as public community, Dr. Doucette was able to forge common goals and shared activities between warring gangs at two East Coast state prisons."

Guyla Rae watched Dominique wipe the stain—no, she was attacking it—as if at any moment the spot might grow by leaps and bounds. Her tablemates looked on with fascination. One of them would say later that they heard her whisper, "Not a single smudge on your pretty new dress."

Someone nudged her forward. Dominique looked around, bewildered.

"Ladies and gentlemen, Dominique Doucette."

Dominique was still rubbing the stain when she got up and walked unsteadily to take the microphone.

Guyla Ray thought the psychiatrist looked exceptionally radiant that day. Dominique filled out her stylish, cool mint jacket and skirt like a model on the runway. Her luxuriant chestnut brown hair was pulled back into a tightly-braided chignon, which instead of appearing severe and old fashioned, served to accentuate creamy dark skin wrapped firmly over sharply defined delicate features, and golden eyes the size of saucers. After vigorously shaking Dominique's hand, the chairman exited the stage. The audience clapped.

But she just stood there. Not moving. Not talking. With a vague wandering gaze, she caught Kevin's eye and tried to place him. Guyla Rae could feel him stir next to her.

"Kevin, do something. She needs you."

Kevin straightened, readying to get up. Just then, as if finally recognizing her colleague, Dominique came to and began to speak.

The words came out softly, slowly. Words Guyla Rae knew were being devoured lustily, syllable after syllable, by each of the two hundred and fifty audience members.

"Thank you for this great honor. I would like to begin by telling you why I started Desire Therapy."

Guyla Rae exhaled the breath inside her stomach, stretched her shoulders and squeezed Kevin's hand tightly. His idiot grin was gone, replaced by a weary knowing smile. His eyes glistened. It wasn't so long ago that Kevin and Dominique claimed their romance in photos on the front pages of tabloids, right next to the stories of scandalous Hollywood comeback kids. They had been dubbed Cleopatra and the Viking. Afterwards, Dominique had let Kevin down easy, assuring him that their friendship was the most important thing. Then she ribboned the deal by offering him a full partnership in the House of Mithras project. Of course Kevin had accepted. How could he say no to the promise of making history, as well as continuing to work alongside his "best" friend. Yeah, he would have it all. All except the love and sex.

Everyone could see Kevin was still very much in love with her. Everyone but Dominique.

Guyla Rae allowed herself a private moment of doubt. She believed she had seen raw fear earlier inside those big glassy eyes. But what in the world could have daunted Dominique into a stupor like that? Maybe she had misunderstood the significance of her boss's reaction. Had it been just a clever ploy used to spellbind the crowd before giving them what they really wanted? When it finally passed, that *frisson* of silence, Guyla Rae didn't give it another thought. And wouldn't think about it again for another month.

Dominique was moving about the stage now, her voice rising, lilting.

"I envisioned a future filled with safe and vital communities. Places where all members, no matter their history or mistakes, could achieve and contribute."

The newly built convention hall, with its unadorned ceiling and sterile white walls, suddenly began to sparkle with excitement. Dominique's signature passionate speechmaking was infecting every corner of the room. The front tables, a contingency of Doctors Without Borders, cheered vigorously. Even the usually stoic group of psychiatrists from Indo-European nations rocked back and forth in their seats. Look out if this woman ever wanted to run for president.

"Victims and criminals alike share deep and rich histories. Before their losses and before their crimes, remember these were all children with dreams. Desire Therapy releases those dreams and prepares the adult for reentry into society."

Someone stifled a cough. That was the last interruption anyone would notice for the next ten minutes.

"In the 1950s, Abraham Maslow founded humanistic psychology, a philosophy dedicated to the full realization of one's potential based on the hierarchy of human needs. An idea that advanced a sound holistic vision. It failed because it did not go far enough. It only considered healthy and motivated folks. Desire Therapy uses the principles of humanistic psychology, but focuses on society's damaged individuals. It moves people through believing they are deficient into a consciousness of safety, belonging, and finally into self-actualization.

"You cannot ignore people's basic needs and expect change. Nor can you fix a criminal in a day. Desire includes intensive written exercises, journaling and counseling, bi-weekly group therapy, hard physical work, the advancement of creative pursuits, and community participation. The only way to grow what is already inside the inmate, is through constructive methodology and vigilant follow up."

Guyla Rae put her head on Kevin's shoulder and began to weep silently from exhaustion. The wait was finally over.

In the beginning, House of Mithras had seemed like a done deal. Trading on the merits of her highly respected therapy modality, as well as a stockpile of socio/political cache, Dominique quickly rallied both Fortune 500 corporations and non-profits around her cause. She received the support of significant medical organizations, and pledges of financial support from everyone she'd ever done business with. Hollywood moguls, trans-national media owners, energy companies, and even a famous former football star. All had stood in line to help her achieve the goal of raising two hundred fifty million dollars for the unorthodox project.

Frankly, raising money was as easy as pie and took no time at all. But afterwards they found themselves mired down at the bottom rung of an impossibly tall ladder. Winning over the hearts and trust of government officials was a different story. They hadn't expected a flood of rejections from so many states. Citing increasingly litigious times, legislators claimed it would be impossible to purchase the kind of insurance that could protect the states from liability. What if something went wrong, they asked. *What if one of the prisoners escaped and murdered again?*

Deep down, what scared the lawmakers most was the thought of a stormy backlash from survivors of homicide victims. Since the 1980s, the country had seen an unprecedented growth of coalitions involved in holding both lawmakers' and perpetrators' feet to the fire. These survivors wanted someone to pay for all the loss and hardship that violent crime left behind: children without parents, parents suffering the loss of their children. In a political climate where the death sentence had been reinstated, no one state could risk the perception of being soft on crime.

And then one day, out of the clear blue beyond, the chief officer of the great state of Louisiana called Dominique. Governor Spike Jefferson said he had nothing but admiration for Louisiana's native daughter. Never mind that she had not lived there since departing for university more than twenty-five years ago, at the age of fifteen. Now he was giving her a chance to come back permanently. With open arms and a truckload of confidence and good will, he and the other legislators saw fit to free up a little ole' plantation northeast of New Orleans. He added that she should come see it right away. He was sure that adorable little spot in Elysian Fields Parish would make a most suitable setting for her new promising enterprise.

And why not Louisiana? Since its recorded history, the territory that Napoleon eventually sold to the Americans had inherited a rich, lurid, and often corrupt social pedigree. Jazz was born in New Orleans and so was the drive-up liquor store. Mardi Gras was still the nation's biggest party, and from 1894 to 1999, Carville, Louisiana, had been home to the only continental leper colony. Wild boars roamed city parks, and one of its recent governors was serving ten years in federal prison for racketeering. Now the family tree would also bear a reform institution for killers, ensconced no less, inside a historic plantation.

Spike Jefferson wasn't worried about survivor victims backlash because he enjoyed publicity. All kinds. He knew he couldn't lose. If Dominique's new-fangled program for prisoners actually worked, then he'd get credit for being a maverick governor. If it failed, all eyes would turn on his state again, drawing the nation's gawkers and their heavily padded tourist wallets.

But for right now, the news would give all the other forty-nine states something to talk about. Every shark knows how to bite down on a gift.

Dominique came off the stage and worked the aisles.

"Let me be clear, Desire Therapy is not a cure, but an important key to opening up human potential. The real test for Desire Therapy lies not in our prisons but squarely inside the gates of our communities, where the healing journey and the search for core meaning can truly begin."

Guyla Ray turned her head to listen. A crescendo of murmurs swollen with anticipation rippled across the room. Tent revival fever.

"I, too, am returning to my core. My roots. To the place where it all began." Kevin was on his feet applauding with hundreds of other well-wishing enthusiasts. At the start of the new millennium, against all odds, Dominique appeared once again to triumph.

"Thanks to the great generosity of private donors and the courage and willingness of Governor Jefferson, the great state of Louisiana and House of Mithras now have the opportunity to seal a momentous partnership. In Elysian Fields Parish, and in the city of New Orleans, my partner in crime if you will, Dr. Kevin Wadell and I, will direct a pilot program using Desire Therapy on prisoners convicted of rage murder.

The simultaneous intake of breath might have been choreographed. Afterwards, only the silence was louder. "Ladies and gentlemen, next Monday morning at 9 a.m., the doors of House of Mithras will open. After that, the world will change."

THREE

The pressure to resolve an ongoing war of words in the media between the directors of the reform prison and Sheriff Leroy Futrell resulted in a hastily arranged meeting with the parties at the governor's mansion. Governor Spike Jefferson suggested that his long-time crony from the Iberia Peninsula and his new politically advantaged buddies from House of Mithras meet up at his place for drinks and hors d'oeuvres.

"Y'all come on up now and bring your party hats," Spike had crooned to Dominique. "We're gonna have ourselves a regular tête à tête."

While Kevin drove his Lexus on I-10 headed east to Baton Rouge, Dominique studied the paperwork on her lap. And he studied her. Meeting at the governor's mansion seemed like a sensible way to try to soften the steel-plated curmudgeon from Elysian Fields. Futrell was the only powerhouse left in Louisiana unconvinced that placing convicted killers at a minimum security setting right smack dab in the middle of his fiefdom was such a hot idea. Even though there were only six men in the pilot program, the sheriff had insisted they were six too many.

"We're almost there. Just a few more stones for the altar," Kevin said.

"The governor doesn't worry me. But Futrell. He requires real blood," Dominique said without looking up.

"Where's all this coming from? You're just a jumpy little jitterbug."

"Question is, why aren't you more concerned?"

"It's over, Dominique. We won. He can't hurt us."

"He's a good old boy with a big ego," Dominique said.

"Does he still think security's a problem? I thought we proved that our technology was the gold standard," Kevin said

"We can't take it with us into the community," Dominique said.

"It's only six convicts. There will be more one-one-one interaction with these guys than in any other state facility."

She faced him and he didn't like what he saw, although he couldn't identify his source of distress.

"We have to be very careful. Nothing can go wrong. Especially now," Dominique said.

It was hard seeing her this way. Dominique was always meticulous, but seldom uptight. Whether they were in New Orleans, New York or globetrotting, his long time companion, former lover and business associate, had always displayed self-assuredness and aplomb in the face of challenge and distress. That's who she was. A consolidator. A peacemaker. Today she was acting like an awkward teenager at her first dance.

Kevin knew some of his perception was colored by the surfacing of long lost feelings. Feelings that Dominique no longer shared. The decision to turn their relationship into a business- driven enterprise had yielded in Dominique an uncharacteristic iciness. She hadn't acted like a friend in a very long time.

Kevin took one hand off the steering wheel and rifled through the back seat. When he shoved a colorful poster on top of her laptop, Dominique squealed.

"What? What's this?" Dominique studied the poster warily.

"It's not going to bite you. The Jazz Asylum is playing on Front Street tonight. I thought after the meeting we could grab a bite to eat and hang out until...well until the music started. Go dancing. It's been awhile."

Dominique stared straight ahead.

"You're kidding, right?"

Kevin placed his hand over her closed fist. "Dominique, it's just dancing. We need to celebrate every victory."

When Dominique turned to Kevin she looked right past him, pretending to eye something beyond the interstate. "That was a long time ago. We're different people now."

Kevin loosened his tie and smiled impishly. "We still have to eat. And I'm willing to bet that you haven't seen the inside of a nightclub in years. It would do both of us good. Reclaim use of some body parts that may be getting a tad rusty."

Dominique threw the poster in the back seat and muttered something about trying to concentrate. The rest of the road trip was spent in awkward silence. Kevin had been unprepared for the shock of rage that coursed through him now. He gripped the steering wheel so hard he wondered it if might crack under his clenched fingers. He had never felt more betrayed. She couldn't see him anymore. Dominique had turned into a machine. He felt like slapping her.

FOUR

Kevin parked in the driveway and looked up at the white-stone Greek Revival mansion before getting out of the car. Its resemblance to Oak Alley Plantation in Vacherie was remarkable. A hip roof supported by Doric columns on three sides, three Georgian dormers, and a sunburst window over the main door. The only things missing were a second-story veranda and a quarter-mile double row of twenty-eight live oak trees.

Dominique was already at the front door talking to the governor's fawning aide, who kept patting the psychiatrist's hand. When Kevin got to the steps, the aide quickly ushered the psychiatrists to a mahogany paneled vestibule where she offered them identical winged leather chairs. She said breathlessly, "I'll let them know you're here."

Down the hall, in a larger version of the waiting area, sat Governor Spike Jefferson, neatly attired in a Panama suit. He was a bulldog of a man, short and stout. In his mid-fifties, the governor sported glorified muttonchops and a shocking head of wild white hair. One particularly unruly lock always fell into his eyes, which he took great care to remove by shaking his head to one side, like an aging rock star.

The governor was equally famous for both his bigger-than-life smile and a penchant for good malt whiskey. Today was no different: he smiled every time he sipped from his highball glass.

"You need to turn down the butane some. These are nice folks who are bringing our state economic largesse and some much-needed positive promotion," the governor said.

Sheriff Leroy Futrell was as physically different from the governor as one could get, even though the men were first cousins whose mothers had been identical twin sisters. He was tall and wiry, wore rumpled jeans and a faded western shirt, and always kept his hat on in order to hide thinning dark curly hair. Today the lawman smoked his cigar and leaned rakishly against the casing of the wide mullioned window, where he could watch Kevin and Dominique come inside the mansion. A corpulent ash fell on the high-gloss wide-planked wood floor.

"You might want to open the window. My staff will sue me if they smell tobacca," the governor said.

Just then the phone rang. Spike picked up, listened and hung up. "Show 'em in."

Even as the aide made introductions, the governor dismissed her by clamping one hand heartily over Dominique's wrist and lobbing the other meaty limb on top of Kevin's shoulder.

"Dominique, so lovely to see you again. And a pleasure to meet with you again, Kevin." While maintaining a grip on the guests, he nudged them gently forward.

"Leroy. Sheriff. These are the good reformists I was tellin' you about. Dr. Dominique Doucette, and Dr. Kevin Waddell. Native born, Louisiana's pride and joy."

Futrell turned slowly to scan the interlopers. Cigar stuck firmly between straight, even teeth, hands clasped behind his back. Kevin extended his hand. The sheriff observed him coolly as they shook hands.

"Sheriff, we've been looking forward to meeting you. I expect we'll be seeing a lot of each other."

Kevin kept talking, but Futrell had already dismissed him from his mind. His eyes were locked firmly on Dominique's. Expecting this, she moved confidently into the battle zone. When she was only an uncomfortable foot away, she spoke.

"We all know why we're here. You have concerns and so do we. So let's start with…"

Futrell strode away, also dismissing Dominique. He stopped and seemed to stare at his reflection in the floor, puffing away.

"You come waltzing into my jurisdiction, snatch up one of the state's oldest landmarks, and then you turn it into a shithole prison." Futrell looked up and started pacing again. "Now, you expect me to be nicey-nice."

"Whoa! What's done is done. We want to work with you. Not against you," Kevin said.

Dominique pulled a syrupy sweet smile and followed the sheriff's march.

"I get the distinct feeling Leroy here forgot the welcome mat. He just can't hide how much he dislikes us."

"What I *dis*like is you piling up that mansion with pieces of shit you pulled out of a drain sewer. Murderers basking in minimum security.

Dominique shot Kevin an "I told you so" look.

"Your failure to respect the law is matched only by your complete lack of common sense. Just don't forget, your little ass is mine if there's even a single crime perpetrated by anyone living at Club Med."

Kevin could not believe his ears. Dominique's stride came to a dead stop. The governor studied his empty glass.

Kevin said, "Minimal security matches the reform prison model. When you show inmates respect, outcomes improve and recidivism drops dramatically."

Futrell's brassbound stand on the law was only strengthened by the appearance of compromise in Kevin's tone. He dropped his smoldering cigar into Spike's highball glass, sauntered past Kevin and positioned his face inches away from Dominique's. Using the remaining room between them, he stuck his index finger below her nose and wagged it back and forth.

"You liberal whiners always mess things up. I bet back in New York they actually let women like you run the show. Just as long as there was someone else to clean up the mess."

Dominique swatted the finger away like it was an insect. Kevin and Spike stayed transfixed in their spots.

She leaned in closer, her breath overlapping his. "Guess what Leroy? While you were napping, the world shifted. I'm now one of the state's highest-ranking corrections officers. That makes me your boss."

As she stepped back, Dominique picked up her briefcase. "Just so you know, my door's always open. But if you threaten me again, I won't hesitate to personally hand you your walking papers. Along with an indictment for sexual harassment," she said, burning her image for all times into Futrell's surprised face.

Kevin followed Dominique out the door while Futrell looked away and smirked. When the door shut, the sheriff strode back to the window and waited.

Spike opened a lower desk drawer and pulled out a fifty-dollar bottle of half drunk whiskey. He tossed the wet cigar out of his glass into the trashcan. In another drawer he found a clean glass. He lined up the glasses and poured liquor to the top in both. Then he walked over to the sheriff and handed him his cocktail. They watched as the car eased out of the driveway and Dominique's profile in the passenger seat faded from sight.

"I could be wrong, but Leroy? That could've gone better."

Kevin was pulling out onto the street just as Futrell inhaled a long pull of drink. "You were right about one thing, Spike."

"Yeah, what was that?"

"She's definitely one of Louisiana's treasures. Oh my, yes."

———————————————

A few hours later, the Lexus pulled up in front Dominique's house in Uptown, where the psychiatrist declined Kevin's offer to see her to the door. As soon as his car was out of sight, Dominique reached for her cell phone and dialed. Her eyes blazed with anticipation as she listened to ring after ring, and then squeezed shut in disappointment when she heard: "Darnell's out. Leave him a present."

A few miles away, a shadowed man listening to a ringing cell phone, smoked hard and tried not to feel anything. Why had she come back, he wondered? Why now?

FIVE

Kevin couldn't shake the heebie jeebies.

On Monday morning when he got to the surveillance room at House of Mithras, it was 8:00 a.m., and he was alone. Too bad he couldn't drink a beer. If only he were back in New Orleans he could get one at the drug store. But since it was too early to drink and he was the first one there, he thought he might as well use the time to collect and examine some of his orbiting thoughts. And calm down.

Something had crawled inside his skin and was twisting in place like a rabid insect. What was it? He thought carefully about the meeting at the governor's mansion; at the time it seemed more like a badly-orchestrated wrestling match. Now from a distance, Kevin saw that if he wanted to, the sheriff could be trouble. But underneath it all, he was still a lawman and could be reasoned with. Maybe it had been what the sheriff had said, *Murderers basking in minimum security.*

Kevin had been burying his feelings in work for so long that he was surprised what a few quiet moments alone could unleash. When it hit him, it felt like a pitchfork stuck between his eyes.

Basking. There was only one prisoner that could fit that description. One guy who could throw everybody off. And hadn't he always known who that was?

Although he and Dominique had poured over the criminal resumes of over two-thousand candidates, and together spent six months cautiously, meticulously, whittling down the list to six, he had always expressed doubts about Lerance Lemartine. That the convict was a perfect contender for Desire Therapy was never in question. That he was a bad choice for the group, was.

Lerance had been a rich doctor whose parents had also been rich doctors. When they died they left him a sizable estate, but he himself continued to earn his daily bread. As an orthopedic surgeon, his patient list ran the gamut from Washington insiders to nationally renowned athletes. Everything had gone swimmingly for the pedigreed professional until the day he emptied his small caliber gun into his wife's chest. After Clarissa confessed to having an affair, neither stood a chance against the eruption of volcanic rage that had followed.

Kevin remembered the case well. It had made national headlines when the media learned that Lerance had called the police immediately after the killing and confessed. With all the clout and money in the world, the doctor not only refused a trial, but when his lawyer tried to negotiate a shorter sentence at a minimum security facility, Lerance insisted on being treated no differently than any other convicted killer. He was quickly remanded to Florida State Prison to serve out a twenty-five-year-to-life sentence.

Even Kevin had to admit the guy was fascinating. Why would someone who had everything, throw it away blindly in one fell swoop? Cheating was normal fare among the titled and rich, so what had Clarissa's confession really triggered? Why had Lerance chosen the SuperMax when his clean record and reputation could have greased an easy skate? Since he never gave interviews, people concluded Lerance chose the harsh sentence because he felt great remorse for his actions and wished to expiate his sin. Kevin believed people were more complicated than that.

Lerance almost didn't make it into the program. A technical mix up resulted in lost paperwork. At each prison they visited, Dominique and Kevin deposited a ream of application forms along with strict guidelines. Only convicts who had been model prisoners for at least two years could apply. Dominique was hot after Lerance from the beginning, even before he had ever applied. She, too, knew of his history. By some miracle of the fates right before the deadline, she found his paperwork and authorized it. Then after only one interview, he had made her short list.

Kevin had been present at that interview and he remembered that the former doctor had shown no discernable interest in relocating to House of Mithras. He answered their questions but remained stoic behind a mask of sullenness and a mountain of entitlement. Prison hardened men; for most it would take more than a quick chat to elicit emotions. But not so long ago Lerance had been a popular figure in Miami's social circles. He knew all about grace and decorum. Now it seemed he lacked even basic manners.

More importantly, the disparity between Lerance's station in life—his wealth and education—would by definition segregate him from the rest of the group. The other inmates would eat him alive.

Beneath that truth lay another. Whenever Dominique argued in favor of Lerance, she said all the right things, always carefully weighing his future contributions to the group against all possible deficits. Her arguments were impeccable and had it not been for just that hint of barely-disguised eagerness, Kevin might have been completely persuaded. Then and now, he felt regret in giving in so easily because he knew deep down that Dominique was far too invested in this prisoner. That might not bode well for Lerance. Might be worse for Dominique.

Kevin gave up this self-examination when the door snapped open letting in a small procession. Dominique, Guyla Rae and Jody Johnson, the young intern from LSU, joined Kevin at the long table. Dominique immediately began scrolling through her laptop. Guyla Rae passed out prisoner's files. Jody operated a small recording device and signaled to Dominique to start. Dominique closed the computer, glanced at her pile, straightened it and pulled some papers from the top. The rest did the same.

Dominique said, "I'd like to summarize each inmate's history before they get here."

Kevin, Guyla Rae, and Jody all stared at the materials in front of them. They knew each convict's story by heart, but the briefing gave the staff an opportunity to add observations or express concerns. Kevin knew what he had to do.

Dominique said, "As you know, these men, like most perpetrators of rage crimes, were once children who suffered repeated abuse and neglect. They wore their anger like masks to hide deep loss and pain. In the end fear and rage sealed their fates.

"Julius Lucky was a lowly mobbed up accountant working for the surviving Marcello family. One day, during a routine IRS audit, he had a psychotic breakdown. Terrified, and believing that the agent sent to look into expense irregularities might at any moment run out and tell the crime boss that he was cooking the books, Julius shot and killed the fed. In the past, he always carried a gun to look cool in front of his criminal colleagues, but never thought of actually using it. To this day, he doesn't remember firing the weapon. He once said a guy looking a lot like GI Joe came into the room, took his gun and fired it. When he was a child, Julius' stepfather used any excuse to hit him. After the beatings, Julius always turned to his collection of GI Joe dolls to avenge his bruised limbs and broken spirit.

Dominique reached for the second stack of papers and a thin smile passed her lips.

"Emile Joxieus suffers from Body Integrity Identity Disorder or BIID. Since childhood Emile has been a wanna-be amputee."

Wanna-be amputee. Those words sent shivers down Kevin's spine. Was BIID even a legitimate psychiatric disorder? Or was it a paraphilia? A perversion? Limited studies showed that apotemnopheliacs, those that are attracted to the idea of being an amputee, as distinguished from acrotomophiliacs—persons attracted to amputees—were usually highly educated people, successful in their careers and otherwise mentally and emotionally stable. Nevertheless, it would take some effort for him not to judge someone whose life's dream was to dismember a limb.

"He almost got his wish. Eight years ago, Emile had a shotgun neatly pointed at his kneecap. But when a neighbor intervened, he shot him instead."

"Are we in a position to let him have the surgery while he's incarcerated at House of Mithras?" Jody asked. Guyla Rae's mouth dropped.

Dominique said, "Elective amputation is illegal in the United States, as it is in most countries. We can, however, provide him with substitutions. We will discuss those options after he's been here for a while."

"We picked up a few extraordinary cases, didn't we?" Guyla Rae looked around at her colleagues, "You know what I mean. Take Eduardo Santana for instance. You can't make this stuff up."

"No you can't," Dominique agreed. "Eduardo was born in Arizona to undocumented parents, and spent his childhood moving from town to town. Often he missed meals and homework assignments. When his parents were deported, he found himself deposited on the doorstep of some well-meaning older relatives. By then, Eduardo was thirteen and running with thugs. When he turned eighteen, he managed to turn himself around by enrolling at a local community college. Had his sights on becoming a paralegal.

A few months later, a vindictive ex-girlfriend fingered him for a cop killing. Eduardo was convicted and spent five years of his young adult life with hardened criminals. But a few years ago, a court found him not guilty because new DNA evidence cleared him of the murder. And then right before his release, Eduardo strangled a guard twice his size before he could rape him.

Kevin said, "After that, Eduardo kept himself busy at night studying the law. Now one of his goals is to get a college degree online, and after he leaves here, to apply to law school.

Dominique said, "Next we have Vincent Delavon. Vincent's a gangster. High ranking, and one of the oldest to survive his hood. He grew up on a farm near Vicksburg, Mississippi. Points of light for him were his grandmother, plants and animals. He loved nature, the earth, and the hard work it took to make things grow.

"After his grandmother died, Vincent left for Jackson and the gangs. Ten years ago he shot a man whom he suspected of killing his step-son in a drive-by."

Kevin looked at his own copy of Vincent's profile and wondered how in hell a gangster could relate to a doctor born with a silver spoon in his mouth.

"Speaking of extraordinary." Dominique glanced at Guyla. The cross dresser was the administrator's favorite.

"While his mother left for New Orleans looking for tricks and drugs, Billy Jo Love spent most of his teenage years growing up alone on the Mississippi Delta in a rickety tent, living off scraps the villagers left behind. When he was older, he got a job as a dishwasher at a nice restaurant in the city. When a waiter made fun of Billy Jo's raggedy clothes, he killed him by snapping his neck." Dominique turned to Guyla Rae.

Guyla Rae pointed at the files and said, "It's not in there yet, but I did a little research on Billy Jo. I found a particularly meaningful event in his young life.

"Above the batture where Billy Jo lived, a Gypsy woman called Fifi parked her medium-sized trailer and started up residence. He used to watch the trailer from the river bank as collections of people moved in and out of there throughout the day. There were adults and kids, dogs and cats, too. No way to tell who belonged to whom. A week went by, and Fifi came down the hill and left a sandwich and a Coke next to the tent. After that, she came every day with a different meal. When it looked like it might snow, she left a blanket and a note. He read the note, wrapped himself in the blanket, grabbed his rucksack and climbed the hill to the trailer.

"Inside, people were laughing, smoking and drinking. After a while Fifi showed Billy Jo to a small sofa where he could sleep. Billy Jo couldn't sleep because he liked to watch Fifi too much. She was a small round woman who wore bright dresses and big gold heart-shaped earrings. She had thick blonde curly hair, dark blue eye shadow, false eyelashes; her cheeks were rouged like a clown's. She was a jolly sort, drinking and laughing with the others, usually until two or three in the morning.

"Each night he watched her from his makeshift bed. Once when he thought everyone in the trailer was asleep, he crept into the kitchen and rummaged through her purse. From another room, Fifi watched as he stole her rouge and a compact mirror. That night she opened a trunk in her bedroom and withdrew a yellow feather boa, which she neatly, secretly, folded into his rucksack.

Dominique said, "Tell us Guyla Rae, the meaning behind this remarkable story."

She said, "Billy Jo's dismally stark life was thrown a wild card. I think Fifi's intervention briefly brought the boy color and meaning into his world. It kept him from becoming feral, kept him basically sweet. That, in spite of the killing."

In a voice that brooked no contradiction, Dominique continued. "Lerance Lemartine was a celebrity doctor in Miami where he ministered to the wealthy and famous. One day he caught his wife cheating and killed her in a jealous rage."

This was Kevin's final opportunity to voice an objection that he knew would bear no weight, but might ultimately clear his own conscience.

Kevin said, "Would you please explain again how he fits in with the others?"

"Lerance grew up fulfilling his assigned role. Just like the others, his circumstances robbed him of his true nature and desires; he was born to a fate without any freedom to make choices for himself. His narcissistic parents created his personality and shaped his future. They hollowed out his soul and substituted it with theirs," Dominique said.

"But he did have advantages that the other guys couldn't dream of, and now it seems he wears his arrogance like a badge of pride. How is that going to help him here?"

"Lerance's arrogance is what he shows us when he's covering up his shame. He's simply hiding his feelings of helplessness and lack of power."

Kevin said, "It didn't stop him from killing his wife."

If Kevin knew he had gone too far, he didn't show it. But Guyla Rae and Jody signified the transgression by turning into statues. Dominique behaved like it was a mock trial debate and moved in for the kill.

"Let us not forget one of the guiding principals of Desire Therapy. When a person whose being is filled with toxic shame gains power, that shame can easily turn to rage, to violence. He's not so different from the others. Same virus, different rash. The boy hides his rage and the man kills."

Without another word, Dominique got up and called the technician to tell him that they were ready to launch the surveillance equipment. Guyla Rae took the opportunity to coax Kevin into the hall. He was too numb from defeat to resist.

"Why do you keep doing that to her?" she asked.

"What?"

"Getting in her face about Lerance. Why bother? It's a done deal," she said.

"Seems nothing is ever a done deal." Yesterday, didn't he tell Futrell just the opposite?

"Yeah, tell that to Dominique. Look I don't know what motivates you to poke her like this, but it's childish. Impetuous. It looks like jealousy," she said.

"I don't give a rat's ass about perception. We've worked too damned hard to get here. I don't want a grenade exploding in our faces," Kevin said.

"Why would you say that?" she asked.

Kevin still had Lerance's file in his hand and waved it at Guyla Rae.

"Have you read this?" Guyla Rae glared at him. "No, I mean really read this?"

"You know I did."

"It's in there. Dominique's reason for picking him. Guyla, she chose him for all the wrong reasons."

"What are you talking about?"

"I didn't see it before either."

Guyla Rae tentatively took the file from Kevin.

He said, "It's like looking in a mirror. She looks at him and she sees herself. She identifies with him. Guyla, they could be twins. Dominique and Lerance could be twins."

"How? You're not making sense."

"They have the exact same history. Both were child prodigies. Superior education. They both had parents and communities who used them as vessels for vicarious successes and acclaim. Similar star-struck careers, and nationally famous reputations within their fields. The only difference: the side of the railroad tracks they were born on."

Guyla Rae shook her head and handed the file back to Kevin. "You're forgetting something else. One of them is a cold-blooded killer."

SIX

Billy Jo had enough of Julius' stinky, dripping sweat.

It was like a new form of Chinese water torture. When they fell on him, the droplets soaked right through Billy Jo's prison-issued surgical scrubs. He hated wearing another man's scent. The prisoner showed his dissatisfaction by pushing his bony hip into the other man's meatier one.

Julius pushed back, hissing, "If you do that again I'll fucking kill you faggot. Move it or lose it."

Billy Jo and Julius had been at it for the last ten minutes. The driver's Plexiglass window had opened several times with warning shouts from the guards to be quiet. The last time, as added incentive, a riot-wielding baton pummeled their seat, coming dangerously close to breaking both offending hips.

"Your fucking mother, you fucker," Billy Jo hissed.

The specially-crafted prison transport was making its maiden voyage on the way to Elysian Fields Parish. It had been built for better en route prisoner control. Its main feature was a low profile interior that restrained prisoners from standing. But that did not keep them from colliding with each other. Sometimes the men pushed each other on purpose, but a prison transport is only a glorified van, and ever since the convicts left the staging site at Dixon Correctional Institute almost four hours earlier, the vehicle had jounced over the highway like a wayward ride at the county fair.

The other problem was lack of oxygen. The air hung like greasy smog. The transport was supposed to be air-conditioned, but Billy Jo suspected the guards had closed off the vents to the holding area just to make the prisoners miserable. It was only when they opened the safety window to yell that he felt any breeze at all. Getting to breathe sweet air, if only for a moment, was worth the risk of getting whacked.

Billy Jo looked around him. No one would meet his eyes. He didn't care because he just liked to look at people. It was better if they didn't look back. That way he could thoroughly examine their features.

He was sitting in the middle of two facing metal benches, between the sweating hog and an older guy who appeared to sleep. His nemesis on the right was short, round and swarthy, with the thickest hair he'd ever seen. It was dark with mahogany highlights. He liked that hair. Just wished it would stop dripping on him so much. The guy on the left was cool. He never complained when Billy Jo accidentally bumped him. He had a girl's name. Emily, or Emile. His hair was cut like a helmet with a touch of grey at the temples. At the back of his head a small bald spot was beginning to show. Like a monk. Emile had kind grey eyes under granny glasses, but there was something strange about his legs. Or leg. Whenever Billy looked down it appeared the man had only one. But he had seen him walk normally into the van. As normally as you could when you're shackled. Pretty good trick though, Billy thought. He wondered if he could make the rest of himself disappear, too.

Next he studied the two men across from him. One of them was the biggest guy he'd ever seen, and the only black guy in the group. Vincent. Now that was a good name. He had a lion's nose that flared at the nostrils and looked far too small for his face that began and ended with sharp cheekbones. His large copper eyes looked troubled. His head was shaved bald, and Billy Jo could see thick neck muscles ripple whenever he exhaled.

Next to him sat a youngish guy like himself. But a Latino, named Eduardo. Good looking with sad, almost black eyes. He had a short concave nose, perfect ears and nearly poreless skin. Both men usually kept their gazes on the floor, but occasionally the black guy turned to stare at the perpendicular seat by the back doors, where one lone prisoner sat. The way Vincent looked at the guy, it was as if he knew him.

The man in the back, Léonce, or Lawrence, fascinated Billy Jo the most. His handsome features: olive skin, slightly slanted-downward hazel eyes, eyelashes so thick and long they looked false, didn't jibe with his scowl. It was as if he were *trying* to appear menacing, but didn't quite have what it took to pull it off. Vincent noticed, too, and it bothered him — Billy Jo could tell. Twice the two men's eyes had locked and Billy felt the air get hotter and muskier. Animals marking territory through their pores. There would be trouble between them. Not like the kind between him and Julius. That was as dangerous as a swarm of mosquitoes. No, real trouble. Like hunter and prey trouble. So, who would get eaten?

Even though he compulsively studied people, Billy Jo didn't judge others by their looks, not wanting to inflict the same pain that he had frequently endured. He worried because his own appearance was definitely a cause for concern. So far, except for Mr. Oily next to him, the other four seemed disinterested in Billy Jo's looks. But like all the others before them, these men would eventually send him questioning stares. His six-foot frame weighed in at one hundred and thirty pounds. His hair was wavy and styled like the iconic young Elvis'. With his round, gemstone blue eyes, long pointy nose, and a small mouth whose corners sagged slightly, he might have passed for normal. But he was born with eyebrows that doomed him to a lifetime of unwanted attention. They were black and thick, shaped like sharp arches, and gave him the perpetual look of a clown or mime. Some thought he was a homosexual. That would be okay, but he wasn't one. He just liked to put on makeup and dress up like some of them.

Dominique and Guyla Ray stood in the psychiatrist's office arm in arm looking out the bay window past the protestors—they had arrived along with the sheriff a few hours earlier—and beyond the sugar fields. The women concentrated on a distant road where a van carrying their subjects would soon crest the hill to turn onto Ayrshire Boulevard, the two-lane leading to the plantation. The six prisoners would be there in less then fifteen minutes.

"Now that we have a moment alone, I want to show you something." Guyla Rae dropped Dominique's arm and winked at her. She strode to the back of the room where she picked up a wooden box and her satchel. She set both down on the desk.

As Dominique started towards her, Guyla Rae detected a flash of anger flit inside the bewitching eyes just before the director leaned over and clasped the edge of her desk with both hands.

"Oh no. No you don't Guyla."

The wooden box was open revealing a blue-plated pistol. Guyla Rae said, "It's a beaut. Registered to House of Mithras. They said at the sheriff's office you refused to sign for it. So, I did."

"I don't need it." Dominique straightened and folded her hands on her hip.

"It's a Smith & Wesson Sigma 40VE. See here, it has a polymer frame stainless steel slide." Guyla Rae demonstrated, playing with the slide a few times. "Best part, it's ergonomically designed. That means it shoots straight. Every time. They say it's as easy as pointing your finger. It also has a matte finish on—"

"Were you listening?" Dominique asked.

"Were you? I know how distasteful this seems to you, but it's about insurance."

"I don't need insurance."

Guyla Rae placed the gun carefully back in the box, closed it and picked up her satchel. "A different kind of insurance. The real kind. You know, liability, indemnity and all that. Besides, think of it as giving your good buddy—that would be me—a separate peace of mind."

Guyla Rae followed Dominique back to the window and put an arm around her shoulders. "The gun's not loaded. The bullets are in a separate box. Lock it up. Hide the key. Don't think twice about it."

It was still as small as a fly, but they could clearly see the prisoner van crest Ayrshire Boulevard three miles away.

Something in the tall thin woman reminded Guyla Rae of a thoroughbred right before she breaks out of the starting gate. She felt something leap between them. It was their simultaneous beating hearts. They stood with the knowledge that within minutes things would never be the same again. And then Guyla Rae remembered the strange letter inside her satchel.

"This came for you today."

Guyla Rae watched Dominique's face morph first into childlike anxiety, then into complete bewilderment, and finally into a wolfish grin. The psychiatrist took the letter in her hands and started to probe it like some small child's errant toy.

When the hands stilled, they both stared at the return address—a drawing of Delilah blinding Sampson with a burning sword. But Dominique didn't say a word. The bemused psychiatrist would not dignify this sudden intrusion into her life.

Guyla Rae said, "Hmm, a Biblical reference. Probably from the protestors. Open it later. Let's go, it's time."

The two women walked out of the office quickly, but before Guyla Rae could pull the door shut behind her, in what seemed like one practiced motion and without even turning around, Dominique arced her hand back and high, depositing the envelope inside a metal trash can just inside the room. The administrator thought she heard a hiss, like the striking of match and the odor of burning paper. Or maybe Sampson's scorched flesh.

SEVEN

A man across the road from Louisiana's last standing Creole plantation, now the infamous House of Mithras reform prison, raised his binoculars and began motioning frantically to the protestors. The sorrowful group favoring overalls and spattered sneakers, raised hand-painted signs with names of murder victims, and formed a circle in the middle of the road. All at once they began singing the civil rights song, "We Shall Overcome." Fifty feet away sitting inside his vintage Crown Vic, Sheriff Leroy Futrell also spotted the prisoner van. He pulled on his shades, took one last swig of coffee, and reluctantly said goodbye to the only cool calm air left in the vicinity.

With two House of Mithras guards bringing up the rear, the prison staff marched single- file down the wide, wooden staircase to the lawn. Two more guards, with rifles positioned to fire, stood on the second-floor balcony. When the sheriff opened the gate to let in the prison transport, the protestors ran towards it, but stopped short when the lawman shut the gate behind him.

Dominique, Kevin, Guyla Rae and Jody couldn't help themselves. When the prisoners finally stepped out of the van, they eyed them hungrily like they were items on a restaurant menu. The men did not return their gazes, but kept their eyes fixed solidly on the ground while the transport guards led their shackled line to the brick courtyard in front of the staff. The House of Mithras guards, guns holstered, expressions tentative—as if embarrassed by their roles and thereby appearing less menacing than their law enforcement peers—met them on the lawn.

"Take off their cuffs." Kevin's order fell on deaf ears. The guards who recently had enjoyed unchallenged authority over the prisoners stiffened as they stared straight past him. But now twelve pairs of eyes searched Kevin's handsome face. Wondering if he'd reverse himself. *Just kidding folks.*

"What are you waiting for?" Kevin wasn't in a kidding mood.

While one transport guard stood back with his shotgun aimed, ready to shoot any and every transgressor, the second guard in an exaggerated show of shock and some amusement, began removing the restraints. The prisoners' eyes wouldn't leave Kevin's.

"You've been sitting in a hot vehicle for more than six hours; I bet your muscles are cramped and you'd like to stretch. Go ahead. Stretch. There's nothing to be afraid of."

Billy Jo Love bent over and touched his toes. He straightened and stretched his arms over his head, but quickly dropped them, because like the butt of a practical joke, he was embarrassed to find out that he was the only one availing himself of the so-called new freedoms.

Dominique moved forward. "My name is Dr. Dominique Doucette. I am co-director of House of Mithras. Mithras. The name the early Persians gave to their god of contracts. For the next two years, together, we will fulfill the terms of *our* contract."

In the distance, the protestors began shouting.

"VICTIMS NOT KILLERS!"

When Dominique looked in their direction, she saw the sheriff shrug and tip his hat lightly. She nodded back because only Futrell could keep a short lead on that group.

Dominique said, "Your part is to follow a rigorous program of therapy and work. Everyday you will complete assignments recollecting and describing your childhoods. You will recall your parents and family and what they expected of you, how you were treated, how you treated others. You will record the worst times, the best times. If you were able to distinguish between sadness and happiness. Or safety and fear. These are important assignments that will lead to the Desire portion of the therapy, where the goal will be to liberate your true and authentic selves. The real key to rehabilitation.

"You will take classes as a group so you can learn about the causes of anger, values training, and cooperative skills building. People learn faster and retain more if they can work together, bounce ideas off each other. If you're connected to people, your rehabilitation multiplies, and so does the ability to make good choices for your life."

"VICTIMS NOT KILLERS! VICTIMS NOT KILLERS! VICTIMS NOT KILLERS!" The protestors' chant escalated into a curtain of wails.

"Each day you will be expected to do hard physical work that will not only benefit the local community, but will also keep you healthy and fit. Finally, you will volunteer service at one of our partner agencies in New Orleans.

"Our part of the bargain will be to guide and help you achieve your goals, and in the end, to assess your progress and make parole recommendations," she said, raising her voice slightly.

"VICTIMS NOT KILLERS! VICTIMS NOT KILLERS! VICTIMS NOT KILLERS!"

Dominique moved closer to the prisoners. "Once you've completed the program and demonstrated that you can readapt into society and live as a nonviolent and productive citizen, you will become eligible for a sentence reduction and considered for parole."

One roaring shout followed another. A wiry rumpled youth with thick glasses slipped by the sheriff, cracked the gate open and ran onto the grounds. After he broke through, neither the guards nor staff had a chance to react, because Futrell already had his arm around the distressed protestor and was leading him easily, collegially, back to the fence. When they were on the other side of the latched gate again, the sheriff took off his sunglasses and began speaking to the crowd. The protestors became very still and then a man laughed. The crowd moved back in a wave, swaying in time to the sugar cane behind them, but lacking its certain grace or color. When they were on the road again, the protestors raised their signs and resumed singing. The sheriff nodded to Dominique. What was it about him, she wondered.

"I'm Dr. Kevin Waddell, the other director of House of Mithras. We want y'all to feel ownership in this program. You can do that by building trust. But I'll tell you true right now, we're not fools." Kevin pointed to the roof.

A bank of cameras lined up awkwardly, marring the golden roofline and its gables. While the prisoners scanned the building, Guyla Rae worked with the first transport guard, exchanging paperwork and signatures. As fast as he could, the state correctional officer signed each page, relinquishing all responsibility over to her, to the scant human security detail, and the cameras above.

"Our state-of-the-art surveillance system more than makes up for the relaxed rules and minimal ground security. It was mighty expensive and this building is covered in cameras, inside and out."

When she spoke before, the inmates had not looked directly at Dominique. Even though each of them had met with her at least once—director or not—right then she was a woman out of reach. In prison, the penalty for fraternizing with female correctional personnel had been crushing: solitary confinement or worse. But now they did tear their eyes away from the rooftop to study Kevin. Nothing in their experience had prepared them for a warden who looked like he just stepped out of the pages of *GQ*, wearing a casual suede sports coat, no tie, and perfectly creased tailored pants. Yet he was smiling sincerely, acting like becoming their best friend was the only thing he'd ever wished for. For the prisoners, there could be no choice but to ride out the amusement car to its final destination.

"Not only are there monitors in reception, technicians will follow your whereabouts and actions within the surveillance center itself. There are dedicated phone lines to statewide law enforcement. We can have six-dozen baton-wielding riot police here within minutes." Even though everyone knew the last statement was an exaggeration, it got the inmates' attention.

As if hearing their cue, the transport guards made their way quickly to the prison van, got in and turned it towards the gate. For the last time, the sheriff opened the gate and when the van cleared the grounds, he walked back to his car.

"Unless you are told otherwise, surveillance will exclude individual therapy sessions."

The Crown Vic roared to life and by the time it was halfway around the estate, all but the glinting tips of the 1957 bat fins remained visible; the rest of the car disappeared inside a fast-moving screen of pulverized dust and smoke that would hang in the air long after Dominique finished speaking.

She stepped forward. "Tomorrow is a big day. You will go in pairs to start volunteer work in the city. Guards will show you to your dormitories now. Good luck, men."

There was something reassuring about the last words, *good luck*. So reassuring that when the prisoners got to their rooms, they quickly forgot everything they were told about surveillance.

Dominique, Kevin and Guyla Rae put on their headsets. Jody typed in a command on the computer and three screens came to life. The staff watched and listened with feral interest, only mildly aware that they were spying on their subjects. Dominique reminded them that they were professionals, and what they were about to do was both appropriate and necessary.

Another click and on the first screen they saw the faces of Julius Lucky and his roommate Billy Jo Love. Inside the doorway, the inmates were getting into a shoving match. The guard only inches behind them, waited stoically.

"You don't want to mess with me. I was the Mancusso family bookkeeper, "Julius said, blocking the doorway.

"I should give a fuck about you! You seen my sheet? I got sent to the Farm cuz I killed a man with my bare hands," Billy Jo replied.

"Enough. Get in there, now," the guard shouted. The inmates stepped inside the room and looked maniacally around. Billy ran for the bed on the left, while Julius made a big show of laying claim over the bed on the right. The guard watched them for a while longer before leaving the room and locking it behind him.

Inside the surveillance room, the team watched in astonishment as Julius and Billy Jo, each from their own beds, began a stare down, the kind that can frequently be found on school playgrounds when five-year-olds fight over a toy, one that will be forgotten only minutes after returning to the classroom.

Guyla Rae said, "Oh boy."

Dominique said, "It's a ritual. Establishing pecking order. But also saving face."

"Fuck you."

"Fuck your fucking mother."

On a second monitor, Emile and Eduardo were already inside their room.

Emile pointed to a bed, "Mind if I take this one?"

Eduardo answered without looking at him. "I don't care."

After heaving his duffle bag onto the bed, Emile began removing articles of clothing and neatly placing them inside a dresser drawer. When he turned back to the bed he saw Eduardo pick up a pair of his trousers out of the duffle bag. The younger man held them up high so one pant leg dangled down, but the other was so short it could only have been cut to fit an amputee. Emile snatched the pants back and stuck them inside the dresser drawer. Eduardo looked like he might say something. Like he might say a lot. But he only shrugged and moved to the other side of the room to begin his own unpacking.

"Will you get a load of this?" Kevin was following the images on the last monitor where Lerance and Vincent had just entered their room with another guard standing outside the opened door. "I'm going to rewind it so you can see it from the beginning.

The guard watched for a moment through the doorway, then pulled the door shut and locked it. While Vincent unpacked, he dropped a copy of Organic Gardening magazine. Lerance bent over to pick it up, but Vincent grabbed it first. Disgust briefly creased Lerance's eyes and then he lifted his arms up as if to say, "it's none of my business." When Vincent stepped into Lerance's personal space, the two convicts stared each other down for almost a minute before Lerance gave up and turned away. Vincent continued staring at the back of Lerance's head and slapped the rolled up magazine against his thigh.

Guyla Rae asked, "What are they doing?"

Kevin said, "Sizing each other up, storing weapons for another time."

Guyla Rae said, "Dominique, I'm beginning to think that tomorrow might be a bit early for volunteer work. I mean, shouldn't the inmates get to know each other some before we dump them on the community?"

Without taking her eyes off the screen, Dominique said, "The sooner they start doing meaningful work, the quicker they rehabilitate." Then, turning a weary smile on Guyla Rae, she added, "Besides, the guards are like trained pit bulls. They'd be crazy to try anything stupid."

EIGHT

Dominique seemed to be driven by twin forces: the need to stay safe in her own skin—unfortunately that meant being cold and dismissive to everyone around her, including her loyal friend Kevin—and the fear she was turning into a harpy whom no one could love, not even steadfast, loyal Kevin. She could ill afford to lose him now.

The day after the opening, Dominique was determined to make things right between them again. She began by exchanging her designer suit for a comfortable pair of jeans and a cotton shirt. She scrubbed her face clean of makeup and let her hair fall into a loosely gathered ponytail. And then she surprised Kevin by suggesting that they take a trip up to New Orleans to meet up with the old neighborhood kids.

Kevin offered to drive, and they left in plenty of time to get to the city before dusk. Watching Dominique return to a former version of herself, Kevin relaxed and spoke amiably, eventually ticking off a series of sappy jokes. Dominique responded with laughter and threw in a few of her own. With each passing mile, she felt her crusty exterior melt and give way to a mushier, kinder inside. The pleasure of life was returning. When you acted the part, you became the part. But why had she, Dominique wondered, been repaying Kevin's friendly advances with so much indifference? If he wanted to socialize with her once in awhile, well then who in Hades was she to mistrust his motives?

An hour later, when the car turned onto dusty Claiborne Avenue towards the Desire neighborhood, she felt some of her old anxiety return. It had been years since she last visited the neighborhood, but today the streets looked like they had succumbed to a rotting away disease, now in the terminal stages of life. Burned and abandoned buildings lined the main thoroughfare. Crumbling facades and broken windows left nothing to the imagination. Muffler-missing-smog-billowing cars maneuvered potholes big enough to snag whole wheels and break axles. Rolling debris slapped against the fenders and occasionally flew inside the car. As far as the eye could see, discarded cans and bottles of beer and whiskey, newspapers, old diapers, trash of any flavor, and at times broken-down furniture hugged the gutters and rare parking spaces. Once they had to steer around a twin mattress lying in the middle of the street where a family of kids played keep-away.

But mostly it was the people themselves. Baby-faced teen mothers pushing strollers. Small children with hollowed-out eyes hanging onto older siblings, who hung around corners brokering deals for their daily supper. And daily fix. Her childhood home was being eaten alive from the inside by poverty and crack cocaine. It was a filthy mess, and now she was sorry she'd suggested the trip.

Worse than that, she had begun the blaming game. Suddenly it was all Kevin's fault. If it hadn't been for him, they wouldn't be here at all.

Building community partnerships to achieve common goals was a key component of House of Mithras. Because she had grown up in Desire, Kevin said the neighborhood was an ideal place to set up their adjunct programs. She argued against Desire, because she thought it might show favoritism, and Dominique didn't want appearances to derail community confidence and trust. But Kevin had an ace in his pocket. He knew that they both had an unbreakable tie to the area.

Ten years earlier and almost out of whole cloth, Dominique and Kevin had started a street corner mental health clinic in Desire. Using the financial and social power of more established medical institutions, they were able to provide much-needed relief to struggling working parents, pregnant teens, and ADHD children. The cost to clients: working a few hours each week at the clinic. It was modeled after other initiatives up north, but unlike those ventures, there just wasn't enough support, in-kind or financial, to balance out the number of clients who needed to be seen each week. Right about the time the reserves started drying up, Dominique had been offered a once-in-a-lifetime consulting position with New York State Corrections. After only six months, she resigned her position as director and clinician, handing Kevin and a team of recent graduates from Louisiana State University, the reins. Kevin had stayed on an additional six months wringing out every last sweaty penny from the original grants. He contributed his own savings and waited while his volunteer staff tried to raise money from foundations. It never happened. Fifteen months after it opened, the clinic closed its doors forever.

Even thought the clinic failed, Dominique's reputation as the consummate psychiatrist, able to work the gamut from beleaguered civil war survivors, to highfalutin' spoiled

Hollywood celebs, was legend. When you've appeared on Oprah, and were regularly quoted as often in *Essence* as *Cosmo*, you would remain popular and admired.

Kevin was just as popular, but even more loved because he had stayed longer, working without pay. And he didn't just work behind a desk at the clinic. He had rolled up his sleeves and got to know the neighbors. Whenever someone needed a car jump-started or a lawnmower fixed, he was there to lend a hand. Kevin volunteered at the local food bank, gave people rides to work, and occasionally watched over latchkey kids while counseling their parents. They called him Albino, Whitey, Mr. Pillsbury Doughboy, and sometimes, Mr. New York. But they all respected and trusted him. And missed him.

Dominique knew it wasn't Kevin's fault. There was something about returning to her past. And if she were really honest with herself, she would have to admit urban decay was not the root cause of her discomfort. But she couldn't afford to be honest. At least not that honest.

As they drove, purple haze streaked through scorched trees. Deep shadows fell on single shotgun houses making the people standing in front of them disappear. In a movie, these scenes might neatly showcase a slice of Americana; to Dominique they were lonely eyesores.

Kevin pointed to a dilapidated structure canting to one side, "Look, our old building. Has it really been that long?"

"So long ago, I can remember being young and idealistic," Dominique said.

He braked as a tall, skinny teen-aged boy walked down the middle of the street hoisting an old boom box on his shoulder. The tape started and sputtered, but his solution was to pump up the volume. They waited for him to go around the car before moving forward again.

Dominique said, "This is a hell hole. What happened? Once, crime around here was virtually wiped out." When they turned left, Kevin had to brake again, this time for a group of kids whose average age looked to be less than seven, several of whom weren't wearing pants or underpants. They looked like they would rush the car, but at the last second ran away. "That's when people really invested in their neighborhood," Dominique added.

Kevin listened patiently to Dominique's rant. He had heard the speech before. Pretty negative coming out of the woman who created Desire Therapy. But the 'hood was family to her, and aren't we always harder on our own families?

Dominique said, "Now this place is a night deposit for registered sex offenders, drive-bys, drug deals. Abandoned children."

Kevin said, "It's not their fault. Lack of money, dried up resources. You do the numbers. Or the lack of them. Everything grinds to a halt."

"Don't give me that. You don't just stop caring. And when did it become fashionable to give up on parenting?"

"You're missing the point. There's generational warfare..."

"When you protect your kids, you also teach them right from wrong."

"And socio/political struggles," Kevin said.

"I don't need a history lesson from you. For God's sake. Kevin, this neighborhood is no better than a snake pit."

"I think there's a world of pain and hurt here that you can't identify with."

"You're right. I can't identify with becoming a victim. I would rather die."

"Not fair, you were a spoiled and pampered little girl."

"My family and community scraped together every last nickel so I could have opportunities. Do you really think that makes me spoiled? Pampered?"

"What price did you pay?"

"You think my people sold me out? Because they showed me love and protection? What the hell do you know?" Dominique stopped suddenly, remembering her promise to herself to be nicer.

"Most of your childhood was buried in textbooks and music lessons. When were you ever part of the community? When did you have time to play with other children?"

Kevin parked the car in front of a two-story grey clapboard house and looked earnestly at his friend.

She said, "Everyone sacrifices something."

NINE

The twins, Jerome and Keisha Davis, weren't even born when Dominique and Kevin ran their free clinic ten years earlier, and their older sister Yolanda was too young to remember what the pair had done for the neighborhood. But when the door screeched opened, turning loose a small tornado of three galloping kids, the event played out like it was some long overdue reunion. Though they had never met each other before, in their hearts—thanks to the stories their mother and her friends told—the children felt as close to the psychiatrist as if they had grown up with her.

Earlier in the day, Kevin called Marsha Davis to let her know he and Dominique would be stopping by, visiting the old 'hood. She told them she would be at work, but to come by anyway because the kids would be overjoyed to see them. The kids also learned from their mother that they could expect treats.

Jerome and Keisha dashed around the car jumping up and down, chanting "Dominique," "Kevin." Even Dominique brightened as she took in the sights and sounds, summer's youthful exuberance. Yolanda, who until then had tried to appear respectable and ladylike, began laughing girlishly from the stoop. Kevin swooped up the squirming twins, one in each arm, while Dominique pulled the ice cream chest from the trunk.

After the younger siblings finished unwrapping their ice cream cones, they nestled themselves between Dominique and Kevin. Keisha, eventually making it onto Dominique's lap, and Jerome onto Kevin's. When Yolanda came down and extracted a cone out of the ice chest, Kevin made a whistling sound and slapped his leg.

He said, "Nah, can't be. Is that really you...Yolanda? Last time I saw you," he lowered his hand to his knee, "You were this high. Only six years old. But I'd recognize those big beautiful eyes anywhere. Just look at you. Almost all grown up."

Yolanda smiled bashfully, but turned her gaze to Dominique. "My mama told me what you did for me. I'm so lucky, thank you very much."

Dominique arched her eyebrows and shrugged. "I should be thanking you. We're lucky to have someone as bright as you on our team. Come here." Dominique threw open her arms and Yolanda let herself be hugged and kissed by one of the most famous black women of her time.

Kevin said, "That's right, you start tomorrow night at St. Francis homeless shelter." He glanced at Dominique. "Helping us with a new computer program that tracks residents, and babysitting the kids when their parents look for jobs."

Jerome rolled off Kevin and began making faces. "Yolanda's gonna start working with homeless people and con men." Kevin picked him up and twirled him around until the child begged him to stop.

"What did you call them? Tell me I didn't hear that." Kevin clamped the small boy onto his hip and they sat down again.

Jerome was still giggling when Yolanda playfully punched her brother's arm. She said, "They're called convicts, dufus." To Kevin she added, "My Mama told me that the staff and residents would be safe cuz they're guarded all the time."

Kevin said, "Yes ma'am. Nothing to worry about."

Dominique said, "I used to live here. This is my old neighborhood. My street. Did you know that your Grandpappy was a friend to me when I was little girl?" She pointed to her left. "And see that house next door. That used to be Treasure House. Once when the owners went away for a while, I played inside that house every single day. It was my favorite place in the whole wide world. I can't remember having that much fun since."

Jerome wanted to know, "How come Grandpappy was your friend?"

"Because he was in charge of keeping the house clean and safe until the Treasures returned. One day when he saw my friend and me playing inside, instead of scolding us, he brought us treats instead. He never told on us once. And I knew your mama, too. She was my age, just a little girl."

Jerome asked, "Who did you play with in that house?"

"My best friend in the whole wide world. A little boy like you."

Across the street, curtains and blinds opened and closed. Slowly men and women walked out onto their porches to stare at the unconventional group. No one made a move to say hey until a man in his eighties hobbled across the street to shake hands with Dominique. She clasped the old man's arm warmly and kissed him on the cheek.

"Handsome George. How long has it been? You haven't changed an iota. Lordy, a sight for sore eyes. How is that lucky wife of yours, Janey?" Dominique asked.

"Mighty fine, ma'am. We're all fine ma'am."

Handsome George was a legend because he was old school and never took any crap from the young kids, or the gangsters. Here it took a legend to break the ice. Gradually more people drifted in to either wave, or get a better look at the psychiatrists. Some older folks stayed and reminisced about bygone days. As they all stood chatting, the air around them hung heavy in clumps of heat and stench. Dominique wished for a breeze, and then she got one.

Abruptly, the kids and adults began rushing away back to the safety of their own porches and homes. Before anyone could hear the sounds, they felt them inside their chest walls and in the dirt under their feet. In the distance, a slow-moving-filled-with-pulsating-music, black Hummer was turning the corner, a few boys on bikes hanging onto the bumper. When it stopped in front of the stoop, the bikers fled. Four doors opened simultaneously, but only three men got out.

Dominique, Kevin and the kids, stood up at the same time. Yolanda moved slightly behind Kevin and to his side, the younger ones each grabbed one of his hands. As the large man clambered up the steps the kids froze, but Dominique and Kevin broke out into huge grins. Then the big guy picked up Dominique and kissed her on top of her head.

To Kevin's amazement, Dominique could still do it. Flip a switch and play any role. A new role, a traditional one, whatever, she could fit in anywhere. Back on the ground, clutching her chest dramatically Dominique cried, "I'll be. If it ain't the posse Boucree! Elijah, y'all still behind street patrol?"

Elijah said, "How do you think we knew you were here? We run a well-oiled machine." To Kevin, "Hey."

Kevin walked over to shake the big man's hand, but Elijah clasped him sturdily around the shoulders like they were brothers.

Yolanda walked her siblings to the edge of the porch where they sat down quietly, and then turned back to offer an ice cream cone to Elijah, which he politely declined. But when she extended the offer to the younger men flanking their leader, they grabbed the cold treats eagerly.

"This here punk is Sadizfy," he pointed to the teenager on his left, "and the other sorry twerp's my cousin from Georgia. His name is Henry, but he goes by Gemini. Not even his sign, he's actually a Cancer for fool's sake." That got a chuckle out of the kids, and almost no one noticed that a fourth man had gotten out to walk to the back of the Hummer. Except Dominique.

And Sadizfy. He wasted no time marching after him.

"Darnell, what's wrong with you man? Don't you know who that is? Dominique. You can't be disrespecting her like that."

Darnell who was twice his age and size, said, "Get away from me. You don't know. We had something once."

At first Sadizfy looked confused, but when he looked back at Dominique and then at Darnell again, he fell out laughing. "Give it up. With her? You wish you had something."

Sadizfy sashayed back to the newly-formed crowd surrounding the stoop, shaking his head, still chuckling to himself. That's when Darnell turned all the way around and locked eyes with Dominique. They stayed that way for a while, and no one spoke. No one moved.

"Elijah. What's going on?" Dominique said.

"You didn't hear? Darnell just got out of central lock up. Some trumped up loitering charge. Now he's pissing in short jerks."

"Did he get busted for drugs?"

Elijah looked at Dominique like she had said something funny. "Worse. Our boy's been practicing sobriety. Sometimes he's so ornery, I just wanna beat him across the head." He looked back with an exaggerated scowl at Darnell. The man at the end of the street continued to stare at Dominique.

When Dominique started to move, Elijah cut her stride by lobbing one long arm onto her shoulder.

"You don't want to go there. Now's not the time."

"Oh, yeah? Then why'd you bring him?' Dominique asked.

"I'm sorry, it was a mistake."

"Let me by. He's family."

The hand dropped on command. "Your funeral."

When Dominique got close, Darnell tuned his back to her and what seemed like the whole world. He crushed a cigarette under his feet and lit another. Inhaling deeply, he pretended to be interested in his shoes.

"Hey."

Darnell inhaled and studied the sky.

"It's me. Look at me. Me, Niqui."

"Are you sure?"

Dominique stood so close only fabric separated them. The scent of her old friend smelled like childhood. She raised her hand to touch him, but after a moment lowered it down to her hip. She tried again, but couldn't steel herself against the unspoken rejection. Sensing desperation, Darnell turned all the way around and looked at her. She nearly fainted.

His face was at once of the boy and the man she had loved all of her life. Her skin felt like it was melting off her bones. Something inside her was struggling to free itself, clawing its way to the surface. Suddenly Kevin ceased to matter. House of Mithras didn't exist. Her neighborhood's blight problems—gone. This was her chance. She only had moments to convince him. If she didn't, he'd be lost to her forever. There were just so many times a human could endure abandonment.

Dominique said, " Listen to me. I know I fucked up. Real bad last time. And I know I don't deserve you, but I love you. You know that's never changed, don't you?

"I don't think I've ever loved anyone else. Ever. Not really. Please, you have to help me one last time. I need you." As she listened to the wretched echo of her words, she was reminded of a strung-out heroin addict.

Darnell surprised her. She watched him struggling to maintain some unspoken promise to himself. *Come on, she thought, give it up. It's me. It's us. You don't have it in you to run away. Not from me.*

"I need a friend. I need you," she said.

Darnell said, "What kind of friend leaves and doesn't call or write for ten years?"

"Not a day went by that I didn't think about you. But I worried that I might—"

"I didn't think about you once."

Dominique's eyes grew wide and filled with dread.

"Darnell, *she* stayed. She stayed right here, waiting for me to come back. I don't know what to do now. Tell me what to do."

Darnell dropped his gaze to the cracked macadam searching for an answer. None came.

Dominique said, "A letter came yesterday."

Darnell trained his steel blue eyes on her and Dominique thought she saw real concern. Her heart leapt. "How long had it been?" he asked.

"Not since I left the last time. See, that's why I couldn't contact you. I couldn't take the chance. You'd been through too much."

"You mean *you put me* through too much."

Dominique looked like she'd been slapped.

"Okay, what'd you do with it? Did you read it?" he asked.

"No. I threw it away."

"Now that's good. That's thinking smart. Ignore her and she'll go away."

"No. That's not right. You know she doesn't just go away. She won't give up this easily."

She had pushed too hard and watched as Darnell turned into someone she barely recognized. Someone who could stand up for himself.

"You disappear for ten years. And you expect everything to be like it was?"

"Please, please," she cried.

His voice was so soft she had to strain to hear, but it hurt too much to listen. "When you left, I thought I might stop breathing. But look at me. I'm alive. I live. And now, I can't go through that shit again. I've changed."

"What if next time, there isn't a letter? What if she decides to show up?"

He dropped his gaze once again to the ground and this time it rewarded him. "Then you should've stayed gone."

While he drove her home, Kevin tried a couple of times to make conversation, but Dominique had once again retreated inside another indecipherable mood.

In front of her house, Kevin said, "I'll pick you up in the morning."

"Don't bother, I've got a car here," Dominique said, getting out.

"I could never understand your obsession with him."

"We go way back."

"Even so. He's a thug. I'd watch myself around him."

"You're wrong. Darnell would never hurt me."

TEN

Dominique Doucette could have chosen to live in any house, in any part of New Orleans. A double gallery home in the historic Garden District, a raised Greek revival manse on St. Charles Avenue, or a soft brick Creole cottage in the city's culturally diverse Vieux Carré. Or even in a sealed-off fortress in nearby Metarie, where rubbing shoulders with local celebrities, as well as nationally famous musicians and movie stars, was a time-honored tradition.

Instead, the psychiatrist picked an unassuming shotgun on Prytania Avenue in Uptown. After seeing it just once, she hired a preservationist architectural firm to reverse the interior deterioration, and restore the exterior's vintage architecture.

She didn't give a hoot that it might be the smallest house on the block, and like its owner, ill-fitting indeed, among the established white social elite—those card-carrying kings and queens of Mardi Gras, and leaders of the venerated and ancient krewes. Her new home might have only been a mid-nineteenth century adaptation of an earlier simple Haitian style, but it reminded her of the old neighborhood and Treasure House, where she and her best friend had played so long ago. And sometimes when the sun creased them just right, looking at the soft lemon-yellow clapboards could transport her straight back to those earlier times.

She stood in the driveway looking absentmindedly over at a low brick parapet that ran along the side of the house, where a new conflux of pass-along pots had sprouted—that day's gifts from neighbors and other well wishers. At the bottom of the steps, Dominique ran her hand over the castle-shaped finial on top of the porch railing. Her gaze poured tenderly over the glass-paned doors on either side of the front porch, and the leaded glass double-hung windows in the middle.

Dominique took a minute more to look over other ornamental touches that gave her house the look and feel of a traditional New Orleans home, before her heels scraped the original cobble-stoned porch. Normally, she found the atmospheric clicking sounds of hard leather against soft brick comforting, but tonight the porch sadly reminded her of another brick porch at her mother's house, where the matriarch once held so many soirees. Back then, the invitation to play cards and socialize was a thinly disguised excuse to have folks over to learn about Little Niqui's enrollment in the latest avant-garde programs.

One evening in particular, when the women sat dressed to the nines, sipping rum punch and mint juleps, they were treated to Nadine's world famous Banana Fosters. Even the voodoo priestess seemed to enjoy herself that night. Between the sugar and liquor, tongues had rolled.

"You know Nadine just hired herself a Cotillion expert to give Dominique elocution lessons."

"She coming here, or the girl going out?"

"Coming here, of course. Laws, she might be light skinned, but still too dark for that society."

"Mmmhummm!"

"Juanita says Little Niqui's almost fluent in French. Imagine after only a year with that tutor."

"I heard the gangsters dropped off a boat load of drug money for her summer program in Paris, France."

"The Panthers ain't no gangsters. No no! And it ain't drug money, no how, that helps her. Those are charitable donations."

"If you say so."

`"Last week, Bessie Long drove her jalopy all the way to Natchez to hear Dominique play piano inside that big theatre."

"You see how she runs every evening to play with Darnell?"

"I know her mama don't like that too much."

"There, her mama don't have a choice." That was Miss Marta.

"She sure done us all proud."

"Mmmhummm!"

After the dessert plates were cleared, with a little urging from Nadine, Dominique had belted out *Puccini's Quando Me N Vò* for her admirers. Dominique remembered the incident like it had happened that morning. It wasn't the gossip, or the memory of the pressure to perform that got to her that time, but the words to the tragic song. The aria from *La Boheme* was written for the character Musetta, so desperate to have her true love back, she resorted to lewd schemes to make him jealous in front of all of her friends.

Just like tonight. Dominique tried to persuade Darnell to talk to her, to listen, to love her again. And he had flatly refused. In front of all of her friends and his. Why would he do that? How could he possibly hate her that much? Hadn't there been good times, too? Why would he choose to forget about those? Or could it be that Darnell had finally listened and heeded her warnings.

Deep down, Dominique understood that she was poison to him, that she had used him for her own selfish reasons for far too long. Even though she loved him fiercely, she was no longer worthy of Darnell. Until today, it hadn't occurred to her that he knew this, too. Not until he had turned those wary eyes upon her.

Reluctantly, Dominique took another step towards her door and remembered with a jolt that she had forgotten to turn on the alarm system. She looked to her right where a strangely-constructed purple two-story loomed only a few feet away. The monstrosity, like her eccentric neighbor, Mrs. Marie Dillard, seemed to be sagging from the middle. She smiled despite herself, because it occurred to Dominique that having a nosy neighbor living this close was all the security she would ever need.

Once inside, Dominique was pleased with the last of the contractor's work. The foyer and living room walls were restored to original tongue-and-groove wainscoating; above them wide barge wood slats painted a creamy mint. A wide-leafed patterned sofa and love seat surrounded a lacquered antique sofa table and book storage. Bright table lamps stood on matching stands, and a set of recessed energy lights hung like dew drops over a narrow bar and dinette combination.

Down the hall, the bedroom was sparse and airy, with a few tall plants. A plain queen-sized bed ran the length of one wall. A large bookshelf with evenly-set books and files filled up the other side. In the kitchen, a real cypress tree, cut and fitted for use as both a breakfast nook and a mega-cutting board, defined the space. Warm red walls, and delicately white-trimmed windows and crown molding, framed the cozy room.

From inside the refrigerator, Dominique grabbed a bottle of white wine and a platter of cheeses. She opened drawers and cabinets, found plates, a glass and a cheese cutter. After carefully placing all these items on a tray, she started for the living room.

That's when she heard the crash.

It came from behind her, inside the attached three-season porch. Dominique barely had time to set down the tray when a big tomcat vaulted onto her shoulder. She felt his sharp claws digging into her silk shoulder pads. The frightened animal simultaneously meowed and hissed in her ear.

Dominique shrieked. "Tiger Lily! What's gotten into you!" She knew the feline to be a cool, unaffectionate creature. But just then, the harder Dominique tried to extricate the cat from her neck and hair, the more he fought to stay pinned to her. Something had scared the wits out of the cat. Finally, after several pats and reassurances, Tiger Lily dropped to the floor and began rubbing his body against her legs and shoes.

The porch's only light came from outside, and when a cloud left the full moon she saw the source of the trouble. One of the earlier pass-along pots she had brought in lay broken on the floor. Its contents, a large maidenhair fern and dirt, lay scattered a foot away. The whole thing had been forcibly knocked off its wrought-iron stand that stood next to the open window.

Oh crap, thought Dominique. One of the workmen must have forgotten to latch the windows and shutters. And they still hadn't put in the screen. For better or worse, this was

New Orleans, and not since the eighties, did anyone ever leave their windows or doors open anymore.

"Bad Tiger Lily! You know better than to come in here and frighten me." Dominique opened the door to let him out and stared at her tiny courtyard. The crickets sang and the mild wind laced the humid air with earthy scents. Except for a few wispy clouds, the sky and stars were bright tonight.

After closing and shuttering the window, Dominique started for the kitchen when she saw the door. It was cracked open and led to the stairs and the room she knew was the real reason she bought the house. Almost a lifetime ago, in a similar camel back bedroom, she and Darnell had played so many games. She tried the light switch. Nothing. She hoped there was enough moonlight spilling through the dormer window so she could see around the room.

Each step squeaked and echoed in the darkness. Once inside the room, she gingerly made her way to the mission-style bed and slid her hand over the cool brass frame. She had eventually found the bed on eBay, but it had taken her months before she found the exact model replica that the Treasures had owned. She lay down on the bed and watched through the window as the moon disappeared under yet another cloud.

The instant the moon reappeared, she knew she wasn't alone.

ELEVEN

The bright light flooding the room cast his shadow on the floor and partly up onto the bed. A silhouette twisted and spread over her and the chenille bedspread like a lizard. Dominique rolled off the bed and slipped behind the frame to work her way along the wall towards the door.

But he was too fast. He reared from a dark corner and slammed the bed into her chest.

She stopped breathing. Summoning invisible strength, Dominique scraped her torso down the bars of the headrest and crawled underneath the bed.

For what seemed like minutes, neither of them moved. Dominique lay on her back and could see part of the ceiling. Way up in a corner, a tiny moth flitted in the air and batted its wings against the closed window. Then it repeated the movements. It was a prisoner just like her. At least it was trying to get out.

Without warning, he pounced on the bed. Each time he threw his weight on top of the mattress, the springs beneath tore at her legs. This never happened when she was little and used to hide from Darnell. As she lay curled up in a ball, the young boy had bounced endlessly on the bed to try to coax

Little Niqui out. But she had been only seven, and he weighed forty-five pounds.

Each time the springs lifted, Dominique edged a little closer towards the back of the bed until she was completely scrunched against the protection of a solid bracket. She squeezed her eyes shut and tuned out everything, so she hadn't known the precise moment she became exposed. Until he grabbed her. While she was pretending to hide, he had lifted the thin mattress and the coil spring box, shoving them against the wall.

The moonlight fell on his face like quicksilver. Rather, onto his iridescent mask. Mesmerized, Dominique examined the mask: the left side was predominantly black, the right was white. Both were painted with a patchwork of red and black diamonds. Across the skull-like, chalky white forehead, eyebrows arched with golden rivets met up in the middle to form a small crown. The vision at once melted and froze.

She stifled a laugh. Before her stood a harlequin.

As a child she learned about the character in one of her gifted classes. The first harlequin was Alberto Naselli, from Bergamo, in 1572. Typically a scrounger, intrusive and greedy, he was always the liar, but at the same time clever and flirtatious. Everyone knew he was mischievous, but rarely dangerous. Unless of course you counted his antecedent from the French Medieval miracle plays, when he was called Hellequin, because that one had been sent by the devil himself. When he dragged her by the shoulders and threw her across the floor, Dominique knew for certain which one her attacker was.

She was so close to the window; it would take almost no effort to raise herself up to touch it. She could break the glass and scream out. She didn't.

Instead she turned over and watched the monster. There was something familiar about him. But it wasn't in his height or weight, because in the moonlight his physical proportions kept changing. One minute he was tall and lean, muscular, the next—short and square. There was a presence about him. Of arrogance, entitlement, and a kind of narcissism that belied deep, deep rage.

Oh, whom was she kidding? She had worked with hundreds of men like this, maybe more. It was the other way around. He was the one who seemed to recognize her. This was not random. And this monster desperately needed her approval.

He wanted her to like it.

The slitty eyes she turned on him were full of mirth and coyness. Dominique was betting that inside this funhouse room of distortion and disorientation, he would not be able to read the mockery pressed between her thinly-smiling lips.

He breathed and lowered his head Again, maybe it was a trick of the light, but the shape changer appeared to shimmer and writhe. She could smell his arousal.

Harlequin was off his square and she used the distraction to push past him and run for the door. She would pay dearly for that trick. When he caught up to her, he punched her so hard in the small of her back, Dominique crumpled instantly.

He sat down on top of her and started ripping her clothes like a predator tearing the flesh off a carcass. He groped her violently everywhere, as if making sure she still had all of her parts.

Abruptly, using supernatural strength, or maybe she was too stunned to resist anymore, he lifted her into the air and then flipped her onto her stomach. The force of the movement jostled the coil spring box away from the mattress. When it fell on top of the wood floor, it sounded like a small-engine plane had crashed into the room.

She couldn't move. His body felt like hot cement on top of her. His breath, like a dragon's.

Why was this happening to her? Was this the end? Was she going to die?

Adrenaline, like a thousand prickles of vigilant sentries coursed through her torso and limbs, giving her irrational mind a command. She pushed up on her arms and used her hips like a hammer, aiming at his groin. Something tore and cracked in her spine.

He moved slightly and growled. Ignoring her pain, Dominique began to fling her arm backward and pull at his mask. And just like that, he was off of her. She swiped to grab it again, now having turned almost all the way over. When she sat all the way up she tried a third time. But he was already on his feet staggering backwards. Both hands on the mask, trying to reposition it on his head.

Dominique was possessed. She got up after him and swiped and pulled. He punched and retreated. Still she wouldn't let go. She felt it rip slightly and then everything went black. The punch to the side of her head sent Dominique back to the floor. Blackness swimming back and forth.

When she came to a minute later, she was surprised to be alone. Except for the music. Still trying to clear the stars before her eyes, Dominique crawled to the door trying to ascertain the source of the strange notes. She listened disbelievingly at the top of the steps. Not music. Chimes.

Doorbell chimes, and Marie Dillard.

Clambering down the steps, Dominique was aware of throbbing pain all over her body. The noise wasn't helping. It sounded like something was stuck inside the doorbell itself, so that the peels could go on forever.

Dominique was dizzy and nauseated when she reached the bathroom to put on a bathrobe. One quick look in the mirror frightened her, but not answering the door frightened her more.

"Miss Doucette! Miss Doucette! Open up!" The importunate ringing stopped and was replaced by a thunderous battering noise.

Good God in heaven, the old battle-axe was actually attempting to break the door down.

Standing in a pink flannel dressing gown bedizened by rows of lavender marabou feathers, Mrs. Marie Dillard looked at first like an unlikely hero, but the baseball bat in her hand told a different story. The next-door neighbor glared pit bull eyes into Dominique, then traced her appearance as if she were a market chicken. The old woman wasn't pleased with what she saw, signaling her disapproval with head shaking and clucking.

Mrs. Dillard was so old and wizened, her race and nationality had become indeterminate. The soft white curls and slaty cardboard skin could have belonged to a sixth-ward African-Creole, a European French descendant, or a Sephardic Jew. At last, the bat-wielding crustacean relaxed her grip on her weapon, but not the scrutiny of her glare.

"Is everything all right? Are you hurt? Do you need help?"

Dominique looked so bewildered, Mrs. Dillard tried softening her tone, but she still managed to cackle like a hen.

"What happened here? I heard screaming, things breaking. What's going on? Miss Doucette, say something."

Dominique felt calm return, at least to her breathing. Yet, she did not speak.

"Somebody break in? Are you hurt, Miss Doucette? That's it, I'm calling the police."

The neighbor had already turned to go when Dominique put a hand gently on her shoulder. "Tiger Lily."

Mrs. Dillard turned around and now something akin to shock, replaced her irritation. "What did you say to me?"

"Your cat startled me. Must have turned over some pots. That's when I tripped and yelled. Tore my leg up a little." This in case the bathrobe did not adequately hide her bloody legs.

Dominique held a steely gaze on Mrs. Dillard, while she pulled her robe collar tightly over her neck. "It's getting chilly out here. Best get back inside."

"Tiger Lily? How did he get into your house?" Mrs. Dillard moved a step closer to the door and tried peeking inside.

"Don't you worry none. I put him out back. He'll come home. Good night."

"Are you sure you're all right? You look terrible, Miss Doucette."

Taking a step backwards, Dominique said, "I'm sure we'll both look a whole lot better after we get a little sleep."

"Let me in. We can talk. Then you'll tell me what's troubling you."

"I'm fine. You go on now."

Dominique closed the door, narrowly missing the bony pincers. She turned to look inside her house. The cordless phone stood just inches away on a magazine rack. She was a mandated officer of the law. And a psychiatrist. It was her sworn duty to report the crime. She could not do that.

Just as she had not screamed upstairs, nor confessed to her neighbor, so she would not tell the police, and by proxy the whole world that she, Dr. Dominique Doucette, was molested in her own home. Attacked by a monster. The same kind of criminal element she was mollycoddling in Elysian Fields.

Because that's what they would say, if she picked up the phone.

No thanks. After all the years and all the sacrifices, after giving up every genuine part of herself for the causes of others, she would not lose House of Mithras. Not like this.

Dominique Doucette would rather die than become the laughing stock of the nation.

TWELVE

Dominique had no recollection of walking into the bathroom. When an orange-yellow light struck the glass block wall above the shower stall and illuminated the glass door, she woke up to find herself sitting on the floor of the small enclosure. Water from the showerhead pounded the tiles next to her. Even then, Dominique was only mildly surprised to find her body huddled in one corner, while yesterday's clothes lay crumpled in another. Both wet, both wrinkled.

She wasn't even sure if she got clean, or how long she'd slept. But she did remember that this was late July, which meant sunrise came around 5:10 a.m. Perfect. There would be time enough to dress and make a few calls, before heading out for House of Mithras.

An hour later, Dominique was driving on Napoleon Avenue blocking out all of the events of the night before, focusing only on today's first group meeting with the prisoners. A few blocks before the entrance to the freeway, the traffic stalled. Sirens roared past the early morning commuters, giving Dominique a start. Without warning, her stomach clenched and it became hard to take a full breath. She lay on her horn until the car in front of her moved forward enough for her to edge out and complete a U-turn. Missing an oncoming car by a coat of paint, she jumped the neutral ground boulevard in the direction of a street that would take her into the French Quarter.

She cried all the way to her destination, alternating between hitting the steering wheel and slamming the seat next to her with a closed fist. Dominique felt like she was on fire. The pain was searing her from inside.

She had to find out what was happening to her. After so many years, she couldn't remember whom to blame, or why. In her entire life, Dominique had trusted only two people completely. Darnell and Miss Marta. She knew the older woman would not turn away from her like Darnell did, but right now she had to get a grip. She couldn't just walk in on the poor woman behaving like a lunatic. Not again.

Across the street from Louis Armstrong Park, drug dealers were dragging their sorry asses out of bed to stake out corners. Each waved to an old man who muttered to himself as he zigzagged across Rampart Street. After Dominique parked, she stared for a long time at the familiar duplex with overgrown bushes and clinging trees. She didn't have a lot of time. Might as well get it over with.

Most people went to the front door to meet with Miss Marta. Most people made appointments to see the voodoo priestess. Dominique never did either.

Before getting out of the car, she checked her face in the mirror, dried her tears and erased the smudges. Then using lipstick, Dominique created happiness on her face.

She followed a path to the back of the house, climbed the long stairway and leaned on the door. Before she could knock, the door opened and a small, thin, dark-skinned woman in her early seventies stood beaming at her. "I wondered how long it would take before you graced my house again."

Dominique fell into her arms and they embraced warmly. Just then, a few tears exchanged complexions.

They drank tea, and Miss Marta listened as Dominique regaled her with stories about the meeting at the governor's mansion. She roared when Dominique repeated her parting words to Futrell. When they both ran out of small talk, Miss Marta braced her heart and waited.

"Something bad happened. Somebody needs help, Miss Marta."

"Which somebody we talking about, child?" asked the priestess.

"Little Niqui. Little Niqui. Bad trouble."

Miss Marta couldn't meet her friend's gaze. Not just yet. It was too early in the morning. She took the teapot into the kitchen and refilled it. She would need another strong cup of Japanese green tea to hear the rest of the story.

"Start from the beginning."

Dominique talked and sobbed. She gave up most of the details of the attack. Described the harlequin mask and how she almost ripped it off. Then she jumped to the part about finding herself in the shower—naked, cold and numb.

"I know it in my bones, like I know I love you, that I was set up. Somebody out there wants to ruin me. It wasn't an attempted rape against my body, but against me. Someone wants to stop me."

"That sounds—" Miss Marta felt afraid. Both of insulting Dominique and of facing the truth. "Honey, but that sounds crazy."

"At first, I thought so, too. But think about it. The whole country, almost every state in the union was against my program. Sure, I had my share of supporters, but the weirdos just kept saturating the media with messages that the therapy went against the laws of God and nation. Rabid, scared, opposition groups."

"You think an opposition group did this to you?"

"I don't know if it's organized, or if there's a lone rogue operator out there. But I was supposed to fall apart. I was supposed to fail. I was supposed to call the police and tell them what happened."

"Why didn't you?" asked Miss Marta.

"Because then the attention would turn on me, and what happened to me. Not the work I'm doing. I would have become a soiled object, a scourge of society. No one would believe in me anymore."

"But why rape?"

"It's the most effective weapon. The ultimate humiliation. But they, or he, or she...didn't count on my commitment to House of Mithras, or my determination," Dominique said.

Miss Marta said, "Explain to me why after all this time, you picked this place to come back to?"

"I never applied to Louisiana. It picked me. I didn't want to come back."

"Then why did you, Dominique?'

"I was invited. No one else wanted me. I had no choice."

"You always had a choice."

"You of all people, how can you say that to me now, Miss Marta?"

"I'm sorry, it's just that I worry. I always worry about you."

It was hot. July hot in New Orleans. The women stayed silent in the familiar damp, feeling a temporary insulation and safety.

"May I ask? Did she follow you here?" Miss Marta asked.

"What? Don't tell me you can't say her name. Say it. Say it."

Dominique felt ashamed. She was badgering the only person left who cared about what happened to her. "I'm sorry. I'm just on edge."

"Did *Delilah* follow you here from New York? Did she, now?"

Dominique began laughing. "No. How could she? She never left Louisiana. Miss Marta. I'm the one that left. Don't you know she's always been here? Right here.

"But if you're asking me, could she have crawled out from under some maggot-infested rock and conjured up my attacker? Who knows? Maybe she gained strength by staying behind."

After a few more cups of tea, Dominique followed Miss Marta into the voodoo temple. Nothing had changed. This was still Dominique's church, her sanctuary.

While Dominique sat cross-legged on pillows on the floor, Miss Marta began lighting candles at the altar.

"Wake up, gorgeous," Miss Marta said to Gede, who sat watching them in front of a shrine of deities, "and see who I brought you today. A visitor from the past. You recognize her don't you? And you can be real proud. She's all grown up now and a very famous woman. But today she comes to you as a child. Always as a child. Have pity on her, your honor."

THIRTEEN

Testimony of Guyla Rae

The file on her lap made for an unreliable ashtray. Guyla Rae puffed and watched while erratic revolutions of the ceiling fan turned her exhalations into a flotilla of curlicues. The sheriff also watched and waited.

"Whatever Dominique touched usually turned to glitter. Yet, according to this," she said stabbing the file with her manicured fingernail and allowing an enormous ash to fall, "there could never be a prize big enough to make her *happy." She flicked the rest of the ash into her lap and looked away.*

"It seemed she had a hole in her heart the size of the Grand Canyon. No amount of success could fill that gaping wound. What she concealed even from herself must have been the real reason behind Desire Therapy. I guess she thought if it worked on killers, it just might work on her."

Guyla Rae ground her cigarette on the cement floor before looking back at the sheriff, the crumpled file teetering on her lap. Blowing off the remaining ashes, she read out loud: *"The Delilah Case. The Delilah Case. "She looked up and blinked several times when the sheriff spoke.*

"You were the beating heart of the prison, and her friend. Surely she could have confided in you," Leroy Futrell said.

"Not about this."

Futrell said, "I don't buy that she couldn't call the police. With her sort of weight and stature, Dominique could have had the authorities investigate the incident discreetly. This is Louisiana. We're used to doing things below radar." The sheriff took his time, pulling his chair in closer and leaned his face into his hands. "She could have left things out. No one ever had to learn the savage details."

Guyla Rae said, "You'd have to walk a mile in her shoes to understand why. The toll and pressure of being the most celebrated psychiatrist of your generation. Having the country's eyes boring into your most important work. Waiting, just waiting for something to go wrong. And besides, according to the file, there were only two people she could really talk to."

"Then why didn't she?"

"You already know why."

"I want to hear it from you."

Guyla Rae sighed raggedly,"I think before she left New Orleans the last time, Dominique must have warned Darnell about the danger signs. She made him promise to never, never, help her again, no matter how much she begged. She told him it would ruin him for good if he didn't do as she said.

"In the end, even she was surprised that he'd paid attention."

"And Miss Marta?"

Clutching the file to her chest, Guyla Rae pulled another cigarette to her trembling lips. "You read the Delilah Case just like me. You had to know that it wouldn't have mattered. Sheriff, it was too late. Dominique was being called to the reckoning."

FOURTEEN

The staff watched the convicts on the surveillance monitors; a lone guard stood behind the closed door to the group therapy room where all six men had just sat down. While Dominique focused on the inmates, Guyla Rae stared at her friend. Puffy eyes, ashy skin, and even the psychiatrist's normally ramrod-straight back slouched like it had been punctured, and was now slowly deflating. Until today, Guyla Rae had never imagined that Dominique could look bad. But right now she was a mess.

Jody asked, "How long before we go in?"

Dominique said, "Give them a few more minutes."

Guyla Rae said, "I don't know about anybody else, but this feels mighty creepy. Big Brother and all. Besides, I don't know how much more I can take of Vincent grabbing his balls, or Billy Jo touching his hair."

Kevin said, "Are you kidding? This is the easy part. Wait until they start grabbing each other's balls. That'll show you creepy."

Dominique glared at Kevin. "Stop. Listen."

After nearly five minutes of looking at one spot on the floor, Eduardo shifted in his chair and broke the silence.

"What do you suppose we gotta do in here? And where are the shrinks?"

Emile sat with one leg under him. Everything below the left knee had all but vanished. "Maybe this is our time. We can get to know each other."

The other five returned stares of disbelief.

"I bet you're hoping to be teacher's pet," Julius smirked.

"Which teacher?" Billy Jo asked, snorting in time to Julius' escalating guffaws.

Straightening and puffing out his chest, Julius slapped the empty chair next to him. Each convict had purposely left an empty space between himself and the next man. "I think this is supposed to be a bitch session. Where we register grievances."

Eduardo asked, "Did you say register?"

Julius said, "Shit, I was a bookkeeper. We registered everything." While Billy Jo and Julius started their laughing frenzy all over again, across the room, Vincent burned holes into Lerance's averted face.

"Hey Doc, what do you think?" Vincent asked.

"Excuse me?" Lerance did not turn his face.

"Why do you think we're in here? Or are your thoughts privileged information?"

Lerance lifted his gaze warily to Vincent and said, "I don't understand."

The convicts, including Lerance, almost jumped out of their chairs when the big man shifted in his and then burst out laughing. His sniggers sounded like they came with their own echo chamber.

Vincent switched off the laughter and said, "The Doc don't get it. Maybe he thinks I don't talk right. But that don't make any sense, since we sound the same."

Quizzical exchanges from Julius and Billy Jo. Emile and Eduardo looked alert.

Vincent said, "Even if you say you're from Florida, you still Mississippi to me, Doc."

Lerance said, "You're mistaken."

"You calling me a liar?"

"What the hell is everyone talking about?" Billy Jo crowed.

Lerance looked around the room carefully. He took his time stretching and straightening, and then smirked before he replied, "What do you want from me? I'm just minding my own business. This place. You people. Big mistake. I don't belong here."

Billy Jo rose suddenly and turned to Vincent. "You're right. He thinks his shit is too pretty."

Lerance glared at Billy Jo. "What do you know?"

"I know you don't act like no doctor I ever met before."

Gesticulating wildly, Billy Jo addressed the other inmates like a circus ringleader.

"Should've seen his prissy ass yesterday. He acted like, like he might catch cooties at the shelter. We were supposed to hand out bowls of soup to the homeless. Only he wouldn't, because he was too afraid of getting germy. He actually asked if he could wear gloves. So I told him to fill up the bowls while I handed them out."

Before anyone else could comment, the door swung open. Jody took his place between Eduardo and Emile; Dominique sat between Julius and Billy Jo and directly across from Lerance. For what seemed like minutes, but were only uncomfortable seconds, the convicts could only move their eyes. First their gazes landed on Dominique's face, then Jody's, finally on the floor.

Dominique said, "Come on guys. It's your first meeting. I promise you, this will get easier. In no time y'all will start looking forward to being here. It's the place where you can unwind, let it all hang out. Even as Julius pointed out, register grievances."

Jody said, "It takes time to get to know each other. To build trust. But we'll chip away at it, session by session, week by week."

"But you heard the Doc. He doesn't even want to be here," Billy Jo said.

No one looked at Lerance except Dominique.

Dominique said, "Okay then. Each of you take five minutes to talk about your first day. You don't have to get deep or personal, just describe it. Who wants to start?"

While the men shifted and rolled their eyes to the ceiling, Lerance studied Dominique.

Dominique smiled warmly at him, but she spoke to the group. "Tell me. Do y'all have something better to do? Someplace to go? Expecting visitors?

"No? Really? Okay then. Vincent, why don't you begin."

FIFTEEN

He watched everything she did.

When Dominique's head tilted, he calculated the degree and then computed the time it stayed there. If she picked up a pen, he memorized its make and color before she could put it down again. He tracked her breathing to see how well composed she was, whether perhaps she practiced meditation, or only breathed shallowly like someone who routinely felt anxious. He viewed life in pictures like an animal, but stored the individual scenes like a robot. Lerance's visual recall was total, preternatural and essential. A skill he had acquired years ago as a child. The younger Lerance figured out very early in life that to be able to anticipate the enemy's next move was to survive another day.

Now he was stockpiling pictures of the meeting with Dominique like ammunition, in case he might have to actually remain in this godforsaken place. Legally, he knew, she couldn't make him stay. And that was the only thing that kept him from leaping over the desk and thrashing her.

He didn't want to look directly at her face. All his instincts warned against memorizing those features. But he was who he was and he had to look. In his whole life he had not seen a more perfect creature. Eyes like liquid amber. Eyes you could dive into. A soft nap overlaying the skin, even finer than suede. Skin you had to touch. Bone structure at once flowing and delicate. Normally he wasn't even attracted to a forty-something, but then black people didn't seem to age.

He forced his gaze away from her. His eyes swept the room, the pupils like swift shutters of a concealed camera documenting anything of importance. Initially, the office resembled an international furniture bazaar. Dominique's desk was Asian Beachwood. Quite long with graceful legs. A matching armoire and bookshelf sat on the opposing wall. The walls were painted the color of a rich setting sun and held objects of meaning. One wall was entirely plastered in framed portraits of local jazz musicians. Above Dominique's desk hung framed mementos from former clients. The original wood-plank floor, laid two-hundred-fifty years ago, was now partially covered by thick, colorful South American rugs. The view from the south window led past the front lawn, past a half-dozen live oaks, all the way to the sugar plantation on the other side of the highway. It was a beautiful room inside a beautiful mansion, run by a beautiful woman. Lerance could taste bile swimming up his throat.

He looked back at the desk and tried to guess how many drawers covered the front and what lay in them. Dominique began to shift in her chair, raising her left hand to her head. He played poker and he recognized the tell. It was something she did right before speaking again. The bile was gone, replaced by a sack of rocks pressing against his chest.

When Dominique looked up, she was surprised to see such an intense look of concentration on the prisoner's face. When she handed Lerance a sheaf of papers, he wouldn't take them.

"All we need now is a couple of signatures. Read it all over carefully and sign. When you're done, hand the papers to the guard and he'll drop them off at the front desk for me," Dominique said.

Lerance took the papers but shook his head. "What happens if I don't sign?"

Dominique said, "What's going on with you?"

Lerance wondered if he were going insane. Why had he agreed to come to this place? Then as quickly, he remembered she'd tricked him. Maybe leaving wouldn't be as easy as he had originally thought. Was returning to the Florida state prison really the best thing him for him now? Would it be so bad if he stayed? The fact that he was questioning his resolve made him shudder. A stranger was taking over his mind.

"You know that you can begin working any part of the program as soon as you've finished the Desire exercises," Dominique said. She took a moment longer to finish. "But first, you have to give consent. Do we have a problem here?"

He didn't trust himself to speak but managed a grotesque leer before averting his face.

"Look, I know you are extremely well-defended. But that's not helping you now. The personality is the thing we show to others; the mask, it's all an illusion so—"

Lerance found his voice. "You can peddle that psycho babble to Billy Jo and Emile. But I'm a doctor. And it's not gonna work on me."

"Well, doctor, how could it? You won't even try."

Lerance looked up at the clock. "Oh, darn, look at the time. I gotta run if I'm going to finish chores."

Dominique didn't argue, nor did she look at him again. Instead, she buzzed for the guard.

After Lerance left the room, the psychiatrist removed a file from the armoire and took out a photo of a handsome young man clipped to a yellowed five-year-old newspaper article. Then for the third time that day she began reading the story, hoping to glean something new.

PROMINENT DOCTOR ADMITS KILLING WIFE

...On the eve of Lerance Lemartine's sentencing, friends of Clarissa Lemartine are privately reporting that the couple had been having marital problems before the shooting. In addition, neighbors said they heard heated arguments and loud noises such as glass breaking, at all hours of the night in the days leading up to the shooting.

Dominique turned to the jump page where she was more interested in the prisoner's family background.

In 1978, after twenty years of operating a successful practice, Drs. Lydeah and Morris Lemartine closed the doors to their medical clinic in Dauphine, Mississippi, suddenly, leaving the small town of 1,200 without a doctor. Flush with a sizeable inheritance from Morris Lemartine's deceased uncle, the couple moved to a quiet block of newly-built mansions in Cocoa Beach. Their only child Lerance, 14, was immediately enrolled in a Jesuit preparatory school, where he remained until he left for Harvard University three years later.

Schoolmates remembered Lerance as an affable yet solitary student...

Had she made a mistake? If he didn't want to stay, she couldn't make him. And wouldn't Kevin just love that?

While a guard took Lerance downstairs to start kitchen detail, Julius Lucky walked with another guard from the opposite direction for his own appointment with the director. Halfway down the hall, the guard stopped and grabbed Julius' arm, pushing him against the wall.

The guard said, "Dead zone between here and the next hall. They can't hear or see us. I know because I monitor these cameras three times a week." Letting go of Julius, he added, "My name is Dave."

Julius said, "What the hell, Dave?"

Dave said, "Look, I'm gonna make this fast. I got a message for you from the sheriff."

Julius had seen and heard a lot in his thirty-something years of life. But he wasn't even sure that this guard was speaking English. So he just shrugged.

"He wants you do to do something for him. If you can find a little dirt on Dr. Doucette, or round up anything at all suspicious around here, you'll be well-rewarded."

"Shit. I'm not your pigeon. Not your stoolie. Get my meaning, Dave? And besides, you know as well as me, if I do everything Dr. Doucette asks, I can be out in two years. Compare that with twenty-two, at Rikers."

Dave said, "The sheriff also knows you're a smart guy, one who could pull something like this off. He wants to sweeten the pot for you, is all. Just keep your eyes and ears open."

"For what?' Julius was curious.

"I don't know. Something out of the ordinary."

"Are you serious? Something out of the ordinary?"

Dave said, "And remember, just keep your cool, and everything will turn out all right."

When the door opened to Dominique's office, Julius swaggered as he walked in. Dave wondered belatedly if his uncle, the indomitable Sheriff Leroy Futrell, had just committed his first career blooper.

SIXTEEN

Dominique had never felt more worn out.

Not once during the day had she reflected on the events of the attack, nor did she remember that she'd barely slept at all the night before. She blamed her exhaustion on the session with Lerance, namely on the energy it took her to parry his belligerence with an equal amount of indifference. At the time she wasn't sure whose mask had tightened more. She reasoned if he didn't want to stay in a cushy manor home where practically all he was expected to do was keep a daily journal while therapists and guards waited on him hand and foot, well that was one thing.

But why suddenly throw a bucket of contempt at the person who had gone out bounds, risking the integrity of the Desire project in order to give him a break? His combativeness was almost militaristic; Lerance treated her like she was a combatant of an enemy state, one who needed detaining or perhaps worse.

It didn't help that she still had many hours ahead of preparatory work for the next day's marathon therapy sessions. Dominique might have given up and fallen asleep right then and there at her desk, if not for the inmate who looked especially thrilled to see her. It was just enough spark to jumpstart a renewed sense of energy. And it was a welcome relief to feel something other than harassment or regret, even if the source of pleasure stemmed from the smiling oily face of crass and fatuous Julius. Then she remembered she had called him in for a reason.

"Julius, I'm glad you're here. I'll get straight to the point. I heard you asked for a roommate transfer. Is it true? Did something happen between you and Billy Jo?"

"Yeah, about that. I kinda jumped the gun there. I don't really want to move. Besides, who else is there? Emile, he's a joke. Eduardo, I know he doesn't like me. And frankly, both Vincent and Lerance scare the crap out of me.

"No thanks, I'll stay where I am."

She waved a sheet of paper at Julius. "Then why did you turn this in?"

"To show Billy Jo that I meant business. Ah, the guy's all right most of the time. If you can accept that he's a weirdo. And not in just the way he dresses, either. Did you know he's a klepto? Well, he is, and I'm getting really sick of it."

"Did he steal from you? Something of value?"

"Valuable to me. First, he took one of my mystery books. And then, after I pressed the issue he gave it back, but without the cover. He was so nervy. Billy Jo actually said he should keep the cover because he liked the picture on it more than I did. But right after that, he looted an old photo of my sister at a costume party. I should've known because I caught him staring at it a few times. Even after I told him to knock it off, the picture disappeared out of the frame. He stole it because it was taken at a Halloween party. My sister and her friends wore these bright red wigs and sparkly dresses. Dr. Doucette, Billy Jo will steal anything with color in it. He's a color klepto.

"Just tell him to give it back, and we'll be square," Julius said.

"Thanks Julius, I'll talk to him."

Dominique saw Julius studying her. Earlier when Lerance had done it, was as if he were trying to read her thoughts, or maybe even send her thoughts. Julius on the other hand, wasn't trying to freak her out. He was eager to engage her. She'd play.

Dominique said, "Something on our mind?"

Julius said, "Yeah, I got a question for you."

Dominique had to be careful. She knew full well how manipulative prisoners could be, especially with women. Under normal circumstances, she would not have allowed this, but these weren't usual circumstances.

"Go ahead. Ask." Julius straightened and leaned forward with his arms spread out. "I know why I'm in here. I did a terrible thing, and the law says I have to do my time. That's cool. I deserve it. But you? What's your sin?

"What terrible thing did you do to end up in this hick town, spending all of your time with rejects like us?"

Dominique had not seen this coming. Julius was treating her as an equal, expecting an honest answer to his question. After all, she had left the door wide open, hadn't she?

Julius said, "I know all about you. You used to be on Larry King and Letterman. Shrink to the stars, they called you. What happened?"

Dominique slowly closed the folder in front of her, leaned back in her chair and crossed her arms.

"Nothing happened. I moved on because I'm very committed to the Desire Project and wanted to expand its application. Having success here, in House of Mithras...well, that could change the face of—"

"Don't you miss the lunches? The parties? Jet-setting with other celebs? I think you must have had a pretty good motive to give up those bennies just to come here."

Dominique pushed away from the desk and looked out at the setting sun over the fields.

"Motive? If you must know, I was born here. My community moved heaven and earth to see me succeed." She turned back and held him with innocent eyes. "Along with a lot of hard work, I was also very lucky. Now I have something to give back."

Julius said, "There's a saying in my family. Every time you bury a secret, you disturb a crime in progress."

Dominique nodded and smiled like she enjoyed the platitude. But she'd had enough. Time to go, Julius.

She stood up and grinned. "I have an idea. Rather than speculate on someone else's past, let's get started on your present assignments." She handed him a thick folder.

Julius looked sheepish as he reached for the fat wad of paperwork. He was quickly running out of steam when he got a fresh idea. As he stood up, he tucked the folder carelessly under his arm and soon the pages started falling to the floor. Julius apologized and quickly got down on his hands and knees to pick up the scattered sheets. While he put most of the papers back inside the folder, he pushed a few sheets under the desk, letting a small edge of white peak through. Wouldn't Dave be proud if he could see him now?

Julius stood up, looking flustered and concerned. Dominique shook her head as she rang the buzzer for Dave. When Julius was leaving, she wondered if he and Dave had exchanged a look. After the door shut, she got up from her desk and noticed a few pieces of paper peeking out from her desk. She sighed as she picked them up and stacked them neatly on the edge of her desk.

Dominique looked out the window and watched the sun go down. In less than a half hour it would be dark. There were only a few cars left in the parking lot. Most of the staff had gone, leaving only security and Dominique in the building. Lerance and Billy Jo had left for the city to work the night shift at the homeless shelter, and the other inmates were back inside their rooms. She walked back to her desk intending to begin work on the next day's sessions, but felt compelled to take a painful detour into the past.

Dominique put Julius' file back and pulled out another one. A much thicker one. In small cramped letters at the top, it read. *The Delilah Case*.

The cover was worn and covered with coffee stains, its edges frayed. Normally, neat-freak Dominique would have already replaced something so tattered, but in this case, she liked its familiarity. Kept her honest. She turned on a small lamp at her desk and began to read. Dominique felt the usual emptiness grow in the pit of her stomach, followed by a sudden onslaught of melancholy when she got to Delilah's childhood. She knew no matter how much she had accomplished in life, how many awards or trophies she'd won, how much money she earned, or even how many lives she might have changed for the better, she would never be able to help the little girl who needed it the most.

As she read, Dominique alternated between laughing and crying. She was so absorbed in the faded wrinkled pages that she didn't notice the car that had stopped on the highway outside of House of Mithras. The occupants had watched the small light in the second-story room come on, and were certain that the psychiatrist was up there working alone.

When her door creaked open, Dominique jumped out of her chair and let out a shriek. When she saw who it was, she flopped back down and joined her visitor in a round of uncontrollable giggles. With one hand over her chest and the other wiping the tears from her eyes, Guyla Rae walked unsteadily towards the desk.

"Are you nuts? You scared the hell out of me. What are you doing here?" Dominique said.

"I'd be scared too if I spent all of my nights in a two-hundred-year-old haunted mansion, surrounded by present-day killers," Guyla Rae said.

Guyla Rae would never know how much Dominique envied the administrator's carefree, loosey-goosey approach to life. Guyla Rae was happy in her work, never took it home, and was always up for partying.

"Actually, I feel pretty safe here."

Guyla Rae looked around the room and sighed heavily. That's the problem. And I have just the solution.

"Me and my husband Richard, we were slumming on the country roads when we saw your light. So we decided that we would like you to stop working right now and join us. Leave all this behind and come with us, for once. What do you say?"

Dominique said, "I'd say you're drunk."

Guyla Rae hiccupped. "Very perceptive, doctor. But you know what? You should be too. That's why Richard poured you a single malt scotch into a fancy glass that he's keeping on ice for you in the back seat." As if remembering the real reason for being there, she added, "If we hurry, we can still catch a show in town."

Some things never changed, thought Dominique. In certain parts of southern Louisiana you could still drink while riding in a car.

"And don't you fret none. My husband is a dependable designated driver. Come on. Come with us."

Dominique realized the Delilah file was still open. She closed it and tried putting her hand over the label. But Guyla was too quick. Before Dominique could put the file back inside the armoire, Guyla Rae was right behind her.

"I really appreciate what you're trying to do. Really, I do. Some other time. I still have a lot to do to prepare for tomorrow," Dominique said.

Guyla Rae eyed her boss suspiciously and crossed her arms.

"Is this how you prepare?" she pointed accusingly at the file. "Who is Delilah?"

Dominique turned around and walked back towards her desk.

"You can tell me. Is it a new identity for Billy Jo? Or maybe Emile?"

"No. It's an old case. I pull it out sometimes, to remind me."

"Remind you? What do you need reminding of?"

Dominique wasn't sure how much she could say. But it was a relief to say anything.

"That sometimes the damage is too deep. That not everyone can be saved."

"And that, my dear, is just too goddamned depressing. Even for you. I don't see anyone else working these late hours."

"I'll be all right. I promise. Just go back and have fun with Richard. You deserve it. I'll see you in the morning.

SEVENTEEN

Right after breakfast, the guards took their places and surrounded the entire perimeter of House of Mithras. Dominique had promised that if the weather held up, the counseling sessions could take place outside on the front lawn. Promptly at 10 a.m., six prisoners and their attending counselors would descend on the outdoors.

Marathon therapy sessions were supposed to get the inmates to lose their inhibitions in a hurry. Using challenging board games, puzzles and computer-simulated tournaments, all of which changed every forty-five minutes, invited the prisoners to act spontaneously; they would have little time to second guess themselves, correct their answers, or worry about what others thought of them, because in short order, they would be on to something new. Today they were like small children, or animals, not capable of holding grudges or even remembering what made them mad only moments earlier.

Plus, there would be entertainment, in a manner of speaking.

Billy Jo and Emile had both turned in the first Desire exercises and, as a reward, would get an opportunity to describe as well as enact their childhood fantasies. They could be as creative as they wanted, and were encouraged to use a combination of props and story telling to share their secret childhood fantasies.

"Jesus Mary Joseph, can't you sit still for just one more cotton picking minute? I can't get these on you if you keep squirming like a little baby." Julius tried to look threatening as he stood over a seated Billy Jo, dangling a new box of false eyelashes in front of an agitated face.

"You're trying to poke my eye out. What if you drop glue in it. I'll go blind," Billy Jo cried.

" I did just fine with the first one, you dope. I'm warning you, if you move even one more muscle, I'm quitting. And then you'll have to go out there with just one eye done."

"Nah ah. No way. Dr. Doucette will do it for me. Tell him, ma'am," Billy Jo batted his eyes at the psychiatrist.

Dominique affected helplessness by raising her arms above her head. It was all she could do after finding out the hard way that she had the fine motor coordination of a rhinoceros attempting to walk on a tightrope. Each time she attempted to stick the first set of eyelashes onto Billy Jo's lid, they'd fallen off. Then when she tried to spread more glue to the rim, she dropped them. And there they still lay, stuck to the floor, ripped in half. In this case, her long slender fingers were no match for Julius's short stubby digits. Perhaps years of keying on adding machines made Julius dexterous and confident, because he handled Billy Jo's entire costume ensemble like someone who'd worked as a professional dresser all of his life.

The day before, Guyla Rae had dropped off armfuls of dresses, wigs, make up and accessories, at House of Mithras. Getting up earlier than anyone else, the dueling duo met Dominique in her office to get Billy Jo ready. After much hand wringing and mind changing, Julius picked the perfect outfit for his roommate. And when the eyelashes were finally set in place, Billy Jo emerged wearing a gold sequined gown, a shoulder-length auburn wig, eyelids dusted with blue eye shadow, and a Mardi Gras boa in purple, green, and gold. Even his stylized eyebrows found a purpose for his face, because Billy Jo had transformed into the spitting image of Betty Davis, Louisiana style. Dominique detected a glint of pride in Julius' expression as his roommate and sometimes nemesis walked across the lawn to the cheerful hoots and hollers from staff and other prisoners.

After parading in front of the crowd for a few minutes, Billy Jo curtsied before beginning his story of survival as a young boy on the batture. He spoke tearfully of abandonment and hurt, and then looked as joyful as an evangelistic tent-revivalist when he described Fifi, the gypsy woman whose fondness for loud clothes and bright makeup not only made him appreciate and trust another human being, but sent him on a life course searching for glitter and color. To Billy Jo, it was like digging for and finding love.

When Billy Jo finished, counselors led the inmates in pairs to separate tables to start the games. Jody unwrapped a couple of handheld gaming devices and gave them to Vincent and Eduardo. Vincent picked a baseball game and Eduardo, a poker contest. Kevin's team, Lerance and Julius, both chose Sudoku. To Dominique's surprise, Emile and Billy Jo picked a mystery-solving game that required them to choose strategies through consensus decision-making.

After lunch, the games turned traditional. Julius and Billy Jo played checkers, Eduardo and Lerance began a game of chess, and Emile and Vincent got busy with the first of several rounds of the card game Speed.

At three o'clock, it was Emile's turn to confess his life-long fantasy. He spoke briefly, describing the physical and emotional pain he felt whenever he became aware of his left leg. He admitted he had been dreaming of amputation since he began making memories. Then he got up on a ten-speed bike, one-legged.

Billy Jo tried to get a better look, but his high-heels kept getting stuck in the thick grassy lawn.

With Jody and Eduardo's help, Emile's left leg had indeed disappeared because his team had taped the lower half tight to his thigh, to simulate amputation. Even after several dozen tries, Emile could only peddle twenty feet. But he had his onlookers spellbound, and every time Emile stayed on more than five seconds, they clapped and held their breaths. Billy Jo found a pair of pompons and waived them every time Emile got up to ride.

Julius said, "Betty Davis wouldn't be caught dead acting like a dumb cheerleader." Billy Jo hissed at him.

Just before dinner, Dominique and Kevin facilitated a group session with all six convicts. For the first fifteen minutes no one talked. The directors let the prisoners know that they would not be able to go onto other activities until each inmate participated at least once.

Julius was the first one to speak. "I'd like to know why Vincent is always in such a bad mood." Instantly, all eyes flew to Lerance.

To everyone's surprise and Julius's relief, Vincent faced his questioner with a non-threatening grin. "Why do you think that?"

Billy Jo said, "Because you're always scowling. Now I think if you'd just put on costume and makeup, it would be hard to stay mad." With that, Vincent resurrected his glower, turning it first on Billy Jo then on Lerance. Lerance ignored him. When asked to voice a thought or opinion, the former doctor said he thought marathon therapy sessions were a joke. That statement gained him many groans and a few more dirty looks. Emile thanked everyone for giving him an opportunity to be himself; Eduardo and Julius said they had enjoyed the games, and thanked the staff.

One-on-one sessions followed with Jody showing Eduardo how to use Lexus Nexus to access law briefs. Kevin took Lerance aside to journal for thirty minutes. Afterwards, Lerance surprised Kevin by reading out loud for a few minutes from his notebook.

A final game of volleyball showcased Kevin and Eduardo's skills. They were the only ones who scored points, albeit on opposite teams. Julius couldn't serve the ball over the net; Billy Jo who had taken off his dress and heels and was now playing in a pair of shorts and a tee, continued to trip over his feet and fall down. After attempting several times to play one-legged, Emile gave up. Vincent always slammed the ball out of bounds, and Lerance shuffled in place, but never actually hit or passed the ball. At the end they all sat down to the final group session. It appeared to begin very much like the first one. Vanished were the pleasures of earlier shared company and the inchoate signs of mutual trust. Replaced by a new round of silence.

Finally Emile spoke. He admitted to everyone that his greatest desire was to climb Pike's Peak as an amputee. He added that if he couldn't have a legal amputation while in prison, he would seek one in Mexico when he got out. Either way, he was going to climb that mountain minus one leg. Emile didn't get a lot of response, but neither did anyone ridicule him.

When the inmates were back in their rooms, Dominique found herself once again alone at her desk. She was feeling good. Even hopeful. Her team, the prisoners, were all making breakthroughs. Just twenty-four hours earlier, every bone in her body screamed she would never be able to do this. It seemed for now, her bones had been wrong.

Dominique felt giddy dialing Guyla Rae's number. So strange were her sensations, she almost didn't recognize them as happiness.

"Hey, I'm calling to make a date," Dominique said.

"I just got off the phone with Kevin. I could hear him grinning ear to ear. Sounds like you all had a great day," Guyla Rae said.

"Actually, better than even I could have predicted. It never fails, though. When you treat people like people, well, what can I say, they respond in kind."

"But not Lerance," Guyla Rae said. "Kevin said that except for a few charmed moments, the guy stayed clammed up like a shell."

Dominique said, "I didn't say it went perfectly. There's time for him to come around."

"You said something about a date?"

"As soon as you can clear your calendar, I want to join you and Richard in sampling some of that fancy scotch y'all drink. I want to celebrate," Dominique said.

"Sure, I'll let him know. And then you know what? We can all frolic like Bacchus." Guyla Rae hoped Dominique's sweet laughter was not a figment of her imagination.

"You're on. Remind me to ask Billy Jo for your boa. I think I would like to be Betty Davis for a night."

Guyla Rae said, "I would pay a hundred dollars to see that."

Dominique was about to say, *make it a thousand and I'll really do it*, when she noticed a blinking red light on her phone. She studied Caller ID. "This is strange," Dominique said. "I'm getting a call from outside the prison. Who could be calling me this late?"

The unfamiliar voice kept repeating, "Dr. Doucette? Dr. Doucette. Is this Dr. Doucette?"

Dominique stayed calm while the nurse spoke, her words married to a background of loudspeakers and sirens. When the caller finished, the psychiatrist asked only one question, "Is she going to make it?"

EIGHTEEN

As she drove to New Orleans, Dominique felt compelled to beat the hell out of her car again, but this was about Yolanda, and she would spare herself a temper tantrum out of respect for the young girl.

Dominique had always believed that your past defined you. If you could leave part of it behind, then it would be easier to create healthy psychological connections in the future. But Yolanda's past and present were inextricably linked. Her neighborhood remained a dangerous and camouflaged obstacle course, inside an increasingly more and more violent New Orleans. The psychiatrist knew the teenager had volunteered at St. Francis homeless shelter the night before. So what happened? Had Yolanda walked home alone in the early hours of the morning? Had the perp been waiting for her when she finished her shift?

The emergency room at Charity Hospital screeched with activity. People in various stages of care were either sitting or lying on cots. They moaned and groaned; their friends and family members huddled at the circular help desk asking the same questions over and over of doctors and nurses, but never seemed satisfied with the same answers. Emergency medical technicians rushed back and forth between talking with patients to reading their mounting paper work. Orderlies routinely announced lost and found articles. Sometimes children.

A tall African-American nurse walked quickly through the corridor, pulling Dominique with her.

"I'm Larissa Johnson. You see how insane it is here. Been that way since last night. Normally I don't make calls to anyone outside the family, but the girl insisted. Just kept calling your name, saying she had to talk with you. Had to talk with her boss. I got the strange feeling that she felt guilty about what happened to her. I think she might be worried about losing her job."

Dominique couldn't stand it anymore. She tried to keep her voice normal. "Oh God. What the hell happened?"

Larissa said, "They found Yolanda in the alley behind her house early this morning." The nurse stopped and faced a blanched Dominique. "Say aren't you...?" She stopped mid-sentence remembering it was not a good time for celebrity gawking, and continued matter of fact, "Yolanda was beaten and raped. Her condition is critical. We're doing all we can to stabilize her. She's extremely traumatized, so promise me, you won't stay more than a few minutes."

Larissa pointed to the far end of a curtained row of beds and moved hurriedly towards it. Dominique started to follow her, but stopped when she spotted Elijah, Sadizfy, and Gemini, sitting together with a dozen other people inside a makeshift waiting area in the hallway.

She walked quickly over to the men and noticed Sadizfy was crying. He wasn't even trying to hide it. Elijah got up and put his arms around Dominique.

"I came as soon as I heard." She looked around the room. "Where's Darnell?"

"He took Yolanda's mama to work. You know it happened on his watch and that he's the one that found her?" Elijah asked.

"Thank God he was out there," Dominique said.

"We'll see about that. Something's very wrong in there," Elijah pointed to the last cubicle. "I heard them say something about a pre-existing condition." They all froze when they heard wailing sounds coming from the hospital bed.

Dominique pulled the curtain open and gulped the air. Yolanda lay like a ragged doll, wrapped up in a mish-mash of cords that led to several monitoring units. Her face and arms were covered with purple bruises and bandages. One of her eyes was swollen shut. The other blinked rapidly.

A young white resident, Dr. Alex Moore, was watching the monitor while Larissa wrote down the numbers inside a chart. A black uniformed female officer stood in one corner of the small space, talking quietly on her mobile unit.

"Please try to make this brief. In a few minutes a bed will open up in the ICU and then we'll have to move fast," Dr. Moore said.

"Why?" Dominique look alarmed.

The doctor practically whispered, "We need to follow up with an EKG."

Dominique wanted to know more about Yolanda's medical condition, but if she only had a few minutes, she had to hear what happened from the source. Gently, she knelt down next to the gurney.

"It's me, Dominique. Baby, I'm so sorry. Don't worry. You're going to be all right. They're taking real good care of you here. I promise."

Yolanda's said, "I tried to fight him, Miss Doucette."

Dominique's heart cracked. "Hush, it's not your fault. Some sick bastard. We'll find him and we'll make him pay."

Larissa placed an ice chip on Yolanda's tongue and gave Dominique a stern warning look.

"I didn't want to wait for the escort. Darnell was almost home when he found me. He likes to cut through the alley, just like me. That's why I went that way, thought it would be safe with him around."

Dominique asked, "He's still staying at your house?"

"Yeah, ever since Mama started working nights. Except when he's on street patrol," Yolanda said.

"Do you have any idea who did this to you?" The policewoman looked alert when Yolanda started talking. Moments earlier, when she tried questioning the girl, she'd gotten little more than her name.

"I couldn't see his face, cuz he was wearing a mask."

If Dominique could have stopped time she would have, because then she could permanently rewind this moment back to last week, and then run to any state, any place—far, far away from Louisiana. But it was too late for anything like that.

"What kind of mask?" Dominique asked.

"You know, the kind they sell in all those tourist shops on Canal."

"A Mardi Gras mask?" Dominique asked.

"Yeah, a clown mask." Yolanda began to cough and sputter. Dr. Moore signaled to move the gurney out along with the crash cart. Yolanda clutched Dominique's arm. Startled, Dominique said, "Don't be scared, what is it?"

Yolanda closed her good eye and said weakly, "What do you call them jokers?"

"Harlequin."

"A harlequin mask."

"Did he say anything? Did you recognize his voice?"

"He didn't talk at all. But I did. I begged him to stop."

NINETEEN

They were back.

Dominique saw them on the wrong side of the gate as she turned her car into the driveway. This time the protestors were better dressed, wearing suits and standing on the lawn. It was as if they decided that making a stand at House of Mithras was one sure way to ruin her morning. What they couldn't know was that was not up to them any more. Her morning, and possibly the rest of the mornings until the end of her life, were already ruined. Or would be if Yolanda didn't get better. And if the authorities failed to find her assailant.

Maybe not even then. What happened to Yolanda was all her own fault. All her fault. If she had reported the bastard, he might have been caught before he could rape Yolanda. The assaults were connected. And this one could have been prevented.

Dominique noticed the protestors' hand-painted signs were replaced by professionally- printed slogans blasting everyone, from judges to police, for their failure to protect citizens. And there it was. Flying like a banner: today's *Times Picayune*, featuring Yolanda's photo with a headline of her attack. Dominique noticed the sheriff sitting in his car across the road.

Near the front entrance, Guyla Rae and Kevin were working alongside Emile, Billy Jo, and Julius, making repairs to the front porch. They all stopped to look at Dominique's car pull in, and then at the protestors who rushed it. Everything appeared to happen in slow motion. First, several young men took out plastic toy guns and sprayed Dominique's windshield. Next, a woman uncovered a basket and began pelting the other windows with tomatoes. Dominique slammed hard on her brakes, flew out of the car and lunged at the demonstrators.

"You craven lunatics! If you really want to make a difference, then go home. Take care of your families. Help your neighbors. Vote. But get the fuck out of my prison yard. Now."

Sheriff Leroy Futrell had to admit that Dominique had some gumption. Not that she didn't deserve the wrath of these righteous men and women—that woman had no business fouling up their little hamlet with a disgraceful institution—but she stuck to her convictions, and was as plucky a gal as he'd ever met. He got to the gate just as the fracas began to escalate.

"It could have been one of your guinea pigs up there in those fancy rooms that got Yolanda last night," a woman in high heels yelled.

"There's a special place in hell for people who help criminals commit more crimes." This from a boy who couldn't have been more than fifteen years old.

When the group leader saw the sheriff saunter towards them, he began herding the most offensive of their members.

"Ma'am, would you like me to arrest them?" The sheriff asked, smiling.

Dominique said, "Very funny. You would love that, wouldn't you?"

"Ma'am, I'm just here to serve."

"Yeah, then, serve this."

Billy Jo, who had watched every bit of the disturbance, turned wild-eyed to Kevin. "I think she just gave the sheriff the finger."

Dominique got in her car and drove slowly to the back parking lot.

Billy Jo asked, "So why didn't she have them arrested? They were trespassing."

Julius said, "Wake up, airhead. She's a prison reform activist."

"So?"

Julius continued, "So, say you're someone trying to protect the rights of cons. Cons like us. It ain't gonna win you points to jail folks who might actually be the *victims* of some of our crimes."

Emile, who until that moment looked like he wasn't paying attention to the bickering, looked up and said, "Now that's ironic."

Dominique parked her Toyota Prius next to a fresh-off-the-showroom import. The Audi was black and gleaming, top-of-the-line, and from were she sat, she thought she could smell drying factory paint. Who did it belong to?

Guyla Rae greeted Dominique as she came through the back entrance. Her desire to hug and comfort her friend was cut short when she saw Dominique's expression. It was tired, frazzled, on the verge of combustion. On the drive to work, Guyla Rae heard about Yolanda on the radio, but now she knew her boss would be facing even more bad news. She might as well get it over with it.

"God, I'm so sorry about Yolanda. I can't imagine anything that horrible happening to a young girl. Is she going to be okay?"

"I wish I knew. I have to believe they are doing all they can for her. How could this have happened? I don't know what to do anymore, what to think." Dominique slumped down in one of the visitor's chairs and looked out at the parking lot. "Do you want to tell me that German engineering is about to bring us good news?"

"I wish." Guyla Rae handed her a business card, then tilted her head towards the stairs.

Dominique read the card and frowned.

"Alain Dupree. Just got here. The guard took him up," Guyla Rae said.

"You're joking," Dominique said.

"I'm afraid not."

"I thought he moved his offices to Los Angeles."

"Dupree, Marchand, Lafayette, PLLC, have branches all over the south. The big man just couldn't resist coming back himself," Guyla Rae said.

"Let me guess. To represent one of our inmates? Pro bono?"

"Hitching his star to the celebrity wagon. Probably hoping to become an overnight television sensation," Guyla Rae said.

"So who's the lucky murderer?" Dominique asked.

Shoe gazing wasn't second nature to Guyla Rae, but Dominique was in a really bad way. So it was out of respect for the psychiatrist that she continued to avert her eyes as she announced, "Lerance."

"Great."

Dominique clambered up the stairs and when she got to her door, leaned on it and shut her eyes for a moment before inserting the key. When she opened the door, Dominique froze. Not two feet from her, an envelope lay on the floor. She could tell from where she stood what it was. A letter from Delilah. The second one in two weeks. Instead of using the postal service, this time the woman had broken into the building and prowled in her office. Delilah was getting bolder. Just as Dominique had always suspected she would.

At her desk, Dominique found a letter opener and read.

What visible wound disappears when
Death is your only friend
Set loose from those
Who might make you them.
Damn the vampires.

Delilah was pulling out all the stops, bewitching the psychiatrist. Daring her to walk the gauntlet of moral turpitude. She was showing Dominique a way out; she could kill herself for the things she had done, or rather, not done. For not calling the police after her own attack. For continuing to keep silent after Yolanda's.

It wasn't supposed to end like this, Dominique thought. Hadn't she been doing good things at House of Mithras, giving people another chance at life, at joy? None of that mattered anymore, but there was one thing she could do. Kill Delilah.

And this time, she would to have stay dead.

TWENTY

Alain Dupree dressed like a dandy.

Today he had on a tan Panama suit with matching hat and a purple bow tie. He sported a salt-and-pepper mustache and goatee, and rimless granny glasses that accentuated sparkling pools of blue behind them. Everyone knew that the sixty-five-year-old lawyer had become obscenely rich by handling all the oddball cases the state of Louisiana, then California, handed him. He got a woman acquitted of trying to sheer off her husband's balls, had more than one mafia felon's case thrown out on technicality, fixed a famous investment banker's gambling debt, and then surprised everyone by taking on the tobacco companies.

Once, he won a case for a New Orleans musician who stood accused of growing marijuana in her basement with the intention to sell. The woman's electric company had reported high watt usage at her home residence to the feds. Dupree countersued and won an undisclosed amount of money for his client, by proving that the utility company violated its own privacy policy when it divulged its customer's personal data. But this was the first case he could recall where a client was demanding more punishment rather than less. Dupree reasoned Lerance Lemartine was suffering from brain damage.

They sat in leather-cushioned chairs around a handsome Louis XV table. Paintings of antebellum ways of life covered the walls, and the view from the bay window was spectacular. Dupree thought he would be dealing with the same kind of spoiled, entitled personality he was used to. But there was something far more unsettling about the handsome prisoner in front of him. Lerance didn't just think he was better than others, he was convinced. Dupree would have understood if the inmate had manipulated or charmed him, but Lerance didn't even try. From his slouched posture to lack of eye contact, Lerance's disdain for other members of his species rang loud and clear. Dupree wondered secretly what had happened to the young man to have his light go out so irrevocably.

Lerance said, "Did you read the whole thing? The part about being qualified to apply to the Desire project? It stipulates that a prisoner must first apply for parole. I didn't do that, which means I am here unlawfully."

Dupree steepled his fingers under his chin and began to speak in a low conspiratorial voice. "Son, I know what it stipulates. I know whatchya did and din't do. By the way, how did you get access to the entire text of the contract?"

Lerance was running out of patience. "Another inmate here has some home school law training. He showed me where to look."

"I'm a reasonable man. But let me be real honest with you. In all my born days and nights, I never seen nothing like you before. As your lawyer, I must tell you, any hasty decision on your part could and will be fatal to my health."

"You can just cut that homegrown folksiness. I know you're a shark. I hired you because you can do this for me. So do it. And start talking to me like an adult."

Dupree never heard Lerance. "I mean lookie here." He spread his arms wide like Jesus. "A little therapy, the occasional work assignment. You get to live in a *dorm*itory. I even hear the food tastes good.

"Tell me true, do you have some kind of mental problems? Mad cow disease? When you were a kid, did you fall down in the playground and hit your head on the cement? What happened to you, son?"

Abruptly, Lerance sat upright and said, "I changed my mind. And under the law, I have that right. Because I was brought here under false pretenses. Someone was very sloppy. And we're going to take advantage of that. Okay, hot shot?"

Dupree said, "You know that you could be out in two years? Free and clear? Why don't you just hush up and put up until then? Would it kill you?"

Yes, it might, thought Lerance.

"Son, spell it out for me in the clear and precise English you're so fond of. Someone screwed up, yes. But you willingly went along on the tour. Can you explain that?"

Dupree dug into his satchel and popped a couple of orange pills. "What precisely happened to change your mind?"

"Just get me out," Lerance said, getting up.

In dramatic fashion, Dupree stood up and sighed, then he walked over to the door with his client. He tried to find Lerance's eyes but settled on speaking to his forehead, "Okay, but this is not good for my reputation or my heart.

The paperwork's already started. I'll have you out by the weekend."

TWENTY ONE

Although he might never completely get over Dominique, Kevin took refuge in the knowledge that not only was she out of bounds for him, but most likely for anyone else who might have the audacity to fall in love with her.

Dominique's gift to the world was broad and wide. She was great with groups, villages, and people she would never see again. To say she had intimacy issues was an understatement. Truthfully, she had never clocked in a lot of face time with personal relationships. When she was a kid, there was her mother, of course, and Darnell, and some childhood girlfriend. Later, Dominique hooked up with Darnell when she was in college. After that, there were a few short-lived trysts during medical school, and then Kevin. Then Darnell, and Kevin again. Kevin wasn't even sure anymore in what order the liaisons transpired, but the idea that the gangster still meant so much to Dominique did make him a little crazy.

That didn't stop Kevin from looking for a good time. Life was here to be seized. He was healthy, thirty-eight, still capable of turning heads, and in the mood for love. As he drove his car towards Desire, his breath caught a little when he thought of Marcelle. The sexy minx said she would be at

Camille's tonight, and had asked him to meet her at ten o'clock. The bar and pool hall was also a favorite haunt of Darnell's. New Orleans was small, but the way Kevin saw it, Darnell would just have to do what he was doing right now. Trying to get over himself.

Bumper-to-bumper cars crammed the dark street. After circling the block a few times, Kevin found a vacated parking spot kitty-cornered from the club. He wouldn't have even noticed the darkly-clad homeless woman if a glint from her metal pushcart hadn't ricocheted off his rearview mirror. While backing up the Lexus into the narrow spot, Kevin had missed hitting the ghostlike female by less than a foot. Startled witless, he flew out of the car to apologize. But the enigma had already strode past him across the intersection and disappeared around the corner. He stood shaking, listening to shrill laughter bouncing off the empty street. A minute later, the caterwauling subsided, calm returned, and Kevin walked confidently through the front door of Camille's.

When Dominique got out of the car, a gang of older teenagers was waiting. At any other time it would have been a problem for a lone woman in the dark. Not tonight, though. After the young men got a good look at her, they cleared the street quickly. It wasn't just the wild hair or the tortured look in Dominique's eyes—most of the boys had seen that same look in hurting addicts—it was in the way she moved. Jerky and spastic, like someone unfamiliar with her own body or its movements. To the gangsters, Dominique could have been an alien from outer space, or a mental ward escapee. Someone like that was dangerous, because she was so unpredictable.

Dominique took her time climbing up the long flight of stairs to Miss Marta's. Again, before she could knock, the door creaked open. Once, Miss Marta might have been as shocked as the boys downstairs, but she was used to this side of Dominique. She had seen it too often.

Often people think that a privileged life authors opportunities that others can only imagine from a distance. Like watching two people fall in love and living happily ever after on the movie screen. What they can't fathom is that each success costs something, and your connection to the past never lets you forget your debts. No matter how far away Dominique managed to run, the burden of being wrapped inside the panic of an inchoate nightmare never fully left her. Here in New Orleans, it was paying her a proper visit.

It had been a while since either of them moved. After all of the traumatic events of the past week, to her surprise, Dominique found she could finally relax here, mostly because of Miss Marta's enduring patience, and because the apartment still had the look and feel of her childhood. Next to Treasure House, Miss Marta's was the best place to be.

The psychiatrist sat on a familiar piece of furniture: a seventy-five-year-old royal blue mohair mahogany-framed sofa. Across from her, Miss Marta occupied its companion piece, a commodious ribbed chair. When Dominique first started coming here, the parish priest down the street had decided to update his rectory with the cleaner lines of modern nineteen-seventies furniture. He told everyone he was going to donate his old-fashioned sofa and chair to a needy family in the neighborhood. In reality, the donation went to Miss Marta for her part in helping the priest exorcise his so called "impure thoughts". Before the priest underwent a series of pagan rituals and cleansings, the poor man had been painfully torn between serving God and his church, and falling head over heels for one of his parishioners. Eventually he gave himself over completely to God, and the furniture to Miss Marta.

Dominique bent over to touch the intricate wood frame on the couch and bit back a painful memory. Years ago, Little Niqui used to stick her tiny fingers inside the scrolled arms and trace the floral design down to the cabriole feet. She was content to do that all day long, over and over, until she felt *fine*.

Every so often, when she *didn't feel too fine*—or what Nadine described as her temporary sickness— her young self was dropped off at Miss Marta's. Sometimes the transformation came instantaneously, other times it took all day, but eventually Little Niqui, under Miss Marta's tutelage, got *fine*. She had wondered so many years ago, if Miss Marta's indeed was the place to feel fine again, maybe it was also the place to stay fine. Next she asked herself, why couldn't she just feel fine all the time, then? Why couldn't they just leave her there, maybe forever? Once she had plugged her fingers firmly into the carving, believing if she pressed them deep enough, no one would be able to pry those fingers loose.

"Don't make me leave, Miss Marta. Tell them it's not time yet," Little Niqui cried.

"It's late little one. Your mother and Bobby are waiting for you downstairs."

"I don't want to go. I want to stay here with you forever. Please. Please let me stay."

"I wish…but you have to go now."

"Why? Why can't I stay? Just a little longer. Please. Please. Oh, Please," she wailed.

"If they hear this racket, they won't bring you around next time. Is that what you really want? Think, Little Niqui. For your sake, splash some cold water on your face, and let's get downstairs."

"But you're Miss Marta. You're so powerful. You're a voodoo priestess."

"Yes. But I am not your mother."

"Oh, I wish you were."

In truth, both knew well why she couldn't stay.

If Little Niqui had remained at Miss Marta's, she could always be who she wanted to be. But that was against the plan. Nadine's and everyone else's. As long as she came back home, the little girl could continue to do and be all the things they couldn't achieve by themselves. She was their vessel. Dominique's destiny had never been to individuate. From the beginning, she was their pet group project, and could never be allowed to be her own person. Laws in heaven and earth, if she was permitted to go wild and free, what would happen to them?

For the last three hours, the voodoo priestess had remained cool, determined not to absorb any of Dominique's poison. In order to help her, Miss Marta had to wait until the younger woman completely exhausted herself and regained composure. It was now past midnight, and until a few minutes ago, she had listened nonstop to Dominique rant and cry, and repeat the same story over and over again.

"You should have seen her face. The bruises. All of those tubes. The ER doctor looked real scared.

"I'm to blame. Everything that happened to Yolanda is my fault. I wish I'd let him do that to me. Maybe if he had fed on me, he would have left her alone."

Finally, Miss Marta had had enough. "You just found one more way to beat yourself up. Can you stop for a minute? Can you start thinking rationally?"

"I'm rational enough to know who's to blame. Me, I'm to blame for what happened to Yolanda. I was so stupid. All I had to do was pick up the phone and say I'd had an intruder in the house, and that I chased him out. Of all people, I should have known that he would attack again."

Dominique turned on Miss Marta with eyes that seemed both vacant and bottomless. They were like Venus flytraps. The closer you got to them, the more you had to lose.

Miss Marta said, "But you didn't know, did you? How could you? And you had your reasons. Besides what could you report? That he was wearing a mask that he could dispose of immediately? And become someone else? You thought you were protecting your program, all that time invested, all of your hard work. The work of your colleagues, people depending on you. Even the inmates."

"But he didn't dispose of the mask, did he?"

Dominique sank into the couch like a Raggedy Ann doll, her limbs drooping from her joints like they'd finally lost their stuffing. But she had quit raving and probably did not have the energy to shatter another glass against the wall or tear up any more pillows.

It was always like that. Right before the calm, the storm had raged and raged. Not once had Miss Marta ever scolded or turned her away. Afterwards, Dominique always apologized, cleaned up everything and left money for repairs. Tonight Miss Marta couldn't help thinking that this shouldn't be happening anymore. Dominique was too old. Had been through it too many times. With all of that practice, why couldn't she show some self-control? Someone needed to put a stop to it. Once upon a time, Miss Marta recalled, Dominique had.

"There's more isn't there?" Miss Marta said softly.

"Twenty-four-seven, I'm terrified. She's so close. Moving so fast. I know she's just around the corner, ready to—"

"I know all about the she-devil. I asked about something else. Someone breaking your heart."

"Oh, Miss Marta. It hurts so much. My Darnell is gone. Always before he could make things right between Delilah and me. I think I've lost him for good. He won't even talk to me. Or look at me. He hates me. Darnell hates what I've become."

Miss Marta said sternly, "You know that's not true. He could never hate anyone, especially not you. He loves you, and he will love you until his last breath."

Dominique took the broom out of the closet and swept up the glass, and then on her hands and knees mopped the floor with wet towels. She had suffered for all of us, Miss Marta reckoned. And now, she was paying us back.

"Listen to me. You don't need any of them. Not Delilah, not Darnell. You are Dominique. Look at what you have accomplished in your life."

Dominique said, "And it's killing me. It's killing Yolanda."

They moved together like kindred spirits into the temple. Dominique saw instantly that Miss Marta had prepared for this visit in advance. Instead of a dozen different voodoo deities filling up dressers and tables, now there were only paintings, drawings and wooden likenesses of a single lwa:

Gede. Dominique's own favorite tattered likeness of the deity, her old Gede doll, took prominent position on the main altar. The women found consolation staring into the broken glasses, trusting that the deity did not judge anyone, and unlike the humans, would unconditionally forgive Dominique and give her another chance. Miss Marta began to pray.

TWENTY TWO

Every so often white people could be seen mingling inside Camille's.

Young men who stopped by during happy hour to unwind and play pool with work buddies; neighborhood organizers living down the street hoping to mix it up with the regulars; the doctor renting a room above the bar looking forward to his one scotch on the rocks, promptly at seven o'clock, Monday through Friday; Caucasian jazz musicians that the locals affectionately dubbed light-skinned; and on weekends, older mixed couples, who had been hanging around Camille's since Hurricane Betsy.

Tonight it was only Kevin, but his skin color simply didn't matter at Camille's. For as long as anyone could remember, Kevin had been a friend of the bar owner and much of the clientele, mainly because of his association with Elijah's street patrol. The patrons drank and broke bread with him, played pool, and, on occasion, unabashedly asked the psychiatrist for counseling tips for their kids or friends. Sometimes they set Kevin up with dates. That was not the case with Marcelle.

Courtship in this 'hood had its rules. Especially if it involved dating the baby sister of a well-known gang leader.

Kevin first met Marcelle when she was eighteen and had just finished high school. She volunteered that summer at the clinic, babysitting and doing light office work. In the fall, she began college and the pursuit of an education degree. Marcelle had won a scholarship to Loyola University, and, along with low-interest loans and a work-study program, for the next four years the teenager should have had the financial freedom to study hard and earn her teaching certificate. But Marcelle's hopes for a college education terminated at the end of her sophomore year when she found out she was pregnant. Her baby daddy was a good guy she didn't love, but Marcelle married him anyway because it was the right thing to do for the child, and the next one that followed a couple of years later.

Last year, when her youngest turned six, Marcelle divorced their father—he remarried and stayed close to his kids—and for the second time, Marcelle started school. This time at LSU, in the nursing program.

A couple of weeks earlier and almost ten years to the day since she last saw him, Elijah reintroduced his youngest sibling to Kevin during a community action meeting. Ever since, sparks flew between them. Respect and tradition dictated that the infatuated couple should get their liaison vetted by Elijah before moving forward. But as the collective hormones raged, Kevin and Marcelle began their relationship by doing a fair amount of sneaking around. When Elijah finally did hear about the affair from the cousin of his car mechanic's wife, his response came rather quickly in the form of a phone call placed in the middle of the night.

Checking caller ID, Kevin was grateful Marcelle was not lying next to him because when he picked up on the second ring, Romeo was sweating like a pig.

"Kev. Kevin. Kevin Waddell," Elijah sounded like he was speaking through an extra wide grin.

"Elijah. How's it hanging? To what do I owe the distinct pleasure of your very late night phone call?" Kevin hoped he sounded unruffled.

"Hell man, can't friends just call each other up and shoot the breeze?"

"Sure they can. Look, by the way—" Suddenly Kevin felt like he was five-years-old again. He knew for certain that there was nothing he had done or could do that would make Elijah hate him enough to hurt him, but at that moment, if there had been a hole deep enough for him to crawl into and stay hidden forever, he would have jumped in happily.

"I should have talked to you sooner. I mean no disrespect, but I think I'm really falling for your sister."

There he'd said it, but that hadn't done anything to alleviate the guilt. Kevin had been a coward hiding a simple truth from a man who loved him like a brother. Who trusted him completely. Now Kevin wondered if the words that followed were tinged with hurt because Elijah guessed the feeling wasn't always mutual.

"I see how Marcelle looks at you. You're all she talks about. I'm glad, really Kev. Her ex, a good man, but you know they married young. Turns out she's spice cake and he's still collard greens. It makes me feel good, her with someone like you. You're an upright man. Just Kev...I only have one baby sister."

"You're giving advice?" Kevin said.

"Don't worry, it's not so bad."

"Yeah?"

"Just don't do anything I wouldn't...if I were in your shoes."

"Elijah. What kind of food am I?"

The grin deepened. "Pork, the other white meat."

For everything it was worth, Kevin had been very happy to receive the cautionary approval. Because Kevin needed to be here. Finally, with or without Dominique, he had found a place to hang his hat. Right smack dab in the heart of Desire he felt more at home than some of its residents. No one should have been very surprised.

Kevin was a perfect blend of mismatched belief systems descending from two generations of Waddells. First there was the example set by grandfather Hiram, who because of his dogged spirit worked tirelessly until he achieved millionaire status in the 1940s. He was a savvy entrepreneur who invested in a Standard Oil refinery near Baton Rouge. At the same time the country was growing rich in oil reserves and refineries, a dangerous soup of toxic chemicals began threatening the health of refinery workers and anyone living close enough to breathe in the assorted cancer-causing agents. Hiram, following in the tradition of other newly-made oil tycoons, moved himself, his family, and his offices as far away as possible from all of those environmental hazards that had garnered him so many riches. Far east, to the salubrious shores of Nantucket.

But neither Hiram nor his wife lived very long to enjoy their newfound prosperity. Hiram died of a brain aneurism the next year, and his wife followed with a massive heart attack. Their only son Marcus had been away at Columbia University when the tragedies occurred. A sizable inheritance and a guilty conscience prompted Marcus to quit school and move the family business back to Louisiana, where he hired a bevy of topnotch managers to run the refinery. Then he set out to research and implement his real ambition: philanthropy.

Marcus's first foundation set up college scholarships for the children of refinery workers. Next, he pioneered and developed medical research to study the effect of petrochemical exposure on children living near refineries. While testifying before congress, the oilman-turned-philanthropist met his wife, a spirited junior senator from northern Louisiana. The courtship was short and sweet, they married and soon their son Kevin was born.

After a few years, while the money poured out of his family corporation into needed trusts and research organizations, Marcus began to enjoy life more and more from the bow of his thirty-four-foot luxury sea cruiser, marlin fishing in the Gulf of Mexico. It wasn't that Marcus wasn't one-hundred percent committed to the humanitarian works he began and promoted, it was that he found out he simply detested work of any kind, and just as he had turned over management of the refineries to highly qualified folks, he now employed financial wizards to run his foundations.

Kevin was just finishing his residency in psychiatry when he came into the first leg of his inheritance. By then his eccentric father had divorced his mother and moved to a remote atoll in the Pacific. Straightaway, Kevin began his medical career among poor and dispossessed Americans, sometimes paying for medicine and equipment, staff salaries, out of his own pocket. But he also worked. Day and night. His aides would have to remind him to eat and sleep. He had the constitution of two people and a heart as big as Alaska. Kevin inherited equal slices of Hiram and Marcus, and spent his life merging his ancestral parts, their strikingly different profiles notwithstanding. Kevin fell in love with the communities he worked in and tried to help. He also fell for their women.

Marcelle was waiting for him in the back booth by the popcorn machine. When Kevin arrived, her cousin and his new girlfriend were sliding into the opposite seat. He took his place next to Marcelle, setting down a pitcher of beer. The waitress followed, bringing over plastic cups for everyone. They drank and smoked, letting the accumulated tensions from the week slip away. Then Kevin and Marcelle got down to a serious game of craps.

The haze from the smoky poolroom hung over the horseshoe bar like a hovering spacecraft. By midnight, the bar counter was three-deep with folks waiting for drinks and a place to sit. When Darnell stomped in from the street, even before he was fully inside the doorway, a small partition appeared at the end of the bar. A man got off his stool and Darnell took his place. It was just what people did when Darnell came into a room.

"I almost gave up on you. Your boys come and gone a few times already," the bartender said.

"What, am I supposed to be on some kind of schedule now?" Darnell was crabby.

"You know you don't have to be that way with me." The bartender had known Darnell since childhood and admired him, but lately even he had to acknowledge the nights floated by a bit more pleasantly when the gangster kept himself away.

"My man, what would you like?" A dumb question aimed at a recovering addict, but it was what he said to everyone.

"Coke, no ice." This time the words were not followed by the usual withering glance or any sort of sarcasm, because Darnell had already swiveled his stool around, so he was no longer looking at the bartender but at the booths lining up the far wall.

While peering through the cloudy air and aimlessly studying the throng of people, he glimpsed Kevin. He stared at him, stupefied, coaxing the shrink to meet his look. When he did, Darnell gave up his stool.

Something was different. To Darnell, Kevin looked boyish tonight, not professional. He had traded his usual suit coat for a jeans jacket, and his whole face was suffused with a goofy grin that was probably the result of the time-honored tradition of sneaking out back for some reefer madness. Or maybe it was Marcelle.

Elijah's medium-skinned sister was easily the most beautiful woman in the room. Darnell noticed she filled in her low-cut tank top under a tight leather jacket like always. Exceptionally. He felt a dizzying spiral of emotions kick him in the teeth. In that instant, a long history of sadness and torment clasped him around the chest like a straight jacket, bringing with it the strongest urge to drink yet since rehab.

Kevin was already standing when Darnell strode up to them, but Marcelle clutched Kevin's shoulder, urging him to sit back down. "Ignore him," she said.

"How dare you show your face in this bar. Get the fuck out," Darnell spat.

"You're way out of line, dude," Kevin shot back.

"Where do you get your nerve?" Marcelle was up now, too. Jabbing the air near Darnell's face with stiletto nails, she yelled, "Why don't you do the world a favor, and die. Die, Darnell! Die and go to hell."

Darnell grabbed her arm. "Get up out of that booth. Where's your self-respect?"

Easily shirking him off, she said, "Don't touch me or I'll tell Elijah you put your hands where they didn't belong."

"Elijah's whacked out on glue if he thinks," Darnell eyes swung wildly from Kevin to Marcelle, "this is okay." He was about to say more when he felt a hand on his shoulder. As he turned around, the bartender was looking at him kindly, as were the two giant bouncers next to him.

A couple of hours later when Kevin emerged from Camille's, Darnell was across the street watching him walk to his car. He had been standing in the shadows, thinking of what he wanted to say. Waiting for Kevin had sent his flight-and-fight chemicals into the ionosphere, along with most of the urge to use again. Now he only felt a strange unease that was kept alive by what he knew he could not do. Some of that was compounded by intense dislike of Dominique's friend. Was it jealousy, or that he couldn't trust him? He wished he could, because then he could tell him what was worrying him. He could warn him about future trouble. Kevin would want to know all about that. Hell, the task was impossible. Where would he start? Could he really do that to Dominique? Maybe. But what about the memory of his childhood friend? And if he did unburden himself, whom would he really be helping? Dominique or himself?

Darnell watched helplessly as Kevin drove off with Marcelle following close behind. He knew that his decision to stay quiet wasn't the right one to make. But it wasn't up to him. Ten years ago on the phone, he helped Dominique construct an emotional DNR agreement between them. But was it binding? Do you let your best friend get herself killed because she thinks she deserves it, or do you save her for the next time she decides to go off the deep end? There was another truth. Darnell was worn out. Although he could never

TWENTY THREE

Miss Marta's cleansings always had an immediate restorative effect upon Dominique and provided temporary insurance against further madness. She might expect to feel good and normal for as long as a couple of weeks; once it lasted ten years. Even though the psychiatrist had emotionally stopped reliving her own attack as well as Yolanda's, Dominique still felt responsible for what had happened to the girl, visited her everyday in the hospital, and swore that she would look after her interests for the rest of her life. She also began her own inquiry into the assaults. Dominique was determined to get to the bottom of the crimes if it was the last thing she ever did.

She did not call the police. It was too late for that. But like any good detective, she laid out all of the facts in neat timelines, starting the day she landed in Louisiana. Using Excel and iCal programs on her Mac notebook, Dominique carefully listed each person she had met with face to face, and those she had communicated with electronically or by phone. Her layout looked like a grade school grammar diagram with subjects and actions, adjectival and adverbial descriptions—some from memory, but mostly derived from the detailed notes she wrote after each individual or group session. She studied all of the prison personnel and inmates to establish their positions within the prison, their means of opportunity, and past connections to Yolanda and herself.

No one escaped Dominique's scrutiny, not even Kevin or Darnell. Not that she suspected either of them, but she could ill afford to miss anything. But she did feel stabs of pain and embarrassment when she keyed in the names of Guyla Rae and Richard. What surprised her was the unexceptional work and personal history of Leroy Futrell. So far, the only thing interesting about the sheriff was a long and unfortunate relationship to his notorious cousin, Spike, the governor of Louisiana. CPAC (The Committee to Protect Citizens Against Crime), whose members regularly showed up in front of House of Mithras, included all the usual suspects: fanatical religious leaders and their followers, finding one more battle to fight against the steady drum of a liberal agenda hell-bent on depriving good Christians of god, country and traditional marriage. But there, records showed up nothing at all—no harassment charges, not one restraining order, not even a recent parking ticket.

As much or as hard as Dominique looked for evidence that could lead to the attacker, nothing tangible or provable popped out at her. Still it had to be in there. Somewhere among all those names and dates was a link, a walkable path that would lead her to the truth. Yes, she or he was in there, wanting, no demanding, that she, Dominique Doucette, get her proper comeuppance for the deeds or ill effects of some former indiscretion. Dominique was sure she was the target of a yet-to-be-identified revenge strategy. Once she got that feeling deep in the pit of her stomach, she knew she was close.

But what had she done to deserve all of this? Who could hate her so much? What really frustrated Dominique was that the perp was still out there somewhere, possibly even close by, watching her.

In addition to a methodical clinical study, Dominique began fieldwork. For the last two days and nights she had stayed in New Orleans, shopping for a mask. In total, she visited eighteen souvenir shops inside the French Quarter. Carrying with her a copy of the police sketch Yolanda had provided, she showed the Harlequin mask to managers, clerks and customers. No one she questioned ever seemed to remember that particular mask. A couple of times Dominique had asked the shop keepers if anyone else had stopped by inquiring about the mask. The answer was always no. That meant that police detectives hadn't taken this course of investigation. Was it because resources were stretched inside the murder capitol of the country? Or maybe finding justice for someone like Yolanda wasn't at the top of their list.

Towards the end of the second afternoon, Dominique decided to change direction and began hitting establishments where New Orleans' creatives—the artists, writers, and parade organizers—hung out. During Happy Hour, the bars were filled with gracious and accommodating sorts, but no one admitted to ever seeing a mask like that. After a few hours, the psychiatrist decided to pack it in and head home. That's when she noticed a very tall woman with purple extensions standing erect, arms akimbo, next to her car. She was about to be handed her first clue.

"I know that mask. I used to sell it," a rich baritone announced. Dominique studied her informant and guessed that with a couple of more regiments of female hormones, the transsexual should fully cross over.

"I used to work at the Presbytere, you know the Mardi Gras museum? On the first floor there's a little shop." Pointing to the drawing, "A couple of years ago, we got a shipment of some beautifully hand-painted full-faced masks. I'll never forget their intricate craftsmanship. That was one of them."

Dominique inhaled. "Does the museum still carry them?"

"Not a clue. But my old boss, Tammi Lynn Sonnier, still runs the shop." She looked at her watch. "Tammi should be there for another half hour."

Dominique raced her car towards Jackson Square Park and parked behind St. Louis Cathedral. She ran the short two blocks to Chartres Street and was breathless when she finally pushed herself through the heavy glass door.

The small room was brightly-lit, lined with glass-fronted cabinets, each displaying dazzling Mardi Gras memorabilia: tasteful jewelry, post cards and books, beads and doubloons. On each wall, colorful Venetian feather masks stared down at the psychiatrist, but she did not find a Harlequin among them.

"May I help you?" asked a friendly voice belonging to a diminutive, sixty-something, wearing a dark tailored suit and perfectly coiffed platinum hair. Dominique thought the woman should have been called Doris, or Mabel, not Tammy Lynn.

After Dominique finished explaining what she was looking for, the museum manager appeared embarrassed before saying, "I got these in about two years ago and haven't been able to reorder them since. They sold like hot cakes, but then some problem between the suppliers and artist put a kibosh on future deliveries.

"It's too bad because they were unique, each one hand-painted just a little differently from the others. The one in your drawing had those beautiful gold beads sewed into the top. And the black and white diamonds were very distinctive."

Seeing Dominique's crestfallen expression, Tammy Lynn added, "Perhaps I could show you some unique paintings of Harlequins that we carry in the back. They're done by a local artist and all one-of-a-kind."

"I need this particular one. Perhaps you could tell me who bought it?'

"Normally I would not be able to tell you because we honor the privacy of our customers. But in this case...

"You see there were six masks in all and I bought two of them. One I gave to my Aunt Pearl. She still has it because I saw it in her living room this morning when I stopped in to drop off her groceries. She would never part with it, because I gave it to her. I'm her favorite niece, her only niece. Besides, neither mine nor hers is the exact one you're looking for."

"And the other four," Dominique prompted.

"That's not really a secret either. All four were bought up by Father Pierre Lormond at St. Francis, just before Mardi Gras, in 2003. I remember because they were celebrating their first year anniversary."

Dominique froze. Father Pierre Lormond had been a fixture at St. Francis Church for more than thirty years and was wholly responsible for starting the church's most ambitious project, the St. Francis Homeless Shelter for Families. The adjunct program to House of Mithras. The last place Yolanda was seen before she got raped.

"I don't understand."

"I think it was a couple days before Fat Tuesday. Father Pierre had already purchased boxes of beads and eye masks with sticks for the children of the homeless residents, but he

wanted something extra special for the volunteers to wear.
They were very beautiful, especially the one you are looking
for. You might check there and see if those masks are still
around.

"May I ask why you are so interested in that particular
mask?'

Dominique's uptake was quicksilver. "When I found this
image I was drawn to it, hoping I could purchase one for
myself."

Back in the car, Dominique did not know if she felt relief
or grief. If the mask had been at St. Francis, chances were
that one of her inmates had found it. And done what?
Escaped the locked premises to begin a raping frenzy? No, it
seemed more likely that a worker or a former resident would
have committed the crimes. That didn't feel right either.
Shelter workers were usually college-aged kids getting field
experience in either social work or psychology. Homeless
people were notorious for committing petty crimes of
thievery such as stealing lunch buckets from work sites, or
lifting purses when their owners weren't paying attention. But
violent crimes against women? It just didn't add up. As soon
as she could, Dominique would pop into the shelter and begin
a new round of inquiry. Right now she needed to get home to
rest up for tomorrow's sessions with inmates. She was
already dreading the first one.

TWENTY FOUR

The room was achingly hot and damp. The plaster walls shone with condensation, the wooden chairs felt thermal. A ceiling fan whirred, lazily redistributing the moisture while the two challengers sat staring at each other, each beginning to sweat, adding their own contribution to the collective wetness. Even though Lerance would be gone in a few days, he was still required to attend daily therapy sessions. They sat unmoving across the large desk until the inmate did something Dominique had never seen before.

He smiled.

The length and breadth of the wattage unsettled the psychiatrist so much that she was unable to stifle a gulp. That had not gone unnoticed, because the inmate quickly turned up the brilliance. As soon as she collected herself, Dominique's mind started in the direction of analyzing the man before her. He had what most people would call smoky good looks, a dark sullen handsomeness. Lerance's tawny skin and dark eyebrows only enhanced slightly drooping cat eyes, yellow-rimmed with green centers. Bedroom eyes. His face was gaunt in the manner of a nineteen-fifties movie star: hollowed out cheekbones, a straight nose and perfectly defined lips. But when he flashed his pearly whites and stretched his mouth into a lusty grin, Dominique thought that look could unscramble eggs.

And that made her suspicious. Dominique wanted to know why Lerance had chosen this particular moment to become disarming. Had he been saving it? For what? Why hadn't he tried to influence the judge who sentenced him, or the team that recruited him for House of Mithras? Why wasn't he beaming friendliness to the other inmates? His kind of magnetism had the power to shift paradigms. And Dominique knew something about that. She enjoyed a similar power.

Whatever Lerance's game was, Dominique would not allow it to circumvent her agenda. She had to find a way to derail the inmate's efforts to leave the prison, otherwise her goals at House of Mithras could not be met. Either fiscally, or organizationally. She needed six inmates. Lerance *had* to be one of them. She began with prepared remarks.

"I heard you met with Dupree. Was that really necessary? You could have come to Kevin or me. We could have worked things out. Still can."

Lerance said, "Don't worry, I *already* have it all worked out. By Sunday evening, I'll be history."

Dominique said, "I really want to understand why you want to leave the program. Tell me, is it the therapy, the rules? Do you have some specific concerns about safety, security maybe?"

"I found out that I'm only here because you pulled some strings way back when. I'm not interested in taking part in your little experiment, so I suggest you stop making a fuss before anyone else finds out about this." And then the smile was back.

Aha! It became crystal clear to Dominique. The calm, smug, affect was actually a self-appreciating punctuation mark at the end of an emotional victory. Lerance wore his enchanting smile like a banner of conquest. This called for a new strategy. Dominique always had a secret bag of tricks she carefully stowed away for such occasions. He couldn't know in advance that she was about to unveil the same stunt he'd used on her.

Dominique's own bewitching ear-to-ear grin showed off her sparkling jeweled eyes, beautiful white teeth, and skin that began to flush just noticeably. Lerance drew in the corners of his mouth and narrowed his eyes. At least he was curious.

"I'd like to explain why I did what I did."

"Be my guest, but you won't change my mind."

"Desire Therapy is my most important work. I believe it can help anyone anywhere to lead a better, more fulfilling and productive life. To prove its merits, I chose the hardest subjects to test it on. Rageful men."

"Hey, don't take this so personally. It's just not my cup of tea."

Dominique felt the room get hotter. She got up slowly and moved over to Lerance's chair. He smirked when she hopped up on the edge of the desk to confront him. She crossed her legs, folded her arms, and began.

"We profiled at least two-thousand prisoners. Eventually we settled on five. One left. And then I saw an attorney on television talking about you to reporters."

Lerance said, "I bet that was a turn on."

Dominique leaned in and said, "Your parole board decision made headlines because you were a fortunate son who was turning down parole. I read as many articles about your case as I could get my hands on. You intrigued me. That's how I found my sixth subject."

"You took a big risk. Your career, the entire prison project. All that for little ol' me? Geez, color me flattered."

"You were paying an enormous price for a disastrous mistake. Yet when offered, you always persisted in turning down help. I believed that guilt and remorse were crushing your true nature, your humanity, and for that reason alone I thought you'd make a good candidate for House of Mithras.

"So I pushed your name through. The screeners never flagged it. After a while, if someone did find out you hadn't initiated the process yourself, you'd be well into the program. It wouldn't look good to give you back. Especially if progress was being made."

Lerance screwed up his face into a question mark and leaned back in his chair rakishly, head cocked to one side, hands clasped behind his head. "Wow. And that justifies what you did, does it?"

"You justify what I did. Have you noticed something about the other inmates, Lerance?" Dominique asked.

"Only that they're crazy."

"The others are as different from each other as you are from them. But the six of you create a complete flawless picture."

"You've got to be kidding. Really, is that your best shot?"

"I can get someone to replace you," Dominique said.

"Be my guest."

"But then the picture would appear lopsided. And what happens to the group? You're already part of their family."

"What are you talking about? They hate me. You've seen the digital tapes."

"You're wrong. They admire you. And you're leaving before you've given them a chance to care. Before you can care about them."

Lerance straightened and made to get up. "Sorry, as good as you think you are at enticing violent men to do your bidding, which by the way I think strays towards the demented…well, let's just say it's not working on me."

Moving with predatory speed, Dominique jumped down, walked around the desk and slid two thick files towards him. Lerance automatically shot his arm out to stop them from falling onto the floor.

"You want the truth. The real truth. You remind me of someone." Dominique slapped the top file. "You were a child prodigy. Class valedictorian at age sixteen. Passed medical boards at twenty-one. Impressive academic career. But there was never any mention of friends, hobbies or interests. Your parents, family—where were they when you needed them?

"Oh, I bet they were near and dear when they asked you to perform for the purpose of making them look good and feel good. But what about you? Who cared about you? Who stayed back to love the brilliant little boy?"

Lerance was up now, glaring at the file. He was about to grab it when Dominique pushed it off to the side revealing another one. She flipped though several pages before speaking.

"This one's mine. Except for a few bends in the road, our two case histories are identical. I understand you better than anyone. I can help you. Let me try. Don't leave House of Mithras."

"You don't know me. I killed my wife. I'm dead inside."

Lerance seemed suddenly unsure. He sat back down and started rubbing his forehead.

"Don't you see that we have a perfect storm here? You have gifts that you can share. But it's really what Emile, Eduardo, Billy, Julius and Vincent, can do for you."

Lerance shook his head. "I'm not who you think I am. I can't."

"I know who you are. We're the same. I'm certain of that."

"And I'm going to make you a deal. Finish up the Desire exercises and then pick someone, either staff or inmate, to demonstrate your dreams to. After that, if you still want to, you can leave. I'll even help you pack."

Lerance turned to go. Dominique held her finger just above the call button for the guard. Lerance turned around slowly and she saw a puzzled expression on his face. The look of bewilderment changed to one of acknowledgment. He smiled thinly and then nodded almost imperceptibly.

"Just like Lady Macbeth. She too, was incapable of showing any restraint in pursuit of her goals," Lerance said.

What was that for, Dominique wondered. Did he think she had said something more? He certainly acted like it. When she finally rang the buzzer and Dave appeared, Lerance vanished from the room like a flash. The psychiatrist stood as still as a statue for a long while, staring at his afterimage in the open doorway.

TWENTY FIVE

The topic was memory. The assignment was trolling for and uncovering the happiest moments of their lives.

Today the inmates sat in a circle on padded metal chairs around an Early American braided rug. Dominique chose the room for advanced group therapy sessions because it had once been the personal library of the former plantation owner and had retained the feel of a learned man's quarters. A high ceiling with oak beams looked down over two walls lined with tall narrow bookcases. Some held actual books, but most of the shelves were now repositories for matching plastic bins, accordion-style file folders, and a slew of electronic accessories and sundry surveillance components. Two hanging ferns and the view from the leaded bay window onto the lush back gardens also made the room feel restorative and tranquil.

Personal and emotional space between the men was still being observed, but the empty chairs that used to separate them had been removed, replaced with two feet of empty wood floor. Per usual, the inmates began group therapy with a series of grunts and belches, far away looks, and open hostility. The noisy prologue came from Julius and Billy Jo; Eduardo and Emile studied the windows the ceiling and the floor, for the seventh sign of the apocalypse; Vincent viewed Lerance with a paler, softer hostility. One that seemed to say, *I have something on you now*, rather than the old and tired, *I will kill you and your entire family as soon as I get the chance*. Playing his part dutifully, Lerance inspected his fingernails, pretending to ignore his nemesis. But his slouch also had sent out a message: *Bring it on, asshole*.

Dominique and Kevin waited patiently, occasionally sneaking peeks at Emile, hoping he would break the yoke of the macho grandstanding before too much time had passed. When he finally spoke, Emile looked directly at Dominique as he quoted Gilbert Parker.

"There is no refuge from memory and remorse in this world. The spirits of our foolish deeds haunt us, with or without repentance."

All of the faces dilated with curiosity and just as quickly deflated.

"Okay then, I've got something good," Eduardo said. He shook his head when he saw everyone was staring at him.

"Relax, Eduardo," Kevin said. "Never easy when you're the first one to share."

"We were like Gypsies," Eduardo began in a whisper, eyes darting between the inmates. "Moving from town to town. Usually in the middle of the night. By day my parents would find work while me and my brother Al played in the streets; sometimes we even went to school. Once after we hit this long patch of unemployment for both of my parents, we found ourselves at an old-time gas station in the desert. Mom had just traded her gold watch for a full tank of gas and some bucks for the next toll fee. Just as we were about to take off, an ice cream truck pulled up.

"I nudged Al who was older, to ask our poppy for money. We both knew that the only change left in the kitty, deeply hidden inside mom's purse, was just enough to pay for a motel room later that evening. Poppy said no, but Al was like a dog with a bone. He wouldn't stop. He just kept on and on, begging and crying and torturing poor poppy. Then I started in. Any other time we would have been whooped for our selfishness, but that day our parents gave in, and we all got to eat ice cream."

Eduardo was talking louder now, looking at a distant spot outside of the bay window. Dominique followed his gaze and saw Sheriff Futrell strolling on the front lawn, smoking a cigarette. He looked lost, adrift. After a moment he sat down on a wooden bench and looked off at the cane fields.

"The desert had been like an oven set to broil. The cold from the ice cream was heaven-sent. I licked until every drop was gone. I couldn't get enough. None of us could. Afterwards it was like we were really high on drugs because everyone just started giggling hysterically.

"It didn't matter that when night came we would all have to cram inside the car like sardines in order to get some sleep. That we might not have enough gas to get to us to the next job site. That mom and poppy might not even find work there. We just couldn't stop feeling happy. First, it seemed that nothing could erase the cold and sweetness from our minds, like within the memory alone we would remain cool and full forever. And second, even though it was possibly the most insane decision the family ever made—to spend our last pennies on ice cream—it felt like we were playing hooky from the rat race, thumbing our noses at failure and loss. Just then, we were the winners."

Billy Jo fought to keep back the tears. Instinctively, Julius scraped his chair to his right overlapping Billy Jo slightly, effectively hiding the cross-dresser's hand when it lifted to wipe his cheeks. Without a thought for himself, Julius had risen to defend his roommate from an ugly and possible permanent humiliation.

Only Dominique noticed that Billy Jo and Julius watched out for each other. She thought in their own way, Emile and Eduardo did, too. Vincent and Lerance on the other hand were planning each other's funerals.

No sooner had Eduardo finished than Emile began his tale. This was not your typical nurturing psychotherapy group. Cheers of support did not immediately follow deep revelations. The purpose of the Desire exercises was just to get the information out. To share a happy history and have someone around to witness your disclosure.

"When I was five I watched our next door neighbor, Mr. Jimmy Jansen, return home from war. His house had a big lawn broken up by a skinny concrete path leading up to the front door. The seams in the concrete were chipped and had become home to lots of little weeds. But it was just the right width for Mrs. Jansen to push her husband's wheel chair. A lot of people carrying balloons and casseroles lined up the walkway. They came from all around—family, friends and neighbors. Somebody had even traveled by airplane for the homecoming. This was a big celebration for the returning wounded and crippled soldier.

"A little boy my age ran out the front door and jumped into the wheelchair hugging and kissing the man. Jimmy wrapped his arms tight around his son, and every one clapped and cried. I began crying, too. No one, but no one in my family, had ever been that nice to anyone else. When my stepdad saw what I was doing, he grabbed me hard by the shoulders and pulled me inside. I remember thinking he was afraid that those nice people were going to invite me over. He didn't want me to get infected by all of that goodness.

"That moment has a permanent place in my heart. It gave me such pleasure and serenity just to know that a person could be adored like that. I wanted to be that person. I sensed Jimmy, Mr. Jansen, was a very nice man, a good father and husband, and of course a decorated war hero. But even at five-years-old, I knew his true lovableness came from losing his leg. I wanted to be just like him, but figured I would have to wait until I grew up before I could lose a limb. Now, whenever I fall into depression and think that there is no reason to go on, I try to imagine Mr. Jimmy Jansen's homecoming. And myself without my left leg."

"What if you don't have any memories like that?" Lerance asked, not quite looking at anyone.

For a while, Vincent was like everyone else, eyes down, soaking in the revelations. That changed as soon as he heard the inmate speak. Then with his eyes popped open and alert, his chin bullishly pointed forward, he dared the other man to go forward.

Lerance said, "You guys are talking about a moment filled with joy, the kind that sweeps you up and doesn't let you go for the rest of the day. Where you lose yourself completely and for what it's worth, become someone else. And no matter what happens next, you just know you're going to be okay."

Kevin said, "Are you saying—"

Lerance said, "I'm saying I can't think of a single happy time. Is that such a big deal?"

Vincent snapped, "You gotta be shittin' us."

"I only remember doing what I was told. I guess I was good...at a lot of things. They expected a lot. I don't recall having many choices."

Dominique said, "It's fine, Lerance. This isn't a contest. Sometimes it takes a few tries to come up with happy memories."

"For a shrink, you don't listen well. I have no mushy moments to mention. I can't think of a single instance of altered reality joy. The kind of bliss that Eduardo and Emile talk about—doesn't exist for me, never has," Lerance said.

"Fucking bullshit. Not enough that you were born with a silver spoon up your ass, but now you expect us to feel sorry for you?' Vincent's mad dog glare was back.

Eduardo said, "Maybe he really was an unhappy kid."

Vincent said, "Really. Really? Okay, tell us Doc. What do you need? What would make you happy here? Right here, right now. Tell us what."

Lerance said, "It would thrill me to no end if you shut the fuck up. Yeah, that would do it. Just shut your stupid ugly mouth once and for all."

The sounds that Dominique would remember afterwards always began with a chorus of eight chairs scraping in unison across the wooden floor—everyone getting up in slow motion—and culminating several decibels higher with an onslaught of not-too creative invectives. It had happened so fast.

Vincent and Lerance, who had been sitting the furthest apart, were now standing close enough to inhale each other's raging fumes. The room quickly divided: Emile, Billy Jo and Julius stood with Vincent; Dominique, Kevin and Eduardo flanked Lerance. Bluster and threats grew on both sides intensifying the already palpable adrenaline ripping across the floor.

Kevin delivered a series of sharp "no's", while Dominique began slapping the top of a nearby desk. When Billy Jo jumped up on the same desk waving the peace sign with both hands and singing *"Hare Krishna, Hare, Hare"*, he was still partially dressed in the outfit he had worn to an earlier counseling session: leotard and shorts, his eyes streaked with melting black eyeliner, cheeks rouged. Those were the things Sheriff Leroy Futrell saw when he and the guard burst in. Both had guns drawn.

The hush that fell over the room was not because the inmates were afraid for their physical lives, but was due to the instant regret they felt after seeing the complete look of mortification on Dominique's face. She looked like a ghost. They had failed her.

"What in tarnation is going on here? I could hear you clear across the lawn." Futrell's eyes burned darkly, but his gun was now at his side.

Futrell holstered his pistol and then brandished all of his disgust at Dominique. "What were you thinking? Didn't anyone teach you that you need rules to run a prison? Otherwise your little experiment here's going to end up just another dingbat idea," the sheriff said.

Dominique turned away from Futrell because she was too shaken up to play a posturing game with the lawman today. "Thank you sheriff for your concern, but we can handle it from here." To the guard she merely sighed, "You can go back outside, we have this under control."

With barely concealed impatience, she addressed Kevin, but the message was clearly directed at the inmates. She couldn't face them. "Sit down, all of you. Now. Take a deep breath. And start over. Kevin will facilitate the rest of your time together." Dominique left the room.

If she hadn't left, Dominique's face would have betrayed her. Dominique felt very ashamed and too fragile and transparent. The last thing she wanted was for Vincent to find out exactly which fiery road to hell her imagination had dispatched him to.

TWENTY SIX

In the afterglow of the disappearing sunset, the Creole plantation had taken on a sacred luminescence.

The steeply-pitched roof, the raised gallery, and the adorning gingerbread fretwork trim all cast their reflected images onto the surrounding gardens and orchards. A mild breeze soughed the leaves high up on the live oaks, allowing the remaining sunlight to sparkle through them like teasing Morris code. Dominique swung restlessly on an eighteenth-century rocker on the gallery, watching the flowing sugar cane across the motorway. She tried to remain positive, but unlike Eduardo and Emile earlier, she had trouble conjuring up a single happy thought. Hidden tensions beneath the surface and a new habit of frowning had etched irreversible lines on the psychiatrist's face. Her face contorted as she pictured the almost-fight between Lerance and Vincent. It stunned her to realize that she had lost Lerance. But her anger was reserved for Vincent alone. If it hadn't been for his taunts and threats, she might not have completely lost her dwindling hold on the former doctor.

There was something else clawing at the surface.

Dominique was known for throwing her energy a hundred percent at projects; her strategy of efficiency and persistence consistently reaped higher than expected results. But when it came to Lerance, she had taken it an even-greater distance and still failed. Meanwhile, she had run afoul of her business partner and friend, and now, possibly, one of the other inmates. She could not tamp down a surfacing fear that Lerance might actually be the one responsible for the former gangster's sudden transformation from the earlier mild-mannered farmer to ruthless provocateur.

When the sky darkened and the moon slipped onto the horizon, Dominique got up and began to pace. She glanced at her watch and saw it was almost nine p.m. Exactly twelve hours ago the day had begun with sweetness and promise. Before it went all-cockeyed. Had she missed something? Something said or overheard or seen? Whatever it was, it had happened before the group meeting.

I'm not surprised your undies are in a bundle. You've been losing your touch for some time now.

That was the kind of negative statement Delilah might make. Dominique didn't want to engage in self-pity. The only thing that would help now was good sleuthing and decisive action.

It's because you've been careless. If you had paid attention to the signs, you wouldn't be in trouble now. If you didn't absolutely have to have Lerance in the program...you could be concentrating on the future of Desire applications, not their demise.

No. It's not too late.

Time is not on your side.

You're wrong.

She needed to spread out all the events of the day and study them. Something had occurred which hadn't seemed significant, but was. She was sure of it now. All she had to do was to travel back twelve hours and find it.

In the morning, white clouds had drifted like creamy quiffs across a surprisingly deep blue sky. Usually at this time of year the scorching temperatures in southern Louisiana bleached out everything in their wake, including the heavens. Despite the heat and humidity, the front grounds of the prison estate were filled with relaxed prisoners attentively working their Desire exercises. Inside her office, Dominique facilitated a special counseling session with Billy Jo. He had earned her time by volunteering to shore up a crumbling brick wall of a tool storage shed. He also turned in extra homework assignments and hadn't stolen anything from Julius for almost a week.

When the guard deposited Billy Jo at Dominique's office, the inmate practically lunged at the iPod so he could play his favorite 70's disco songs.

For forty-five minutes Dominique had alternated between laughter and praise as Billy Jo, dressed in a black spandex leotard, matching high heels, short shorts and a red chiffon shawl, danced energetically. When *Stayin' Alive* started, the psychiatrist stood up and from behind the desk, leaned over and grabbed the shawl away from the inmate. Then she did her best impression of John Travolta in *Saturday Night Fever*. This time Billy Jo showered the applause. When Dominique started giggling she didn't quit until her face was entirely streaked with tears. She had almost forgotten how much fun it was to lose all sense of control.

When they finished, Dominique told Billy Jo she was proud of him because it had taken a great measure of courage to exhibit and celebrate his love of costume and dance. He asked if he could go out and join the others.

"I'll call the guard as soon as you change your shoes and wipe off your make up." When the guard came in she added, "Oh, and drop the shawl." Billy Jo affected hurt and surprise as he left with Dave down the corridor.

When she opened the window, the warm breezes floated into the room bringing up the sounds of overlapping chatter and laughter. The guards on the front lawn were corralling the inmates and counselors into a designated semi-circle where Emile was getting up on his bicycle. One leg was bent back 180 degrees at the knee, the ankle bound by duct tape to his thigh. In just a few short days the inmate had mastered simple one-legged peddling and was riding almost as well as he did when he still operated with both legs. Dominique was surprised to see Sheriff Futrell hanging out in the middle of the crowd that waited for the inmate to perform his next trick.

It took only two tries before Emile began racing the bicycle down the brick path towards the gate. At the last possible second, the genteel murderer popped the front end of his bike into the air like a thoroughbred rearing its front legs. His first practiced attempt at a wheelie was momentarily successful and was quickly met by a large round of whistles and applause. Then he lost his balance and plunged back to earth—bicycle on top of him. Emile got up, clumsily at first, dusted off his pant leg and bowed from the waist, one-legged, to the group of admiring fans.

Wearing his uniform look of bemusement, the sheriff stole a glance up at Dominique's window; seeing nothing but glare, he began moving among the prisoners and their activities.

Eduardo and Jody sat on a bench operating a laptop, paging occasionally through a thick law book for guidance. Julius worked at a table under a live oak, sanding and gluing pieces of a large wooden boat. In a private session he had confessed to Kevin that he secretly wanted to race sailboats and that the only class he hadn't skipped in high school was shop. It looked like Kevin had found the perfect outlet for Julius's creativity. Soon Billy Jo sauntered by and the roommates began anew, squabbling and teasing each other good-naturedly. When Dominique saw Vincent walk down the front stairs with the guard, the director quickly left her office.

Because he had been one of the last holdouts to begin Desire exercises, Vincent surprised the staff by catching up on all his assignments the third week, and just like Billy Jo had, handed in extra work. He applied himself in other ways, too. When he was at the shelter he worked diligently to complete his evening chores, which meant ladling meals to the residents, and also washing and putting away all of the dishes. Then, after everyone was asleep, Vincent stayed up sanitizing the kitchen like it was a hospital ward. Cleaning was something the guards at Mississippi State Penitentiary taught him to do to pass the time. One night he emptied every cabinet and cupboard, before washing them thoroughly and then putting everything back.

They walked quickly across the field. Dominique was telling Vincent she had something to show him near the old slave cabins. When they came to a scrubby field fenced off by rope and chicken wire, Dominique abruptly stopped. In front of them gaped a twenty-by-twenty enclosure filled with shovels, a hoe, rake, several trowels, a tall pile of bags of sheep manure and a box stuffed with seed packets. In one corner, two ten-gallon plastic worm bins for composting kitchen scraps and organic waste sat next to a wooden crate labeled RED WORMS.

"I realize this is August and planting season is at least another month away, but you can get started by tilling the earth and getting your worm bins ready. I have arranged for a volunteer from LSU's Ag Center to come out in September to work with you. It's a win-win. The student can talk to you about the newest organic gardening techniques, plus he can actually help you start and maintain the plantings. At the same time you can share your personal knowledge of farming with him. You get free labor, good advice, and vice versa.

Vincent didn't move a muscle. He held his breath. Dominique continued, "You might need more than a shovel. Look." Dominique bent down and scratched at the dirt. "The ground here is packed down like cement, and I'm sure those grass roots are tough. But there's an honest-to-goodness roto-tiller in the tool shed at your disposal. It was a donation...you might have to tune it up first."

It took awhile for Vincent to speak. He was afraid if he did, he might betray an unmanly emotion. "For me? You did this all for me. I can't believe it." Vincent stared hard at the garden spot, to make sure it wouldn't disappear on him.

"All the things you told us and wrote about in your journal showed that farming was your one great joy from childhood. We can't let that go to waste. Besides, in the fall you will be able to produce a vegetable crop that might finally balance out the worn-torn diet of Louisiana beans and rice, and the artery-clogging red meat diet we've all been on."

"I'm a strong man. If it's all right with you, I can just use the shovel for now. I want to feel the earth under me."

"I've scheduled time every week for you to be out here. Right now you have an hour and a half until lunch. After that, it's group."

He finally found her face. "I don't know what to say. No one outside the family has ever even come close to..."

"You can show your appreciation by working hard at what you love. By the way," Dominique pointed to the worm bins, "the staff in the kitchen will report directly to you regarding vegetable scraps."

"Thank you, Dr. Doucette. Thank you."

She watched him for a minute. With his eyes Vincent seemed to scoop out neatly-lined rows and fill them with seeds. He laid down mulch between the rows to keep the weeds down. When he turned on the sprinkler, he heard bubbles of water penetrate the dried cracked earth. When the tiny sprouts finally appeared, he fed them organic compost and watered again. Then Dominique walked twenty feet to the shed to check on the roto-tiller.

Vincent's brief stint with euphoria was replaced by a dark vision in his periphery. Two men walking quickly towards them. One of them, Lerance. Dominique did not actually see anything, she was on the backside of the shed now trying to find a key to fit into the ancient hanging Yale lock. When she heard the clipped cadence of the former doctor's speech, she listened, but at the time gave it no regard.

That's when it happened.

Lerance had asked for and received permission to walk around the grounds before lunch. When he spotted Vincent alone in the garden, he and the guard walked over to see what the inmate was doing.

"You really from Mississippi? Vicksburg way? Or more inland?" Lerance made it sound like a question on a game show. The wrong answer might prove to be fatal.

Vincent sliced through the desiccated soil with his shovel as easily as if it were a sandy beach. Though it was slightly less humid that morning, the heavy air didn't move, and with each shovelful, Vincent's shirt soaked up a spoonful of sweat. He stopped to mop his face with his forearm before leaning on the shovel.

Vincent asked, "What do you want?"

"What are you, about forty-five? You would have been a teen-ager when those boys started disappearing. But not you, right? You escaped? Or maybe you were just a kid who never got sick." Lerance hadn't even bothered to look at Vincent. With his arms crossing his chest, he talked to the bin of worms.

To the guard, the words sounded like gibberish. He was busy thinking about the plans he had made with his girlfriend for the weekend, and never saw the fear move across Vincent's eyes as he knelt down heavily to remove small rocks from the dried earth.

"Hmm? Ever wonder if you might have passed up a great opportunity? Maybe if you'd seen the doctor, your grandmother would have been able to keep the farm, and her grandson wouldn't have ended up in *gangland*."

That got the guard's attention. But before Lerance could say another word, Vincent had walked to a far corner of the plot to set the rocks down.

Vincent was stunned. *Nana had been right about me after all. I got that special gift. I can know all about people even though I never met them before. And I was right about him.*

But what do I do? How could I ever prove what I only know in my heart to be true?

When Dominique returned she saw the guard and Lerance walking in the direction of the main building. Vincent would not look at her. Just kept arranging rocks in order of size. From his cowed posture she knew with certainty that whatever Lerance said to Vincent had been filled with just enough toxic residue to knock over the big man's short tower of burgeoning dignity.

The shoe was on the other foot. Lerance was no longer afraid of Vincent. Even though he could not have survived fisticuffs with the gangster, he owned something now much deadlier than muscle or brawn. Or why else had Vincent climbed over the chicken wire to throw up? Vanity caused her to conclude that the gift of the garden had simply overwhelmed him. But now she saw that Vincent had been seized by panic. A horror unleashed by Lerance.

TWENTY SEVEN

Vincent's voice always surprised people. It made you think of a warm and sensitive soul trapped inside a big granite mausoleum. When he spoke, each syllable hit a perfect note of melting sugar and sandpaper, bringing with it the ability to momentarily put anyone listening at ease. The pitch and rhythm never gave away his temperament. If you wanted to find contradictory evidence of discomfort or anger, you only had to look into his eyes.

"Are you going to take my garden away?" Vincent's question held more curiosity than combativeness. Dominique was relieved to see that for now his eyes were wide open and blank.

"No, you earned that. But I do want you to tell me the truth," Dominique said.

"The truth about what?" Vincent padded across the wide oak floorboards, over the rugs, and lowered himself into a chair beside her desk. He smiled thinly and nodded knowingly at the psychiatrist. She knew the calm was only skin-deep.

"Why do you hate Lerance?"

"Pardon me, ma'am?"

Dominique said, "Don't ma'am me. I want to know what started all of this hostility between you two."

Vincent asked, "Am I talking to the shrink or the warden?"

Dominique said, "Everything in here is confidential. Now tell me. Why do you constantly pick on him? What is it? What's he done? Do you have history? Did you know him before?"

"No."

"Does he know you?"

"Ask him yourself." Vincent shifted into predatory mode. His eyes hooded over leaving only a dark slit that shifted back and forth.

Once again, it was too early to be this hot. Dominique tapped her pencil to the tempo of the croaking ceiling fan and felt her cheeks burn. Her hands and arms were already covered in dewy film only oppressive humidity creates, and at any minute she feared she might jump out of her skin and clothes.

"What happened yesterday?" She asked intentionally leaving the time frame ambiguous.

"Wasn't no thing."

"It was something if Lerance decides to leave House of Mithras."

And just like that the big man slumped deeply inside the chair that was already too small for him. He groaned, "So losing your pet is supposed to be my fault, now?" The accusatory words contradicted his tone. He sounded like a man arguing over whom was responsible for leaving a tube of toothpaste uncapped.

"I don't have pets. I fight for everyone in here. Listen to me, Vincent. I need to find out what is going on. Tell me what I'm missing." When the most in-your-face inmate folds in like a lethargic lizard, "What she might be missing," could fill up a country.

Vincent said, "Maybe you should be looking somewhere else."

It occurred to Dominique then that the sweltering heat might be playing tricks on her. Like a mirage, all of Vincent's hard edges were melting. The room had become an echo chamber pinging his hollow words off the walls and ceiling. Only sad sleepy eyes returned her stare. It took forever for the words to come out. "He's a freak. Acts like he walks on water."

"Did it ever occur to you he does that for self protection? He might be just as intimidated by you as you are of him."

"Doubt it. He's different."

"Vincent, y'all just got here. It takes time to get to know each other."

"With Lerance, there's nothing you want to know, ma'am."

"Nothing?"

"You may not believe me, but I got this bad feeling. He reminds me of an evil creature right out of one of the books my nanna used to read to me as a kid."

Vincent made to get up and Dominique nodded her assent. He walked over to the window and studied the lime-green fields in the distance.

"Sugar cane. Funny, they say it's a sign of good fortune. We had ourselves a small cane farm once. Nice house, too. Small, but we were so happy there. Until the day the sheriff came with papers, telling us we had forty-eight hours to vacate. I think that day I cried up my lifetime allotment of tears. I believed we were about to lose the best part of us.

"But my nanna told me not to fuss. That things could have been a lot worse."

"What could be worse?"

"Disappearing."

With his back to the psychiatrist, Vincent looked like a stone sculpture of himself. He was giving her time to let the answer soak in. *Disappearing*. That's what she heard Lerance say near the garden plot. What or who exactly had disappeared?

Vincent continued, "She warned me to steer clear of a particular kind of folk. Nanna said that even though that kind had everything money could buy, they were always looking for another kind of satisfaction.

"I guess she must have been pretty scared for me, cuz so many kids were gone by then. Boys. A few girls, too," Vincent spoke to the front yard.

"When was that, exactly?" Dominique asked.

"Oh, I expect I was about fifteen or sixteen. They weren't killed you know. Just used. People sometimes ran into them years later in other towns, in others states. By then it was too late. They had changed too much."

"The mid seventies. How many?"

"Nine."

"Why haven't I heard about this before?"

The obelisk turned around. "Are you serious? They weren't exactly on anybody's to-do list. Just some poor throwaway kids."

If no one had paid attention to missing black kids three decades earlier, why did Lerance know about them? She would have to proceed cautiously. Could it be that Vincent had just become her last hope?

TWENTY EIGHT

Only fifty-four hours and twenty-five minutes until he could leave. Or a grand total of three thousand, seventy minutes. Lerance stopped having fun ticking off the minutes and he no longer cared how much that translated into seconds. The doctor was experiencing the first twinges of real doubt.

Life is one long discovery. But the first person you meet on the way is yourself. If early on you find out that your identity, your sum total worth, is completely dependent on the achievements your family expects from you, you learn to relegate your personal desires and needs to a dark corner. Your achievements become addictions: the more you achieve, the more your have to do it again. When you finally face the fact that becoming famous and rich and accomplished will never be enough, you find other ways to feed your needs. Because before he killed his wife, someone else had murdered his soul.

The first time he won a national contest, Lerance was seven years old. His abstract drawing of an elephant had been created against the background of classical music and won the attention of gallery owners and art auction houses. Contest after contest, awards after medals, firsts and top grades, none of these things ever garnered praise from his parents. But that hadn't been the goal. Success was simply a tool to ward off their disapproval, because their kind of disapproval could threaten his very survival.

When he was a toddler, Lerance still hoped he could win his mother's love. Once he placed a Tinkertoy creation that he'd worked on all morning into cold hands and then jumped onto an equally cold lap to look into her face. He wanted to catch a glimpse of his own reflection inside his mother's eyes. A sign of unconditional love and approval from the woman who had given him life never came; the only thing Lydeah Lemartine was capable of was projecting her own image. Lerance was never her precious little boy. He was just offspring, an annexed wing of whatever was next on her agenda. She swatted him away like a bug, because at that moment she hadn't wanted him for anything. She was thinking about her next patient. Afterwards he found it hard to form real relationships; only the imaginary ones that he could control were satisfying. Lerance wasn't sure if he ever loved his wife, but he thought he had tried to make the marriage work. At least in the beginning.

Lerance's history dictated that he inherit all of the characteristics of a commitment- phobe, so it was unlikely that Lerance would have ever freely chosen to live in House of Mithras, what with all of its emphasis on interpersonal therapy, expressing your feelings, and developing better people skills—all the things that had been wiped out of his emotional toolbox long ago. But that was before he met Dominique.

Prison had been tolerable. A place to hide and nurse his wounds until it was safe to move on. House of Mithras, conversely, reminded him of the open schools of the nineteen-seventies. Far too lax in discipline to actually make any difference in a child's education, it was more like a porous vehicle ready to invite outside temptations. Lerance didn't understand why he hadn't simply refused Dominique Doucette. He could have. Not showing enthusiasm wasn't the same as saying no. Lerance had to admit that in the end she had worn him down. She was as persuasive as she was famous. Just like the Greek goddess Ariadne who had swooped down and promised Theseus safe passageway out of the Labyrinth, the psychiatrist wooed the inmate with enticements of healing his psychic scars by venturing on a less-traveled course, one that led directly back to your first hopes and desires. Desire Therapy. He had vacillated because he was curious. He surrendered because she was black.

His own past remained murky with an endless string of unanswered questions about his progeny as well as the mystery of possible descendents born to both his mother and father, all of whom he had not been allowed to meet or know. And this was exactly why reform prisons, like their antecedent open schools, were dangerous entities in civil society. They gave you a false sense of security, because when you least expected it, they could coax out of you old family secrets — some, if exposed — could cost you your life. Better to inhale molten lava than become that vulnerable.

When he finally managed to relax enough to lie down on his bed and read the newspaper, the big man appeared in the doorway sucking up all the light in the room. Lerance hoped the guard was right behind him. But he knew he wasn't. Things were getting pretty lackadaisical around the prison. He tried not to show fear by pretending to read.

"I heard you getting ready to move on. It ain't right man," Vincent stood with arms akimbo, his face screwed up into a question mark.

Lerance said, "What if it's right for me?"

"See that's what you always do."

"What?"

"Make everything about you."

"Whom should I make it about?"

"We're in this together. We all made the same deal. Why would you leave anyway? You're gonna make out better than anyone else.

"You have advantages, already knowing how this system works. As soon as you finish doing a few assignments, you get your freedom back, get to pick up on your very nice life you left behind. It's all good for you."

"You're sure about that?"

"You're gonna throw it all away."

Lerance snickered. "You mean I'll miss out on all your philosophical musings?"

"Is that what your fancy education taught you? To be a smart ass? What about honor? Where's your honor, man?"

Lerance got up and strode to the window. He looked out at a grassy field painted yellow by the radiant setting sun. He thought of Lydeah and realized he could no longer recall her face. His mother had so often stood with her back to him.

Lerance said, "You're a gangster. You sell drugs to children. And then you kill people over drug deals. Why are you talking to me about honor?"

Before the last word was out, he felt Vincent sidle up against him, breathing and exhaling air, his air. In that moment, Vincent had gained something. An extra-credit confidence. No longer afraid, and reading him. Even as

Vincent might know what Lerance was thinking, he wasn't judging him anymore. He stood so close Lerance didn't know where he ended or where the big man began.

Vincent whispered hoarsely, "I walk a jagged line. What I take, I must replace. But you, you're like a ghost. Your feet ain't even touching the ground."

"What do you really know about me?" Lerance asked.

"I know you're still burying secrets."

TWENTY NINE

How far do I have to go before I can free my pain? How will I know when I get there?

After working all night patrolling the streets and alleys of Desire, at dawn, Darnell changed guard with Gemini, went back to the Davis' to drink three cups of coffee, and then headed for the French Quarter. Darnell volunteered for night shifts because it suited his insomnia. This affliction started in high school shortly after Dominique left for Princeton and he hooked up with the local gang. Back then, the normal routine was to catch an hour of z's after midnight, get up and read, get up and listen to music, or get up and walk. In the early years, he had walked for hours on end around his hood with no purpose at all. Later, his night ventures would lead him all over New Orleans and neighboring suburbs, and to several arrests.

Most of the arrests happened just after Darnell had stopped walking long enough to inspect something that intercepted his interest. Like the time the night watchman found him sitting on top of a mausoleum in an exclusive Catholic cemetery in Metarie. He had been examining the inscription of its permanent dwellers: a long line of deceased Louisiana plantation magnates and former slave owners. Or a year later, when a trucker spotting a young black man walking barefoot against traffic on Lake Pontchartrain Causeway, on the way to Mandeville, reported the sighting to the local constabulary on his CB. Darnell's longest ramble, spanning twenty-seven hours, occurred in 1992. Thinking he'd only be gone a short while, he had pulled on his new Nikes, adjusted his headset and pressed play. Only after the last set of batteries died and the sun rose for the second time, did Darnell realize he had come up on the shores of Morgan City. Along with the eye of the storm that would forever be known as Hurricane Andrew.

These infractions were small potatoes though, compared to the absolute toll that insomnia played on his physical and mental health, as it steered Darnell to a lifetime affair with booze, pot, downers and finally his own personal siren, heroin. Now, while serving a sentence of sobriety, reality seemed just a bit too sharp-edged. He needed walking more than ever to stay calm and focused, especially for the task ahead.

When Darnell came out of treatment the last time, he turned over his firearms to Elijah, promising his good friend and mentor that he would not buy or carry any kind of weapon in Desire, especially while he was on patrol. His promise was a lie. But only a partial one. Even if one day out of duty and loyalty he was compelled to shoot someone in Desire, it could not be linked to a gun that he had purchased there, because that violated his personal code of standards. Too much was at stake: the example he passed on to his younger counterparts, and the all too real possibility of implicating Elijah and the patrol in some future crime investigation. No worries, Darnell had connections all over New Orleans and the best place for forbidden dealings was still in the French Quarter, where you could buy anything from a puppy to a stolen merchant marine vessel.

And any gun under the sun.

Besides, Yolanda wasn't getting any better. Worse really, and the police — no surprise there — were no further in either apprehending or even identifying her perp. It was time to take the 'hood back. One rapist at a time. The attack happened under Darnell's watch; it was his responsibility to avenge the innocent young girl. Because no matter how long the community waited, no one else was coming. Not like last time.

Before crack cocaine beleaguered and then permanently sealed its venom inside the arteries of the crescent city, New Orleans had been the usual mobbed-up town, whose economic nerve center revolved around the French Quarter. Drugs were sold, prostitution flourished, but if you had the chutzpah to rob a visitor in the tourist areas, you'd better be prepared to say goodbye to your kneecaps, once and for all. Mugging an old man or woman in downtown New Orleans was tantamount to napalming a village of innocent women and children, and was always rewarded with an unexpected two-week stopover at Charity Hospital. And if word got out that someone even looked at a child wrong, that fool's seeing days would be over because he'd be dead, thanks to an unwritten criminal code established years before. Crime in certain segments of New Orleans had an ethic, because crime bosses looked well after their interests.

Unfortunately, no such corresponding scenario could be found within the black barrios that held the majority of the populace. The mob largely ignored the men and women of African descent who experienced rampant poverty and life-threatening street crime every day of their lives. So did city government and its tyrannical counterpart, the New Orleans police department. In 1970, the Desire 'hood in the upper Ninth Ward arguably was the poorest, most forsaken neighborhood in the city. That year the BPP (Black Panther Party) of New Orleans, also know as N.C.C.F. (National Committee to Combat Fascism) moved in, and for the first time in memory the population felt hope for its future. The radical group endeavored to get it to thrive.

For a short time it achieved its goals. Although the BPP movement enjoyed wide-ranged support throughout New Orleans, its ability to endure eventually crumbled and ended due to a prolonged campaign of city and state harassment, and police brutality.

The BPP had started out by launching service programs that included free breakfasts—at its peak it fed three hundred children a day—cleaning homes of the elderly, visiting and writing prisoners, spreading political education, and most importantly, providing security. Before that, Darnell and his little friends were only impersonating the lives of innocent children.

Kids had been allowed to play outside during daylight hours, and for those whose parents had jobs, only under the watchful eye of a grandparent, if they were lucky enough to have one living with them. The alternative was staying indoors, where it was only slightly less dangerous. Then one day they appeared; men and women in black berets patrolling the streets and distributing food. Soon after, the adults began acting differently, they smiled a lot more and yelled less. The Panthers looked out after all the children, but they went all out for his friend, Little Niqui. That suited Darnell just fine, because it meant he could spend more time with her.

These days, although he knew he probably would never see her again, Darnell walked so he could stop thinking about his old friend. More often, so he could remember.

While he walked, Darnell's childhood came back to life, along with the little girl who always accompanied him in the back alleys. Darnell, in his big boots slurping water out of the puddled-craters, she scissor-kicking her way across the narrow passageways, expertly avoiding each and every rut. Dominique always ran ahead, cleats pinging on the tarmac, the switch of her ponytail slapping against the wind, like that of a young colt. When the humidity peppered the night air with spicy perfumes, most people smelled Night Jasmine or Magnolia trees, but Darnell could make out Johnson's baby shampoo and Dial soap—Little Niqui's bath time toiletries.

On these walks, they talked a fair amount. She always asked how he was doing, if he was really straight, did he attend his weekly AA meetings. He allowed the nagging to go on because she had earned it from all the times of picking him out of the gutter, literally saving his life numerous times.

When Dominique came home for her first visit from university, she found out Darnell had been tossed in the clink for loitering and resisting arrest. Nineteen years old and already hopelessly hooked on smack. She already had influence, but where she got the money to pay for his treatment and subsequent prescription of methadone, he never found out. The following spring she sent for him to stay with her in Princeton. It was always like that: for a few months Darnell stayed sober, but soon was back using and landing in jail. She'd bail him out again, and he always promised to do better. And then the cycle repeated.

Ten years ago when she returned to Desire to open her clinic, only slightly less famous than she was now,

Dominique declared her undying love for Darnell and they hooked up like Romeo and Juliet for six months. Despite the fact that just like the tragic Shakespearian duo, they were doomed from the start, it still shocked Darnell to his core to wake up one morning and find her gone.

She called him from a New York hotel later that night. On the phone they cried together over all the lost opportunities and faced the truth, that each in their separate ways could hurt the other more while together, than if they stayed apart. She told him she loved him too much to risk his life or sanity for her ever again. And then she extracted that final vow from him, the same one she asked him to break a few days ago. Had it been a test? Or had she always known the truth? That one day, she would weaken.

"Promise me, Darnell. Promise that no matter how much I beg you to do different, you'll stay strong. That you won't give in next time. I can't bear to see what happens to you when I'm around. You know you're lucky to be alive?"

"No Dominique. You're the reason I live."

"You know what I'm saying. Can't hide from what's plain on your nose. Promise me. Just say it."

And just like that, he swore on a stack of bibles, the same way he'd promised all those other times. Except this time, it was to *not* be there for her.

It was as hard for Darnell to resist his first love as it was to shun drugs. He could imagine himself easily sliding back. Allowing himself to feel her arms around his neck, her kisses in his hair. Like a baby swaddled in fleece. Would it be so wrong to take Dominique back for a short while? Compare that with never being able to touch her face again. Yes, she was like a big shot of happiness inside his veins. The first plunge proving that you were born to do this, the rest, making you wish you were dead.

If Yolanda hadn't been brutally violated, he could easily have broken his resolve. But it was too much of a coincidence that a young girl in Desire was nearly killed so soon after Dominique's arrival in Louisiana. Darnell wasn't big on introspection; he never wasted time analyzing problems from different angles. And he didn't believe in coincidences. He only relied on his instincts, which were especially keen when he was sober. Darnell knew in his gut that if he didn't avenge Yolanda soon, it might be too late to save Dominique.

As soon as Darnell crossed N. Claiborne Avenue into the Fabourg Marigny neighborhood, Dominique disappeared. She didn't know the territory like he did, and wouldn't follow him all the way into the French Quarter.

Darnell found Georgette sitting inside a cafe on Royal Street. She didn't look particularly surprised when he sat down next to her, only flicked her gaze up briefly and then back to her pancakes and syrup.

It was Darnell who appeared nonplussed. The singer had packed on the pounds in the last year. A telltale sign that the Bettie Page look-alike had joined the ranks of other maturing and talented musicians who had undergone sobriety, substituting their old habits with calorie-dense, vein-clogging, New Orleans-style cookery.

"Knock it off."

"What?"

"What you're thinking. We're all getting older and fatter. Just wait until it happens to you."

Darnell wondered if down the line, Georgette would eventually favor her father. Now in his sixties, the man's physique resembled a bowling pin. Georgette would make a buxom bowling pin, he thought.

"Darnell, were you planning sometime in this new long century to let me know to what I owe the pleasure of seeing your fine face, so early in the morning?"

"I need to score."

"Word on the street is that you're clean. What gives?"

"I am clean. I need a gun."

"Jesus, shut up. People will hear you. I got a gig here at noon."

"Forget you, I need Elgin."

"No. He don't get into it no more. Didn't you hear? Daddy had a massive heart attack and then by-pass surgery. He almost died. Leave him alone."

"But I need his help."

"He doesn't need you."

"Come on girl, give it up. It's me, Darnell."

"Na-ah. He can't handle the stress of the business. You know, like always having a lawyer on retainer. That's what did him in, not the police, not the competition. It was the damn lawyers." Georgette abruptly looked away from her table companion and said, "He can't help you. You've come to the wrong place."

"Give me his number."

"What did I just say? Bother someone else."

Darnell grabbed the woman's arm, pulling up her sleeve to reveal a history they both knew she recalled like it happened yesterday. It amazed him how much of the ugly red scar that had been carved into her forearm had disappeared under the craftsmanship of a new snake tattoo.

Abruptly he dropped Georgette's arm. "The last thing I want to do is cause you or your family aggravation. But y'all owe me. Elgin said if I ever needed anything to come calling. I wouldn't be here if it wasn't important."

Georgette looked around before quickly writing down her daddy's number on a business card and then handed it to Darnell along with a weak smile. She couldn't say no to Darnell. They did owe him. Her whole family might have been torched to death by a firebomb if it hadn't been for Darnell and Elijah. The duo and its posse crossed neighborhoods to warn her father that the new boys on the block—so anxious to take possession of the gun-smuggling territory—had decided on a very public display of overthrow. The new cartel had been quite surprised when a black gang came to the rescue of an old established white hoodlum and his tribe. But then, they didn't understand how New Orleans liaisons worked.

"Sorry, Darnell. Actually I think Daddy will be happy to see you. You've such a way with people."

Darnell might have noticed, but nevertheless didn't acknowledge, the sarcasm in the last statement because just then a cop walked through the door. Upon seeing Darnell and Georgette huddled together at the small table, the uniformed man did a double take, especially after Darnell raised his hands over his head in a mock exaggeration of being arrested. The cop studied him for a moment before ordering a cup of coffee to go.

An hour later, Darnell was at the Franciscan church in front of the shrine of Our Lady of Prompt Succor, praying for a miracle. He jumped when the retired arms smuggler clasped him around the waist. The obese, grey-haired man led Darnell down a couple of blocks to his newly-built mansion. Darnell could only shake his head. He had no words for the things he felt about the changes that had come to the neighborhood. To

Darnell this was the strangest part of New Orleans. The new houses on the northern edge of the Garden District all looked like they might have been dropped from the sky by Martians. For three blocks, the architecture looked forlornly out of place amidst the elegant influences of nearby French, Spanish, and German structures. Here, new, sprawling, one-story brick ramblers that would have been much more at home in the Midwest than in one of the densest historic sections of America had uniformly sprung up. More and more, many things seemed upside down to Darnell.

When they were inside Elgin's spacious living room, the older man studied his friend. "What's wrong, son?" Elgin handed Darnell a glass of lemonade while the younger man examined the Browning M1911.

"Nothing. It's just been a while since I seen one of these."

"You want to tell me about it?"

"Nah. Some neighborhood mess. It'll be good soon."

"I heard Dominique's back. Some fancy prison project. You seen her?"

"Your daughter seemed right out of sorts when I asked about you."

Elgin was no better in getting through Darnell's defenses than anyone else. So he didn't challenge the younger man's not so-subtle change of topic. "She's just being protective. You remind her of what might have been. I see it different."

"How do you mean?"

"That piranha was going to skin her alive, before he burnt the rest of us down. You and your boys arrived just in the nick of time. I'll never forget that. It's just that Georgette can't help reliving the scene over and over. The cutting, she feels like it's happening in real time. I think because you walked in and saved her, she can't extricate you from the horror."

"Sounds wicked, man."

Elgin asked, "Are you really clean?"

Darnell said, "Seven months. Longest time ever."

Elgin asked, "Then why do you need a gun?"

"Shit, dude, what does one have to do with the other?"

What indeed? Elgin shrugged and let Darnell out of the house. They both looked up and down the street that seemed to be transforming right in front of their eyes.

"We all got to get used to it. Everything's changing," Elgin said.

"Not everything."

Back on State and Magazine streets, Darnell's cell phone rang. This time it wasn't Dominique. It was his mother. Another call he couldn't answer.

THIRTY

All night long, ugly pictures rioted in his head.

They spilled into his dreams and contaminated his awakening. Lerance watched as frightened melting faces from his childhood chased him through hospital corridors, out into the street. There he tried to outrun crazed cars whose screeching brakes always failed, and metal crashed into metal. The cars turned into writhing naked bodies whose limbs and torsos mercifully again changed into ancient burr oaks. He hid under the trees until emaciated cat-like creatures with red eyes jumped out from behind branches onto his chest and poured sand into his nose and mouth and eyes. As he struggled to breathe, a thick bubbling white liquid began to gush out of his fingertips. He knew that the distance between the terrifying images and the present was shrinking. Whenever he tried to break free, his younger self always found the older Lerance at the finish line. The dream was showing him how pieces of the past could escape his mind, leak out somehow and, like quicksilver, course down all of the world's vacant cracks and crevices, filling them up with putrid truths. Available for anyone to come see, to poke and examine.

Less than forty-eight hours ago, Lerance knew with absolute certainty that the only way to stop the madness was to leave House of Mithras forever. Even after Dominique had encouraged him to stay, he'd managed to parry the gesture with a quick call to his lawyer. But when she upped the ante and showed him a brand new map, one peppered with possibilities. Now instead of clear direction, he faced a fork at the end of the psychic roadway.

She had torn open an old thick file and cried, *"This one's mine. Except for a few bends in the road, our two case histories are identical. I understand you better than anyone. I can help you. Let me try. Don't leave House of Mithras."*

Grasping for the right words, he managed, *"You don't know me. I killed my wife. I'm dead inside."*

But she kept on. *"Don't you see that we have a perfect storm here? You have gifts that you can share. But it's really what Emile, Eduardo, Billy, Julius and Vincent can do for you."*

"I'm not who you think I am. I can't."

"You're wrong. We're the same. I'm certain of that.

"And I'm going to make you a deal. Finish up the Desire exercises and then pick someone, either staff or inmate, to demonstrate your dreams to. After that, if you still want to, you can leave. I'll even help you pack."

He had walked towards the door. Dave was on the other side. Safety. When he tried the knob, it wouldn't move. She hadn't pushed the call button because she wasn't done with him. Her kind always held another card. He waited and listened. What he didn't expect was a seduction of words.

I understand you better than anyone because I recognize what it is to be you. Don't you know? I can hear the creeping termites under your skin. The ones can't silence or scratch out. Or tell anyone about. I know about them because every night I go to bed with demons and wake up on fire. I know what you need. I can help you.

"*Just like Lady Macbeth. She too, was incapable of showing any restraint in pursuit of her goals.*"

This was a different Dominique. But how could she know? If she did, she had to be as messed up as he was. And if that were true, what might she expect of him? Would remaining at the prison take on a different form of liaison? Still, if he and the shrink really were twin sides of the same coin and Dominique's desire to help was sincere, that could mean that sometime in his very near future, Lerance could straighten to full height and become human again. Since incarceration, he'd only been crawling on all fours, slinking and sliding through required routines and activities, all in the name of staying safe. Maybe this was his chance at redemption. At freedom. Then again, if he were wrong about Dominique's true intent, he could be making the biggest mistake of his life. Only one way to find out.

By the time Lerance had finished splashing cold water on his face he knew what he had to do.

THIRTY ONE

To Dave, Lerance had always seemed unfinished.

What really puzzled him was that on the outside the inmate seemed to have it all: a great education, wealth, and a preponderance of smoldering good looks. But it was all surface, nothing underneath. Like a joke without a punch line. Stan minus Ollie. Or that big chocolate bunny with the disappointing hollowed-out center inside your Easter basket. So it surprised the guard that on this sweating-from-the-armpits morning, while on the way to see the director, Lerance's gait was noticeably jaunty as he swung a heavily-packed cardboard satchel, much like a young boy might do on his first day back to school.

"You threw me for a loop, Doc."

"How's that?" Lerance wasn't used to guards talking to him, nor for that matter, answering them back.

"Well, for one, I hadn't taken you for the wishy-washy type. I thought your kind always made snap decisions and then stuck to them like glue, no matter what—even if they were spot dead wrong. You being a card-carrying member of the established hoi polloi, and all.

"And yet, I see I was mistaken. You know how to teeter-totter as well as any other little girl in the park." Dave snickered, clearly enjoying his analogy. If life had turned out differently, he might have had a career as a stand-up comedian.

Lerance thought for a second, then decided not to respond. It was only when they reached Dominique's office, that he surprised Dave by firing off his own mocking salvo.

"If you truly understood *our kind*, then you'd know we can get away with just about anything: let's say murder for example, and oh yeah, changing our fucking minds."

A few minutes later, Dominique watched as Lerance emptied the contents of his satchel onto her desk. Satisfied that the case was empty, he set it on the floor before pulling up a chair to sit next to her. Dominique ignored the thick sheaf of paper to study the inmate. Today he seemed to be playing at yet a new character, happy and open, and she wished she could slap the perkiness right off of his face. Watching his expression brighten with expectation, Dominique deeply regretted agreeing to meet with him.

The night before, Dominique slept in her room at the prison, waking up early to check for phone messages and emails. Lerance's email had read like a distress call. He said he had a matter of great urgency to discuss with her. She replied immediately telling him to come see her after breakfast. Then she sat down at her vanity to carefully arrange her hair, which now lay in soft loose curls around her face and shoulders. She had also dressed in her favorite white silk net blouse, a vintage garment with small pearl flat buttons and a front panel of tangerine chiffon appliqué flowers. As she leaned back in the high-backed silk brocade Louis XIII chair, Dominique looked less like a psychiatrist counseling rage murderers, rather more like the original proprietress of the colorful manor house—a Victorian landowner. Ironic.

They sat in silence for a while, each occasionally stealing glances at the stack of papers. Dominique's mouth was set in a thin pinched line, readying to let loose a snarl. Lerance crossed and uncrossed his legs.

"I don't get you. I thought this would make you happy," Lerance finally said.

"It's not enough that you manipulated the system to get out of the Desire program, but you had to dream up some emergency just to be able to watch me sign your exit documents. That's what they are, aren't they?"

"Looks like somebody got up grumpy," Lerance said.

"We didn't need a meeting for this."

"Aren't you even curious?" Lerance asked turning his palms up, a final petition for understanding. She looked again into his face and saw that although he was still smiling, the mouth curved with strain. Fine lines creased his eyes and his skin looked waxy, empty of the usual underlying arrogance and belligerence. Just a deep weariness. She saw how very, very tired he was.

Lerance hunched forward, heavy-lidded eyes closing. When he opened them again, they were yellow and slitty, like a waking cat's. She thought he might slither to the ground on all fours and stretch. When she flipped through the top few sheets, she too felt like stretching. "I don't get it. These are the forms I've been waiting for since the first week." From the middle of the stack, she slid out a red folder and peered inside. "Your Desire exercises. When did you find time to finish all of them? Don't tell me you stayed up all night? Lerance, what made you change your mind?"

Lerance closed his eyes again and said, "Actually, Vincent. Something he said reminded me of an incident in my youth. That's why I'm here. I want to tell you about it. I really think it just might be the key to unlocking my . . . what do you call it?"

"Potential. Unlocking your potential."

"Yeah, it's going to sound strange, and I don't want you to take anything the wrong way. Still there's no easy way to say it."

Dominique couldn't believe her luck. She'd won. "Go on," she said.

"It's just that...I want to be black. I am black. But I want to *be*...black. Like you. Well, not like you, but like me, if I was. Because I am. All over, inside, outside, I am. I am black."

The urge to slap him snapped back in her along with a desire to flee the room. She wasn't sure she could manage either activity because just then she felt her feet and legs sinking into the floor like it was made of quicksand, and just like the heat, the sensation was mildly intoxicating, keeping her bonded to the chair, to the floor, to Lerance.

"You better not be having fun at my expense. If this is a joke, I'll call the guard and we'll be done. And this time, permanently."

"Forget it. Just remember this was all your big dumb, Desire idea." Lerance rose to leave.

"What do you want from me?" Dominique asked.

"I want you to listen."

Dominique couldn't help it. She did want to listen, more than anything on earth, to his every word. Why did it feel so wrong, then? She recalled Vincent's words when he accused her of favoring Lerance. Were her psychic seams of abuse and neglect, once plastered over with achievement and celebrity, finally cracking? Was she looking for new armor inside this murderous inmate, or was he perhaps just the most perfect foil to draw Delilah back into her life? Either way, this was one breakneck rollercoaster she had to stay on until the very end of the revolution.

Lerance sat back down and placed his trembling hands on the side of his chair to steady them before taking a deep breath.

"It happened at our house. I was in second grade and we were celebrating my grandpa's sixty-fifth birthday. Everyone was there, mama, daddy, cousins, friends and neighbors. As usual, my Aunt Lucretia and Uncle Dwight were seven sheets to the wind. When I went inside the kitchen to fetch snacks for my mama, Lucretia grabbed me.

"She was always doing that. You know hugging me, pinching my cheek, slapping my butt. But this time it was different. This time she grabbed me by the shoulders and then pushed me into my uncle. I was sandwiched between them and couldn't get away. It was horrible, the liquor reeked on their clothes, in their skin, made me want to puke.

"Lucretia said, 'Why Dwight, do you know where young Lerance gets his dark handsome looks from?"

Dwight swallowed what was left of his whiskey and said, 'Tell me true, where from, baby?'

"Lucretia said, 'Could only be one place, and one place only, Dwight. That fine nigger his great grandpa Smoky hitched up with.'

"Dwight said, 'I know who you mean. Oooh wee. Labelle Monset. Rumor had it she was the prettiest girl in the county, even if she wasn't white. Also heard Smoky made her tie up her hair, so none of the other men folk got ideas.'

"Lucretia said, 'Either that, or to hide those extra tight curls.' Dwight pondered this as he stepped back to pour himself another couple of fingers and added, 'Yep, dawalin', we sho' got us a fine-looking boy here.'"

Lerance walked over to the bay window and sat down on the ledge, staring at the cane fields. Dominique whispered, "Go on."

"Just then my mama came flying through the door. Dwight dropped his glass, splattering liquor all over the floor, and I saw another kind of wetness begin to spread across the front of his pants. Lucretia ran terrified for the door, pulling Dwight behind her. I tried to do the same, but my mama grabbed my hair and pulled me to her. She started hollering for what felt like hours, but only minutes had passed before Dwight and Lucretia, and most of the other guests were inside their cars, their tires squealing, flying out of our driveway.

"In the end she turned to me and whispered, 'They're barbarous folk, you hear? I'll see to it that they never set foot in my house again. You boy, just forget what you heard today. Now get outside and join your grandpa. This is his birthday party."

Dominique said, "It's all right Lerance, come back over here."

Lerance came off the window ledge and leaned across the big wide desk, fixing Dominique's gaze with his own.

"Can't you see how I was robbed? My family shamed me about my heritage, about my people. Just think about it, I could have a whole town of cousins, uncles and aunts, somewhere near Vicksburg."

When Lerance straightened, Dominique noticed his hands had stopped shaking. They were resting on his hips, his face and eyes turned back to the window, "Hell bells, you and I could be related. They said Labelle was real pretty."

Whatever Dominique had hoped for, it certainly wasn't to be regaled by a narrative woven with tales of scandalous black mistresses and lost opportunities. The story was a good one, even believable, but how could she truly trust Lerance now? How was she to reconcile the inmate's earlier behavior, when he had eluded her every attempt to help him, with this about-face performance, behaving like the prodigal patient: showing remorse and asking for understanding? It was, after all, something male felons frequently did when they attempted to manipulate women, even their therapists, for hidden personal gains. She finally decided there would be time enough later to sort out all of these pesky details. For now, she would give him the benefit of the doubt. All that mattered was that Lerance remain at House of Mithras, and her Desire program continue like nothing happened. Spotless reputation. She would have to remember the next time she was at Miss Marta's to lay an extra cigar at Gede's altar, for bringing her such good fortune.

Dominique hoped she sounded sincere, "Lerance, you have real choices now. About anything. Your friends, family, career, it's totally up to you. This is a huge breakthrough. But even though you've talked about it, it's only the beginning. Any time things get tough you can't go calling on Dupree. You come to us, the team. You come to me. Understand?"

Lerance nodded, but looked disappointed, as if Dominique had not shown enough appreciation for his efforts. Dominique didn't care. She was losing steam. Even as Lerance got color back in his face, she felt an irresistible urge to shut her eyes and go to sleep. Instead, she reached into a drawer where she pulled out a notebook and scribbled a few notes.

"I'll make sure Dupree and the Florida prison are notified. Lerance, it's Saturday, you're free to go back with Dave to the grounds and use the time for recreation." When she got up, he did, too. They were moving towards the door together, only inches apart when Dominique abruptly stopped, forcing Lerance to nearly bump into her. She said, "It's hot. Hot this early means we're in for a scorcher." She glanced up at the clock above the door, "We actually have a few minutes left. Do you have any questions for me?"

Lerance shook his head and moved back. He began to circle her, first in a wide arc, and then narrowing the space between them. She closed her tired eyes and smelled musk cutting through the humidity. It smelled like fear. Fear and loathing. Privately she chastised herself for recoiling, because the odor seemed wrong emanating from such a handsome and composed man. It should have belonged to someone else, someone like Julius Lucky.

He was still circling her when she opened her eyes, turning her face to him. It was shiny with perspiration. Just like that, the putrid aroma had vanished, in its place good old musky body heat. As he rounded her, she twirled in the opposite direction. For a few minutes they were like attracted magnetic fields caught up in a rotational dance. The ceiling fan slapped Dominique's hair across her face where a few strands stuck to her neck and cheek. Lerance looked like he wanted to pull back each individual hair off her bare skin. She wondered if she might faint. It was too hot. Without warning, a cool draft scraped her arms and back. Impossible. She saw his eyes. Lerance's glare was animalistic, changing from still to alert, and then finally turning rageful as he lunged towards the door. It was slightly ajar when he pulled it wide open. Julius Lucky didn't have time to catch himself before falling on his knees to the floor. Dave was on top of him instantly, swearing hoarsely under his breath.

"I'm sorry ma'am. This idiot has ants in his pants. I guess he just can't wait to be in therapy." He held Julius firmly as Lerance let himself out.

If Dominique wondered that her patient might think it strange that she was dripping with sweat at nine thirty in the morning, she didn't show it. She smiled and waited a beat.

"Good morning, Julius. You're a little early so I'm sure you won't mind waiting until I finish writing my notes." Without looking at him again for the next ten minutes, Dominique composed herself by writing down observations and making recommendations for the next leg of Lerance's program.

It was midnight when Dominique finally finished writing her day's summations. After rereading the entry on Lerance, she stowed all of them away in their respective files. It felt good to lean back in her plush chair, close her eyes and review the events of the day. Today, it seemed all of the dots connected. So this was to be her reward. No bells or parades of cheering fans, just a dollop of tranquility offset by the slightest thrill of smugness. She deserved it; she worked damn hard. That she had used unscrupulous tactics to keep Lerance didn't bother her, because he was after all a rageful murderer, completely clueless about what was best for him. Rationalizing seemed easier when she recalled what a friend from Minneapolis had told her about her daughter. When the child was five, the mom bribed her with a new Barbie doll in order to entice her to attend a beginning theater class. The mom knew in her heart of hearts that the little girl was a born actress, and if she just went to the first class she'd finish out the summer semester. The bribe worked, because for five years, the child never missed a Saturday class at The Children's Theater.

Dominique's heart skipped a beat and she felt afraid when she noticed a red light flashing on her phone. Then it started to ring. She glanced at Caller ID and saw a familiar number.

After introducing himself, the caller waited.

"Dr. Moore? Hello, how is..." Dominique did not get a chance to ask.

"Yolanda died an hour ago. I'm sorry to have to have to tell you this on the phone, Dr. Doucette. Yolanda was a heroic fighter, but her heart couldn't withstand the surgery to repair her valve. She was under anesthesia when she died and did not feel any pain," the doctor said.

Dominique hung up and glared at her desk. All the pens lined up. Matching accessory caddies holding neatly filled paper clips, rubber binders and staples, started to blur in wavy rows beneath swimming tears. A stack of perfectly stacked files anchored one corner, while a handsome silver tea set with a decorative porcelain cup and saucer hugged the other side. It took the psychiatrist two seconds to hurl the entire contents onto the floor.

THIRTY TWO

Testimony of Billy Jo

All eyes were on Billy Jo. He knew it was his turn, but he wanted to be sure he said everything just right. Just like it happened. For the third time he looked at the pages he had marked in the file. Finally he met the sheriff's eyes.

"Am I in trouble Sheriff Futrell?" Billy Jo asked.

"Just tell me about the day you and Dominique went into the city a couple of days ago. What happened when you worked together at the St. Francis Shelter?"

Billy Jo found out it was much harder to talk about important things when Dominique wasn't around to encourage him. Especially now. In therapy, the inmates were asked to talk about their past. But here he had to explain what happened just a few days ago. And the topic was Dominique. He did not want to say anything that might besmirch her good name. But he had to tell the truth. She would have wanted it that way. He twisted uneasily in his chair and then sat up straight. He knew he looked good this morning. Julius had picked out a neatly-pressed blue and white striped shirt, and his best dark blue jeans for him to wear. His eye shadow was subtle, a light powder blue to match his shirt. Time to go on stage.

"Ever since I can remember I've loved dress up. I like girls okay, probably a lot more than they like me. But I was always jealous of their clothing styles, and the colors they got to wear.

"It was all those bright colors and gold beads. That's why I took it. I just had to have that mask. I never dreamed that it would cause her so much pain."

Except for the director and a few volunteers, the homeless shelter was always empty during the day. The main sleeping room was especially dark, and dreary. The only window, narrow and high on the wall, was heavily draped when Dominique and Billy Jo walked in. As soon as she turned on the lights, Billy Jo gasped.

"Dr. Doucette. Oh my gosh, what happened? Where are all the people? And the beds. What happened to the beds?"

"The homeless residents are required to leave by 7:30 a.m. Many have jobs; others look for work. This morning all of the beds were pulled up so maintenance could shampoo the carpet. I agree with you, Billy Jo, I always thought this place looked very sad when it was empty. Come on, we have to put everything back."

Billy Jo thought it was the psychiatrist that looked sad and empty today. He wished he could think of a way to cheer her up. He followed Dominique to a tall cabinet on the south wall and together they began pulling out deflated air mattresses and air pumps out of big cardboard boxes.

Billy Jo asked, "Dr. Doucette, why did you come with me today? How come it wasn't one of the other inmates?"

"Ten years ago when Dr. Wadell and I had our clinic in New Orleans, we found out that many of our clients were living in homeless shelters. After that, we spent a lot of time working in them, getting to know folks, trying to find out what we could do for them during the day.

"I like coming back and working in here. Makes me feel useful."

"But that's just silly. You're always doing useful things. You help everyone."

"It's different. Maybe here I can help myself."

Dominique not only looked different, today she was talking strangely. He wanted to know why, but he didn't ask, lest he offend her.

For two hours they blew up beds, put on sheets and blankets, and then arranged them across the freshly-cleaned floor. Dominique had gone into the kitchenette leaving Billy Jo to put back unused linens, when he noticed Dave checking the window locks. When Dominique returned, he said, "I see Dave is sticking around today."

Dominique looked over at Billy Jo and shrugged, waiting for more.

"I mean we've been here the better part of the morning and he's never left."

Dominique said, "What do you mean, never left? It's his job, he's on security detail with us."

Billy Jo's hands shot up to his head. Dominique watched through narrowed eyes while he tried to smooth down some phantom cowlick. After a minute, Dominique cleared her throat and said, "Enough. Put your hands down. Look at me."

Billy Jo dropped his hands but would not look up. She took a step towards him. In four short weeks, she had learned that when you stepped into what most people accept as personal distance, unexpectedly, Billy Jo always felt more secure and always calmed down, even in the middle of a tantrum. The closed off space was like his own personal blanket.

"Listen to me. The success of this program depends on security. I know we're a little lenient sometimes at House of Mithras, and that's because we have surveillance, but here in the community, inmates are never supposed to be left alone without a guard present."

Billy Jo stammered, "He was always nearby. He just...I guess he goes across the street to get coffee."

Dominique said sharply. "There's no coffee shop around here. Where, where does he go? You know."

"He's never gone long. Really. I don't know where exactly, but somewhere close, and the staff is always here. They see us. Miss Doucette, please, I thought it was okay."

"Billy Jo." She took another step towards him and put her hand on his shoulder. "I'm losing patience."

"I'm not a stool pigeon. I learned from Julius, when people are good to you, you're never to tell on them."

"You have to tell me. I have to be able to trust you. I have to be able to trust Dave. "

Whether it was that Billy Jo could not keep a secret, or perhaps because he felt the director had taken a special interest in him the way Fifi used to, he decided to rat out his favorite guard.

"I think there's a pool joint around the corner. He plays pool. He brings his own pool stick. I saw the case once."

Just as Dominique pulled off her hand, Billy Jo burst into tears. "Are you going to fire him? Cuz he's the only guard I knew that never hit me. Never even yelled at me. Please..."

"You did the right thing by telling me. Don't worry. Everyone deserves a second chance. I'll take care of this. But Billy Jo, believe me, when I get done with him, he will never pull this crap again."

Dominique and Billy Jo exchanged knowing looks; the inmate felt reconstituted. He had not only told the truth, the outcome, it seemed, would benefit everyone. Dominique still trusted him, and Dave would learn how to become a better security guard. For Billy Jo, it had been a win-win situation. But it had not wiped the sadness off of her face.

While Billy Jo continued to put away linens, Dominique again walked over to the kitchenette and began taking down paper plates and cups. From the other side of the room, Billy Jo watched as she absentmindedly arranged plastic knives, forks and spoons. She was putting them in all the wrong spots. How were the homeless going to reach them if they were lying on a counter that was closed off to them? Right then and there, he made his mind up. He couldn't stand it anymore, her acting out-of-sorts and all. He found his knapsack, pulled out its contents and walked up behind the director.

"Dr. Doucette, I been noticing you look very sad today. So I got something here I think you're really going to like. It's going to cheer you up."

Dominique knew Billy was standing behind her, but she did not immediately turn around. Instead, she took down more flatware and started counting it.

"Dr. Doucette. You're supposed to look at me. You're ruining my surprise."

With exaggerated care. Dominique put down the plastic plates and slowly turned around. Her head was down. She sniffed. It looked like a second ago she had been crying.

When she finally lifted her eyes to look at Billy Jo, she was so shocked by what she saw that she couldn't speak. Instead she let out a shriek and then immediately slid down the wall to the floor where she sat down with a thud, continuing to stare wildly at him. Billy Jo tore the mask off his face and kneeled down beside her. "Dr. Doucette! Dr. Doucette! Oh, I'm so sorry if I scared you. I wanted you to be happy again. I thought this would cheer you up. "

Before she could say a word, Dave burst through the cafeteria doors with his hand on his holster. First he glared at Billy Jo, and then looked at Dominique with concern. "Are you all right, Dr. Doucette?"

Billy Jo looked feral as he jumped up on the counter. He had reminded Dave of a cat. He knew Dave hated cats. "Get down, Billy Jo. And don't move again."

Dominique got up and motioned to Billy Jo to stand beside her.

"Dave, it's okay. I was lost in thought when Billy Jo startled me. It's nothing, you can go back to your work."

Dave didn't believe Dominique that everything was all right. She seemed strange today.

"Okay, if you're sure you're fine." With a parting warning glance at Billy Jo, Dave went back through the cafeteria doors.

They were alone again. When Dominique found her voice, she hissed, "Where did you get that mask?"

The question sent Billy Jo into a fresh spastic fit. He paced back and forth like a caged animal and chewed his nails. "I ain't no thief. I just borrowed it. I din't steal it. Not me."

THIRTY THREE

When Darnell returned to Desire it was late and the streets were teeming with bodies. Too hot to go inside yet. The men stood in pairs drinking beer. Women composed larger groups and most had small children running around them. Everyone held up a newspaper or a piece of cardboard to fan themselves.

In front of a brightly-lit pizzeria, a dozen preteens screeched as they ran after each other into the street. Darnell decided to park his car in front of the Davis house and walk. He needed answers. Face-to-face inquiries worked best around here.

Four men playing dominoes smiled toothless grins when he sat down next to their table. The games would go on until two in the morning, or until the beer was gone. Each man shook his head when asked if he saw anything unusual the night Yolanda was raped. Then each stated by turns his regret that any young girl should suffer like that. Darnel thanked them and stood up, declining offers to drink beer with them. He walked towards the women. When he was still half a block away, the catcalls were audible. They were followed by cooing, and several silky breathy invitations: "Come here baby," Where you been keeping your sweet self," "Ooh, don't you look good tonight," "I want some honey on my money!"

The cluster of women ranging in age from twenty-something to sixty, and wearing everything from midriff-baring halter tops and short shorts to long flowing muslin cotton dresses—these women knew how to put on the ritz—looked expectantly at Darnell. He smiled and looked the women over with warm appraisal. His eyes lingered over the hairstyles. Darnell loved the hairstyles the most. The time and care the dark lovelies put into their tresses never ceased to amaze him. Retro hawk cuts to spiked and textured, elaborate cornrowed updos, and long micro-braid styles.

Darnell tried to look cool, tried to stay focused, but when two of the women wrapped their arms around him, and began kissing his cheeks and running their hands over his back, he gave up his indifference by falling out laughing. He allowed himself to be shown to a tattered overstuffed chair and accepted an opened cold bottle of O'Doules. His fan club was nothing if not considerate.

As he relaxed, the forty-something man pondered just how he had become so popular. When he was kid, everyone, including his own family made fun of him for being too dark. Having a set of white-man's colored eyes didn't help him much either. Steel blue they called them. Some people said it made him look like he was blind, still others thought they were signs of witchcraft. Dangerous for the one who stared into them too long. Bad juju.

But not Little Niqui. Darnell was sure she loved him the very first time she laid eyes on him. She once said that he was her prized possession, not just because he was so nice to be with, but also because he was so nice to look at, too. It took ten more years before everyone else noticed. He grew tall and muscular, and his angular face softened and molded to become the perfect showcase for those bejeweled orbs. The same females who disdained him in his childhood now treated him like a movie star, and every single one of them wanted to get into his pants. Not tonight. Staying sober and finding Yolanda's attacker were his sole agenda.

For thirty minutes the women talked about the Davis family and how they had been part of the 'hood for fifty years, but no one knew why anyone would hurt a young girl like Yolanda. Darnell felt deflated; surely someone had to know something. Sensing his defeat, the oldest woman in the crowd moved forward, a sleeping baby on her hip, tapped his hand, then pointed across the street at a one-story establishment. Darnell thanked the women for a lovely time, got up and walked into the Korean grocery store.

The wizened man knew just about everything that happened on the block and beyond, but in those early hours he heard nothing because he was fast asleep. He told Darnell there was someone who might not have been. The owner blinked his hooded eyes at the back of the store and said, "Alley."

Darnell cut through the shop's back door and spied the heavily-clothed woman stowing a large handbag inside her shopping cart, only a few feet away. Daisy Lucrez had been homeless since Darnell was a boy. It was rumored that she had been born homeless, and that her first toy was a child-sized shopping cart. He watched as she held a Po'boy sandwich in one hand, while with the other stuffed several small handbags under a pile of larger handbags. For all anyone knew, she could have been getting ready for a garage sale. When Daisy spied Darnell watching her, she brightened, showing him her hairy chin, freshly lathered in red deli sauce.

After a few niceties, Darnell asked, "You see anything that night?"

Daisy giggled. "I seen plenty. Max sneaking back home 'fore his wife catch him playing craps with the Creighton brothers. Mr. Dieters pacing up and down this here alley, cuz he lost all of his money at the bingo hall. Those Davis kids, harassing me again!"

'What else?" Darnell was running out of patience.

"A car. I seen a car."

"What about the car?"

"It was a fancy one. Too bad about the scratch."

Darnell felt adrenaline course from his brain into his hands. His heart raced like a runaway train and his head felt like it had just exploded. "What color was the car and where was the scratch?"

"Black car. Back quarter panel. Passenger side."

"You got more?"

Daisy finished the Po'boy, neatly folded the sandwich wrapper and placed it on a box on the bottom shelf of the cart. She took out a napkin from the same box, spotted with old brown stains, and wiped her chin and mouth. Next she folded it and put it back to rest neatly on top of the wrapper.

"Maybe, maybe not."

Darnell pulled out his billfold and extracted a bill. "I ain't got time for foolish games. Here's ten dollars. Now give me something good."

Daisy felt the air stir above her as the ten-spot waved near her head.

"That nice white man been around like usual," Daisy snatched the bill.

"Like usual? Who, exactly?"

"You know who he is. The one who used to carry on with Miss Dominique. Now he dating a girl in the 'hood," Daisy said.

"And you're sure he was here that night?" Darnell's voiced cracked slightly.

"Just like every night." Daisy giggled again. "Personally, I think he's kinda cute. Very respectful to me. But I know he messes too much around here," Daisy's hands rippled to and fro, "He's gonna end up ugly. Maybe by you."

Darnell strode to his car and fished out his cell phone. Time to call out the Ken doll.

THIRTY FOUR

After carefully reading each newspaper article, Guyla Rae sat at her desk numbly staring at the computer screen. She wondered with bemusement what Dominique was going to do after she read through the website searches. There could be no denying that Kevin's detection into Lerance's computer pursuits had uncovered the mother lode. He discovered them, but they agreed that Guyla Rae would deliver the findings to Dominique. Because at this point in time, the co-director had lost all credibility with the other co-director, especially when it came to Lerance. Yes, Guyla Rae Gansen would be bringing more bad news to Dominique.

The day before, Kevin supervised computer time with Eduardo and Lerance. The inmates each had thirty minutes to surf the web, to conduct research, or just catch up on the news. Afterwards, when the men went to dinner, Kevin got curious and scrolled through their search histories in Firefox. It was what he didn't find that prompted him to use the computer's backup utility to pull up deleted history. Ironically, if the guard hadn't gossiped and Kevin hadn't heard it, he would never have poked into Lerance's perusals. Or, if he had, he would have written off the web searches as random inquiries rather than systematic studies.

Kevin became intrigued by a guard's tale of how Lerance managed to 'scare the hell' out of big man Vincent near his garden plot. Apparently, Dominique had been in the vicinity, but too far away to hear anything as she struggled with the shed door. The guard said it was mostly a one-sided conversation with Lerance harping about "Mississippi," and "kids gone missing." The guard went on to say that when the former doctor mentioned Vincent's grandmother, the would-be gardener nearly ran to the far side of the garden before collapsing to his knees.

What could have cowed Vincent like that, even if it were momentary? Kevin also learned that Vincent provoked Lerance later that day in group therapy, and might have struck him if not for the sheriff's timely barging into the room. Things just weren't adding up.

Initially, when Kevin pulled the day's most recent searches, he found nine and they could only have belonged to Eduardo: constitutional law case briefs using the application LexisNexis. That was it. What had happened to the rest of the searches?

Kevin didn't think Lerance was interested in constitutional law, but something must have compelled his attention because he had typed furiously for almost the whole half hour, pausing now and again to read a few sentences of text. And then he erased everything. What was so significant or disturbing that he wouldn't want anyone else to see?

Lerance hadn't known that despite his best efforts to hide and destroy, almost his entire keystroke history had been permanently recorded, and like a bloodhound searching for a victim, in less than ten minutes, Kevin found seventeen hidden searches. They all led to the archived content of two newspapers: Vicksburg's *Post,* and *The Natchez Democrat,*

1971 – 1975. The first twelve searches using the key words, *missing Mississippi children* and *Mississippi children disappear,* led to stories on the disappearances of teenagers from Warren County, Mississippi. Another search pulled up Warren County's suicide records. Next, a short article reported the suicide of a teenaged boy named Dean Cobb Jones. The last three search entries showed *no results found for* Vincent Delavon, in Warren or neighboring counties.

Now the administrator wanted to know why something that occurred more than thirty years ago near Vicksburg, Mississippi, meant so much to Lerance today. And why was he looking up Vincent? Had he suspected the gangster of being one of the missing kids? But why would he care?

The only thing the administrator knew for sure was that between 1971 and 1973, seven boys and two girls disappeared from small towns in the Mississippi Delta. During interviews with family, friends, teachers and doctors, police found a few similarities between the kids and one definite tie. Most had come from broken impoverished homes, had truancy records, and suffered from chronic childhood illnesses. Each of them at one time had been treated at Lemartine's Saturday Morning Free Clinic.

According to FBI records, none of the children was ever seen again until 1975, when authorities discovered the body of Dean Cobb Jones in the basement of a Jackson after-hours nightclub where he had worked as a male prostitute. The coroner's report indicated the sixteen-year-old died of a self-inflicted gunshot wound to the heart. One of the last people to see Jones before his disappearance, Dr. Lydeah Lemartine, said he had come in with flu-like symptoms and was severely dehydrated in the spring of 1973. The doctor said she had not seen him since he ran away from their home and was very sorry to hear of his death.

Guyla Rae did her own research into the disappearances. A few sightings and a rumor here and there were the only indications that the other boys and girls might still be alive. A reporter who tried to reopen the investigation in the nineties was told by authorities that the cases had been closed because the kids were deemed delinquent runaways. The reporter thought the authorities dropped the ball because the kids were black and poor. Their families did not have the clout or resources to push for more investigation. If they were alive, they'd be around Vincent's age.

The last thing Guyla Rae wanted to do was unload this bombshell on Dominique tonight. The psychiatrist had a lot weighing on her since Yolanda died a few days earlier. Ever since, Dominique and staff were fielding nonstop calls from reporters, community members, and of course the CCAF. Strangely, the only call from the sheriff's office came directly from Leroy Futrell, who simply told Dominique that he was sorry for her loss. And now the director had a funeral to prepare.

It was late in the evening at the prison when Guyla Rae finally called Dominique to explain generally what was in the internet searches, specifically, their connection to the altercation between Vincent and Lerance in the garden and possibly to a thirty-year-old suicide. The psychiatrist surprised her by saying she'd come by in a few minutes to look over the information.

When Dominique walked into Guyla Rae's office she looked tired but relaxed, something Guyla Rae hadn't seen for almost a month. The old Dominique, her friend, was finally making an appearance.

"I wish I didn't have to dump this on you right now. But Kevin and I thought it was too hot for us to handle. Maybe you'd know what to do with it," Guyla Rae said.

With only tepid sarcasm, Dominique asked, "You mean too hot for Kevin to handle? Never mind, I'm sure it's my fault. I've been riding his ass for too long now."

Dominique's sudden candor made Guyla Rae self-conscious. "Perhaps this can wait for a few days, at least until after we bury Yolanda."

Dominique said, "No. If it weren't important, you wouldn't have taken the trouble to vet everything. Look, I don't want you or Kevin to blame yourselves. I have not been very approachable or cooperative these last few weeks. But I promise you, that's all going to change. Now show me what you have."

Guyla Rae stared hard at Dominique as she turned over the computer disc to her.

"You've been a good friend and a great colleague. So has Kevin. Sometimes, I'm just too stubborn, too set on getting the ball across the field that I can't see the people I'm mowing down on the way. But now, my eyes are wide open. I promise."

"What happened? What changed?"

"I'm not sure exactly. First, Lerance gave up his legal battle to leave. That should have made me happy, instead it just made me suspicious. And then there's this story that I can't get out of my head that Vincent told me. It was about his grandmother and her fear of losing him. His disappearing. It's all come down to this hasn't it? You know what I mean, Guyla?"

Guyla Rae didn't know what Dominique meant at all. "Come down to what?"

"The final showdown. Life's enduring battle between good and evil. You know like the cautionary tale that's found in a hundred children's books. Written in simple words, illustrated in bright colorful scenes. Why don't we remember these lessons when we become adults?"

Dominique continued, "The lost lads. Even though they grow into men, they are forever the agents of their unfulfilled boyhoods, stopping at nothing to seize what they think is rightfully theirs. But what they ache for the most, what they cannot find, has always been lost to them."

"Why, honey?"

"Simply, because their wells have no bottoms."

Despite the intense heat in the room, Guyla Rae began to shiver.

"Who will win? In this battle, who will win ultimately?" Guyla Rae wanted to know.

"It can't matter. Good just has to try. Staging the battle is what counts. Trying to *do* good is what matters most."

THIRTY FIVE

"Stop right there and turn around. Look at me. You know I can't let you do this."

"Try and stop me."

"You really think putting those people through hell again will change anything?"

"Don't know unless I try. And since when do you worry about other people? Let alone, me?"

"Are you serious? I was born to protect you."

"You serve yourself."

"You've got some selective memory, girl. I hate it when you get to sounding uppity. Makes me feel like I never mattered. Like I wasn't even part of you."

"I wish to heaven you hadn't been."

Time and space felt disjointed and irrelevant. One minute she was Dominique, the next, Delilah. The formerly shrouded and secretive alter was making her first appearance. This was not a visual or aural hallucination. There were no colors or symphonies or voices from the Bible. More like a performance piece where light and movement roamed freely behind diaphanous curtains. And like tectonic plates, the two personalities seemed to move together now along the same plane, an unseen friction determining their final destination.

For Dominique, it seemed like she could easily slide the alter right off the planet, and for good. She decided to take her time though, since this would be Delilah's last appearance. The surreal encounter began with a squabble about moral authority and quickly escalated to a war of words over control and dominance.

"If you pretend I didn't exist, then it's a slippery slope to believing it was you who created yourself. Your fame, your wealth. Your good name. That honor rightfully belongs to me."

"You're a piece of work. How do you figure?"

"Because I'm the one who made it possible for you to go on. Day after day, week after week, all those grueling hours of homework and tests and getting put on display for teachers and selection committees, after all of that, who made sure you were able to get up the next morning and do it all over again? Do you really think you would have survived grade school if I hadn't spent all of my energy distracting you from your colorless and loveless life? What if I hadn't filled your dreary days with spirit and expression? What if yours truly, Delilah, hadn't fought to keep you out of the loony bin? Where do you think you'd be now?"

"No, that was Darnell. He was my only friend."

"Ha. Some friend. Where is he? Why don't you call him up and tell him what you're up to? See what he says. What? Cat, got your tongue? Oh, wait, you have been calling. Mmmhmm. But he won't pick up, will he? He won't talk to you anymore, because he doesn't love you anymore."

Dominique sucked air through her teeth. That wasn't true. She and Darnell had a bond that united them until death. They promised they would look after each other. Even if he wasn't speaking to her, in his own way, she was sure he was still looking after her. Oh, Darnell. Why can't it be you here, instead of her?

The intolerant voice of the scold continued. "No one loves you. No one cares. If it seems like they do, it's only because they want something from you."

"You're wrong. I have friends. Many friends who back me up and support me, unconditionally."

"Would they give a shit about you if they knew what you really were? Face it, you only have me."

"Shut up! Get out. You don't live here anymore."

"Really? Then why are you still talking to me? Can't you understand that without me you're nothing? Nothing at all. Just an empty sorry shell!"

"Now you sound like them."

"How dare you compare me to your mama and the rest of the bootlickers. Those gigolos made it clear from day one that you were only as good as your next A. They sucked out your excellence for themselves, but left your soul to starve. They stole your glow, honey. I gave it back to you. I showed you how to play. I taught you to dance."

"And then you tried to kill me."

"Now why do you always bring *that* up? An unfortunate glitch, and it was only because I got tired of watching you suffer. Miserable, crying all the time. I had to do something. And don't forget, that little incident off the balcony bought you extra time with Darnell for the rest of the spring and summer."

She was every bit as flamboyant as Dominique had imagined. When the other *straightened to full height, spread her feet apart and crossed her arms, she struck a pose like Yul Brynner in the* King of Siam. "But here you are, doing it again. Going off the deep end. You don't know how to swim, *but you want to be a big fish. If you go out there, I promise, you will drown. It's too risky for someone like you."*

"Or maybe it's you that's afraid of risk. Maybe you were weak and gutless all along. And we both know that if I succeed, you'll be out of my life forever. If I fail, you will still be out of my life."

"Listen to me. If you walk out that door, you'll get ripped to shreds. There will be nothing left but the funeral, little missy. You CAN'T make it without me. Don't you understand that yet? Don't you get that's why you came back here? You came for me!!"

Too stunned to respond, Dominique stumbled to a nearby chair and tried to catch her breath. Delilah was right. She did come back for her. She just didn't know why, after all this time. Something very wrong must have occurred even before she came back to Louisiana. It had to have happened somewhere else, during the planning stages for the reform prison. Dominique tried countless times to sequence those events, but couldn't because she lacked the normal memories to make sense of her life. This wasn't new. Since the time she began facing repeat emotional abuse for the crime of being a child prodigy, Dominique coped with trauma by dissociating.

Dissociation. During childhood and in later years, it had been a series of stroke-like occurrences from which she ultimately escaped and survived, but rarely ever fully recovered or remembered.

All myths and fairy tales include stories about shapeshifting and shapeshifters, many of which transform into someone or something else in order to find escape and freedom. In a nineteenth century Italian fairy tale, a princess escapes her incestuous father by taking on a bear's shape. Dominique, following in the footsteps of ancient heroines, was grateful to be able to become someone else for a awhile, even if it meant trading places with crazy Delilah who tore at her skin, threw hysterical tantrums at Miss Marta's, destroyed furniture, and beat on walls until her tiny little fists bled and turned black and blue. If that's what it took to stop the all-pervasive sense of shame that came from feeling defective—because that's what always happens when someone expects you to be perfect—well, it had been worth it. The problem was that the transformation into Delilah was in itself traumatic, and therefore subject to blackouts. By the time an episode ended, it was like waking up from a dream. Dominique always chased after those vaporous scenes, only to grasp at fragile, fading tendrils.

Dominique stood up and began pacing around her office. "That was a mistake I'm paying for dearly. But now I see clearly how much damage I caused, and that's what gives me the strength to let you go. If I have one regret, it's that I didn't bury you earlier."

She had been far too young and fragile when she first unleashed the alter. Dominique couldn't have guessed how much trouble she'd be and couldn't ask for help afterwards, because so few people ever met Delilah. Dominique recalled that she had kept her appearances to a select few. She rarely showed herself to Nadine or the neighbors, or even Bobby Beale. She saved her full-on episodes for the people that Dominique loved the most. The ones she trusted. Darnell and Miss Marta. Whatever Dominique knew about the alter, she learned from them.

Delilah had been a sly and surly teenager who in the beginning was only a bit on the wild side. She smoked cigarettes, had tasted beer, knew how to play adult card games, and sneaked mystery books, just for fun. As Little

Niqui's academic demands increased, the alter's games grew proportionately more destructive. She taught Little Niqui to overeat and binge, and to cut herself in places where no one would see. The worst thing she did was to introduce her to the notion of suicide. First came ideation, then experimentation. Little Niqui discovered a dozen different ways to die, but usually stopped before anything bad happened. Delilah had made it very clear, Little Niqui could think about it all she wanted, but that suicide was a last resort measure, to be saved for the worst of times. When they took Darnell away from her, she jumped off the balcony.

Delilah's most striking talent was her ability to quiet thoughts, something Little Niqui could never do on her own, and perhaps the best argument for letting her stay. On a day when Little Niqui, passed a test with flying colors—she always passed tests with flying colors—later on, the event repeated itself in her mind, manifesting in seemingly-real-time images, as if she were still in the classroom filling in multiple choice answers with her sharpened no. 2 pencil. After playing a piano concert in the afternoon, that evening, her fingers could not stop tapping out the score, or her mind the melody, because she wanted to make sure every note, every key sounded perfect. Once transpired, these things lived a second secret life inside Little Niqui's head, tormenting and telling her she still wasn't good enough. Delilah could temporarily expunge those doubts, and allow her brain to rest on other things. Childhood fairy tales, school gossip, fancy balls she would attend in the future. Afterwards, Dominique always felt an eerie calm that allowed her to sleep.

Eventually, Little Niqui grew up, leaving the adult Dominique to struggle with guilt. Not for creating Delilah, but for allowing the alter to consume her. When Dominique went away to college, she began researching her own illness. She examined Sybil's case, the split personality from Minnesota, inside and out. She might have gotten help like Sybil did, but she was still too cowed by her childhood wardens: mama and the 'hood. She knew they would not want to see the great Dominique prostrate herself in front of some shrink, like ordinary folk. Still, that wasn't the real reason for not seeking help. She didn't think anyone would believe her.

Every psychiatric professional knows that disassociation stems from childhood trauma. Little Niqui however, was never sexually abused; no one had laid a hand on her. But she was traumatized. She'd been fundamentally and materially abused through psychological oppression. Didn't that count? When someone you love and trust eviscerates your past, present, and future, and then refills them with exploitation, manipulation, and corruption. How do you explain to someone how it feels to have your innermost desires, your defenses, and real thoughts removed?

When life finally got unbearable for Little Niqui, she found a way to fantasize happiness. She pretended she was someone else, an older girl from another neighborhood, someone she could stand for a while. She must have gone too far, because one day she couldn't snap back. She'd lost control over the entity and it was too late. She couldn't get home because the last train had left the station.

Who would ever believe that? Better to find another way.

Dominique applied to medical school, and threw herself into psychiatry like it was the last meal on earth. It appeared she wanted to study the human condition, but in reality she was searching for her own cure.

Delilah interrupted her thoughts. "Fine, throw me away like rag doll. But you owe me an explanation. Why are you doing this?"

Someone like Delilah would never understand. Two things now drove Dominique. First, getting the monkey off her back. For once, she'd like to face problems head on, without worrying what her actions might do to or for her image. LET THEM THINK. Second, she wanted Delilah's power for herself. Not the hostile, hurtful personality, but the one with panache. Oh, to be spontaneous and vital and flamboyant! If Guyla Rae and Richard wanted to go slumming, next time she'd drive and bring the booze. And if Kevin ever asked her to go dancing again, she'd take him to a real New Orleans honky-tonk, where the musicians didn't even begin jamming until after midnight.

The last question came like a faint murmur. Dominique had to strain to hear and realized she was really finally alone, listening to her own thoughts. "Are you absolutely sure you need to go to Mississippi? Why are you putting everything at risk? Whom are you doing this for?"

Dominique picked up her keys and satchel and road map, and strode out of the historic manor. "For Darnell, who risked everything for me. I want him to be proud of me again. He's got to see that I was worth it."

THIRTY SIX

"She got reborn rolling in a deep river."

Listening to the opening line of Marta Ettlin's title song "Mama Delta" on the car radio, it occurred to Dominique that someone with musical talent and flair for the dramatic could easily romanticize any place under the sun, no matter its state of decay. People believed that it was here in the Delta that popular American music originated, including Delta blues and jazz. But few could fully appreciate the true cost behind those rich melancholy notes. Who wanted reminders that their inspiration had risen from the bowels of desperation? Out of endless hardship for black sharecroppers and indentured farmers? Pain, racism and poverty, each in their own way, contributed to the shine of the enigma that is the Delta today.

No one knew this better than Dominique, yet even she wasn't prepared for what lay ahead outside of Vicksburg and Highway 61. Earlier, the old confederate city had emerged like an elegant sprawling matron, showing off historic bridges and parks, museums, restaurants and mansions. Maybe it hadn't been a town at all, but a mirage. Or a Hollywood movie set made up of cardboard and papier-maché, cleverly built to hide the big bad joke on the other side. A screen cover decorated with irony: starving people living on the richest soil anywhere in the United States. Now, as she searched for the unincorporated village of Dauphine, the ghosts of the American dream for African-Americans mocked her at every turn. Abandoned cotton gins, rampant weeds, overturned skeletal cars and trucks, rusty barbed wire fences, houses layered with torn plastic covering broken windows, clapboards so completely bleached of paint they looked liked strips of starched ironed fabric. Tar paper roofs, here and there a lone shingle dangling.

But was this really a big surprise? The psychiatrist had always had a firm grasp of socio-economic issues. She understood that when machines replaced human farm labor and textile mills moved overseas, an area's economy usually collapsed. And that in the Delta, because of intergenerational poverty, it seemed to fixate in ruins. But seeing it in person produced in her a strange out-of-body experience. And then, a full-on panic attack. She braked and stopped.

Finding it hard to breathe, Dominique rolled down the window and was immediately greeted with a blast of steam. Even the air was implacable here, a punishing fortress of heat and vapor unfit for human habitation. Her attention turned across the street. A small shotgun house, dotted with flecks of cerulean paint that the rains and sun had not been able to vanquish, leaned eerily to one side. The only house for blocks, a shack really, it looked like it had been set up as a prop for a really cheesy horror flick. And that might have seemed funny if it had not been for the ragtag knot of adults and children surrounding a burn barrel, not a hundred feet away. It was ninety-nine degrees outside with the humidity at ninety-nine percent, yet each of these folks resolutely held a stick with something on the end of it over an open fire. Lunch.

Dominique guessed it was too hot to cook inside. Or perhaps the house was no longer hooked up to electricity. Did that mean that the afternoon meals could only arrive through the creation of yet another inferno on the already scorched earth? Dominique sagged in her seat watching a picture form in her head. She saw why she was freaking out. Far from the sheltering arms of her career and milieu, the psychiatrist apparently had just crashed smack dab into the middle of her birthplace. These broken homes, this lack of basic resources, and the inevitable hopelessness she saw in people's eyes, comprised the ingredients of her childhood. Okay, maybe Desire hadn't been crushed or isolated to this extent, but at that moment it felt like someone had flung a giant time-traveling mirror into the middle of the road, forcing her to scrutinize the past.

One of the children seemed to recognize her. A skinny seven-year-old with long pigtails shaded her eyes to take a better look at the stranger. Suddenly she dropped the stick she was holding and began running towards the car.

This couldn't be happening, Dominique thought. Wasn't it just this morning that she valiantly fought off Delilah's threats? Hadn't she fully believed with all of her mind and heart that she had dispelled her and the hallucinations forever? Still it *was* happening. The layers were peeling away like they always did. Her whole head felt hot and swollen, the familiar bile rising in her throat. What had she done? More to the point, how fast could she turn the car around and drive back to where she belonged. Surely it was time to give up all this nonsense about missing children and questions surrounding Vincent and Lerance. What had she been thinking? That in one fell swoop, the golden girl would be able to alter history? With a simple visit from her, a beaten-down family would find miracle salve and succor for its broken hearts? That overnight, she could extinguish a lifetime of her own pain and grief? No, she just needed to find her way back to the highway and head home to House of Mithras. When she was safely back at the prison she would immediately resign. Quit. Make up a story about some emergency where her skills were badly needed. She would cite a hunger crisis on a desolate Caribbean island and make plans to move there. Then turn over the reins to Kevin just like before. Because Kevin was trustworthy and dependable. The institution would not only survive, but would run like a model reform prison, and eventually it would be on him and Guyla Rae to sort out the other matters. Yes, it was time to get the hell out of Dodge.

But when she turned her head and saw the little girl standing in front of the car, she knew she wasn't going anywhere.

The girl slid to the driver's side and peered in. Dominique met the bejeweled eyes and gasped. "Oh god. Where do you come from?"

"You know where." The little girl pointed behind her. "You saw me in the field."

Dominique studied the child. Puffy eyes from lack of sleep, probably from too much crying. Smudges of soot running ragged across perfect chamois cheeks, but it was the hands that raised the hair on Dominique's neck. They were her hands. As she rocked back and forth on her heels, they clenched and unclenched spastically. A fierce response to repeat victimization.

"I'm sorry, I thought I could help but I can't stay. Not this time."

"Why? Why do you say that? You're already here. Don't leave."

Dominique felt ashamed. "I really thought I could do this. But it's too dangerous for us. I have a feeling that bad, really bad things will happen if I stay."

A twisted smile creased the little girl's face. "You mean bad like the things your mama did to you, or Delilah? Your whole life ravaged by those self-centered bullies. Remember how they ripped your thoughts and wants right out of your head and heart? And made you their beast of burden. To carry their sins. That's how come you missed out on love. And sleep. And peace of mind. You think that Dean Cobb Jones' parents, or for that matter anyone else, could hurt you like that ever again? Nah, they're just going tell the truth." She stopped smiling and thinned her lips. "When you finally do the right thing, Dominique, it will feel so good, you won't hardly believe it."

"And if you're wrong? What then? Besides, don't you think it's too late? That too much time has passed?"

The little girl rocked back on her heels and thought. "Nothing's ever too late. Not for us. And you're so close. That tells me that you understand how important this is."

"Well, I did have good intentions, that's true. But there are other ways of being good. I can make up for what I did by helping—"

"I think part of the reason you're scared is cuz you're doing new things. Of course everything's going to feel strange. Finding the confidence to right wrongs must seem to you like wearing a scratchy sweater. But you'll see, soon you'll grow new skin and the sweater will stop itching. No one can tell you what to do any more. You're in charge.

Because you don't have to be perfect anymore. I believe in you, Dominique."

"To do what? What am I supposed to do?"

"Take back your freedom, of course."

Dominique froze. This slip of a girl was feeding her moral courage while she used old excuses to try to run away. She was facing a terrible choice. Accept the madness and live like she always did, half in and half out of the world. Or find out who was responsible for the attacks in New Orleans and put a stop to him once and for all.

"What else?" Dominique asked.

The little girl draped her with a look of pure clarity. "Find out who's wearing a mask."

THIRTY SEVEN

The car started moving. Slowly at first, then speeding up with a mind of its own. Dominique felt for the brake and wondered briefly why her foot wasn't on it. No longer on the motorway, the car surged down a pebbly surface. The shoulder was narrow and ran parallel to a razor-edged gully deep enough to hook a whole cadre of cars. Dominique did not think the trunks of the spindly cottonwoods or willows would break the fall if the car suddenly changed direction. She didn't think anything could stop the careening until she felt the front end hit something solid. Numbly, Dominique marveled at her savior. A large metal steel container, a dumpster of sorts that someone had pushed halfway between the shoulder and a stump of trees, almost completely covered in kudzu.

Not much of a savior, after all. The car rocked unsteadily. On the driver's side the wheels clung clumsily to loamy earth, while the other two teetered between air and rocks. She tried looking down, but turned quickly away, the serrated gully filling her with terrifying possibilities. A minute ago, after being visited by her younger self, Dominique had been vacillating between two unwinnable scenarios. Now as her life see-sawed beyond her control, she wondered if she might live long enough to make any decision at all.

Sudden truths floated from her memories like embers from the ruined dreams of youth. The little girl had been right. They had used her. But she had used Darnell.

Each time Little Niqui screamed and cried, he had torn off a piece of himself and applied it lovingly to her tears. Those pieces that the small boy willingly gave up for his best friend happened to be the inchoate makings of a man. Without them he would never grow up, never reach manhood. The first time Darnell noticed something was off kilter was right after Dominique left for Princeton. The absolute emptiness he felt from that moment on filled him with a dread greater than all of Dominique's former tantrums put together. Where his friend had the burden of balancing two distinct personalities living simultaneously inside her body, Darnell could not find even one.

Once he confided in her that he could always touch his material self: flesh, muscle, bones, eyes, mouth. But they had felt like imposters, didn't fit right, seemed to belong to someone who had once lived on another frontier. He was a peeling onion with no center. A separate, conscious, bobbing ego miles adrift from his doppelganger's cold clammy flesh. Darnell had tried the usual things: self-help books, vigorous exercise, community-ed classes. Nothing helped. Nothing worked. After that, he stepped into the footsteps of other hollowed-out souls from the 'hood, when he found himself knocking on the door of the local dealer on the block.

As soon as the smack hit his bloodstream, the ringing in the empty cavities of Darnell's brain stopped. Only to be replaced by yawning holes of disproportionate grief that on a daily basis threatened to tear his heart wide open. Darnell didn't mind though, because this was a human pain he could deal with. As long as he had access to a steady supply of the white stuff, he could get through anything. Dominique knew too well that but for the sacrifices of her only true friend, she would not be here today.

The vision was driven away by scratchy voices closing in on her. In the rear-view mirror Dominique noticed a small crowd of men and women descending on the car. Angled all wrong. Like they had learned to walk sideways and were now showing off their skills. Then she remembered she and the car hovered above a dangerous slope and the only one skewed wonky was her.

The top of a very dark-skinned teenaged boy gleamed into view, but disappeared quickly, replaced by a twin, albeit thirty years older. The father's face showed up inside the driver's window, unshaven, concerned.

He said gruffly, "Don't move an inch. Don't even breathe. We called for a tow truck. It's coming now."

Something tall and rumbling came up behind her, obscuring the view of the crowd. The behemoth smacked into her, giving her and the car a sudden jolt forward. Noisy commands. Metal scraped metal. The car moved an inch and then backslid. Somewhere an engine labored and then thundered. She moved another two feet before sinking into the loam. The crowd bellowed its sorrow and then cheered as the metal monster rumbled anew, firmly wrenching its prey away from the maw of the gully.

Dominique, shaken but grateful, got out of the car and thanked her rescuers. The same motley group that minutes ago played at rallying cheerleaders now stood confused and shy, staring at the ground, wanting very much to leave. She thought it was strange that no one had asked her why she'd gone off the road in the first place. She opened the passenger car door and pulled out a crumpled sheet of paper. She gave the hand-drawn map to the tow truck driver. He squinted in the light and then became alarmed when he recognized the name and address.

"Who are you and whatch you want with them people?" The crowd rumbled back to life.

"I have an appointment this afternoon with Paul and his wife Deneeta. I'm from New Orleans, Elysian Fields Parish, really. I run a prison there."

A very small round woman opened her sleepy eyes and asked, "What kind of trouble they in, ma'am?"

"Oh no, they're not in any trouble." Dominique said. "I contacted them because I'm interested in an old case. One that involved disappeared children."

The crowd tightened and froze, protecting itself against the intruder. Dominique thought if they stood still too long they might turn into stone. Finally a man in red pants and a black and white checkered shirt, with *Nascar* emblazoned on the front, walked forward and spoke. "Paul and Deneeta don't give interviews anymore. What makes you think they'll see *you*?" The man had appeared out of nowhere. He was older than the rest, in his sixties, and bent at the waist. He shuffled towards her, poking the sharp end of his cane firmly into the dirt as he stepped. Not a cane, but the stick he used to cook his meal a minute ago.

When he was within a few feet of Dominique, the round woman exclaimed, "Damien's Deneeta's brother. They haven't spoke in fifteen years. Those people just stopped talking one day. Now they keep to themselves. You be wasting your time. You should go back now." She banked snappy shoo motions at Dominique, suggesting to the psychiatrist that in the recent past the woman had raised and killed chickens.

Dominique considered how much to reveal. Why not the truth? She owed these people that much.

"I wrote them and told them exactly what I wanted, and I wired money. I promised there would be more after I got here. They gave me permission."

Dominique had sent the Jones a cashier's check for one hundred dollars wrapped inside a handwritten letter. In it she promised two-hundred more in cash if she were allowed to come by in person to ask them a few questions. Politely, she also promised not to stay too long, and included an overnight-stamped, self-addressed envelope for their reply. As soon as it arrived, she got in her car and drove.

The plume of skeptics swelled back to life. Its collective head bobbed like a wave across the afternoon heat. The round woman stopped waving at her like she was an unwanted animal and closed her eyes in thought. The stooped man offered a small sermon. "You best watch yourself good. That house has powerful sickness. You can go in one person, and come out someone else."

Dominique brushed back a sweaty lock of hair and took one last look around. The skinny little girl was nowhere in sight.

THIRTY EIGHT

The noonday sun managed to scald the color right out of the world. Dominique stepped out of the car and onto a brand new page just as everything was being erased. Today, only she would fill in the details, arrange shapes of truth with tints of courage. Today, the inescapable heat would double as her co-defender and warden, while it locked out every possible means for escape or rebellion. As if in a dream or in shock, she made her way towards the shack.

On the tiny porch, a wilted man wearing a faded aquamarine t-shirt and a grey knit stocking cap inhabited the doorway, partially interrupting woven shadows created by numerous hanging planters, each one filled with nothing but dirt. She couldn't make out the expression on his face, but the uniform bobbing of the red coal of a cigarette between clenched teeth signaled her welcome. When he spun around and walked through the doorway, Dominique followed. Recently, someone had swept the raised dirt apron leading up to the porch steps. The welcome mat.

Inside, she immediately felt hemmed in by the room. Four walls, each one pressing its case to win her attention. Together they murmured their secret in unison. *It wasn't always like this. We were happy here once.* Draping her gaze over the bare, scarred wooden floor, she imagined a litter of toys and small piles of stuffed animals, some new, others dragged through the dirt so many times—obviously the favorites. Inside a tall wardrobe, drawers opened and closed, revealing neatly-pressed school clothes. Despite cracked plaster, and floor-to-ceiling exposed tiers of lath, each wall spilled tales of crayon marks and drawings so bright, but for the boy's disappearance, they might never have vanished.

A child died and a murderer was safe.

"Have a seat," a dark finger pointed to a white oval Formica breakfast table in the middle of the room. Nestled around it, four matching leatherette chairs with cracked seats held up by surprisingly clean and polished chrome legs. Dominique scraped a chair back and sank her weary torso down. Her eyes drifted in every direction. Just inside the doorway stood a wood shelf unit filled with a few canned goods, a bottle of bleach, and a torn bag of charcoal. On the other side of the room, sundry laundry stretched suspended from a PVC bar. The same wall held another shelf-unit with mismatched metal doors tied together with clothesline, holding back whatever precious cargo rested inside. On the floor, a newish looking commode, and in front of it, a lawnmower. To her left, a narrow doorway led to a cramped room, its only occupant, a double bed covered by a faded-pink patchwork quilt. She looked up. The corrugated ceiling sagged above criss-crossed, two-by-four rotting planks. A parade of exposed, snaking metal tubes ran over and under the wood, carrying the water and electricity for the house. She saved the best scene for last, to examine.

Not four feet in front of her, a sixties Moffat stove, a thirty-year-old refrigerator, a freestanding stainless steel sink, and a butcher-block table. The Joneses pattered between the utilities in an effort to finish preparing lunch. Deneeta was tall and substantial, clad from head to toe entirely in orange. From turban to slippers, each garment was a shade or texture different from the next, but everything fit together like the pieces of a finely crafted mosaic. Her mumu flowed like linen in a gentle breeze as she stirred pots, commandeered lids, and sprinkled spices and herbs. Next to her, the stick-thin Paul began assembling cold cuts and tomatoes for club sandwiches. She sniffed the air. The couple had used some of Dominique's money for a proper lunch.

She continued to watch as the woman trundled bowls of steamy soup to the table while her husband set down mismatched plates filled with sandwiches and chips. Out of nowhere, a pitcher of lemonade appeared, followed by glasses, newly-filled salt and pepper shakers, and bottles of catsup and mustard. When they were all seated and staring at each other, Paul asked, "Why come all this way to ask a few questions about our boy? Why bother? Dean Cobb is dead and buried in Poorhouse Cemetery without so much as a headstone. Can't nobody help us now."

Dominique peered kindly into the man's eyes. "I'm very sorry about your loss. I know I'm powerless to change things for you. I'm not here for that." She picked up her spoon and delicately sipped delicious broth. "I've come all this way because I thought maybe you could help *me*." While Dominique continued eating her soup, the man and woman silently arched eyebrows at each other.

Deneeta seemed to gather her thoughts while alternating between stirring and blowing on the soup. "Help you? Why could we . . ." voice faltering. Her face shot up and glared at Dominique's. "It's happening again? But that can't be, they be dead and gone now for a long, long time."

Dominique set her spoon down. "Not everyone died. And I don't think it ever really stopped. Just got put on hold for awhile."

Paul asked, "Does this have something to do with your prison?"

This was the worst part for the psychiatrist. She needed answers quickly. But the cost of extracting them would mean more heartache and suffering for these already dejected parents.

"A young volunteer in New Orleans was raped going home from work, and then later died from complications due to her injuries. Before that, a woman was attacked in her home."

"What makes you think those attacks are connected to what happened here?"

"I'm not entirely sure they are. But for my peace of mind, and the safety of a community, I must investigate. Would you please share your story with me?"

The man set his empty bowl aside and picked up a sandwich. "What kind of bad luck you stumble across that makes this your problem?" Deneeta groaned.

If only it had just been luck and not fate, Dominique thought.

"Please, just start at the beginning and tell me in your own words what you remember."

Paul and Deneeta nodded slowly, knowingly, like they had always suspected this day would come. They seemed to be reading each other's thoughts so they could coordinate their stories. After clearing his throat several times, the man put his hands on top of the table. When Paul began speaking, the psychiatrist noticed the walls had relaxed their vigil and the room grew bigger.

"Our son was thirteen when the fever started. Before that he was hardly ever sick. Just some childhood colds and stuff. But this fever, it went high and lasted two weeks. He wasn't getting any better so we took him there."

"To the free clinic," Dominique added.

"We didn't have the kind of money to take him to a big-city hospital. They were such kind folks. And he always looked happy when we came back to visit."

"Wait, you left him there. Overnight?"

Before Paul could react, Deneeta rested her hand on her husband's arm. "It wasn't like that. He was so sick. Burning up. They told us they could give him proper medicine, keep him hydrated. And that he had to be under observation. We were welcome to stay the night."

The man said, "The next morning the doctors said he was stable, but the fever was still too high. He had gotten himself a serious internal infection. They told us to leave him, so we could get on with our jobs. They promised to take good care of him, take some tests, and they would call us at the end of the day.

"It went on like that for a month. We visited on the weekends, when we could borrow a car. After a few weeks he looked better, was stronger, and the fever finally came down. At first, he always liked to run up to us and show us the latest book he was reading, or video game he just learned to do."

His mother said, "They even bought him new clothes and paid for a fancy tutor to come to the house in the mornings."

Dominique asked, "But if he wasn't sick any more, why did you let him stay?"

"Lydeah said that on the outside he looked better, but in the inside his kidneys had stopped working right. They said they had to give him drugs intravenously to save the kidneys.

We trusted her and the other doctor. Anyways, it was getting on May. School would be over soon. We figured he'd be home by summer. We didn't have anything to complain about, you see. Imagine if we did. How ungrateful we would sound, and what if we took him home too soon and he got sick again?"

Paul grabbed the table and whispered, "They never asked us for a penny. Sometimes when we were leaving, they would hand us gift baskets filled with food, home baked goods, freshly caught fish. Even clothes. A nice sweater for me, a dress for Deneeta. They thought of everything."

"Still, it must have crossed your minds that even charitable people did not usually go that far." Dominique said.

"Nothing crossed our minds at first. Just our boy's health and safety." Deneeta laughed joylessly. "The summer came and went, and one day when we drove over there with our own car...the doctors helped us buy our neighbor's jalopy. It wasn't a lot of money because the car was old, and Paul here, a real handy mechanic. But still, they bought us a vehicle. That day I'll never forget."

Dominique learned how in one fell swoop the Jones' lives changed irrevocably. When the parents went over to the Lemartine's, Dean and the doctors' son were playing chess on the floor. Lydeah came over and per usual explained in detail Dean's progress. She said his kidneys were now ninety percent back. She had looked triumphant when she exclaimed that he would most likely make a full recovery. It was just then that they noticed their son still hadn't gotten up to say hello. He wouldn't even look at his mom and dad when they called out to him. But the other one did. There was nothing on earth as frightening and domineering as those cold mean eyes. They seemed to say, "Do what you got to do and leave. Leave now. This ain't your hangout no more. This ain't your son no more." When they finally shook the boy's hold on them, the Joneses turned to leave the house, looking back once at the boy. By then his expression had changed. He was smiling politely now, waving goodbye.

Paul got up, taking with him everyone's soup bowls and plates, and gently setting them down in the sink. He ran a little water, then turned around, his hands gripping the sink's rounded edge.

"By then, the ugly talk had begun. We didn't want to believe nothing bad about the doctors. They had done so much for us and Dean. We ignored it. At least in the beginning."

Dominique asked, "What kind of talk?"

Deneeta said, "People from neighboring towns saying kids gone missing. These folks started coming down here, making rumors about the clinic. Saying to whoever would listen, how it made zombies out of their children. Even if they gone back home, they acted like someone else in their bodies. Strange and uncommunicative. They said whether they got them kids back or not, they were still disappeared. All of them were telling the same kind of story. That it be the doctors at the clinic doing evil things behind closed doors. How could we believe something like that?"

Paul said, "Dean turned fourteen in September. They gave him the biggest grandest party we ever been to. There was food on tables that ran the whole length of the back yard. They had badminton, croquet. A small band of musicians played real good jazz. A lady read poetry, and Dean's teacher gave a speech that made Dean sound like the smartest kid in the county. Towards evening, the kids started dancing. It was a beautiful sight.

"But we felt like intruders because we were ignored. Especially by Dean."

Dominique asked, "Who all was there?"

Deneeta recalled, "The doctors, Dean, their son, and a few boys we had seen hanging around before, all black teenagers. A few girls from the local school. Some older white boys and white girls, too. They were mixing it up, not something you usually see around here. We didn't pay too close attention because we were still hoping our son would talk to us again. We couldn't understand what we did to make him go away from us like that. When he finally looked at us, it was late in the evening. But we know what we saw. His eyes told the whole story. He was a lost boy. To us, himself, to the world.

"You probably seen it in your own work," Deneeta played with her sandwich like it was a toy to be assembled and reassembled. "The dead zone. My boy's eyes were dead. We knew then we had been invited for one reason and one reason only. To understand once and for all how much we were no longer needed."

Paul said, "How could something like this happen? Those people saved his life. For what? To take it away again? Does that make any kind of sense to you?' He turned away again to tinker with the dishes before one teardrop fell.

To Dominique it was clear as day. The fattening of the calf before the great sacrifice to the gods. "Did you keep in touch?"

"Oh, yes," Deneeta said. "We called every week. Once in a while Dean got on the phone and tried to reassure us. Said he was doing real good with the tutor. That he might go on to college someday. He wanted us to be proud of him. We were.

But we had stopped asking him when he would come home. And he stopped lying to us about it."

Paul sat back down and without emotion told the end of the tale. The following summer, their boy ran away from the Lemartine's. Took a car and drove to Jackson. Nobody knew it at the time, but Dean quickly got involved in the sex trade. They started to suspect something, because after a few months he began sending money home. Regular like clockwork, five hundred dollars would arrive at the end of each month. This went on for eleven months until a Jackson detective called them. They found out on the phone that their only son had shot himself in the heart with a nine-millimeter Beretta. The following day he would have turned sixteen.

A light patter of rain tapped on the windows. The sun shower fell like crystal teardrops against the brilliance of the pale blue sky. Deneeta got up to look outside. "The doctors were gone six months by then. They just up and closed the clinic one day, sold their house and moved away. I guess they couldn't take all that gossip flying helter-skelter. Shortly after they left, an FBI man came here and asked a few questions about Dean. About his sickness, how long he stayed at the clinic. Did we know how he could get in touch with him? We didn't say nothing because of the money..." She turned around and looked at Paul. "We didn't want to get him in trouble."

How much actual joy did a human being experience in a lifetime, Dominique wondered suddenly. Could it be calculated? Its numbers compared to those of tedium, frustration, or even sorrow? And what kinds of joy were there, really? Substantial joy, like giving life? Or pointless joy, like observing plants growing, birds flying, children singing. How could this joy not be pointless, if the things it gave rise to could just as easily, in minutes, suddenly and finally vanish. And what about a child? What is the point of loving your child if one day it's snatched from you like a purse full of money? Dominique was startled to be able to feel so much so fast. From here on now, this was to be her fate. That at any moment she could be ambushed and cankered with the capacity to feel so much pointless joy, and so much mutilating sorrow. Life without Delilah would be a trip.

Dominique asked, "What about the other children? Any word about them?"

The man considered and spoke. "We heard two others passed. The Felix boy died joyriding with some older boys in Tampa. And a girl who returned to New Orleans was killed in her own house by some gangbangers that had taken over the block."

Dominique pulled out the trump card. "What did you think when you heard about the son's legendary career? His being a famous doctor in Florida. Did you think there was a possibility you might have gotten it wrong?"

"Ma'am, we were dumb for such a long time. Partly because we loved Dean so much, and also because we had the wool pulled over our eyes real good. But that don't mean we stayed that way. It's just like that fairy tale, you know. There's a very good reason why wolves wear sheeps' clothing. If they didn't, then everyone would be able to see their big ugly sharp teeth."

THIRTY NINE

Dominique wished she could run over to Miss Marta's to tell her all about the little room inside the Joneses' house. The way it had made her feel welcome and alive. The things it whispered to her about love. How love could be as delicate and translucent as a queen cicada's wing, but that it would live on in people's hearts long after the person who created it vanished.

The room showed her something else, too. She had sensed emotional happiness passing swiftly through the walls and over the counters, across the floor, and when it spilled onto her, she was left with a certain revelation. That in comparison to the hailstorm of sudden tragedy and its companion, enduring grief, joy was but a mere spit in the ocean within the great tenure of a human life.

When the room came to life, the things she had once tried to conceal even from herself jostled loose. Even surrounded by so much pain, for the first time ever, Dominique felt like a full-fledged participant in the world and not just its lonely observer. That's what she really wanted Miss Marta to know.

She had already turned the car around and was about to step on the gas when a screen of orange filled her windshield. Deneeta floated quickly over to the driver's side. For the first time that day, the woman's eyes had had lost some of their clarity. They beseeched Dominique's.

Dominique rolled down the window allowing the AC to wash over both of them. "You've seen him then, haven't you? You've stared evil in the eye." It was gospel. "What are you going to do now?" Deneeta asked.

Dominique let the questions stand while she concentrated on breathing. Was Deneeta right? How could the woman be so sure? But isn't that what drove her to Mississippi in the first place? A mother's love could reveal acres. Yet, it was hard to be certain. She would not know anything until she could apply the test.

Without saying another word, Deneeta reached inside the car and squeezed Dominique's shoulders hard. For good luck.

It was early afternoon, but the day was quickly disappearing under a coal dust sky. The rain had let up and the air temperature mercifully dropped ten degrees. While she drove, vapors pirouetted like phantoms across the roadway. Earlier in Vicksburg at a gas station, Dominique had spied a curious flybill that advertised a strange concoction of shopping experiences. The outlet was called Guns and Gardenias. She had felt simple incredulity when she read that it was a "one-stop emporium for all of your outdoor needs". As nutty as it had seemed before, now a similar advertisement above her loomed inspiration. A larger version of the notice, the ad in the sky also included an arrow that read, 2 Miles East. Dominique slowed down, switched on her blinker, and turned down the empty gravel road.

The building was a corrugated pole barn stuck in the middle of an endless, barren, clay-packed desert. The *Gardenia* side was painted yellow-green and was home to the largest plant nursery Dominique had ever seen. Inside, row after row held small and large pots filled with every kind of tree imaginable. Flowering, fruit, hardy, shade, as well as a potpourri of flowers and shrubs ready for planting. Outside — shovels, hoes, rakes, wheelbarrows, and mulch stood cramped together around a motley collection of lawn ornaments. She became hypnotized by the offerings: angels, young boys urinating, rabbits, turtles, doves, deer, and the pièce de résistance, a large assortment of earnest-looking gorillas in every color but pink.

Not to be outdone in curb appeal, *Guns* was painted brilliant lavender. But that's where the cheer and charm ended. The gun shop looked liked it belonged in a 1940's noir film, where the femme fatale could be seen going in to buy a weapon that would soon end the miserable life of her cuckolded but extremely rich husband. The entire perimeter was secured in iron bar. She walked over to a lead-lined, thick steel door with a protruding doorbell that said to push once. After a few minutes, it wasn't Robert Mitchum or Peter Lorre who came to let her in, but a tall skinny, air-dried looking lad whose eyes looked crossed.

When she asked to look at a small gun, the sales manager suggested a sub-compact Beretta. He barely looked at her driver's license before handing over the gun and a box of bullets. That the man behind the counter didn't even hesitate before selling a sidearm to an elegantly dressed black woman slumming in the Delta, mildly surprised the psychiatrist. What was the world coming to?

Outside, Dominique lifted her face to the sky. The rain began like a fine spray. By the time she finished loading her new gun, it felt like she was standing under a waterfall. The parking lot, with its studded rows of tire marks and deeply veined water cracks, would soon become a morass of swirling

FORTY

"Keep your voice down and walk normal."

"How can I, when you got your freaking hands all over me?"

"Shhhh!" Dave shepherded Julius Lucky towards Dr. Doucette's office door. He looked both ways before using his passkey. "Remember, you have thirty minutes before your session with Dr. Wadell. Here's your chance to do something big. Are you excited, Lucky?"

Julius Lucky looked anything but excited. His normally olive-toned pallor paled a few shades down to a sickly grey, and his stomach hurt to beat the band. But a promise was a promise. Dave had given him extra rations and recreation time throughout the week. Now it was time to pay the piper.

"Why can't you go inside with me? Two can work faster than one," Julius hissed.

Dave disliked whining almost as much as he disliked Julius. "Moron, I have to stay out here and act as a lookout. If we get caught, I can lay the blame on you, say you were screwing around in there. That way, I don't lose my job and you only get grounded. Capiche?"

Julius failed to see the logic. "What exactly do you want me to do in there?"

"My uncle wants dope on Dr. Doucette. He said to look in the inmate files. The key to that big armoire..." Julius looked puzzled. "The tall wood unit, you can't miss it. Anyway the key is in the middle drawer of the desk. That's never locked. Scan them quickly. If you see anything weird, photocopy it. Take this." Dave handed Julius a ream of paper. "Use these sheets like I showed you in the guards' office. It's the same kind of copier. When you're done, replace all the files, in order. Take out the sheets you didn't use. And don't forget your homework."

"You gotta admit that was slick, me leaving my assignments in there. Good excuse to go back in. Where are they, anyway?"

"I saw them on a tray on the edge of the desk. Lucky, find me something."

Julius didn't move. "Are you sure she's not coming back?"

Dave shook his head. "Not for hours. Dr. Doucette just called. Still in Mississippi."

Julius trudged in and immediately saw his papers sitting on the desk. He rummaged through them and set them aside. Next, he went to the desk drawer and picked out the key. After unlocking the armoire, Julius couldn't resist looking at his own file first. He skimmed over court and prison records, ignored medical data, and went straight for Dr. Doucette's notes on their last session. He was disappointed to find nothing explosive. He was sure she would have used strong words and recommended harsh punishment for the way he acted during their last meeting. At least that would have proven that there *was* something rotten in the state of Denmark between her and Lerance. Instead, she wrote a whole page about his use of coping mechanisms to offset feelings of inadequacy. ...*Today Julius used compensation to deflect attention from his reluctance to talk about himself. Instead of advancing his Desire goals, the patient asked me pointed questions about my own life and experiences. When I gave him an indirect answer and tried to steer him to topic, Julius became more insistent. Truncated childhood due to emotional abandonment by anti-social and alcoholic parents...* Yeah, he'd heard all that before.

Julius put his file back and reached for Eduardo's. The young inmate's history and medical data read just like his accounts in group therapy. He waded through a long list of family and friends, trying to find a connection between him and Dr. Doucette. There must have been fifty childhood photos of Eduardo and his brother growing up. And what was this? A list of law school internet searches? Well, well. Eduardo, the smarty-pants.

Emile's file was a bit thicker. The man was older than the rest of them and had a long history of amputation attempts. According to medical reports, beginning in 1990, Emile had tried at least four times to amputate his leg. Once he froze it with liquid nitrogen and called an ambulance to take him to the hospital. Once in hospital, they managed to save the leg, even as he threatened to do it again. But he did not freeze it again. Instead, Emile traveled to Mexico, where for two-thousand dollars an unlicensed surgeon, practicing inside a boarded-up concrete bunker in the middle of downtown Ciudad Juárez, promised to chop off his leg at the precise height and angle of his choosing. Emile, who was heavily sedated at the time, and his leg injected with a nerve block, did not hear or move as the Mexican Federales used a front-end loader to storm the ramshackle surgery.

Next, he took his case to England, where voluntary amputation was legal and safe at the beginning of the year 2000. After extensive medical and psychological examination, the former computer analyst was put on a list and told to go back to the States for a few months. He never returned to the British Isles. Within days of learning about the first two amputations, the British parliament, its citizenry, and no less The National Health Service, made their feelings quite clear on voluntary amputations specifically, and on BIID generally. The practice was forthwith abolished. Along with Emile's last chance of getting a safe and legal amputation.

Billy Jo's file looked like a fashion magazine. He had worked ad nauseum on his Desire exercises, and every wish and hope he'd ever glimpsed, was documented. There were scores of cutouts featuring trendy clothes, costuming, make up, hair accessories, and fashion tips. He only glanced at his roommate's harrowing account of living on the batture and his later encounter with Fifi, because he knew it by heart. Giving up hope of discovering anything to damn the psychiatrist with, Julius flipped to the last page and read Dr. Doucette's summary. For the first time in a very long time, he felt guilty. Only a bad friend would violate another's privacy like this.

...In addition, Billy Jo credits his ability to honor his true feelings and desires to the love and support he receives from his new and forever friend, Julius Lucky. If he had been fortunate enough to have a brother, he says he would have looked just like Julius.

Vincent Delavon's case history also traced back to childhood. He was seven when his parents were killed in an automobile collision. An only child, he went to live on his maternal grandmother's sugar cane plantation. She was a loving woman who taught him to work hard, play hard, and pay attention to his studies. When he turned twelve, tragedy struck again. His grandmother lost her small farm in a forfeiture, and the two of them were forced to move in with shirt-tail relatives who lived down the road. A couple of years later, the grandmother died of a stroke and Vincent took off for Natchez and a street gang called the Vice Lords. But just before leaving Warren County, Vincent, who was fourteen at the time, was briefly questioned by the FBI regarding the disappearance of teenagers in the area, specifically a fifteen-year-old boy named Dean Cobb Jones. They had attended the same middle school. A few years later, they became runaways, both landing in Jackson, Mississippi. What the... thought Julius, what is all this mumbo jumbo about missing boys?

Wait a minute. Warren County? Where had he heard that before? Julius replaced Vincent's file with Lerance's. He paged through the sticky thin sheets until he found a stack of newspaper articles. The first few were from the *Miami Herald*. Headlines announced: "Prominent Doctor Kills Wife In Jealous Rage," "Celebrity Doctor Admits to Shooting Wife," "Deep Mystery Surrounds the Confession of Dr. Lemartine." There were also photos: Lerance with hospital staff, some on the golf course, another with his new bride five years earlier.

Another article, "Teen Girl Dies After Brutal Assault." This one was a *Times Picayune* story about the volunteer who was killed after leaving the homeless shelter he volunteered at. And there it was. *The Vicksburg Post,* "... in Warren County, Mississippi, police question Lydeah Lemartine about the disappearance of Dean Cobb Jones. The fifteen-year-old was last seen at Lemartine's Free Clinic, which operated out of the doctors' home in Dauphin, Mississippi…"

The last article was a report on the discovery of Dean Cobb Jones' body in a seedy Jackson bar. The boy had apparently found the owner's pistol and shot himself in the middle of the night, through the heart. According to the coroner, Jones bled out in minutes on the bar's concrete basement floor.

Julius took Vincent and Lerance's files to the copier. After photocopying all of the articles on missing children and the death of Dean Cobb Jones, he put both files back and tried to shut the drawer. At the last second it caught on something and would not close all the way. Julius took the files out again and then put them back carefully, and tried shutting the drawer. It still wouldn't close. He opened the drawer again and this time took out the whole stack, which he intended to put back, one, neatly, after another. That's when he saw it. A tattered corner sticking up from the bottom of the drawer. He set the stack down on the floor and slid out a thick battered buff file. Funny title, *Delilah*.

Julius' heart quickened, and after he read the first few lines he nearly fainted from happiness.

Delilah cried, "He's my twin!! If you don't get me, Lerance, I'll bring the house down. I'll expose you for who you really are. Cooperate, join us, and we'll do everything to keep you safe."

And I was safe. Until he started killing again.

Pay dirt. Eureka. Barnburner. Now his old pal Dave would get a promotion, and little ol' inadequate Julius—instant parole. He checked the wall clock, rubbed his hands together vigorously, blew on them and walked over to the copier. For the next ten minutes the machine labored mechanically, scanning and printing file pages. With each flash and surge, another twisted tangle of secret memories and dark history struggled free.

FORTY ONE

Testimony of Miss Marta

"I tried to tell them. That they would come. The ordinary days."

She sat in the middle of the summoned court looking straight into the eyes of the sheriff. The ceiling fan squawked and canted and no one noticed because what the voodoo priestess knew and understood was legion.

"When sleep returns, just like before. Your mind rests and your heart beats slowly."

The sheriff liked the small old woman, trusted her, and thought this must be what it felt like to interrogate Mother Teresa. He sat motionless while she took her time to look from side to side at the waxy, tear-stained faces, and then turn forward again, brushing dark slender fingers across yards of pleated skirt. In the distance, from inside an adjacent building or home, or perhaps a car, the distinctive sounds of Ella Fitzgerald's scat singing wafted in gently, as she spoke her next words.

"Ordinary days would be back. To begin the first drafts of the first chapters of your new life. I told 'em they would always come. But of course, they didn't come."

The sheriff asked, "Why Miss Marta? Why didn't they come?"

"Because between 'em, as smart as they were, they didn't own one lick of good sense. They were gonna do what they always do. I expected as much of Dominique, but my son, he too never learned how to do things in small measures."

FORTY TWO

Darnell believed that inside each human being lived at least one other distinctive character. Not exactly like in Dominique's case, but more like it than most would want to admit. People were complicated; they had secret thoughts and loves and shame, and unbearable desires. In his case, Darnell was known around town as a foot soldier in the Boucree neighborhood street patrol. Part gangster, part avenging angel. Addict, recovering addict; addict, and recovering addict again. Aloof and self-centered, with a bad temper, and a biting sarcasm. A friend, if you were lucky, loyal to his family and Elijah and to the residents of Desire. Not particularly violent unless absolutely necessary. Like today.

But Darnell also had a strange and wonderful interior life. That other self toottled carefree through the world in books. All kinds: fiction, history, literature, memoir, fantasy and recently, the forty-two-year-old had turned his fancy to science fiction. Whom among even his closest friends would have ever believed that writing a fantasy/sci-fi novella was constantly on his mind. That in his room at the Davis' lay an outline, a ten-page synopsis, and the first chapter of a modern-day *Animal Farm*. He thought his version would be better than the original—more relevant—because it was peopled with lots of street-wise, smart and sassy black kids.

Each day, he read a couple of daily papers, watched MSNBC to catch up on politics, and this he hid from almost everyone: watched the soccer World Cup with the kind of passion most of his friends reserved for the Final Four. But always at his mom's. Less prone to humiliation that way. He knew everything about black history and black people's contribution to America's culture and society. He knew just as much about European history and its tradition of conquest and bloody wars. He read botany books, astronomy books, and thought science and not religion might hold the answers to man's most pressing questions. Darnell gained his appetite for learning about the world when he was quite young and helping Little Niqui study for tests. While she memorized answers to quizzes, he read her books. She told him once that he knew as much about her subjects as she did. Besides his mother, she was the only other person that told him he was smart. But his appreciation for things material and factual came even before his friendship with Dominique. It began with his mother.

And that was why, even though he wasn't a God-fearing man, Darnell loved churches. Since he could remember, he had willingly accompanied his mother to most of the churches in New Orleans. She brought him along because she wanted him to listen. To music, to the liturgy, and to gospel. Later she taught him about architecture and design—before he was ten-years-old, Darnell could distinguish between a Rococo altar and one styled after the Gothic period, he knew how stained glass was made and what it symbolized, and where the wood and marble for the naves came from. They would usually linger together long after the mass was over, so she could talk to him about the shrines dedicated to the Blessed Virgin and the saints. And this was the real reason for his education. His mother wanted him to learn about *the way of the saints*.

Although she was an avid practitioner of Voodoo, it was important that her son understand that the religion was syncretic, based upon a merging of the beliefs and practices of West African peoples and Roman Catholic Christianity. She explained that the African slaves who were brought to Haiti in the 16th century were forced to convert to the religion of their masters, but that in private they still followed and practiced traditional African beliefs. Over time they also fell in love with some of the Christian saints because of the strong resemblance to their own traditional lwa, or deities. Thus Voodoo was created. This was the last thought he had before he found himself once again at Our Lady of Prompt Succor, the Catholic church a few blocks down the road from Elgin's house.

This church, Darnell recalled, contained the oldest image of the Madonna in the city, and had miracle history associated with it. Two miracles that he knew of, and both occurring after nuns prayed to the statue. First, it was well known that in 1788, the Ursiline Convent was spared from the great fire that destroyed most of the French Quarter, all because of divine intervention. And then in 1815, the British soldiers in Louisiana, outnumbering Americans by more than two to one, were defeated. General Jackson himself came to the convent to thank the nuns for their prayers.

Unfortunately, Darnell didn't believe in prayer or divine intervention. When he wanted a miracle, he turned to drugs or books. But since Our Lady of Prompt Succor was New Orleans' first stop for intercession, Darnell figured it wouldn't hurt if he hung around the grounds for a bit, reading the dedication plaque. That way, if an all-seeing, bounty-dispensing divinity hovered nearby, he or she would be able to hear his thoughts and feel his fear.

These ruminations only served to postpone the sickening task ahead. Darnell lit a cigarette and with an unsteady hand raised it to his mouth to inhale deeply. With his other hand he fingered the semi-automatic pistol inside his jacket pocket and smiled thinly. Thanks to a single-stack magazine, this heavier pistol was still the ideal conceal-and-carry gun. It dawned on him that worrying about the existence of a God or Madonna was futile, since neither of them would likely shower him with succor; rather they might send him straight to hell for what he was about to do.

Darnell crushed the cigarette under his foot and tried to land some of his orbiting thoughts. If this thing was going down today, he had to hurry home. It was four o'clock. It would take him another hour to walk there. And if Kevin left Elysian Fields right now, he'd make it to Desire in two hours.

His mind began to fill with images of ghosts. Yolanda already singing with the angels, and Dominique starting to fade away like she might become one soon. He noticed that she didn't even try to call him anymore. No matter, their pact was until death. Even if they weren't on speaking terms, he would always be her lookout. It was up to him to avenge Yolanda and save his best friend. Darnell would be ready for whatever happened because he was sure he was right. He didn't think Kevin could say or do anything to change that.

Darnell figured the psychiatrist kept his phone charged and nearby. With a final look at the spires of the church, Darnell turned and headed for Magazine Street. He thought, not without regret, that now would be a perfect time to smoke a bowl.

As he walked, he took out his phone and began texting.

MEET ME IN DESIRE

LEAVE NOW

I KNOW WHO KILLED YOLANDA

D

FORTY THREE

Kevin's counseling session with Julius did not go well.

To his credit, the inmate had caught up on all of the Desire exercises and talked enthusiastically about his dreams for the future. He still liked the idea of owning and running a ranch, but had scaled his intentions down to the realistic goal of living on a hobby farm, with his sister sharing in his plans for the future. He had even gone as far as writing her a letter, sketching out his ideas for a tree and shrub farm. He had asked her what she thought of raising Alpacas. He explained they were related to camels and llamas but were only three feet tall, with the softest most luxuriant fleece, and had the cutest faces of any animal on earth. To Kevin's amazement, Julius' research had been thorough, because he had included websites that explained where to buy plans and materials to build pens for this type of livestock.

Then, seemingly out of nowhere, Julius lobbed a monkey wrench into the middle of this otherwise halcyon scenario. "Yeah, man. Don't be surprised if our little plan happens sooner than later." After that he straightened in his chair and began nodding his head up and down, eyes as big as saucers, complete triumph swimming in their obsidian lenses. Kevin thought it was much like watching a full-sized bobble-head doll that had suddenly come to life. But did that really happen? Or had he merely imagined the moment and its excruciating bizarreness. Right now he didn't think he was in a position to interpret anyone's expression or its intended emotion.

Kevin did recall with nauseating clarity that once during the session, he had been so completely preoccupied with his own thoughts that when the inmate leaned over the desk and tapped him lightly on the forehead, asking, "Hey anybody in there?" he barely felt it. Only Julius would have been that brazen, but the psychiatrist became terribly embarrassed and apologized obliquely, forcing himself to ask only a few more questions of the inmate before ending the session and dismissing him.

Ever since Dave told him that Dominique had left that morning for Mississippi and wasn't due back until evening, he'd felt uneasy. And Kevin didn't understand why his co-director hadn't said a word to him or Guyla about the trip. What was so important in Mississippi that Dominique felt like she had to sneak out there before the two of them could find out? All he knew for certain was that ever since they had shown her Lerance's computer searches the day before, she had transformed. This time instead of casting the usual excuses around her favorite prisoner, she adopted a conciliatory demeanor and genuinely wanted to know how Kevin and Guyla thought they should proceed. Dominique's colleagues said they wanted to sleep on it, and she had thought that was a sensible idea.

So why wasn't she acting sensibly now? It wasn't her style to be irresponsible, to just leave without a plan, without consulting her partners first. Something she saw in those searches must have spurred her on. Something to do with

Lerance. And Jones. It definitely appeared that Lerance, Vincent and Dean Cobb Jones all had something in common. In the early 1980s, they had been teenagers living in the same county in Mississippi. Lerance and Vincent were still there at the time Jones went missing. Perhaps she was looking for that one shred of evidence that would exonerate the prisoner. Or condemn him.

But of what? What did anyone know about Lerance besides the fact the he had murdered his wife? Until that time, at least on paper, the former doctor had led a model and fortunate life. But he was guilty of something else — everyone felt it — and no one could name it.

Kevin felt increasing irritation when he considered the legal and ethical ramifications to the prison if Dominique acted out of haste on any possible findings. But he also worried about her state of mind if the news on Lerance was damning. What would she do? What would she say? And who would hear it? That was bad enough. It's what Kevin discovered afterwards that began to cripple his ability to concentrate.

Right after he talked with Dave, he went into Dominique's office. He had wanted to take another look at Lerance's files. He had his own volumes on the inmate's history, but Dominique kept the newspaper clippings of the arrest and hearing in her armoire. He thought if he probed carefully enough, he might be able to parse an elusive clue that could potentially upend the whole mystery.

He didn't have to go that far.

As soon as he opened the file, a yellowed lined sheet of paper, unattached to any psychiatric notes, fell out of the folder. It was handwritten in red and black ink and was unlike anything Dominique normally wrote or kept in her files. He read it several times, then pocketed it and left. The entire contents of the note was in his head, in front of his eyes, when Julius came in for his appointment. There had to be some reasonable explanation for it. The note read like it was penned by a crazy person. Or two crazy people. Two types of ink pens, two sets of handwriting, each one similar to Dominique's, but not exactly in her penmanship or syntax. It was the kind of dialogue found between two people arguing in a 1950's melodrama. They had been arguing about Lerance.

It even occurred to Kevin that Dominique was drunk when she wrote it. That would have made sense if she had written it recently. The harassment by the sheriff and religious group, and the too-real shock of Yolanda's death, and now Lerance's mysterious activities—those things combined would have been enough, perhaps after a couple of shots of strong liquor to send her headlong into freewheeling hyperbole. He could even buy that, after writing them, she had forgotten to remove the rantings from her patient's file. The problem with all of this was that Dominique, or whomever, did not write this recently or at any time during the administration of the prison. These notes were written a month before the staff or prisoners arrived in Louisiana.

After the guard escorted Julius out, Kevin reread the note for the last time. The first character wrote in red ink.

SUBJECT: LERANCE LEMARTINE, June 18, 2005, 12:00 p.m.

Congratulations girl, you won! And just in time. I bet he won't even know what hit him. But the best part is that now he really is yours to do with what you want. Don't worry your pretty little head that he might be a complete fake and guilty of who knows what, because look how perfect he's for your program. Another scalp for the belt. Best of all he's so much like me, you won't miss me at all when I'm gone. Yeah, I know I'm not welcome anymore. You've made that perfectly clear. No matter, I am not going to leave you stranded up the creek in that very leaky boat of yours. For that, I give you Lerance, my final gift. From now on, he'll be your paddle. For who you are, for what you always were.

PS Don't ever forget. What Lerance wants and what you need ARE the same thing. Like me, he's your better half. Best part, honey, he's real.

Nothing. He could not make heads or tales of it. That first part definitely could not have been written by Dominique. The next part written in green, must have been.

SUBJECT: LERANCE LEMARTINE, JUNE 18, 2005, 12:45 p.m.

You are not in control and never will be again. I let you go a long time ago, but if you did something behind my back before that, you can be sure I'll figure it out and redress it. As it stands, you have been known to lie to me on other occasions, so I tend not to believe you when you imply that there might be something hidden and corrupt about my last choice for the prison. Either way, the prison must thrive. Any other outcome is unthinkable.

And then he got to the part that curdled his stomach contents and seared his eyeballs.

SUBJECT: LERANCE LEMARTINE, JUNE 18, 2005, 1:00 p.m.

Really? But you and I know perfectly well that I wasn't sneaking around very long before you found out. You and I have always been privy to the same things.

For the last time, what he did, what they did to him, it's what made him who he is. Find out what happened. And

*don't forget that he is capable of unleashing that demon
again.*

And again.

Kevin's cell phone startled him. The ring tone was from
the film, *The Good Bad and Ugly,* which meant a text had
just been sent. Nobody but credit card merchants ever texted
him, and that would only happen to confirm payments. His
friends and colleagues simply called, or sent emails to his
computer. And he hadn't made any payments recently. He
looked at the name of the sender and then promptly forgot all
about the note.

MEET ME IN DESIRE
LEAVE NOW
I KNOW WHO KILLED YOLANDA
D

The challenge hung above him like volcanic ash. Kevin
felt at once smothered and blinded. He didn't think things
could get any worse.

FORTY FOUR

Sheriff Leroy Futrell would never accept the idea of a reform prison. A prison whose sole purpose was to bolster the self-esteem of killers through counseling and Desire exercises. Especially not the one that they had floated in his back yard. Without any of his input or, more importantly, his blessing.

He was old-school and believed whole-heartedly in family, country, and bible. Prison reformists like Dominique Doucette did not figure into his way of thinking because they did not live in the real world. They, therefore, did not suffer normal everyday hardships as did the folks who populated the communities they were supposed to serve. She could never understand, for instance, that if you lost a loved one through violence, abject misery and heartbreak stayed with you until the day you died. Therapy for the bereaved was but a soggy bandage, never completely adhering, and more often than not, something that caused the wound to reinfect over and over.

Dominique had never suffered privation, and at her core believed she was anointed with powers and privileges that allowed her to circumvent traditional customs and mores. If she wanted something, she would always find a way to get it. No matter what it cost others. She preached desires and dreams. Undoubtedly she had never actually lived among real people or she'd have a clue that most folks lived their whole lives without achieving their dreams. Or that they even had the luxury of dreaming dreams. Most folks merely hoped to earn enough money to get by. To put food on the table, clothes on their kids' backs, and to be able watch some good sports on the weekends. If they drank a lot of beer at the same time, well maybe it was to forget that, all too soon, they would have to face the punishing reality of returning to the same thankless jobs that waited for them every Monday morning, year-in and year-out. If they still had jobs.

This never happened to Dominique. If she didn't like how things were going or encountered roadblocks, all she had to do was pick up the phone or open up her checkbook and *voila*, problem solved. That must have been why, after pushing through her cockamamie correctional facility, she really thought she could make it work. Futrell knew that it was nothing but a smoke screen, just a stupid fantasy without any real-world muscle behind it. As far as he was concerned, you'd have to be smoking corn silk on a cold Saturday night with Daisy Mae behind the barn to even imagine you could miraculously turn back the clock for a cold-blooded killer. Like all animals, if a man tasted bloodlust just once, there'd be no turning back for him. Ever.

Dominique was on the wrong side of history and on the wrong side of the law. And not just because of blind arrogance, very little life experience and childish obstinacy. Her intentions at the outset were dishonest because she wasn't motivated by a wish to help people rise out of their dismal circumstances, but by an insatiable need for personal fame and glory. And beneath all that there was something even more unsavory. Futrell was convinced that the director of House of Mithras was a classist who felt nothing but contempt for anyone outside her social strata.

Because he believed strongly in what he believed, the sheriff was as happy as a pig in mud when his nephew Dave arrived at his office earlier in the day with a beat-up, chunky file under his arm.

When Futrell began reading the file he knew at once that he had been delivered the keys to the kingdom. Right away he saw that it contained everything and more that he needed to shut down House of Mithras and Dominique Doucette, forever. Feeling confident, vindicated, he made himself a strong cup of cup of coffee and kept on reading for the next two hours. It wasn't until he had perused the entire contents of the Delilah file, and jotted down his own comments on a separate sheet of ruled paper, that Leroy Futrell stopped feeling happy.

Something niggled at the back of his mind. He knew what he had in front of him was an unorthodox system of recording experiences and reflections. But these pages also told the story of an extraordinary battle, one that had raged for decades. One that was still on fire. It reminded him of something. When he walked overt to the copy machine and began feeding it pages, he recalled one of his favorite passages from *Revelations*:

"And there was war in heaven: Michael and his angels fought against the dragon; and the dragon fought and his angel, And prevailed not; neither was their place found any more in heaven. And the great dragon was cast out, that old serpent, called the Devil, and Satan, which deceiveth the whole world: he was cast out into the earth, and his angels were cast out with him."

God had asked the archangel Michael to put down a rebellion started by Lucifer. Once one of God's favorites, the rogue angel decided to take over the kingdom of heaven. But the evil one was put down, because God's emissary was stronger and braver. It was just like what Dominique had done her whole life. She had battled the possession inside her soul, tooth and nail, and never stopped until she won. Now, so close after her victory of ousting the dragon, Dominique had a new problem. It seemed she was more vulnerable than ever. Because the evil Delilah was like the hydra: cut off one head and whoosh, another one sprouts. Now she had to find and castigate the one who had set so much violence in motion. Unlike her life-long struggle with Delilah, this time the psychiatrist had no idea of what she was up against, and she was going at it alone. Futrell had a real bad feeling.

When he called the prison, he asked for Dominique and got Kevin instead. Kevin told him Dominique was out for the day and that he would leave her a message. When Futrell asked where she'd gone, Kevin hesitated. Finally after a bit of cajoling, he told him she had left that morning for Mississippi. Futrell's heart sank like a brick. Kevin gave him Dominique's mobile number, but said not to bother calling, since she had not picked up any of his earlier messages.

Futrell tapped his fingers furiously against his battered desk and looked up at the clock. If he left now, he could avoid heavy traffic and be in New Orleans in less than two hours. Futrell picked up the file and locked the door behind him.

FORTY FIVE

Louisiana was one of the wettest states in the nation, averaging 57 inches of precipitation annually.

Today was no exception. On the way out of Elysian Fields, the robin's-egg blue sky over East I 10 had been painted with decorative stacks of pillowy clouds in different shapes and levels of illumination. Right before Futrell reached the city limits, the afternoon light disappeared, flattening the sky into a lifeless dark grey. Small, insistent droplets began to beat against his windows. When he switched on the wipers, they fanned smeary bits of countryside against the glass, because he had forgotten to fill the windshield washer fluid tank before he left. On South Claiborne, the drizzle turned to rain and the palms began to sway. People everywhere were running for shelter. He turned right on Tulane Avenue and parked in the first handicapped spot.

Earlier, Futrell had found Darnell's mobile number inside the file and tried calling him. Another call that went straight to voicemail. Next, he returned a call to the New Orleans Police Department. He told the detective he was coming in, so whatever he had to tell him could wait for a couple of hours. It wasn't that Futrell didn't want to know what his old friend had to say, he needed a few hours to absorb the substance of what he had just read. A drive into the city might clear his head.

Before he got out of the car, the sheriff took one last look at the file on the passenger seat. He resisted the temptation to open it and start reading again. Instead, he reached into the back seat and grabbed his Stetson. Then he pulled the cherry light off the floor and stuck it on the roof of his car. Outside, the rain did nothing to alleviate the familiar smells of sewage and heat.

God, this city stinks, he thought. For the umpteenth time, he wondered why on earth anyone would chose to live here, let alone visit. Almost everything about New Orleans depressed him except for the architecture. He looked up at Charity Hospital and studied the sprawling behemoth. In its sixth incarnation since the eighteenth century, the structure looming in front of him was a premier example of Art Deco design. He had to admit that since the 1930's New Orleans politics and civic consciousness did more to preserve city history than anywhere else in the United States. He smiled as he lingered for a moment longer to look at two stone bas-reliefs above the doorway. But he didn't come to NOLA to sightsee.

As soon as he walked through the massive doors, he was met by Detective Anthony Villere and nurse Larissa Johnson. Inside a small waiting area, Futrell studied his hosts. Villere was a handsome, light-skinned African-American in his late forties. He wore a Hornets tee and khaki pants. Next to him, another friend, Larissa, thirty-eight exactly—the sheriff knew her full DOB—stood tall, thin, and imposing. These days she was sporting a short, spiky hairstyle. She could get away with it, Futrell noted, because her dark angular face could support any do, or no do at all. Balls to the walls, she was beautiful. He had heard a rumor that the two had gone out together for a period of time. He studied them to see if they still did.

"Good evening, Larissa. Anthony."

"Glad you could meet us on such shot notice," Anthony said.

"You want to talk about the girl?"

"It's a real shame about Yolanda," Larissa said.

"Sheriff, we hadn't put this together before. Yolanda told Larissa something before she died. I think you might know what it means."

Futrell braced. This day was well on its way to becoming one of the biggest in terms of surprises.

Larissa said, "She got here in real bad shape. But by yesterday morning she looked better. It gave us hope. We thought our prayers had been answered. I can't believe she turned like that. Never should have happened. Not to someone that young."

"Larissa, tell the sheriff what she said. About the badge."

Futrell said, "Badge?"

"Yolanda was feeling energetic and wanted to talk. Why she picked me, I'll never know. She said she remembered something, and had to tell someone. The girl kept insisting that when she struggled with the rapist, she fought back real hard. She wanted me to know she didn't give in.

"She tried to tear his off his mask. And that's when he hit her and started to..." Larissa stopped talking to wipe back the tears.

Villere said, "Yolanda said when the perp threw himself on top of her, she grabbed at his sweater and that's when she saw it, for a second. Then he pinned her arms back and all she could think about was staying alive."

"What, what did she see for a second?" The sheriff met Larissa's gaze.

"Leroy, I would have called sooner but right after, poor baby started having seizures, and then her blood pressure dropped. We spend all morning trying to resuscitate her. She died in emergency surgery, and after she was gone it seemed like everybody and their mother were coming in. I just forgot about it. When I woke up this morning I remembered what she said and called Anthony. I told him to call you.

"She saw a prison ID badge. She recognized it from working at the shelter."

Leroy Futrell tried Dominique's cell again. It went straight to voice mail. He called the prison again and was told that she would be back by six o'clock, more or less. He glanced at his watch. Three-thirty.

The sky was still a dull sheet of grey, but now a thinner pinkish layer in the middle was letting in a little sun to lighten up the world. Despite the return to daylight, the heavens opened up anew, drenching the few people left on the sidewalk with a sudden downpour. This time to the beat of crackling thunder. Once back inside the Crown Vic, Futrell didn't bother to turn on the wipers, because he liked how the world distorted and then disappeared underneath the wall of sluice. The perfect background to reading the last entry in the file.

It was his favorite story. He was halfway through the journey to France, wondering how Darnell's life might have turned out if he'd never known Dominique when the police scanner started clucking.

ATTENTION ALL UNITS IN THE VICINITY OF DESIRE. ARMED STANDOFF WITH ADULT MALE HOSTAGE.

Futrell closed the file and started his car.

FORTY SIX

Only a chump would agree to meet up with one of Desire's most infamous gangsters.

Yet here he was. Alone without back up, without faith, turning off the freeway onto Louisa Street in the Upper Ninth Ward. Looking back on what he did right after reading his cell phone text, Kevin saw only blurry images of himself stumbling out the door and getting inside his Lexus. As if in a dream, he was on the road doing the other man's bidding with no thought to the risks involved. Almost two hours ago, he hadn't even bothered to get an address or directions, and now had no clue where to find Darnell inside Desire's two-square mile neighborhood. Was he supposed to spit in the wind to see what direction it flew? Or maybe he could act like a dog, and sense out the other man's presence by sniffing out the streets for evidence of fecal matter.

But he had gone. Why? Adrenaline. It does funny things to the mind and body.

And how could he have resisted? Darnell had written that he knew who killed Yolanda. Another person would have called the police. Darnell was not another person, but a black man from a black neighborhood which never had and never would share a cozy relationship with the New Orleans Police

Department. Still, everyone knew how much he hated Kevin. There were only two possible explanations for the former boyfriend of Dominique Doucette to seek out her other former boyfriend.

Since Darnell was already part of a vigilante group created to keep neighborhoods safe, it would follow that he would want to be the one responsible for wreaking revenge on whoever had attacked Yolanda, but for some reason unknown to Kevin, he also wanted his assistance. Taking the law into your hands makes for strange bedfellows. Didn't everyone know that? The alternative, of course, was that Darnell had no idea who killed Yolanda, but had used the lie to lure Kevin into Desire so he could hurt him for sleeping with Marcelle. Maybe for sleeping with Dominique. He prayed it wasn't because of the last two reasons.

Suddenly, the earlier drizzle accelerated into a downburst followed by racing straight-line winds. As he drove, the windshield wipers proved useless against the slanting rains; Kevin couldn't see more than thirty feet in front of him. Trees bent over, and trash cans rolled down sidewalks. He swerved to duck flying debris, and once had to slam on his brakes when a man holding up a skeletal umbrella walked out in front of him. Afterwards, he rolled down the window a crack and asked the soggy man if he'd seen Darnell. The man kept on walking. Kevin veered onto Higgins Boulevard and had just passed Desire Street Ministries when he spotted Sadizfy on Piety Street, hovering on someone's stoop waiting out the rain. Kevin got a face full of wet when he stuck his head out the window to offer the teen a ride. Sadizfy waved him off. He tried asking him about Darnell, but the boy either couldn't hear him or didn't want to. Four blocks later, he slowed to wave to Jerome and Keisha who were watching the rain from their front porch. They quickly ran inside the house without acknowledging him. Like they had been warned.

On Metropolitan, Kevin squinted in his rear view mirror to watch an older model car traveling a half block behind him. He noticed the vehicle because it and his own vehicle had been the only two cars on the streets for the last five minutes. He wasn't convinced he was being followed until he turned sharply onto Abundance Avenue and then zigzagged in and out of side streets, before getting up on the main drag again to head for the Industrial Canal. The other car stayed on his tail but disappeared a couple of blocks before the levee. Kevin followed France Road Parkway towards the river. At the end of the road he circled a monster-sized warehouse surrounded by empty semi-trucks and shipping containers, before pulling up tight against a bank of metal garage doors. As he stood under the eave of one of the corrugated buildings getting pelted by hard rain, Kevin thought wistfully of his big plastic umbrella lying on the floor of the back seat. The idea of holding up an umbrella when Darnell arrived was too humiliating to contemplate. Luckily, after a few minutes the rain slowed to a trickle, but that was exactly where his luck ended. An old car, mowing erratically through the parking lot, stopped suddenly, leaving a vapor-thin space between itself and the Lexus.

It was the middle of the day, but looked like full-on night. Both sets of headlights beamed sunbursts over broken concrete, illuminating long narrow streams of oil slicks that flowed like rivers and shone like the inside of abalone shells. Kevin recognized the boot as it stepped into a greasy crater filled with water. Just above the knee, a hand gripping a heavy gun swayed uncertainly.

FORTY SEVEN

Darnell waited for Kevin near the freeway entrance. Slouched in a borrowed car, he tried to plan out his next moves. But ideas only bounced around in his head. He knew finding Yolanda's rapist was righteous and necessary, but that wasn't the reason for tricking Kevin into driving in today. If that honky was responsible for what happened to the young girl, wouldn't he also be tied to whatever was freaking out Dominique? And wasn't she the real reason he was sitting under a bridge in the pouring rain holding an unregistered firearm, ready to put the hurt on another man?

Ever since Dominique stopped calling him, he had begun feeling anxious and afraid. His longing for his lover, his best friend and his reason for being, grew insatiable. This jonesing sat burning on his chest like a brick baking in the sun. Raw-knuckled heartbreak. God, he missed her. She had been and always would be his best of everything. Even his best trouble. But trouble was what Dominique had found by coming back. Real trouble. Not the Delilah kind. Something much worse. He knew this because he wasn't alone anymore. Despite putting up a monster-sized emotional wall, she had been able to crack his crusty shell. Now he could feel her breathing on top of his skin, small thin tentacles reaching inside, tapping out S.O.S. on his heart.

They had both developed telepathic feelers when they were still quite young. It happened soon after Little Niqui started fighting a cosmic war against unbidden forces. And that was the other thing. One day with no obvious provocation, his friend changed from a sweet and gentle child to an unhinged creature that sometimes reminded him of a frothing rabid dog. Someone else had taken over her brain and was driving her actions. After that, it was Little Niqui herself who guided Darnell with secret thoughts, showing him where and when to navigate Delilah's inky hollows. Darnell quickly learned that sometimes the other could be a fun and funny friend who could deliver hours of laughter and good-natured mischief. During those times he would play along, swimming side by side with her as if she were only a playful dolphin. But she could also transform into cruel kin who liked to torture Little Niqui mercilessly. That's when the young boy showed steely ruthlessness and crushed her tantrums. Just before Delilah could wring out the last shred of vitality from her host. By the age of ten, the boy knew more about the inner workings of another human being than most people would if they had lived several lifetimes.

But Darnell was human, and his capacity for energy was finite. Over time, committing knowledge and skills to save Little Niqui from herself began to threaten his own health and sap his strength. Run down like that, he became like Sampson, who never did stand a chance against the machinations of the biblical Delilah.

He lost weight, couldn't sleep; several times his mother found him disoriented hiding in a closet. That's when Little Niqui and, later, the adult Dominique, pulled away in order to give Darnell a break, to give him time to heal. He hated it when she'd leave, but he knew she did it to protect him. So he, too, wouldn't go mad. But he always did go mad with grief.

And last time, Dominique stayed away TEN LONG FUCKING YEARS.

She needed him now and that's all that mattered. But where to turn, what to do? To Darnell, it seemed like all points led to that damned prison. Yolanda, the inmates, and Kevin. All of them linked in some way to the "thing" that made her come back to Louisiana. He had a morbid feeling about it.

It felt ancient. Like an old secret had threatened to come undone. Like maybe Dominique came back to make sure that a bad guy got his day of reckoning. A really bad guy. That sounded right in his head, but it got him scared all over again. He felt she was up to her neck in it, and all alone. The only person she could turn to refused to help her. The least Darnell could do now was try to stitch some of the pieces together to help move the process along. Backing Kevin into a corner might be a good start. Too bad he would not know for awhile if the dumbass was actually a dangerous perp, or just the fucker he had always disliked. There was one sure way to find out.

One thing Darnell knew a lot about was lying. Basically, there were two kinds: lying badly that would land you in jail, and lying so well it sounded like the truth. Mastering the latter was something he only accomplished after many trips to central booking during his youth. Elijah, fed up with bailing out his friend every time, told Darnell to pick up a psychology book and learn the signs. He told him to study the *tells* the police used when they questioned suspects. Darnell went to the library and began studying assiduously, because he knew what everyone was saying behind his back. That he lied like a two-year-old.

He learned that a liar usually squirmed a lot, and couldn't look you in the eye when you asked him a question. Similarly, if a man answered your questions without hesitating and at the same looked you straight in the eye, the dude was probably telling the truth. Another thing, an honest man didn't usually sweat, but he might squint some and look confused. That was okay. Sociopaths, on the other hand, usually stood or sat very still, and looked straight ahead. With them there was no body language. Just silence. Their eyes were literally hollow — staring at them could send you straight down into their dark deranged souls.

Darnell would soon put the test to Kevin. But first things first.

He called Dominique's number several times in a row. It went to voice mail each time, just like it did five minutes before. Darnell resisted the urge to bash the phone against the steering wheel and redialed. This time he left a message.

"I miss you."

He might have said more, but hung up as soon as a late model black car turned down Louisa Street. It looked like a scene plucked right out of an old Marvel comic book. The Lexus was an airship that floated through liquid space, parting the rains like they were sharp curtains of glass. He heard crackling in the streets. He drove after it, enjoying the feeling of redemption in his extremities.

FORTY EIGHT

It might as well have been pouring inside of the car. Wet and exhausted, Dominique strained to see beyond the sheets of rain as she crossed the state line. For the next thirty minutes the psychiatrist crawled behind a line of traffic as unprepared for the downpour as she was. Relentless rains this time of year meant hurricanes weren't far behind.

She looked at the clock. Already four o'clock. At this rate she would be late for her counseling session with the inmate. She knew she should push on, but one more stop was calling her name.

The rain had emptied the streets in the French Quarter. Dominique turned off the ignition and leaned into the passenger window until she spotted a faint light at the top of the stairs. The voodoo priestess was at home. She knew showing up unannounced and drenched would scare her old friend. But she had to see to her. It might be the last time.

I wanted you to see with your own eyes that I'm okay now. She's gone and never coming back. This was your dream for me. You never gave up and always cared about me unconditionally. I wished, and still do, that it would have been my luck to be your daughter. I'm only here to thank you for everything and to tell you that I love you.

Asleep in Dominique's favorite mohair chair, Miss Marta woke to an almost soundless rap-tap. It was the vibration in her head that sent her headlong to the back door. A minute later, she couldn't be sure if she was still dreaming, or if her cataracts were cloudier than usual. Dominique walked into her living room looking like a drowned rat. In the last few weeks she had aged ten years, new worry lines carved across her forehead and cheeks. But her old friend was sitting still. As still as a drowned cat could. Eerily calm. Nothing to do but make some tea. Maybe, while she boiled water, Dominique would start screaming or breaking things.

Dominique said, "No tea."

Miss Marta said, "Look at you. You're soaked through and going to catch your death. Why don't you take off those wet clothes, and put on something dry.

Dominique shook her head, "Please just sit with me and listen awhile. I won't be long, I promise. I have an appointment I have to keep at the prison."

Who would Dominique want to meet looking like that? Miss Marta felt shock waves roll over her heart. That Dominique was in trouble was obvious. But what kind of trouble? A new kind?

No storm, no chaos. Not even a faint current of madness. But something was occupying the still pond. She couldn't say why, yet the aging voodoo priestess got the oddest hankering to get up and lock all the doors and windows so Dominique couldn't leave. She didn't want her to go back. Definitely not tonight.

"Honey, maybe you should spend the night. I could make up the extra room…"

Dominique got up and slowly paced across the living room floor. The soft rhythmic click of her heels on the wood floor contrasted a painful outpouring of words.

"Disgusting things used to happen to our people. I know they still do sometimes. But I've stumbled onto something more depraved than I thought humanly possible. I know—or I will know when I get back—who committed such vulgar acts against our children.

"They were such young innocent babes. Their only sin, poverty. Oh, Miss Marta." For a second Dominique looked like she might accept Miss Marta's invitation to stay.

"Dominique. If what you say is true, don't you think you should call the police? The FBI, maybe?"

"Yes, I will do that. As soon as I can be sure whom is responsible."

"But you already know, don't you. I see it in your eyes." Miss Marta sat down opposite Dominique and shut her own.

Dominique said, "You're probably wondering why things are different. Or maybe you've already guessed. I chased her away. When I started searching for the truth, I realized it would be easier to do it without Delilah.

"She's actually the one that pointed me towards the evil doing. But then she started interfering with my investigation. I know it's hard to believe. But Miss Marta, it's over. I'm whole, and I'm going to make up for a lot of lost time real fast."

"I don't like this. It feels wrong. Bad timing."

Dominique remembered what her young self said just before the car veered into the ditch. "*...You're already here. Don't leave.*"

Dominique said, "Timing is never right. Ask your son. Speaking of Darnell, please tell him I'm good. Tell him it was always him. Nothing ever mattered like him." Dominique squeezed Miss Marta's hands gently. "That I believe in him. Tell Darnell I know he can do it. He *can* be happy."

"Don't go," Miss Marta pleaded.

They embraced and Miss Marta saw Dominique's tattered features lift for a moment. Goodbye dearest child.

Back on the freeway, Dominique stopped trying to fight the rain, stopped trying to focus on the murky white lines to guide her turns. In this weather, she was the only one on the road to Elysian Fields. One hand rested lightly on the steering wheel while the other gently rolled the warm cell phone over and over again against her palm. Tears fell from the corners of her eyes and mixed with the watery world in front of her.

"I miss you."

FORTY NINE

Kevin's strange reaction was not on any list of any psychology book Darnell had ever read.

After Darnell slid out of the car, it took him only five steps before he had Kevin by the throat and slammed up against the metal garage door. If the dude had something to hide, he wasn't exhibiting the usual signs. At all. Instead of sweating and looking away, or dithering and looking scared like a good man might, Kevin barred his teeth and started screaming at his attacker. Then he snapped when Darnell stepped back and pointed the gun at him.

"You stupid fucker. You tricked me," Kevin spat.

"That's the least of your worries, asshole. Tell me about that night, before I forget what I'm doing and shoot you."

But Kevin wasn't listening. "You better have a damn good reason for dragging me down here." Not until he tried moving past Darnell, but couldn't because his own car was in the way, did the psychiatrist notice the weapon. He wouldn't show fear.

"What do you want? Why did you text me?"

It wasn't going the way Darnell wanted. The stupid white man was mad and making him feel like he did something wrong. He would change that. His solid punch connected with a rock-hard stomach, yet he managed to knock Kevin to his knees. Hearing him moan through sharp intakes of breath gave Darnell momentary satisfaction. That's right fool, no time in the gym is going to protect you from another man's righteous anger.

Trying to straighten, Kevin asked, "What the fuck did I do? What? What do you want?"

"Okay, that's better. Now think real hard. What I could I possibly want from you?"

"Is this still about Dominique?"

Darnell wished he had it in him to punch the idiot again. "Why would you ask that?"

"Look, we haven't hooked up for years. Face it, she dumped both of us. I just work for her now. I moved on. Why can't you?"

"Kevin." He said his name the way cops always said *Darnell*, just before they accused him of something or other. He liked the view from the other side. "Are you scared yet? Afraid of dying?"

"You want me scared? Fine. I just pissed my pants. So ask me whatever the fuck you want me to know. Ask me and let me go."

"Is that what Yolanda said? 'Let me go?' Or was it, 'Please? Please don't do this. Oh, God, don't do this.' "

This time he spit out the words with so much hatred, Darnell started to think he'd made a serious mistake. "What are you saying to me?"

"You trying to deny it? I know you did it man. It's murder now. And there's a witness."

Darnell thought Kevin was starting to look like a mangy wolf, readying to spring. Flat wet yellow hair separated and rose in clumps revealing pink scalp. Red-rimmed eyes looked like they could pop out any second, the chest and arms coiled up tight, the hairs on the psychiatrist's wrists and hands bristling. Too much adrenaline. Too close for comfort. Darnell backed up a step, hoping the unhinged man wouldn't grab for the gun. He didn't want to shoot. He only wanted answers.

So did Kevin. "Who?" he demanded. "Who saw me?"

"Daisy can make your car in Desire, the same time Yolanda was raped. Like the rest of us, she keeps good watch."

"That's fucking great. A homeless woman saw a car like mine. There's got to be dozens of cars like mine around here."

Darnell laughed. "Really? Around here? Even if there were, not with a scratch like that." They both stared at a long keystroke across the back passenger quarter panel.

Kevin shuddered. "You did that? Okay, I was here the night Yolanda was attacked. But it's not what you think."

Darnell leveled the gun and shook his head. "What I think is, after I blow your brains out, our streets are going to be safe again." For a moment he had Kevin's full attention.

Darnell shoved the gun barrel into Kevin's ear forcing his head against the metal wall. When he pulled back they both resumed screaming at each other. Their yelling was so loud against the torrent of wind and rain that they barely heard the sirens until the first squad car was almost on top of them.

FIFTY

Futrell didn't mind hard rain. He rather enjoyed what it did to his perception of the world. He liked that it could melt ugly realities into vague harmonies, deconstructing even broken-down streets and neglected houses into impressionistic paintings. The way its slippery lens rearranged the natural world into niches and cocoons, creating in each tree and bush an asylum against the mounting storm of industrial development. He hated it when it played tricks on his eyes.

To the east, the water flowing in the canal looked bright and sparkling and innocent. Not at all like what it really was—a noxious brown water highway that, with each passing storm, pushed further and further down on soil layers. The sheriff figured at this rate, it wouldn't take much more than today's rain to bring down the levee and the floodwall. If that ever happened, all of eastern New Orleans would flood and float away. Another misconception was the crime scene itself. From a hundred yards away, it appeared secured. The sheriff counted eight marked and three unmarked squads, all grouped tightly around the armed conflict. The parking lot danced feverishly with color and sound. It wasn't until he sidled up to the first vehicle that Futrell realized that the flashing and peeling and rumbling were just part of the usual New Orleans dog and pony show. Eight out of the eleven vehicles were still occupied. A couple of the police were smoking cigarettes, others drank coffee and chatted with their partners. Apparently a black gangster pistol-whipping a well-dressed defenseless white man still wasn't considered enough drama to get these officials to leave the comfort of their dry vehicles and venture out into the storm. Maybe if the water on their windshields turned bloody red, and brain and gut spatter tangled up inside the windshield wipers, just maybe then New Orleans' finest in blue might start taking their jobs seriously.

The three police in raincoats standing in front of the fracas seemed as ineffective as the cops in the cars. One had a bullhorn and every few minutes repeated, "Put your weapon down. Raise your hands and turn around slowly." The other two, one female and one male, leaned on their cars, weapons drawn and pointed, but they looked like they were ready to take a nap.

The ringmaster himself, Sergeant George Afreesman, a native of Elysian Fields and Futrell's old high school classmate, sat inside his personal car, a souped-up 1990 Dodge Charger. The stout balding officer—not quite eligible for retirement, but nonetheless trying out the lifestyle for size—was scrolling the pages of his computer, a cigarette in one hand, a half-eaten candy bar on his lap, when Futrell leaned into his window.

"Good afternoon, George. I see you've got things under control here." The sergeant's eyes quickly shot straight ahead. After seeing that Darnell and Kevin were still standing upright, he rolled the window down a crack to face Futrell with raised eyebrows and a surprised smile.

"Christ, Leroy. I swear, you lost or something? Or are you just taking a break from wrasslin' all 'em snakes and alligators?"

"You know me, I like to come up to do a little shopping and sightseeing. Looks like a good show right here."

"Not for long." The cop sucked loudly on his filterless nail coffin. "See that goon with the gun? That's Big-Pain-In-The-Ass, Darnell. Hell, he's harmless. Normally. I just can't figure out why he would put a gun on a white man in the canal. And what do you suppose the white man is *doing* here in the first place?

"Maybe going straight fried the dude's brain? What you think, Leroy?"

Futrell didn't get a chance to respond, because just then a black Hummer lit up with as many lights as a football stadium during Homecoming rolled noisily into the parking lot. "Shit to damn. Elijah." The sergeant shook his head. The sheriff wasn't sure if Afreesman was reacting to the man getting out of the Humvee, or if he'd burned his fingertips taking a final pull on the butt.

An impressive man of gigantic proportions, holding a black umbrella over a diminutive woman wearing a purple flowered coat and white headscarf, walked quickly over to the parade of vehicles. A female officer came out of one of the squads extending her arms in the universal "don't come any closer," stance. Elijah kissed his companion on the head, handed her the umbrella and walked back to stand by his truck. The police could not or would not keep the septuagenarian back. Futrell followed her.

Miss Marta said, "Darnell, you listen to me! Put that gun down. You got it all wrong. It was never Kevin. He comes around here because he's sweet on Marcelle. You can't change things. Get that through your thick head now."

The bullhorn sputtered, "Move away ma'am. He's a dangerous man. Ma'am, move on, now."

Even though the officer was only twenty yards from Miss Marta, he kept on admonishing her over the loudspeaker. She strode until she was practically on top of Darnell. And then she turned around.

"I know he's not dangerous. He's my son."

Futrell watched in amazement as no police moved to restrain the woman. He guessed that not even the law wanted to mess with New Orleans' most powerful voodoo priestess.

Darnell didn't bother to turn around, but the incredulity in his voice could not be disguised. "Mom? Get out of here. You could get shot."

"Oh, don't worry, no one is going to shoot me. These fine police just want to make sure you don't mess up anything here on the levee. Now, what did I say? Put that gun down."

"I know what I'm doing. He killed Yolanda. I'm not leaving until he confesses. Even better that the police can hear it for themselves."

"Kevin's not confessing to anything because he didn't *do* anything. Why haven't you figured that out yet? Listen son, I talked with Dominique today. She and Delilah had a fight."

Darnell smirked. He was a kid again, standing in his kitchen listening to his mother tell some tall tale about a relative he might or might not have met when he was only a toddler. "Yeah, who won?"

"This time, the right person. That's what I'm trying to tell you. She came to me, clear-headed, confident. She told me things. About the one who hurt Yolanda, and there were others we never even heard of.

"Son, the evildoer is not in New Orleans."

The finality of those words caused Darnell to stumble backward a few steps before letting go of Kevin. Before turning all the way around to face his executioners, he handed Kevin the gun and whispered, "Sorry, dude. Seems I was wrong."

The two men looked at each other with disbelief and then at the burgeoning crowd in front of them. Everyone was out of their cars pointing weapons.

Kevin shook so hard his words sounded like they were filtered from a carnival ride. "Where did these...people, police come from? How would they know to come out here, in the rain?"

Darnell raised his hands and turned around slowly. "Man, you can't see them. But they're all around you. In the past couple of years, the homeless made themselves an invisible tent city here among the abandoned trucks and trailers. And thanks to human services, every single one has a cell phone to use for emergencies. When we intruded on their hood, they called the cops."

Kevin wondered if he was going into shock, because despite nearly losing his life and still hanging onto an illegal gun, he began to laugh hysterically. Even Darnell snorted at the idea of getting busted by folks dressed in layers, sleeping in cardboard boxes next to carts that held everything they owned. As he was being dragged to the back of a police car, Darnell saw three of them slither through the opening next to the garage, where for more than thirty minutes he'd held Kevin hostage. Miss Marta said a few words to Darnell through the police car window and when she turned to go nearly smacked into the sheriff. She implored the tall man wearing a cowboy hat with her eyes.

"Ma'am?"

"You the sheriff from Elysian Fields." Then she screamed. "He's in the house. He's in the house." She crouched down to the ground and pointed behind her. "There, right now. The one with the bad gris gris on him since he was a boy. He wears a mask, even when he's not wearing one."

Darnell heard his mother yelling and felt it rain over his heart. He suddenly understood that it was too late. He called the sheriff over. Futrell motioned to the officer to lower the window. "What?"

Darnell said, "My ma's right. You gotta go back now. You gotta hurry, man."

FIFTY ONE

Lerance hadn't thought of his old life in so long, it now felt like rummaging through someone else's history.

Before the shooting, before prison, and before this Louisiana circus tent, there was the unspoiled routine that had started each morning at five a.m. When he was still able to walk into his own private sanctuary: an L-shaped shower decorated in geometric mosaic so intricate, it looked like colorful beading or embroidery. When he stood next to the hand-painted tiles of Andalusian design, under the perfect pressure of the brass showerhead, it had sometimes felt like a religious experience; he wasn't just getting clean, he was having himself a baptism.

The room had no door, only an arched opening that led to his spacious dressing room. After toweling dry, the doctor would put on a two hundred dollar shirt followed by an equally expensive, handmade silk Italian tie. Black Michael Toschi shoes, shined to perfection, waited for him at the top of the stairs. At the bottom of the marble staircase, he smelled breakfast. Cook always prepared some variation of scrambled eggs mixed with in-season sautéed vegetables, sliced oranges and mangos, fresh figs, and toasted Ciabatta bread. When he finished eating, he was served a very tall and frothy cinnamon latté, which he took along with several national newspapers to the screened-in porch, and read for the next thirty minutes.

After checking for messages on his Blackberry, the doctor drove himself in a 2003 Bentley downtown, and parked in the first stall near the wrought-iron gates that heralded Dolphin Orthopaedic of Miami. On Monday, Wednesday, and Friday, he was in clinic. Starting at 8:30 a.m., and finishing at 3:30 p.m., Lerance Lemartine spent twenty minutes making each patient feel safe, comfortable and cared for, just before scheduling them for surgery. Knees and hips were his specialty. He spent Tuesdays and Thursdays replacing them for his golf buddies, movie stars, and every flavor of athlete.

They came from across the country and all over the world to be cut by the young surgeon. He hadn't built his reputation on good diagnosis and skillful operations alone. In the ortho world, Dr. Lemartine was known for research and applied innovation. He believed joint replacements should improve people's quality of life, and strove to minimize recovery times and increase the wear durability of the artificial devices. When his peers took vacation time to sail their yachts in regattas or relaxed in all-inclusive resorts in the Caribbean, Lerance was off to Belgium or Canada, to learn all about new materials and techniques that helped limbs return to natural flexibility and movement. His outcome research had been presented at national and international orthopedic conferences, and he was regularly published in a number of medical journals. Just before getting arrested, he had become a consulting editor for *The Journal of Modern Orthopedics*.

A few years back, the board of directors of his clinic and surgery came up with the bright idea that Dr. Lemartine should start volunteering. If he could be seen operating in underprivileged nations, his own institution would gain a boost in public relations, attracting even more wealthy donors. So he joined Doctors Without Borders, and for three weeks each fall, Dr. Lemartine donated his skills in Bhutan. After that he went to Haiti.

Finding the hospital conditions on the island nation deplorable due to lack of access to water and electricity, Dr. Lemartine arranged to have his patients flown back to Miami for surgery. After staying an additional three weeks, when the last young patient finally left town, Lerance's wife Clarissa began to suspect something was up. Unfortunately for her, she decided to poke around her husband's clinic. As a result, less than a week later, she was dead as a doornail from a gunshot wound delivered to the chest.

Caught up in reverie, hypnotized by the uniform vibrations of steady rain, the former doctor almost fell off his bed when the guard walked into his room.

Dave was uncharacteristically snapping his gum and arching his eyebrows. Something wasn't right. But Lerance got up and walked in front of the guard because he knew it was time for his session with Dr. Doucette.

The jaunt down the skinny hall was an adventure in dampness. The rain pummeled the metal roof overhead like bullets while the humidity inside attacked his perfectly healthy lungs. When they stopped in front of the door, Lerance walked his customary ten paces back so Dave could open it. After the guard used his key to turn the lock, he turned back to face the prisoner.

Dave said, "Dr. Doucette's still en route. She called to say she's running about thirty minutes late."

"Why does she want me here early?" Lerance asked.

"Because she's the boss."

"So, what? Are we expected to stand outside her door until she gets here, whenever that is? Why couldn't I wait in my room?"

"You're going to wait inside her office."

Lerance took a step while Dave opened the door. "Let me get this straight. You and I are going to stare at each other for the next half hour. Or maybe we could play a hand of gin rummy? Don't you think this is a little insane?"

"No, I think that sounds sane. What's really crazy is that I gotta let you inside while I stand out here and wait for Dr. Doucette to get back." Lerance didn't bother to ask why. Dave would only answer, "Because she's the boss."

Dave turned the light on and closed the door. The office looked empty without its mistress occupying her throne at the big mahogany desk. Lerance sat down in his usual chair and tried to make his mind go blank. But the rain would not let him.

The rain slapped tirelessly against the bay window and he thought of his mother. She had once stood in front of a similar window looking for signs of the boy. Earlier that evening so many years ago, she had run out after him in the pouring rain, against the thunder and lightning. When she finally came back, it was to stand alone, wet, dejected, against their front window, willing him to come back. What happened next was all Dean's fault. Because of Dean Cobb Jones, his family had been forced to desert their childhood home in the middle of the night, and look for safety inside the anonymous Florida metropolis. Lerance was happy that Dean was dead.

As far back as he could remember, his mother had never run after anyone before. To say she was cold was a colossal understatement. Lydeah could look you in the eye and still not see you. The woman gave everyone short shrift, including her husband. Everyone, except her pro bono patients. These kids came to see her on Saturday mornings, driven in from miles away by poor bedraggled parents. After a thorough examination and usually within an hour, they were sent home with pills, suggestions and get-well wishes. Some stickier cases spent the night. A select few camped out for weeks, or even months. Dean had stayed the longest. He arrived in May, finished out the school year with the Lemartine's, and remained for the next thirteen months. He ate healthy food, studied with a tutor, swam and fished with other kids who came and went out of the clinic, and generally blended in with his new surroundings. Until the day he took off in a car—the one they bought for him—and never came back. The following spring he was dead, killed by his own hand. When they found him, he was lying on a seedy bar basement floor, far, far away from the touch of the woman who had loved him.

As he watched his mother standing, dripping wet against the window, whispering the other boy's name into the night, Lerance felt his first stirrings of hatred. Because he saw up close what he had been missing. A parent's unconditional love.

Almost unconditional love.

Dave walked in and stared at Lerance. Lerance stared back. When Dave was out in the hall again, Lerance noticed the time. Ten minutes after six. Dave would check on him every ten minutes. Time to get to work.

FIFTY TWO

Dominique caught a break thirty minutes outside of Elysian Fields. It was drizzling when the sun parted the heavens. Islands in the sky appeared, delicate creamy clouds with ribbons of orange and purple lace sewn into their edges. If Dominique had believed in signs, this would be it. But she didn't. She wasn't superstitious or spiritual. She had never sought refuge at Miss Marta's for religious exorcism. She went to the voodoo priestess because the gentle woman loved her fiercely and with all of her heart. But maybe she should have. Without warning the air stilled, the world became motionless, the present and future receded. The car she drove was really a time machine, bringing Dominique back to that fateful summer when she spent two months on the French Riviera with her best friend.

And Nadine.

Bobby Beales had come through. He paid for a plane ticket for Darnell to accompany the Doucettes to France. Although the young boy was not considered part of the grant program that sought to teach the world's best and brightest children, the sponsoring French organization arranged Darnell's accommodations and even supplied him with copies of schoolwork materials. This last part was Nadine. If her daughter had one failing, it was her aversion to mathematics. Especially algebra. Not so for her best friend who loved problems that used numbers and symbols. It wasn't that Dominique couldn't do math, but she hated it so much that having Darnell there would help her daughter concentrate.

In the beginning, Dominique resisted taking the math courses. When she found out that her study companion would be Darnell, she threw herself into learning all she could about the science of measurement. He made her practice, something the little genius had never done before. She practiced her lessons during her free time in the afternoons; afterwards she allowed him to quiz her. By summer's end, she'd gained a strong handle on complex mathematical operations and processes. When she was finally able to do the problems in her head like he could, he complimented her, telling Dominique he was proud. She loved that Darnell was proud of her for practicing, and not because she was smart. Thirty years later she could still see her own look of joy as he said those words, reflected back into his deep-set dark blue eyes.

Sheriff Futrell floored the gas pedal as soon as the rain let up. He tried the prison phone number again. It always went to voicemail. Where was Dave? Normally at this time he was at the front desk checking the screens, answering the phone. Next he tried Dominique's cell. It rang and rang. The last couple of times he blocked his number so she wouldn't see his name. He suspected that in the beginning she hadn't picked up because *Sheriff Futrell* appeared on caller ID. Now he didn't know.

Futrell wished there were time to pull over and read the file again. She fascinated him; the real Dominique came to life in those pages. Even after having been so utterly wounded on the inside, he had never known anyone to fight so bravely to help strengthen the world outside of her. She sacrificed peace of mind and personal love, to find justice for those who, because of the roll of the dice, never had a chance on their own. Normally, the sheriff didn't believe in crackpot liberalism, all that freewheeling gooey generosity that served to keep downtrodden folks—well, down. But he could relate to what she was doing now. She had become an avenging warrior. Completely fearless. Too fearless. If he didn't get to her in time, he would never be able to tell her how proud he was of her.

Dominique's thoughts raced backwards. Before France, there was Treasure House. That's what it would always be to her. Treasure House and all that the words implied: the riches and glory of spending time with the only person that really knew her.

Whenever people thought of instinct or second-sight, they usually attributed the gift to something supernatural, to otherworldly forces. Dominique thought instincts were much more complex than that. What the eye glimpsed and the brain tried to sort and compartmentalize could total a thousand discrete steps. Too many for the conscious mind to grasp and assimilate. A sound carried by the wind, a current from behind, the whispers in the streets, the cries from above. The fresh wounds in one girl's heart thirty years earlier mirrored in the broken spirit of flowing orange. Turned and kneaded, folded and pressed—a fresh idea reconstituted from the deposits of all that the senses tried to preserve and filter.

Dominique had not thought of the young girl, Destiny, for three decades.

The only reason she and Darnell were allowed to play at Treasure House was because Dave and Davina Treasure had taken their severely ill daughter out of state for medical treatment. Little Niqui and Darnell were still in France when she finally came home. Everyone said how much the girl had changed. Once sweet and chatty, the teen withdrew from her parents and everyone else on the block. A few months later she became social again, but truant at school and oblivious of the consequences. She had started drinking and smoking, and dressing seductively. By the time she turned fourteen, right before the school year ended, Destiny was pregnant. She lost the baby in her third trimester, and her own life a few weeks later. Destiny was home alone in her bedroom, listening to music, when teenaged boys broke in looking for drugs and money. When she went into the kitchen to get a glass of milk, one of them shot her three times.

That year Little Niqui was too preoccupied with Delilah's shenanigans to pay much attention to the social woes of others. But her alter did. And it was then that the paths of Destiny, Little Niqui, and the young predator-heir apparent crossed parallel worlds.

FIFTY THREE

Lerance couldn't believe that once he thought this room was beautiful.

He swiveled in his chair, trying to make sense of the oddly juxtaposed artwork and other objects in Dominique's office. He turned around and studied the shadowbox behind him. It contained something like pressed flowers jammed into a weird-looking vase. Upon closer inspection he saw they were actually stick-figured people trying to get out of a jail cell. Why hadn't he noticed the mish-mash of styles before? Collections that must have held meaning, but not a scintilla of design value.

Everywhere he looked he was struck by the vulgarity of color where reds and greens, and bright yellows dominated. Geometric designs clashed with Victorian copycats. And those were just the floor rugs. The crap on the walls took the cake. Where he would have hung his spoils of success, everything from diplomas and awards, to framed watches — gifts from football players — and Tiffany sconces or Palmer glasswork, she had displayed unrelated collections and memorabilia. Lerance almost laughed out loud. Pretty tacky, Ms. Psychiatrist-to-the-World. Next time you decide to move into Southern living, hire yourself a decorator first.

He walked over to the bay window to look at two wanna-be cubistic posters on either side, which were supposed to signify the New Orleans jazz scene. One of them was frayed around the edges, like it had born one too many moves, or maybe it came from a yard sale. Most distracting were the scores of framed thank-you notes that lined the tops of bookshelves and filing cabinets. Written in mostly cramped illiterate scrawl, they were all acknowledgements made by children, the homeless, and a myriad of crazy ex-cons.

She had told him they were cut from the same cloth. She actually thought they were alike? Because they both scored high on achievement tests? Skipped a few grades?

He was born to doctors. She came out of the ghetto. Her streets were flooded by gangsters. He grew up surrounded by woods and orchards. Later his property was protected behind tall fences and a gate, and a guard in a guardhouse. She spent her life's work living in thatched-roofed shacks, ramshackled mud huts, and run-down apartments in all the wrong parts of town. Even in New Orleans, she had picked a small non-descript crib. As a child, Dominique was coddled, maybe even loved. He certainly wasn't. She had bad taste in art. They had nothing in common.

Or did they? He might have something in common with Delilah. With any luck it would be Dominique's double that would arrive late for their session tonight.

He wandered over to the bookshelves. Poetry by Langston Hughes, Emily Dickinson, Sylvia Plath, Raymond Carver. Novels by Toni Morrison, memoirs by Patricia Hample, Frank Conroy, and Zora Neale Hurston. His own bookshelves had held autographed copies of guides to business and finance, and a few biographies of famous athletes—none of which he'd read, but which always seem to impress his patients.

Okay, that took all of five minutes. Lerance tried to find something to read. But there were no magazines lying around. No newspapers, no sports pages. Maybe she kept the good stuff inside her desk. With any luck, he'd find something dirty. He walked over to the front of the desk. He sat down in her chair and started pulling drawers open. The inside of the middle drawer looked like a smaller version of the top of the desk. Neatly lined paper clips, note pads, an extra calendar, pens, sharpener. The left-hand drawers contained phone books, tape recorders and a couple of digital cameras. The right top drawer was empty. The bottom one, locked.

Where was she? And why was she keeping him waiting? He had better things to do than sit here and analyze her unfortunate choice in aesthetics and the all-too-revealing anal-retentive contents of the desk.

Maybe he should try to get inside the locked drawer. Wasn't there a key somewhere? He found it next to the pencil sharpener. But it didn't fit. Lerance ran his fingers slowly under the drawer. Then very gently, he pushed the office chair back and slid onto the floor. Lying on his back, the underside of the desk was dark. He moved his hands along the top and the sides until he felt the corner of a small envelope in the back. He pushed on it until it gave way and fell onto to the floor. He scooped it up, slipping out of the narrow hollow.

When Dave poked his head into the room, Lerance was swiveling to and fro in his chair, eyes fixed upward and blinking at the slow moving fan.

"Hold on to your britches, Bubba," Dave said. "She'll be here in another ten minutes."

FIFTY FOUR

Dominique didn't call Dave when she got to House of Mithras.

She parked in the back and peered out the front window of her car. The antebellum prison looked like a lone sentry planted against a combative sky. Only drizzle remained while dark crescent clouds hovered and separated, offering up the world a lozenge of blue. It was as if the damned and the furious were waging a battle over the only remaining real estate left in heaven. She wished she had the time to stick around to find out who would win.

After punching in her code, Dominique strode down a long corridor until she reached the surveillance center. She leaned on an office chair, hypnotized by the always-moving images across multi-unit video walls. This was where every room, every visitor, all movements were caught, displayed and transmitted to a receiving center in Baton Rouge. Intelligence programs tracked people moving to and from high security areas, and catalogued and separated authorized from unauthorized personnel by areas and times. High levels of noise and sudden and quick movements were checked and analyzed by the computer, and sent by satellite to the receiving center, which was always staffed 24/7 by actual people. If human monitors became concerned by unusual activity at House of Mithras, they would call first and wait for instruction. Barring no answer at the prison, they would immediately alert the nearest authorities to dispatch an army of law enforcement to the site. Normally at this time Dave would be in here, too, a set of human eyes and ears ready to identify, evaluate and respond. But tonight she had sent Dave to her office to stand guard, while Lerance waited inside.

Dominique found the other three guards on the screens. One sat outside the dormitories on the second floor; another kept tabs on the main entrances. The third guard was stationed outside, patrolling the courtyards. She and Kevin had given explicit orders that staff was not to monitor the individual counseling rooms. Kevin's and her offices were off limits to surveillance. They said it was to maintain privacy and respect for the individual, during those vulnerable and exposed therapy sessions.

That didn't mean they couldn't.

Cameras had been installed in the two offices and could be turned on quickly when it was determined that conditions posed an imminent threat to staff or prisoners. All you needed was a code. Dominique typed it in. She waited. Almost a minute went by before her office illuminated the screen. Lerance looked impassive. She heard a door squeak open and saw Dave poke his head in to tell the inmate that Dr. Doucette would be arriving in ten minutes. When the door shut again, Lerance took his bored gaze upward and stared at the unevenly rotating ceiling fan blades. Occasionally they made scraping sounds and slowed down. Dominique smiled knowing Lerance would be obsessing over the noise and rickety quality of the mansion's cooling system. And that it would never occur to the inmate that the motor housing covered by a copper-filigreed encasement was hiding a sophisticated camera outfitted with a fish eye lens.

Dominique stole a glance at her watch. If he didn't do something soon, she would have to shut everything down and split. She was about to quit the program when he got up. And then the penny dropped. The prisoner put his right hand down his pants. When he pulled it out, he was holding her blue plated Smith & Wesson Sigma 40VE.

Before Dominique left the room, she erased the footage and turned off the camera. There had been no transmission of what she had just seen, and no one would ever know about it, because earlier the psychiatrist had neglected to input a series of commands that would have enabled the system to simultaneously share images with Baton Rouge.

————————————

Sheriff Futrell drove quickly, wishing he had brought along his camera. He was following a half-bowl shaped cloud that had just separated from its lighter more brilliant half. In between, a sliver of the bluest sky appeared. Immediately, the Biblical parting of the sea came to mind. The cloud suspended nearest the earth was swollen and heavy, primed by the atmosphere to unleash millions of droplets.

At the guard station, Futrell pushed a speaker button and announced himself. Soon a guard wearing a hooded slicker opened the gates for the sheriff. Futrell nodded to him and started the drive to the back. He slowed down to watch another hooded guard lumber across the grounds on the way to the mansion.

"What the hell are you doing, Dave?"

FIFTY FIVE

Dominique leaned heavily against her office door, shaking her head at the guard. She said, "Dave, I need a favor. I left my satchel in one of the outer buildings. My laptop is in there. While I get started with Lerance, would you please find it and bring it up to me?"

"Dr. Doucette, you know I can't do that. I can't leave you unattended."

"I need my notes from the computer for the session. It will only take a few minutes. I'd do it myself, but I'm already late."

Dave was unmoved. "Dr. Doucette, this is against all regulations. I just can't."

"Yes, you can. Please stop worrying. You have my permission this time. Besides, you'll be leaving me alone with Lerance."

_____

Crazy woman. First she gives me the dressing down of my life about that shelter incident. Says I gotta stay put at all times, or else. But when it's convenient for her, she changes the rules. Now I'm supposed to leave her alone with a freaking murderer. It's probably a test. She must think I'm stupid.

Dave slipped on a slicker and grabbed his radio. Before he went out the door, he ducked into the surveillance center and pressed a few keys.

FIFTY SIX

Dominique strolled into her office, placed her shoulder bag on the desk, sat down, and took out a notepad. She waited for the inmate to question her tardiness. When he didn't say anything, she fixed him with apologetic eyes.

"I'm sorry for being late. I was in Mississippi earlier and it rained all the way coming back. There were winds and backups and we all just crawled through most of Louisiana …"

"Did it rain inside the car? Or do you drive a convertible?"

Dominique said. "Excuse me?"

"You look like hell. Why were you in Mississippi?"

Lerance was showing signs of discomfort. He looked like he wanted to get up and stretch. Or unbutton his pants.

"Why don't you finish telling me your story?"

Lerance cocked his head slightly and smirked.

Dominique continued, "The reason for your fascination with being black. With black people."

He leaned forward and clasped his hands. "You first. What's going on?"

Dominique pulled a sticky strand of hair away from her cheek and smiled broadly. "You're right. I must look a fright.

Normally, I would care. A lot. But today, well let's just say I look the way I feel."

His handsome face was framed in undisguised contempt. "What the hell are you talking about? I thought I...we were going to have a counseling session. Instead, Dave pulls me out of my room and drags me in here to wait alone for more than a half hour. And now you're talking in tongues. It is you, isn't it, Dr. Doucette? Or are you someone else today?"

If Dominique felt a sharp pain stab her in the temple, she didn't show it, instead, she got up suddenly and slung her bag over her shoulder. She strode to the bay window and looked out. Patches of royal blue dotted the sky, a strip of burnt sienna cloud streaked through the lowering sun.

"It's funny how people in small towns always remember every detail of their history. And how they love to gossip. Especially about former famous neighbors." Dominique turned slightly stealing a look at the inmate. He was still in his chair, his eyes were studying the floor.

Dominique said. "In Dauphine, Mississippi, the tales of a doctor husband and wife team are still clear in the minds of those whose wounds feel as fresh today as the day they were cut."

"You went to my hometown? Why?"

Dominique slipped off her shoulder bag and leaned on the windowsill, her back to the inmate.

"You bewitched me. I had to know everything about you. But when I started digging, I came up with more questions than answers. For instance, why would a preeminent surgeon kill his wife and *not* want a trial?" Dominique waved her hand dismissively. "I know what you said, that you couldn't live with the horror. That you deserved punishment. I can still hear the violins, Lerance. People ate up those morsels like slices of American apple pie. I got to give it to you. You're really good."

She glanced back again. Still sitting in the chair, legs splayed, head down.

"But just a few years later, you applied to this program. Forget the part about my tricking you. You came here of your own free will. Then what? After a couple of weeks, you called in Dupree. Saying you wanted to transfer back to the state pen. Now what in the world could have provoked that?"

When he spoke, he did so quietly, hesitating after each word. There had been no time to practice.

"I really didn't think I could live with the guilt. But you convinced me to stay."

Keeping her back to the room, Dominique rummaged through the shoulder bag. Abruptly she turned and pinned him with her gaze.

"Why don't you admit that your obsession with blacks has more to do with your insatiable need to control them, dominate them, even torture. Especially the young and vulnerable ones.

"Why didn't you tell me about the sex parties? Where poor parents were forced to trade in their kids' innocence for life-saving medicine?"

"This is nuts." Lerance tried to follow the scent. He scraped his chair back, stood up and saw her eyes. They had slipped their gaze over his groin. *She knew.*

"Why didn't you tell me that you watched your parents seduce children? Young black boys and girls. Sex toys for mommy and daddy after clinic hours."

"You don't have the right!"

"What were you? Ten, eleven when they began including you?"

Dominique took a step towards him. "You didn't plead guilty out of remorse. You had a much more compelling reason. Avoiding an investigation. You couldn't risk some savvy prosecutor figuring out that the real reason you killed Clarissa wasn't because of jealous rage. Because she wasn't seeing another man, was she?"

Dominique took another step forward and put a hand behind her back.

"You killed your wife because she discovered you were molesting your Haitian patients. Haitian children. She was going to expose you. So you killed her before that could happen. How am I doing so far?"

Lerance opened and closed his mouth several times without saying a word. He looked down and then squarely at Dominique, for a moment hypnotizing her with beseeching eyes, before turning his head slightly, squinting at something in the distance.

Dominique placed a couple of fingers on the side of her head.

"Am I forgetting something? Oh, yeah. You were leaving House of Mithras like a house-a-fire because of something you lost. Is this it?"

Lerance perked up and watched the scene unfold in slow motion. In one smooth movement, Dominique swung her closed fist in front of him, and then like a stage magician liberated a colorful rubbery mass. Lerance lurched forward on his feet, an audible groan escaped from his throat. From her fingertips, the harlequin mask bobbed and danced like a grotesque puppet.

"Have you been looking for this? Because the inside must be burning with your DNA."

For an instant Lerance appeared wistful; he looked like he wanted to reach over and put the mask on for old time's sake.

She flung the mask across the floor. "Fun's over. Where's the gun? Show me the gun."

Shocked into consciousness, Lerance said, "Since when do you spy on your own office?"

"Don't worry, I erased everything. Now, it's just between you and me."

It didn't matter if he believed her or not, because when the sudden rush of adrenaline hit him he felt more alive than he had in years. He was hydroplaning on power again. Nothing could stop this feeling. He had a gun, and he was holding it over one of the most powerful women in the country. A *black* woman. She would do exactly as he said or he'd kill her. At least she would fear that. Now that was real power.

Lerance took a step to the side and scanned the room solemnly. He lowered the gun slightly and moved his other arm back and forth in time with his visual examination. If not for the loaded weapon, he could have been lecturing at an orthopedic convention.

He said, "You have to admit, all this—what you're doing—pretty stupid, if you knew I had your gun."

Dominique sighed. "Not if I have one, too."

Lerance turned sharply. Another gun. Impossible. But the psychiatrist had used his momentary lapse into full-scale bravado to produce her own piece. The Beretta she had just purchased at Guns and Gardenias. It was pointed at his heart.

"Why?"

'Because you killed Yolanda."

"I didn't."

"You raped a sixteen-year-old shelter worker who was sick. The violence blew out her heart."

Lerance shook his head furiously. "No, that was your conceit. You were so busy parading a cure for killers, you forgot what might happen if one of us got out."

Dominique said, "Not everyone is like you. Some people really want to change and use their experiences to help others."

"Is that what you did? Did you help Yolanda? Really? When you didn't report your own attack?"

Lerance took a step closer to Dominique and raised his gun to her chest. The guns faced off.

"No, you didn't, because you knew that by doing the right thing you'd be jeopardizing your precious reputation. Don't look so surprised. I got it straight from Delilah," Lerance said.

For the first time since meeting with Deneeta and Paul Jones, Dominique felt *terra firma* dissolving into sand. Delilah was gone and she was on her own. But what had the other done behind her back? How much had she told Lerance? What did he know? How would he use it against her?

Dominique wasn't afraid to die, she was afraid of moral uncertainty and that one wrong move might catapult her life back into slavery. Her new skin was not even a day old. How could it possibly stand up against the machinations of an inveterate psychopath? Good god, had Delilah slept with him?

Lerance pounced on Dominique's doubt.

"Shit, I studied dissociative disorder in med school, but I never met anyone who had it. You mean you really can't remember? *Any* of those visits?"

"When did you first meet her?"

Lerance laughed. "Oh hell, I could lie and you'd never know. But why should I, when the truth is so much better than anything I could make up.

"Let's see, the first time was right before the proper Dr. Doucette came to persuade me to sign up for the Desire program. She shows up at prison, tells intake she's Dr. Doucette but tells me she's a close friend of yours and that her name is Delilah. That she knows all about me and my secrets, but that doesn't matter because Dominique, that's you, needs someone like me. And not just for the program. If you get my drift.

"She goes on about how you work too damn hard, all that time spent helping others makes you a real dull girl filled with anxiety and stress. Yada yada yada! She sounded different. Unsophisticated, uses a lot of street slang and sexual innuendo. Her appearance wasn't professional either. I'd say it was more on the provocative side."

"Did you see her again?"

"Twice. But I have a question. Your little plan, whatever the fuck you're doing? Have you forgotten about the guard?"

Dominique said, "Guard? There's no guard. No camera. No guard. Like I said, just you and me."

"But Dave…"

"Gone on a thankless mission. He won't be back for a long time."

"Why, you diabolical little witch."

Lerance said the second visit occurred right after he got to House of Mithras. All the inmates were down on the grounds for recreation. She had pulled him away from a chess match with Kevin, and the two walked behind one of the slave cabins where the cameras didn't reach. This time he had smelled the madness. Delilah was so drunk with ego that she practically pimped out Dominique to the killer. She told him where she lived and said he should visit her. She explained how getting in and out of the homeless shelter was a piece of a cake. When he did show up at her house, he hadn't expected Dominique to put up a fight. And he was damn glad that he had worn the mask. But afterwards, that kleptomaniac Billy Jo stole it.

Delilah appeared for the last time right at the end of the counseling session where Dominique had used props to try to show him how much alike they were. Even after her very passionate efforts, Lerance still wasn't convinced. Just before Dave came in to let him out, the psychiatrist turned.

I understand you better than anyone because I recognize what it is to be you. Don't you know? I can hear the creeping termites under your skin? The ones you can't silence or scratch out. Or tell anyone about. I know about them because every night I go to bed with demons and wake up on fire. I know what you need. I can help you.

Dominique let the revelation stand and asked, "Did she tell you where to find the gun?"

"What do you think?"

The shifting sands had reached a crucible. She struggled to recognize a grain of truth hidden beneath all of the jumble. Still, she failed to see what it was.

While she wrestled with questions, he planned his next move. Using a perfumed whisper, Lerance gambled, "Look, you were right. We are the same. We're special. Condemned to live among those who can't understand us. Once we were voiceless and rejected. But now, thanks to you, thanks to Delilah, we've found each other. That's all that matters now."

Lerance took a step forward.

"I've looked inside you, and I've seen what's missing. Someone like me."

Dominique recoiled and took several steps back. But he kept coming.

Her eyes filled with tears. She had to find the missing link. She needed it to guide her to do the right thing, because she might not get a second chance.

"But you already knew that. Otherwise, why go to all that trouble to find me, get me, keep me?"

He was on top of her. Their guns separated by atoms.

"Get back. I made a terrible mistake. But you will always be a monster."

She needed to know why this was happening. She'd give everything up right now for that one elusive discovery. That thing that humans crave above all. Self-knowledge.

Otherwise, why go to all that trouble to find me, get me, keep me?

Lerance said, "You know what you have to do? Don't you? Give it up. Give me the gun. Come on, you don't want to shoot me. I'll keep your secret. You won't tell mine. It'll be good. Two years, you and me."

His face dimmed and so did the words, because just then she was struck by a bright light. The delayed dawn of answers arrived like sweet forbidden fruit, seeding themselves with abandon where only doubt had lain before.

She looked right through him as she spoke. "I know. I see how it happened. I do.

"Delilah knew that her power was fading. That I didn't really need her anymore. So she went to work and found the one force that could ambush me. Her banishment was to become my punishment. And it all stemmed from a childhood story that both of us remembered, just enough to contaminate each other's lives. She conjured you. A parting gift to me."

Lerance said, "Whoa! You sound as crazy as she was."

Dominique continued. "I read the article on you, but she was the one that remembered the missing girl from my neighborhood.

"You see, everyone thought I was irrationally fixated on you. I convinced myself that you were dynamic, and therefore essential to the program. But deep down, the whole time, I wanted something else. Justice for a little girl whose broken existence had given me the best spring of my life. Even Delilah couldn't know the strength of my conviction. That destroyed little girl's name was Destiny...because of her, I got to be with Darnell.

"There were rumors, but only rumors. Yet they lived on so they could be resurrected one day. That day came when I read the article about Lerance Lemartine killing his wife. The one who didn't want a trial. Who volunteered in Haiti. Whose parents had been doctors. In *Mississippi*. I didn't know it at the time, but the whole Desire program was a just a screen to uncover a child abuser.

"As for Delilah, she was only interested in finding someone even more despicable than herself to settle into my life."

Lerance didn't care about the origins of madness. Or final resolutions. He should have.

He leaned into the remaining space between them and began caressing her gun with his. He felt her slump and straighten. He pulled back again, shaking his head. She should have given up by now. They always did.

Lerance said, "This has to end now. Dave will eventually come back. No one needs to get hurt."

"That's right. So drop the gun."

"You know I can't do that."

She cocked the hammer, but he was faster. By the time his bullet pierced her chest, the trajectory of her bullet was already underway.

When the lawmen flew through the door, their bodies were writhing on top of each other, commingling blood spraying and staining the ancient floor. Futrell pushed Lerance off of Dominique and stuffed a fist into her chest wall, already knowing he could not save her. But he started CPR and continued it until the paramedics arrived.

Six hours later, after the police and emergency vehicles had left, Futrell and his nephew walked down to the surveillance center and watched the battle on the screen. The second time around, Futrell took copious notes.

Futrell said, "How did you do it? I thought cameras in the directors' offices were off limits."

Dave said, "My job was on the line. I worked out the code. Same one they use for everything around here. Mithras."

"Did it transmit to headquarters?"

Dave said, "Nah, I didn't have time to look through the manual, they use different software, so different codes."

Futrell said, "Okay now, erase it. All of it."

"Why? It's evidence. Everything you ever wanted on her."

"I didn't want this. The woman died a heroine. She not only discovered the history of these savage crimes, she ended that whole damned era of depravity. Dominique cared deeply about people. And I misunderstood her. She had real guts. If you release these images to the world, no one will ever know how brave she really was."

"But uncle, she didn't follow the law."

"If she had, he would have been a free man in two years."

FIFTY SEVEN

Testimonies of Billy Jo, Miss Marta, Guyla Rae, and Kevin

"That first time we pulled an all-nighter. I couldn't keep my eyes open. When I woke up, Lerance was just coming back into the shelter," Billy Jo said.

The usual suspects, Billy Jo, Guyla Rae, Kevin and Miss Marta, were seated in a semi-circle facing the sheriff. They each had a file on their lap. Futrell watched them from his cluttered desk. His cigar was still lit in the ashtray, sending clouds of smoke towards the noisy ceiling fan. After taking final inspection of his face in a compact mirror, Billy Jo smoothed down his shirt and met the sheriff's gaze.

Futrell asked, " How did he get in and out?"

Billy Jo said, "The lock was a hundred proof, but the hinges, nineteenth century. He had a system of pulling the door open and closed. When he left, it looked like the door was still shut tight. No one ever noticed. When he returned, he slipped the hinges back on. One time when he was asleep, I searched his knapsack and found the mask."

The sheriff said, "Miss Marta, how did the madness begin?"

"We treated Little Niqui like she was our own personal gift. Trouble was, every time she triumphed, we came around sniffing. It was like puttin' your nose in heaven. It forced her to grow up too fast. Always having to please us all. That's when Delilah showed up.

"But let me back up. Most kids get a big head when they're complimented or given special privileges for their good grades and skills. Not Little Niqui. It made her most unhappy. That beautiful innocent child started to believe the impossible about herself. She thought she had been born defective. Like God or somebody was punishing her by giving her such a big brain. She wasn't allowed to play and laugh like other kids. Cuz that would have interfered with her studies. Her progress made our advancements. It wasn't just her mother. All of us were to blame. We acted like her only usefulness was in making the neighborhood look good. She rebelled by creating the other.

"Delilah on the surface looked like a kid only capable of harmless mischief. She provided the goody-goody a break from performing. But Little Niqui had another secret purpose for her." Miss Marta looked around to see if people were paying attention. They were. "She used the other like a mental hair shirt, you know how those Catholic monks used to wear them for self-abuse. Little Niqui wore her Delilah right next to her tender skin, as punishment for being born wrong."

Guyla Rae set down the file and said, "It appeared that, at least in the beginning, the Delilah character represented carefree youth. Just the opposite of Little Niqui's reality. I can see how both the child and the grownup got enthralled in the rapture. Whether it was for escape or punishment."

Miss Marta said, "In the past, when it got real bad, Little Niqui could always come to me to invoke the spirits. To help suture all those heart wounds that Delilah left behind."

Billy Jo took Miss Marta's hand and looked tenderly into her eyes. "Even spirits can't bind a blistering soul. Dominique believed that she had killed Yolanda."

Kevin closed the file and cleared his throat. The prison director didn't look like himself. His eyes were swollen, the skin around his cheeks raw and flaky, and his hair looked greasy. "And she lost Darnell. Dominique gave up everything she loved in the name of excellence, except her best friend. If it hadn't been for him, Delilah would have destroyed her long ago.

"He was her rock. Her core. During the most painful splits, Darnell was always there to put the pieces back. Until he wasn't."

Sheriff Futrell did not relish the drive back to New Orleans. He'd had nothing to eat, was craving sleep, and mostly just hated the city. But he had one last mission to accomplish, and for that, he had to get the gangster out of central lock up.

On the way, he thought about how long Dominique had carried around so much inherited burden. Yet in one single day, she had both exorcised Delilah from her mind and Lerance from the world. Almost from the time they began inhabiting the earth, each villain in its own way began sucking the life out of it. But with their destruction came her own demise. Even so, she died having lived completely. Even if it was for only one day.

Futrell had called ahead to make sure Sergeant Afreesman was around to sign Darnell's release papers. It took some doing, but the sheriff reminded his old friend about what he saw at the levee, and the city lawman acquiesced.

Darnell was waiting for him when Futrell got to the courthouse steps. The small town sheriff told him that Dominique died a heroine's tragic death and that she had dedicated her last act in life to him. Then he pulled the grieving man to the nearest bench and took out his notes. He put on his glasses and read. After he finished his account of Dominique's last fifteen minutes on earth, he took out a lighter and burned the paper.

Darnell asked, "Christ. Who else knows?"

"My nephew, but he'll keep quiet."

Darnell surprised the sheriff by asking about Kevin.

Futrell said, "Besides needing a shower? He'll be okay. You know, he refused to press charges."

"Seeing Dominique like that again after ten years, I lost it. Her and Kevin standing there at the Davis'." Darnell shuddered. "I walked away and keyed Kevin's car. Later, when that old lady told me she saw a scratched Lexus near where Yolanda was attacked, I thought I had it all figured out."

Darnell brought out a cigarette. Futrell lit it for him.

"I almost killed him."

"That's not what I hear. Come on, I'll give you a ride home."

Inside the car, the sheriff handed Darnell a copy of the Delilah file.

"What . . . shit, no, I don't have to read the file to know how the story went. I've been living that story my whole life."

Near the French Quarter at a stoplight, a clanging streetcar rounded the corner. When it stopped, a dozen uniformed African-American children piled inside.

"I was just a little kid. I thought she was real sometimes. She looked like a different girl, smelled different. There were some good times, but Delilah always went too far. So many times I wanted to run and hide. But I couldn't leave Little Niqui alone."

They drove past cemetery city. Block after block of crumbling above-the-ground cemeteries. Crypts, statues, and gates and fences with wrought-iron tracery—subsisters from the last centuries. Futrell asked. "Why do you think they rode her like that?"

"Are you serious? They thought she had the power. They told her that because she was talented and smart, she needed to take advantage of her God-given blessings in order to carve out her future. But she knew it was all a lie. She was made to carry the mantle of spiritual savior. She was Moses of the 'hood. It was on her to redress all the hurt, all the atrocities, any and all our people had ever suffered. She always knew that they had picked her to do the impossible."

Twenty minutes later they pulled up in front of the Davis'. They sat in silence for a minute before Darnell opened the door and got out. Futrell leaned over and gave him his card.

He said, "She wanted you to be proud of her. She thought you gave up your life to protect her from herself. Dominique wanted to show you that it had all been worth it."

Futrell pointed to the file. "It's all in there. You're going to want to call me after you get done reading it."

"Who says I'm going to read it?"

Futrell said, "I pulled the calls on Dominique's cell. Just so you know, that last message you left her. She heard it."

Darnell nodded and walked up the stairs. He turned around and said, "What's going to happen to the others?"

"Oh, I reckon they'll sit in my jail for a while until the higher ups figure out where to transfer them. Their contracts have to be honored. Kevin says he's going to try to keep them together so they can finish out the Desire program."

The following Sunday Futrell decided to reread his favorite passage in the Delilah file. He thought it might cheer him up. Earlier in the day, the guy on the weather channel said that Hurricane Katrina had formed over the Bahamas and crossed southern Florida as a moderate Category 1 hurricane. Meteorologists weren't sure but thought the storm might weaken; more than likely it would make a second landfall in Louisiana in as little as a week.

The sheriff pulled out his cell phone and pressed the numbers.

"I guess you must have lost my card because I haven't heard from you. Say, I was just about to crack open a beer and read my favorite part in the Delilah file. It's all about that summer you two spent together in France. Now be a good man and shuffle off to the fridge and get your self a nice iced tea or Coke. Then we can read it together."

"Dude, you're crazy. I tried reading some, but it just kills me."

"I'll be waiting on you. Don't take too long."

"Why are you doing this?"

"It's better not to be alone when you read her journal."

EPILOGUE

EXCERPT FROM THE DELILAH FILE
August 5, 2005

Earlier today, at an award ceremony in Washington D.C., I told the world about House of Mithras. That I would be opening the reform prison in just three days. But before I got to do that, something very strange happened to me. Just as I was getting up, after the chairman called me to the podium, I accidentally spilled coffee on my jacket sleeve. When I saw the stain begin to grow and felt hot liquid soak through the fabric and scald my skin, I became catatonic. As if I were possessed by a demon. I wasn't sure if that demon had been my mother, or her. *But later, when it passed, I recalled a summer in France thirty-five years ago that I spent with Darnell. When another spot, this time on a little girl's dress, was never allowed to form. The same summer when I still believed Darnell could save me. Even now, as Delilah creeps closer and closer, threatening me once again with annihilation, I see back with crystal clarity to a time when my best friend introduced me to joy. Nothing lasts but the memories. Below is that day, the best one of my life.*

June 17, 1975–Niqui and Darnell, The French Riviera

The Mediterranean rose up with the sun and burnished the world with a silvery radiance.

The children stood at the top of the hill watching the sea writhe and glimmer like a watery coquette. Its swells rolled and surged, calling endlessly to them. But they always waited until the last possible instant to make their descent. When it was only a hundred yards out, they flew down the floury sands to meet the giant wave. Their small bodies pierced the cool solid shoreline with conquering kicks and shrieks, but each time were made to be completely still, while the sea leaped up for the last time smothering them with mighty kisses.

They played their new game on weekends when the school—much to Nadine's chagrin—instructed the children to stop studying and start enjoying the fresh air. They played and played until their bodies gave out, and all they could do was lie panting with tangled limbs arranged like rag dolls, near the water's edge. That's when Nadine, followed by the nanny, called after them, announcing it was time for lunch.

The international school provided a service woman to look after the children, but Nadine didn't let her near Little Niqui and never paid attention to her companion. So the nanny made Darnell her special project. While the mother set Little Niqui down under the beach umbrella to eat small sandwiches shorn of crust, Mademoiselle Moreau opened up her own picnic basket filled with fresh bread, cheeses, and fruit. She had become quite fond of her handsome dark-skinned charge, always making sure he had as good as the girl.

One afternoon, Nadine declared that Little Niqui should build a sand castle.

"Build me a castle Dominique. Fill it with towers and windows, a moat and drawbridge. And a stable for horses. Atop, make sure there's a princess just like you, who waits patiently for her prince." Nadine cast flinty eyes at Darnell, but he was busy eating and looking off in another direction. "Don't forget to pour in the sea that surrounds the fortress. And child, don't let me see even a single smudge messing up your pretty new dress."

Eventually, Darnell and the nanny set their gazes in the direction of the tiny girl digging and shaping sand near the shore. It was a lot like watching a real house being built. First came the foundation, deep and symmetrical, followed by the ground level which contained a large thick door that actually seemed hinged, along with the requisite moat and drawbridge and a few horses. By the time the last stories were up and the towers in place, its princess looking longingly over a crenellation, the castle was so perfect, without defect or blemish, that it looked like it had been poured out of a factory mold.

A small crowd gathered to inspect the smooth contours and flawless square corners. A man who looked like he wished he'd brought his carpenter's level got on his hands and knees to inspect the tiny details surrounding the drawbridge. Darnell and the nanny exchanged glances and shrugged. They'd seen it all before.

The wind kicked up sand onto their blanket and beat noisily against the ribs of the beach umbrella. Nadine and Mademoiselle Moreau packed up their belongings and began the trek back to the house. The children ran ahead of them but stopped short of going up the hill. Little Niqui grabbed

Darnell by the shoulders and regarded him with animal eyes. He didn't resist her and simply stared back. She let go and he nodded with understanding. And for an instant the girl's face flushed with beatitude.

The nanny's eyes trailed Darnell's gallop back to the shore. Mental telepathy, she thought. The French woman was impressed, because until now she had never seen evidence of it in foreign children.

Little Niqui didn't have the strength to kick her imposed life in the teeth; for that she always had Darnell. She wondered what would happen if one day he could no longer read her thoughts? She couldn't imagine, because who would come to her rescue then?

Little Niqui looked back and saw that the jump was high and the dive true. Darnell had become the rocket that sank the fortress. When he had finished with his task, not one grain of sand remained in place to mark a spot of beauty and perfection. And she was happy.

Read an excerpt from **Mickie Turk's** new,
provocative suspense novel,
Made in the Image.

PROLOGUE

Andy O'Keefe knew he was being watched, but not by the
blue-grey uniforms assigned to the lines.

He had felt Sasha's limpid stare tracking him since early
morning. It started when he finished retrieving data from a
frozen hard drive. While putting his tools away, Andy
dropped a screwdriver behind him. When he turned around,
the gangling Russian slave stood like a bird of prey, holding
it in his hands, blinking hard and pelting him with silent
questions. Andy had felt stripped naked, like bait. During
lunch, Sasha watched him eat his whole sandwich before
going outside to smoke. Was the kid onto him? Was this how
it really would all end? After six months of dogged
surveillance, wiretaps, and countless man-hours poured into
undercover police work—now, to be outmaneuvered and
trounced by a twelve-year-old? Or was the boy just curious
about the outsider? A non-Russian, looking anything like but

what he might expect in a techie back home. Andy refused to wear a uniform, just stuck to jeans and a tee. His hair was always in his eyes, too long, and subject to cowlicks. A real live American.

Maybe the kid was lonely and wanted a friend. But he didn't speak English, and they both knew that the illegal factory made for a lousy neighborhood meet-and-greet. It was a cavernous space laid out in twelve rows, eight boys assigned to each. Serious looking goons walked back and forth making sure no one dropped a stitch. A place where young supple hands and small dexterous fingers—ideal tools for quick and efficient assembly—attached small parts to circuit boards. The new startup company, *MotionAmerica*, specialized in motors and drives used in semiconductor technology. Andy had it on authority that since sales had started to soar, more and more of the company's profits had to be laundered. Not much of a surprise when the biggest overhead: salaries and benefits, had been eliminated. When you only employed itinerant workers and human slaves, anything was possible.

Hear! Hear! America was about to be great, again.

No, Andy did not think it was safe to chummy up with one of the boys, yet. Not with so much at stake. But at the end of the day that is exactly what the undercover cop did.

Andy had closed the cover on a machine. The motherboard inside the installation computer was as good as new. He looked at his watch. Just enough time to check in with the captain and still make it to the World Series Game. Not just any World Series, but the first one played at the new Miami Ballpark, where, if there were any justice left in this world, the Marlins would soon be thrashing the Minnesota Twins. But just then, flailing hands and pointing fingers beckoned him to the back of the room. He didn't have time to fix another problem this late in the day. Shit, those tickets cost $250.00 each.

Andy jogged over to Sasha's computer expecting the worst, like a complete system meltdown. But the computer looked okay, and the page was open to Google Translate. Andy glanced once at the screen, back at Sasha, who for once was not looking at him, then back at the screen. With a simple keystroke Russian morphed into English, and Andy felt it all around him: the crust of everyday routine lifting.

I KNOW THINGS. I CAN HELP.

It was time to call in their secret weapon.

Lydia.

Born and raised in Minneapolis, **MICKIE TURK** has worked independently and commercially in film, photography, and journalism, for the past 20 years. She wrote, directed, and produced several films, both short and feature-length narratives and documentaries. Wayward Girls, which appeared in festivals and on PBS, can be found in libraries across the United States and Canada.

Mickie completed three novels, four feature-length screenplays, a variety of short stories and memoirs, and continues to write for a number of Minnesota journals. The next two novels, *Made in the Image* and *The Mortal Coil* will be available in October and December, 2012, respectively.

Visit the author's websites at
http://mickieturkauthor.blogspot.com
https://www.facebook.com/MickieTurkAuthor

Made in the USA
Charleston, SC
24 September 2012